Praise for *The A*

'Paul A Mendelson's humorous and touching stories are a joy to read. He actually made me laugh out loud!'

Leigh Russell, author of the million book
selling *Geraldine Steel* series

'Paul A Mendelson's compelling stories show the author's gift not just for wry observation about family life and curious encounters, but also for moving seamlessly from warm humour to unexpected and often disconcerting denouements.'

David Lister, *The Independent*

'Paul Mendelson has done it again! *The Art of Listening* is laugh-out-loud funny, entertaining and surprisingly moving.'

Karol Griffiths. Script editor. Coen Brothers. Warners. BBC.
Author of '*The Art of Script-Editing*'.

'*The Art of Listening*' makes the art of reading these short stories enormous fun. Maupassant, Maugham, Dahl and O'Henry spring to mind. As with those great writers the tales are highly original, often moving and end in surprising ways. More importantly, Paul A Mendelson's humanity leaps from the pages. His comedy roots are apparent. I laughed out loud in several of the lighter hearted stories. Brilliant!'

Geoffrey Sax. Film and TV director.

'A charmingly witty, well-observed collection of stories that will have you chuckling. Funny and enthralling'

Preethi Nair.
Bestselling author of '*100 Shades of White*'

"There are genuine laugh-out-loud moments and then surprising tenderness. The writer's warmth comes through and there are some delicious twists to the tales. Each story is very individual and as a whole, totally satisfying."

Francine White, National Show Business Journalist

'Tales of infinite humanity and dazzling variety that contain life-enhancing quantities of both wisdom and wit'.

Paul Alexander. Movie, TV and stage writer.

Praise for *In the Matter of Isabel*

'A wonderfully funny debut novel.' *The Independent.*

'A titillating thriller that is both warm and endlessly funny.'

Ardal O'Hanlon

'Fizzes with surprises.' Andy Hamilton

Praise for *A Meeting in Seville*

'An intriguing and moving tale by an experienced comedy writer at the top of his game'.

Charles Harris,
bestselling author of *The Breaking of Liam Glass.*

'A time-travelling love story that challenges us all to recapture the best of our younger selves.'   David Ian Neville, Producer BBC

'A superb achievement. ..Poignant, pacey and suspenseful.'

The Independent

THE ART OF LISTENING

and other
'inspired' fictions

Paul A. Mendelson

The Book Guild Ltd

First published in Great Britain in 2019 by
The Book Guild Ltd
9 Priory Business Park
Wistow Road, Kibworth
Leicestershire, LE8 0RX
Freephone: 0800 999 2982
www.bookguild.co.uk
Email: info@bookguild.co.uk
Twitter: @bookguild

Typeset in Minion Pro

Printed and bound in Great Britain by CPI Group (UK) Ltd, Croydon, CR0 4YY

ISBN 978 1912881 468

British Library Cataloguing in Publication Data.
A catalogue record for this book is available from the British Library.

To Stephen C, Stephen G, Stephen H and Stephen K. And to all my other dear friends who don't happen to be called Stephen.

Contents

'Listening is being able to be changed by the other person.'
Alan Alda

'There is no greater burden than carrying an untold story.'
Maya Angelou

BASED ON A
TRUE STORY

Some years ago my wife and I booked a cheap winter mini-break in Sorrento.

By a chapter of accidents we ended up sharing accommodation with someone pre-eminent in my 'industry'.

Someone whom I would never normally have expected to meet.

I listened in awe to all he said. A few months later, I began to wonder.

What if...?

SEDICI!

.

"Ah, Doctor Patterson, allow me to introduce you to Señora Marquez."

To anyone else on the first Ryanair flight from Stansted to Naples this bitterly cold morning, in that vaguely disconcerting airspace between Christmas and New Year, the shortish, sandy-haired man with the unconvincing continental accent would probably sound quite odd. Especially as there is no Doctor Patterson within introducing distance and no one looking even vaguely like a Señora Marquez to whom he might reasonably be introduced.

Yet to the middle-aged woman sitting in the next seat along, the petite, somewhat worn, olive-skinned lady with the fine cheekbones and still striking, palm-green eyes, this all sounds perfectly normal.

"Pete," she says, more quietly than his original comment, yet hopefully loud enough.

"Delighted to meet you, Señora."

Nope. Doing a Scottish accent now, presumably Doctor Patterson's. Actually, she concedes, it is passably Caledonian. Which, coming from her, is praise indeed.

"*Pete!*"

"*Encantada*, Doctor Patterson."

3

Oh shit, she thinks, *now he's Señora Marquez! Earthy, guttural and... what? Spanish, presumably?* Something tells her that she should know the answer to this but she can't quite get a fix on it. And why the hell should she? They're supposed to be on holiday!

"*PETE!*"

Now everyone is straining round to look at her. She wants to scream that she's not the one they should be staring at. She's been doing a lot of wanting to scream lately. At her family, at her pupils, but mostly at her husband. Who, sadly, isn't Doctor Patterson, or they would most probably be flying business class Alitalia. And staying somewhere better than the poky apartment that someone has described on TripAdvisor as being 'too small for standard spaghetti'.

"Love," she continues more quietly. "We're supposed to be on holiday. See – aeroplane... sky... extortionate cup of tea?"

For the first time since take-off, he turns to her. Despite the escalating frustration, she picks up on how very weary he looks. The lines on his already jowly cheeks seem more permanently etched today, the bags under his eyes perilously near their allowance for the trip. Yet she recognises it as a weariness quite different to her own. She recognises it, but is too wedded to her own brand of fatigue to help. Not that there's anything she could do. Ask Doctor sodding Patterson to sort it out.

"*So?*" asks her husband, mercifully in his own South London accent.

"So can you put that old script away, please?" She has recognised, as she speaks, exactly what it is that he's holding in his hand. The familiar, industry-standard format; the vaguely manic, scribbled corrections; the wrinkled sheets. And she recalls a time when wrinkled sheets signified something totally different. "*And stop with the bloody voices!*" She feels suddenly outraged. "You never told me you'd brought it with you."

"Never asked me."

"No," she agrees, "you're quite right, Pete. I should have said, 'Oh, by the way, love, have you packed that manky old film script you've been fiddling with for the past umpteen years?' What am I like!"

He observes, not for the first time, how much more Hullish his wife of twenty-four years becomes when she's being sarcastic.

"Oh, very supportive," he mutters, eyes deliberately returning to the mangled pages spread over his fold-away table. "Anyway, why am I thinking movies?" he sighs. "Not like I've ever done one. These days I can't even get a sodding telly script past first base."

Here we go.

She really doesn't want to get into this. Julie Dawkins prides herself on being a woman who fixes things, who gets things done. Practical, sensible, in control. Ask anyone. Ask her kids. No, don't, because that side of her drives them crazy, even as they reap the benefits. But this – her husband's career, his dreams, his self-esteem – are way beyond her skill-set, light years from her sphere of operations. And the impotence simply makes her cross.

"Maybe I should just write one about a Bangladeshi homicide detective in Victorian England, who works undercover in a rural Welsh baby hospital. Cover all my bases."

Julie knows that she should simply ignore this because it's not really addressed to her, but rather into that same ether via which expensively produced material is constantly and relentlessly transmitted, but unfortunately not by Pete. Yet she still feels duty-bound to 'be there', even though she knows that whatever she says will be wrong, simply by virtue of her uttering it.

"Oh, love, I do know it's hard. But hey, let's just try to enjoy these few days together, eh? A nice bit of winter sunshine." A huge sigh from beside her. Yet still she presses on. "We *need* this, Pete. Okay, fine, I bloody do. I don't want to talk to *anyone*."

"Even me," he says, twisting in his seat to stare at her.

This time it is her turn to sigh.

QUINDICI!

The moment she sees the rain, Julie knows that Pete Dawkins of Eastcote, Middlesex, self-employed but only rarely, is going to take it as a personal affront. His persecutors will cease to be commissioning editors of the major terrestrial and satellite channels, replaced for the duration of the shitstorm by God.

"Isn't Naples pretty?" she hazards. "Even in a downpour!"

Pete doesn't dignify this with an answer, as they have so far only seen the airport and the hire car depot, neither of which knocked him out. But, of course, he wasn't peering out of the window as they descended jerkily down over the Gulf of Naples, making bumpy contact with the dark lava stone of Spaccanapoli.

She realises that even she is stretching it a bit as the sprawling and reputedly grubby, crime-infested city doesn't really look that alluring. Fortunately this has never been their intended destination. And, anyway, the Mediterranean and the Gulf or Bay seemed lovely – you can't go wrong with seaside.

***

Julie has heard that you can tell the state of a marriage by how a couple behaves in their car. Once you texture this with specifics

6

like left-hand drive in an unfamiliar stick-shift, infuriatingly narrow Italian roads, rain that a grumpy wordsmith describes as 'driving', and a passenger gripping the door handle like a climber's piton, muttering 'move over – for Christ's sake, move *over!*', you might wonder if the union will even survive the journey.

"Just because you once played a driving instructor in fucking *Emmerdale!*" he yells.

"I was very good," she counters, as if this cements her qualifications. "*And* I drove an ambulance in *General Hospital*. Okay, I went through a windscreen in *Holby City*, but I was a diabetic with a really bad hypo and a dodgy seat belt."

"You know the problem here, Jools?" She assumes he is discussing the tiny car and his driving abilities. "The folk who make all the decisions have either got unbroken voices or training bras. Or both."

"Oh Jesus, are you still on about— *Mind that nun!* Sorry. Shouldn't have said 'Jesus'. Please, love. Not here. Not today." More sighing. "Pete, we're only forty-five. It's nothing these days."

"In teaching, maybe. Sure isn't in your old job. Or mine, apparently."

She doesn't want to go there. Not this trip.

Even when he does mutter something, she chooses not to pursue it, content to look out of the window and savour whatever's out there, both God- and man-made; stuff that, despite the rain, is growing more alluringly picturesque by the minute. *How do the Italians do it?* she wonders. *It all seems so effortless.*

It is only when they arrive in the historic little coastal town of Sorrento, perched cockily on a plunging cliff above the sweep of its Neapolitan Bay, that conversation becomes imperative without being contentious.

"What was the name of the hotel?" asks the driver, as traffic slows and the number of aimless strollers increases.

Julie doesn't answer for the moment, although a part of her brain is listening out, as it always does, for the cue. Of course, she is no longer an actress and the dialogue these days is quite some way from uplifting. But this time her attention is captured to an almost disturbing degree by the surprisingly chic place in which they now find themselves. The cheap-flight, mini-break destination has taken on far more import in her life than even its undoubted old-world elegance might merit.

She finds that she can hardly breathe.

"The Hotel Gran Vista Excelsior," she answers, as his question finally registers. "Oh, ooh Pete! There it is. Just overlooking the sea. Oh love, doesn't it look magnificent?"

"Beautiful. And where's our place?"

"Round the back in an alleyway. We're meeting a man called Pasquale on the hotel steps. Apparently that's a first name from this very area."

Pete just nods, involved in trying not to crush an Italian from this very area. Although, in truth, there does appear to be a whole European Union of potential victims around the attractive, café-lined square, arms full of shopping, children and dripping ice-cream, blithely ambling in the rain directly in front of his crawling, yet not quite tamed, Fiat.

"Ooh, there's a man waving! I bet that's him. He looks like a Pasquale."

"How do you know what a Pasquale looks like? Do you mean he looks swarthy and Italian? That's very judgmental, Julie. Look at you. You don't exactly look like you're from Hull."

"Slightly-tanned Yorkshire. And let's please not have a row. It's not my bloody fault that—"

She stops but, of course, it's too late. She knows he'll pick up a slight like a dropped fiver at the slightest opportunity. And riff on it beyond its most imaginable parameters. *'It's not my fault that your career is totally dead in the water, you've got the talent of a retarded vole and you're a pitiful excuse for a husband.'* None of which she actually thinks, or she doesn't think she thinks, but it's patently of no import what she actually thinks. She simply knows he isn't happy. And that neither is she.

"Signor Peter?"

Thank God for Pasquale, shouting at their little car as if they have to be the English couple from the booking form; glum, floundering and out of their depth. They in turn wonder why he – a native – is looking so frantic.

"Doesn't seem too pleased to see us," observes Pete, who isn't that pleased to see the gesticulating young man either, yet is not wholly unsatisfied that something looks like it is terribly wrong.

The instant the car slows Pasquale is there, dark wavy hair dripping wet, tapping manically at the window.

"Signor Peter, Signor Peter!"

"*At least let me stop the sodding car!*"

"Pete," warns his unsettled passenger, "don't get angry."

"Why not? Oh my God, do you think he's Mafia? Am I going to sleep with the seafood linguine?"

"Don't be facetious. Anyway, it's Camorra round here," says Julie, who saw a film about it once.

Pete stops outside the hotel, ignoring looks from residents who wouldn't be seen dead in a Fiat, and eases the window down.

"Signor Peter? Signor Peter Dawkeens?"

"That's me. The one getting very wet. Where can I park, matey – for where we're staying?"

There is silence. They both watch Pasquale's fetchingly mobile face, as it slowly transforms into a mask of deep concern, overlaid with mortifying contrition. Yet he doesn't talk, as if awaiting further questions.

"Er, is there a problem, Pasquale?" asks Julie.

"Of course there's a bloody—"

"*Pete*, let him speak."

"No. No problem… Okay, sì. A little, Signora. A little tiny problem." The young man suddenly opens Pete's door.

"What the hell—"

"I get in your car. Is okay."

QUATTORDICI!

Pete can feel the eyes of the hotel doorman sneering into his shirt as he struggles out of his pod into the unrelenting rain. Shovelling an apologetic Pasquale into the backseat, he hopes the intruder contracts terminal cramp.

The young man talks even as he contorts, but there's already a smile in his voice, although probably not in his message. Julie finds herself warming to him; he's hardly more than a boy. Albeit a boy about to ruin their already fragile holiday.

"I am so sorry, Signor Peter, Signora Peter. There is little mistake. Well, is not little. But you must no worry." Pete glares at Julie, just so she knows that, whatever this is, it is all her fault. "We drive, yes? Up the mountain. Is beautiful drive."

"*Up the fucking mountain! Up the—*"

"Pete!"

"No 'Pete'! Pasq— Pasquale – whatever your name is. We didn't pay for lodging up a flaming mountain. We paid for lodging down in a seaside town. So we can walk everywhere and not have to drive this bloody thimble they rented me."

"Is very nice. Where I am taking you."

Fearing that her husband might stop the car, swivel in his seat and strangle their unsought local guide, Julie gently taps Peter's arm. Firmly enough for him to take notice but not so hard that he'll take umbrage.

"Pasquale," she says quietly, in the calm yet somehow authoritative voice she has sought to develop over years of teaching drama to unenthusiastic and untalented Eastcote youth. "Am I sensing that you may have double-booked us?"

"What is 'double-book'?"

Julie just waits, enjoying – even amidst the rain and the tension – the stunning views, as Sorrento recedes below them and the staggering Golfo di Napoli opens out like an exotic flower to reveal more of its abundant charms.

"Sì," nods Pasquale finally, grateful that his incompetence has been given a name. "I double the book."

"Uh huh," says Pete in an even tone that the young man, had he been slightly older or more astute, would perceive as simply the ill-fitting lid for an almost uncontrollable anger. Yet, fortunately for Pasquale, it is the sort of anger that more often feeds on its host than allows itself to be spent on more-deserving others. "So, what exactly are you hoping to do about this, mate? And why are me and my wife driving miles away from where we are supposed to be?"

"Is not miles!" protests Pasquale, before blowing it with, "Is kilometres. On road. But there is good path, so you can walk down mountain. Very straight. Very nice. Or autobus. Very fast autobus. It is coming every—"

"Ooh, Pete," interrupts Julie, sensing more trouble. "*Look at that view!*" Instinctively, he turns and the car scrapes the tiny wall that is all between them and wondrous oblivion. "No, don't!" she decides.

Pete immediately swerves too far in the other direction, partly to correct himself but also partly to piss her off. He knows this, but feels no inclination to resist.

"It is here! You turn! Here! *Now!*" screams Pasquale.

"Who's driving this car – you or my wife?" Pete retorts, wasting valuable screeching time on an ancient joke that Pasquale is hardly likely to understand and that Julie has heard too often. The car manages to career, with an insurance-threatening crunch, into a small yet surprisingly well maintained drive.

"Oh goodness, Pete. It must be somebody's home."

"Can't see a home. All I see are trees."

"It's a drive of some sort. And I think those are lemon trees. Oh, how lovely."

"Sì," assists Pasquale, grateful for any crumb. "Limoni! They are belonging to Lucia."

"Who the f— who's Lucia?" asks the driver, trying not to do too much harm to Sorrento's future lemon harvest.

"She is my *zia*. How is it? My auntie. Here is Villa Lucia."

"O-kay," says Pete. "So you've phoned your old auntie in a blind panic and said '*per favore* Auntie Lu, get me out of the shit before two angry Brits beat me to a pulp.'"

"Sì," nods Pasquale happily. "Shit."

Three strained seconds later the villa itself appears, heralded by a welcoming wooden sign that proclaims, in one flowing, hand-carved stroke, its name and owner.

"Pete," gasps Julie. "It's *beautiful*!"

Begrudgingly, Pete has to accept that it is. Newly painted in a glistening Mediterranean white and standing proud amidst a vast hillside of lemon and orange groves, the Villa Lucia, with its wooden shutters as blue as the sea, offers an unqualified welcome to the winter sun. Even the pounding rain appears to have diminished out of deference to the tasteful glow of this particularly ample, two-storey property. The early afternoon light, still fractured through some grumpy cloud, is not without warmth.

Pete pulls in to a parking place, next to a couple of cars that he notices are far smarter than his own.

"It must be magnificent in the summer," enthuses Julie. "All the lemons."

"And pricey," mutters Pete, suddenly concerned again. "It's out of our league, Jools. Look at the bloody motors here."

"Is very nice, yes?" pipes a voice from the back, sensing that salvation might be at hand.

"It's beautiful, Pasquale," says Julie. "Your aunt is lucky."

"No, is Lucia. Is Italian name."

This makes Julie laugh. She notices that Pete smiles too, despite his resisting with every facial muscle.

"And this woman," announces Pasquale, pointing excitedly, "she *is* Lucia."

The approaching creature, dressed all in yellow and growing bigger and brighter, as if amassing sunshine on the way, needs no introduction. She couldn't be anyone else. Arms outstretched as if to envelop the eponymous villa, her new guests and, indeed, the entire hillside, she descends on Pete and Julie like a deeply-tanned and sandalled avalanche.

"*Benvenuti!* Welcome to you. I am Lucia. The aunt of stupid Pasquale."

Her guests just nod, wondering whether she is actually going to stop or simply roll over them with tank-like tread and plough off down the hillside, trampling shrubs and saplings in her wake. Thankfully, she comes to a halt, but her arms remain outstretched. Pete is suddenly reminded of Zorba the Greek and wouldn't be surprised if this overwhelming presence began to click her formidable fingers and dance.

The predominant movement, however, comes from her fulsome, incarnadine lips and the whitest teeth they have ever seen. Julie thinks of a goddess of the sun but she can't remember the name. Mrs Booth, headteacher at her school and a serious classicist, would most certainly know – in fact, it was she who so gushily recommended Sorrento – but she'd take the best part of an hour to inform you, in which time you'd lose the will to live.

"You stay here," continues Zorba/goddess of the sun/earth mother. "Is no problem." She registers the concern on their faces. "I charge you only same as idiot Pasquale. Even though this villa is for much more rich people." Sensing Pete's outrage, Julie nudges him gently. "You have big, homemade breakfast every day. I make. We have the jam from our lemon and orange. You like cake?" She looks at Julie. "I think you do."

Julie sucks in her stomach and smiles. "Oh yes, we're… cake people. Can we go inside, Lucia? *Per favore*. The rain…"

"Ah, sì," says their hostess, turning back to the villa. "You are happy here. Very good beds, yes?" She smiles mischievously at Pete and Julie, as if there's something she knows. Pete and Julie smile weakly back, as if there's something she doesn't. "*And* very interesting guests."

Pete ponders for a second, as they enter the cool, tiled hallway, on the patently innocent abutment of good beds and great guests. For some reason, Fellini's *Satyricon* floats into his mind. *I should be so lucky*, he thinks, then decides he hasn't really been up for a bacchanal for some time.

"My wife doesn't talk to anyone," he says.

Julie starts to protest, then realises that her husband is right. When it comes to holidays, her antisocial skills are legendary; most probably because she spends the greatest part of her every working day in crowded classrooms and school halls, talking dramatically. Whereas Pete passes most of his hours alone and in total silence, without even the satisfying clack of an old-fashioned keyboard or a gratifying call from his agent. It makes for jangly suppertimes and protracted periods of adjustment.

"Ah, sì," nods Lucia, adding somewhat cryptically, "you are English."

She throws open a grainy, oaken door at the end of the hallway, like an estate agent arriving at the deal-clincher. Wisely, she says nothing, allowing her unexpected and barely suitable guests to make the right noises.

"Oh, Pete!" repeats Julie, taken aback by the unanticipated glory of the expansive room, with its solid and tastefully rustic furniture. She finds herself dazzled by the low-poster, king-size bed, an impossible plain of virginal whiteness. And this is with her shades on. She feels almost scared to remove them, as if the emotions stirred will be too much for her to endure.

Pete's attention is on the balcony, taking in its elegant,

wrought-iron table – already a writing table, in his eyes – and the magnificent view, even on this gloomy day, down the lush hillside to the bay.

There's that huge, oddly threatening mountain, crowned with cloud and stuck almost in the sea, that he feels certain he should know. But he hasn't done Julie's research, as until this moment he hasn't cared sufficiently to pick up a guidebook. Now perhaps he might, if there's one in the villa he can surreptitiously flick through. The last thing he would want his wife to think is that he seems vaguely intrigued. Holidays don't change things. Pete knows this. They just postpone real life and usually make it worse.

The Dawkinses are aware, on the fringes of their admiration, that Lucia is talking. Julie wonders vaguely where Pasquale has gone; most probably skipping with relief down that very straight path back into town, to meet the poor people who have booked their crappy flat.

"Tomorrow is *Novello Anno!*" announces their host, to instant bemusement. "*New Year night!*" Pete and Julie nod. They've never been big New Year people. Julie hates the stranger-kissing, cork-popping, passing-an-orange-under-your-double-chin jollity, all for an occasion that is not inherently that special. And she is all too aware that it makes Pete feel even more gloomy, confirming with depressing regularity that precious little is going to change.

"We make the big party for our guests!" continues Lucia, even louder, sensing that the date itself is not sufficient to induce the same euphoria in her newcomers that it clearly does in her. "We watch the fireworkings from *terrazzo*. All over Golfo di Napoli. *Boom!*" This last is right into their faces, like a trailer moment for the big feature. "You eat. You talk. You get drunk."

"Sounds lovely, Lucia," says Julie, trying to match the enthusiasm.

Lucia nods in complete understanding. "You no pay for drinking and eating, Signora! Is included." Before Pete can protest that they're quite capable of affording all the champagne in the world, which they're not, Lucia is pushing them with both arms towards the balcony and the view. "*Vieni, vieni*! You see – over there – here is Monte Vesuvio. Much clouding today."

"Ah, of course!" says Pete, who should have known. With the dark ring hovering around its distinctive summit like a Cossack's fur hat, this great and violent mountain, major tourist attraction and historic slaughterer of thousands, evinces an unmistakeable power. "I hope that's not going to be part of the fireworks."

"No," says Lucia, "is volcano." Then she smiles as she gets it. "Ah. Ha! You very funny man. No, you are safe. I think. Who is knowing! I am sorry about the weather."

"*You're* sorry?"

"Pete!" says Julie. "Don't be worrying, Lucia. We freshen up in lovely room then we make drive into town. I am sure nice, big bowl of Sorrento pasta will be helping us to forget all about her." She shakes her head as Pete just stares, silently berating herself for falling so swiftly into another person's speech pattern. It comes so easily but she knows she is often one slip away from unwittingly causing offence. "Will *help* us forget all about it."

Lucia looks at her, as if she has no idea why the younger woman is saying the same thing twice. "I leave you now. To play young."

With a final, bewildering laugh, their hostess slips away, amazingly light on her feet for such a large person. *Or perhaps,* ponders Julie, *it's the sheer scale of her personality making you think she is bigger than she actually is. Signora Vesuvio.* She smiles at this.

As Pete's worn canvas shoulder bag comes flying down onto the maidenly white bed – denting it, defiling it – Julie feels an almost physical shock.

"I'll just sort myself out," he says, "then we can traipse back down the hill for some grub."

"Oh, look," says Julie, suddenly feeling quite angry, "there's even a lovely big rubbish bin."

"So?"

"So you've got somewhere to put that bloody script. Holiday starts now. Get with the programme."

TREDICI!

A mandolin plays *Come Back to Sorrento*, as it has done throughout the day and will continue intermittently to do until the restaurant closes. Or, more precisely, it plays *Torna a Surriento*, as the only words floating in the sultry air, through fake-flowered trellises and over giant red pepper grinders, are those being quietly sung by slightly merry English couples dotted around the cavernous room. And even these are from the Elvis Presley version.

Julie finds herself joining in, although until this point she had no idea she even knew any of the lyrics. "So, my darling, please surrender... la la la la something something..."

"Have you seen how much this costs?" says Pete, staring fixedly at the menu, whilst ignoring silent entreaties from across the table to raise a white flag.

"You don't need to order fillet steak."

"I like fillet steak."

"Then have one."

"Have you seen how much they cost?"

The conversation appears to Julie to be stuck in the same loop as *Come Back to Sorrento*, but the joining-in isn't nearly as much fun.

"Look," she says, "I know we can't really afford this trip..."

"But you decided to book it anyway."

"To get away from things."

"Things."

Julie stares at him, until his head rises from the demonic menu. "This may shock you to your marrow, Signor Dawkeens," she says, "but there are people out there who'd kill for a New Year's mini-break with their other half in Sorrento!" Pete's head returns to the menu, as if the steak price might suddenly go plummeting like a dodgy stock. "Mrs Booth was dead jealous when I told her."

"Fancy me, does she?"

"She's an ancient historian!" Julie munches a breadstick and waves a second one for effect. "Okay, she's fifty-six." No response. *Jesus!* "She *worships* this part of the world. It was her banging on about it that gave me the idea. Vesuvius, Pompeii. Actually, she wants me to do Roman plays with my thirteen-year-olds. You know, Plautus and stuff."

"Maybe I should try something historical."

"That film script must be historical by now."

He sighs. "Can't I just, y'know – tinker?"

"You've tinkered it to death. You've got to move on, love."

Their waitress, whose smile is now rigid, approaches their table.

"Okay, Julie. You win." He holds up his hands. "When we get back to the villa, I'll avail myself of that waste bin."

"Sounds attractive." She offers a gentle smile, acknowledging his pain. She's not sure if he notices.

"You would like drink, Signor, Signora? The wine?"

"Ooh, yes. Sì," enthuses Julie. "Chianti, *per favore*. Just a small glass."

Pete looks at her. "Now who's getting budget-conscious?"

Julie stares straight back at him, green eyes attempting to gaze deep into his soul, if she can find it, as mischief glints beneath long, dark lashes. "Budget wasn't actually top of my mind, *Signor*

Peter." She reckons she can hear the lusty rasp of Lucia in her voice, burrowing through the seven circles of Hull.

"You have chosen, Signora?" asks the waitress, who quietly wishes the cursed mandolins would give it a rest and that this couple, who really don't seem that united, could do at least one thing in tandem.

"Oh. Er… just this salad, please. The Caprese," says Julie, pointing at the menu. "Don't want anything too heavy." She smiles across the candlelit table at her husband.

"A large *Bistecca Fiorentina* and chips, please. And a flagon of Peroni."

DODICI!

The breakfast table is a work of art. Which doesn't prevent the inexplicably ravenous guests at the Villa Lucia from desecrating it.

By the time Pete enters the busy chamber, the residents of the other six bedrooms have done locust-like damage to the fresh homemade breads and preserves, eggs boiled and scrambled, cheeses *bocconcini* through *ricotta*, cold cuts and assorted fruits of the season. All to the sound of rain speckling the sheet glass that forms an entire wall of the room and the gentle strain of *canzone* insinuating through hidden speakers. The panna cottas are shadows of their former selves and those slightly sweet toastie things he rather likes are reduced to crumbly reminders of what could have been.

Fortunately, almost before his face can fully fall, the door to the kitchen swings open with a warming breeze and in sails Lucia, morning-fresh in a blue dress to match her shutters and laden with reinforcements. Following swiftly is an equally laden young woman, who can only be her daughter.

"Ah, *buongiorno* Signor. You like my breakfast table, yes?"

"It's getting more attractive by the minute, Lucia. Can I help with—"

"Of course not. The whole table we have made. Even the *mascarpone*. Even the table – my husband, he is carpenter. And here is my daughter, Maria. We make her too!"

"Mama!" protests the young woman. Pete notices she has the most beautiful smile.

"She learn to be doctor. Very clever." The young woman blushes but not too much. "Where is your Signora?"

"She'll be along soon. Sent me out as an advance party."

The women smile but clearly don't understand.

"You like tea, coffee?"

"Coffee, please."

"I give you special Italian coffee. You stay here and you make friends. Talk. *Talk*!"

She sets down her sumptuous burden and sashays back into the kitchen. Pete shakes his head and smiles to the nearest guest, who is homing in on the newly-arrived provender.

"Wow!" he says, initiating the demanded conversation.

"Wow indeed!" says the woman, who seems around fifty, with crinkly eyes and abundant grey hair, which Pete notices she has done nothing to mask. Unless, of course, the grey itself is the mask; he is never quite sure. Artifice via the lack of it. The American accent he detects is attractive in its confidence, as are her poise and manner.

There is a warmth in this woman, something to which Pete finds himself instantly attracted, but also a steel. He marvels at how, with two words and a gentle smile, a person can convey intelligence, competence and success. Yet, he muses, were she not possessed of such qualities and accomplishments, would she be staying here in the exclusive Villa Lucia? Unless, of course, Pasquale had double-booked her too.

"Try the honey and lemon preserve," she suggests. "You'll think you've died and gone to heaven."

"I will," says Pete. "And yes, there's that tune again. This time on the accordion."

"*Come Back to Sorrento*. They play it everywhere, don't they?"

"And the second line is 'We promise it won't rain next time.'"

"You should have been here at the weekend," she smiles. "It was glorious."

"Oh, thanks." He helps himself to whatever is on offer, whilst trying not to seem too much of the pig he wants to be. *What is it about holidays and breakfasts,* he muses, *that makes people eat like there's been a famine announced for noon?* "Must be me," he smiles. "I bring rain wherever I go. Just look at it out there."

"Ah, but go take a peek out that window at Vesuvius. Catch it before the clouds do."

Pete adds some extra food for the journey and does as he is told. His new friend follows, with her plate refreshed.

"Whoa, it's magnificent!" says Pete.

"Isn't it? You here on your own?"

"No, my wife's right behind me. Give her another hour."

"She's gonna miss Lucia's famous breakfast. Sets you up for the entire day."

"You're Canadian, aren't you?" says Pete.

The woman looks astonished. "Hey, you are good!"

"Not really," says Pete. "I say it to anyone with an American accent – saves me insulting any Canadians."

"Well, I do live in the States now. Connecticut. With an American."

"Don't know Connecticut. Went to New York once. It didn't rain."

She smiles. "Our office is in New York City."

"Oh yeah? So what do you do?" He pauses, a bit uncertain. "Sorry. My wife tells me I'm too nosy. Comes with the job."

"Not at all," she smiles. "Our species would die without curiosity. I produce. For a director called David Joe Jakes. We make small, independent movies."

Pete finds himself hugely grateful that this information has landed in his cerebral cortex between mouthfuls; otherwise he would be choking, gagging or projectile vomiting halfway across the room. As it is, he simply smiles and nods, whilst hoping that the woman can't hear his heart thumping uncontrollably above the sound of accordion, nor see the sweat he is certain now spatters his face like hard rain on a window.

Happily, Lucia arrives with his coffee. "This is good. You talking. Very nice."

Finally, when she has breezed off to encourage more intermingling, Pete manages to put two words together, although not quite his pithiest. "Oh, yeah?" Then, like he really doesn't give a toss but is sufficiently polite to show some interest, "So. You produce films. Movies."

"Well, somebody has to," she laughs. "I don't know if you're familiar with our work. It's not exactly—"

"*OF COURSE I AM!*" he enthuses, a bit too vociferously, as other breakfasters turn in shock. "*The Choice… A Death in the Valley… Counterpoint…*"

The woman's impressive teeth are flashing delight, as the rest of her face registers total astonishment. "Say, I am flattered. It's not like they're major blockbusters."

"No," agrees Pete, more quietly this time. "They're solid, serious, grown-up films. I have to congratulate you. Great stories. Stories that need to be told."

Her face softens more with every word he utters. No one is immune to flattery and he is ladling it even thicker than the homemade jam he's currently slathering over his *sfilatino*.

"Well," she explains, "that's because they're mostly true. And you know what they say about truth."

Pete is almost certain he does, but looks totally blank. He puts it down to the shock.

"Stranger than fiction?" she completes. He nods a bit too violently. "And there's nothing Hollywood likes more than 'based on a true story'. Courage of other people's convictions. Anyway," she continues, "as you may know, David started in documentaries. Old habits die hard. But say, he'll be so pleased you're a fan."

"Please do tell him when you see him," he says, munching some grapes.

"Tell him yourself. He'll be down in a few minutes."

Fortunately the grape doesn't stay rooted in his windpipe for too long, so Peter Dawkins doesn't die. Yet somehow he feels that he may have gone to that heaven the older woman recently mentioned.

"You okay?"

"I'm fine. Thank you. So… he's here. David Joe Jakes. In this Villa Lucia."

"Sure," she smiles. "Our partnership goes some way beyond the professional."

Pete gives what he hopes is a man-of-the-world nod, although he feels like a child in a toyshop. "Okay," he manages to say. "Right. Well, what brings you to Sorrento? Location hunting?"

"Pure R 'n R. We wanted to get as far away from 'the industry' – y'know, the movie business – as possible. Clear our heads."

"Totally understand. Excuse me saying this, but I would've thought someone like yourself might be… well… at one of those swanky, five-star hotels overlooking the sea."

At this, she shakes her head quite vehemently. "David and I abhor hotels. This is so much cosier. We can read, talk, eat – without being disturbed."

"Oh," says Pete, instantly contrite. "Sorry, I—"

"Hey, I didn't mean you!" She smiles, then looks suddenly wary. "You're not in the industry – are you?"

"*Me?*" He laughs at the notion. "Good God, no! I'm a psychoanalyst."

Pete registers the look of faint surprise on the woman's face and is pretty certain that this has to be the palest imitation of whatever is currently colouring his own.

He had no idea that the momentous words were going to spill out of his mouth until he said them and right now, he is desperately spooling back to determine their source. Beneath the shock, he is rather impressed with himself. How fast must his brain have been working to formulate a scenario of which his conscious self is only just becoming fully aware?

As yet, however, he has no idea where his bizarre fabrication might lead, and this time the perspiration is a full-body event.

"Yeah?" says the woman, who has no reason to believe that the amiable and patently intelligent man in front of her is lying through his crooked English teeth. "Shoot, better be careful what I say!" she laughs. "Know what? I reckon David and I are the only folks in our business who *haven't* been in analysis. It's probably how we can still afford to make movies."

"It's never too late," laughs Pete, with a professional grin. "I should give you my card." He realises this wasn't the brightest of offers and laughs it off as the jest it is.

Thankfully, she laughs too. "What kind of work do you specialise in?"

Before Pete can embellish his breathtaking lie with even more desperate falsehoods, he hears a familiar, smiley voice. It makes whatever breakfast he has managed to consume boil like a volcano in his gut.

"*Buongiorno!*" says the psychoanalyst's wife.

UNDICI!

With a speed rarely witnessed in European breakfast rooms, especially those in the southernmost regions, Pete Dawkins dashes away from his new friend and grabs his wife firmly by the arm.

Almost dragging her towards a glassy corner of the room, well away from the bemused Canadian, he announces loudly, "Darling, you must come and see Vesuvius before the cloud comes down." Turning back to his breakfast partner, he smiles. "Excuse us for a moment."

"You won't regret it," calls the grey-haired woman, although Pete suspects that they might.

Unsurprisingly, the room's newest entrant, refreshed by a sleep undisturbed by dreams or passion and ripe with the promise of a less challenging day, is taken aback by her husband's sudden manhandling and his enthusiasm for a vista she can perfectly well admire pain-free.

"*Pete*," she whispers. "What the hell? You're hurting me!"

"Sshh, quiet!" he mutters.

"Am I going to set off Vesuvius?"

"Listen, Jools, you're Venezuelan!"

As no one has ever called Julie Dawkins 'Venezuelan' (although her pupils have called her other inventive things), she wonders if she may have misheard. Or, of course, if her husband has finally lost the plot.

"I'm sorry?"

She stares at him. Never has she seen a look of such quiet desperation on his face; or indeed, on anyone's. Yet his weary eyes are sparkling with what appears to her curiously like excitement – an emotion that has been in short supply for some time in the Dawkins household.

"*You're Venezuelan,*" he hisses once again, as if this fact should be painfully obvious by now. Raising his voice, he adds, "Oh, isn't that magnificent? Look, you can still see the snow on the top."

"That's cloud. Pete, you feeling alright? You did have quite a lot of beer..."

"Julie, do you love me?" This gentle yet earnest question, more of an entreaty, takes her by surprise.

"Look, I know things aren't the best right now..."

"What do you mean? Oh. Right."

"Well," she continues, "haven't been for some while, actually."

"Yes, yes, okay." Pete doesn't want to go into this. Not now. Or ever. "But basically my happiness is your happiness."

"I wouldn't go quite—"

He suddenly goes loud again, drawing the producer woman's gaze firmly back onto him. He wishes he could look her up on his phone – her name is on the rim of his brain. "Oh, the cloud's coming down," he announces, then adds in softer, yet more urgent tones, "Listen Jools, do you want success for me or bitter failure and disappointment?"

"Mm. Tough one. Okay... I'm going for answer A. 'Success'?"

"Then you're Venezuelan."

"Pete, I know I'm probably being terribly thick, but I still don't—" Then she stops. Her mouth opens but no sounds emerge. And, in that moment, Pete knows she's on message, if not exactly on board. "*This is your bloody script!*" she mutters, in appalled astonishment. He tries to calm her down, using what he hopes

27

is a discreet fluttering of his hand. "The one we just binned. Whatserface – Señora Thingie. *You're asking me to be a character in your script!*"

Guiding her slowly back to a small table in the opposite corner, where his quarry has now parked herself, he swiftly explains. "You're an actress, aren't you? Well, you were. Lovely colouring, olive skin – all that dark hair. You did Spanish for GCSE!" She is staring straight at him now, green eyes wider than he has ever seen, shaking her head as if he's just told her he's in MI6 and specialises in wet-work. "Tell you what," he concedes, "you don't have to keep the same name." As she snorts, he gives her one final piece of briefing. "And I'm an eminent psychoanalyst."

"Course you are," she responds. Because there's nothing else to say.

DIECI!

"Hi, I'm Cassie," says the producer, welcoming the couple to her table. She points to the window. "Awe-inspiring, isn't she? And still smoking."

Julie, who is also still smoking, just nods. But Pete is all smiles, as if everything is perfectly normal. It takes a while to notice that the newly-introduced Cassie is staring at him, the friendly smile beginning to seem a tad fixed.

"Oh, sorry – Cassie. I'm Pete. Peter Dawkins. Doctor Peter Dawkins." He turns to his wife, warm smile still on his face but eyes imploring as never before. "And this is my wife…" No response from the woman on his left but a definite quickening of interest from the person in the chair in front of him. "My wife…" he prompts again, in case she has somehow forgotten her marital status. The seconds seem to crawl by.

"Chulia," says Julie finally, her opening syllable not so much hard as adamantine. Pete is certain he can see saliva flying. But she hasn't finished. "Chulia Carmen Rodriguez Gonzales … Dawkeens."

Jesus!

"Wow," says Cassie, with a smile. "I take it you're not English."

"No. I am Venezuelan. From… Montevid—"

29

"*Caracas!*" interrupts Pete, swiftly. "She lived in Uruguay as a child."

Julie simply nods at this, clearly recalling golden days in a city she couldn't even find on a map. She stares at her husband as if she would like to kill him in a particularly South American way. Feeling inordinately famished, she also looks longingly at the breakfast table.

"I must have cham," she announces.

"Ham?" hazards Cassie. "Not sure Lucia laid out any ham today."

"Not cham!" says Julie, with unnecessary vehemence. "Cham!" She notices blank looks, tinged in Pete's case with just a smattering of dread. "Lemon cham. Orange cham. Raspberry—" Before they can respond, she moves away towards the table. "Excuse me. I am very angry."

Cassie looks at Pete. "Angry?"

"No. She's not angry. She's – hungry. So many years in London and she still has that accent."

"Did you meet in England?" asks Cassie, clearly intrigued.

Pete sits himself down beside her. "No," he says and turns towards the breakfast table. By this time the foraging guests have dispersed, never large in number but clearly larger on leaving, so the three of them have the room to themselves. "Darling," he calls, "shall I tell Cassie how we met?"

"No!" comes the reply, still decipherable despite sharing its airspace with a large breakfast ciabatta. He can't help noticing that she bites into it as a lion might a gazelle.

Pete nods professionally at Cassie. "Still raw, even after all these years."

"Raw?" Cassie shakes her head. "Well, I won't pry."

"Oh," he says, barely concealing his disappointment. "Mind you, I bet some subtle prying is what found you all those other great stories."

"You're smart, doc," she smiles. "But hey – I'm on vacation. Until next year."

"Next year's less than a day away."

"How about that! And tonight is *fireworks* night." She picks up her bag and starts to rise. "I'll leave you guys to enjoy your breakfast. Have a good day."

"And you, Cassie."

He tries to ignore his spouse waving her *adios* with a bread knife.

NOVI!

The dark clouds around Vesuvius are gradually obscuring it from view, like a painting of which the artist has grown weary. There's a breeze with a threat in it, warning that it could quite easily develop into something far nastier.

The Dawkinses walk down the gravel drive, through the sleepy lemon groves and away from the Villa Lucia. Pete realises uneasily that he has his own little Yorkshire volcano steaming just ahead of him, molten and on the move, rattling branches, burning bridges and sporadically erupting into the still damp and faintly ominous air.

"*I cannot believe you just sodding did that!*" she yells into the sky.

He manages to catch up with her, although she can move at quite a speed when angry. And, unlike in suburban Eastcote, she has plenty of untamed earth to scorch.

"Hang on, Jools. *Please*," he begs. "I didn't intend to. Honest. She mentioned who she was and the words just flew out my mouth."

"The lies you mean. And who the hell is she then?"

"Cassie McBride. She produces movies for David Joe Jakes."

"Never heard of him."

"You must have. You're an actress for pity's sake."

"*Was.* Was an actress. Until—"

"Yes, okay."

"In soaps. Bit parts. Not Hollywood."

"He works out of New York."

"Like it bloody matters. Mind that lemon tree."

"I'm walking, not driving!" A branch catches his eye and he yelps. If she feels any sympathy, she's not showing it. "His best movies – his classics – they're based on true stories. About real people."

"Well, yours isn't true."

All at once, like a petrified Pompeiian, she stops exactly where she stands.

For the first time on this uneasy walk, she turns to him. He has seen this look of horror only once before – when he brought home that classic green MG Midget before contracts were signed on a big new series the BBC was going to commission. (It never did and the car went straight back.)

"Oh no," she says, as the awful truth about the awful lie sinks in. "This is getting really scary. You're going to pretend to them that—"

"*The Strange Case of Señora X.*"

"That this festering old script of yours is *real*?"

"Well, they won't listen to it if it isn't," he reasons.

"Course they will. It's their job."

"Not on holiday," he explains, as if this is the worst obstacle. "Not from an unknown, 45-year-old limey hack with no track record."

"You've done a *Casualty*," she protests, coming to his defence.

"Hardly *Dead Man Walking*."

"It is most of the time. So, let's see if I'm getting this right…" She can't stop shaking her head, like a mechanical toy from a cheap souvenir shop. "For the rest of my hard-earned holiday, I have to *pretend* to be somebody I'm not! Somebody who doesn't even sodding exist!"

His voice softens as he gently takes her arm. "Only with the two of them, love. You can be plain old Julie with me."

"*Plain old Julie!*"

Shit! "You know I didn't mean—" He feels a desperate need to ease her back on track. "You do remember the story, don't you?"

"Not exactly. You read the script to me and the kids years ago, in the car on the way down to Cornwall. You did all the voices. It was a long journey."

He turns and starts to make for the villa. "I'll have to fish it out of the bin."

It's her turn to do some arm-grabbing. He can't help noticing how strong she is for someone so compact. "*You will do no such thing!* Anyway, just as I was leaving the room, the maid popped in. So it's with the breakfast crap now. And I came here to walk, Pete. Not rummage in bins. Rain or no rain."

Picking up speed, she storms into the descending mist and onwards to the mostly obscured bay. "And to fucking *relax*," she calls back, tensely, before another thought strikes. "Hang on," she cries, turning. "How old is this woman – in your script?"

"Thirty-five."

"Well, I won't see thirty-five again."

"That's okay. It's set in 1998."

"Oh, okay… Whoa! That means I'd be… what? Fifty-six now."

"Uh huh," he mutters, moving on. "And I'm forty-eight. Because, if you recall, the male lead – the thrusting, wunderkind psychoanalyst – is eight years younger than her."

"Do I look fifty-six?"

"You've had a heavy year, Jools."

"Have the Camorra got a branch in Sorrento?"

His answer is obscured by the crunch of an approaching car. They swiftly divide to opposite sides of the path.

"Hey, you guys!"

They hear the car slowing almost to a halt.

Pete flicks Julie a warning look as he turns towards the newcomers, the big beam on his face hopefully obscuring what's going on in his heart and intestines.

"Oh hi, Cassie," he says, casually. "Look who it is, Chulia." He trusts any groans emanating from the partner quietly burrowing herself into citrus are muffled in the dampening mist.

"Need a ride into town?" asks the oblivious driver. "That sky looks pretty lowering."

Pete smiles at her, as if this could be the greatest offer he has ever received, and nods with what he hopes is casual amiability to the tall, powerfully built man at her side. He can't help noticing that the guy has the sort of chiselled, gritty looks that would work equally well in front of a camera, with spiky, attractively silvering hair and eyes that could match the Mediterranean on those sunlit days that Pete feels they have paid through the nose for but have been unforgivably short-changed.

Although, of course, he cares far less about the elements now that something infinitely better has come along. Yet his killjoy wife is about to spoil it all.

"I want to bloody walk!" she grumbles.

"We'd *love* a ride with you, Cassie. *Grazie*," says Pete, leaping to the rear of the car and opening the door for Julie. He can't help feeling slightly embarrassed that his own hire car would probably fit in their glove compartment. Hopefully they haven't deduced which one has been rented to the eminent psychoanalyst and his exotic wife.

As she slides grumpily in, Julie manages to mutter a swift "You're sick and I hate you", but fortunately Cassie has already set the engine purring. And David's voice, when he introduces himself, has a resonance and timbre that would drown out any ambient sounds within miles.

"Hi, I'm David," he announces, from somewhere near his boots.

"*Enchante*," says Julie, "as we say in Patagonia."

Fortunately she colours this nonsense with her newly sourced accent, so Pete can laugh as if it's simply his 'sport' of a spouse being ever so witty. Thankfully, their hosts think so too.

David stretches back over the plush leather seating and takes her hand. She immediately yelps.

"*David!*" chides his partner. "He's got a handshake that could crush a bear, Julia."

"Sorry about that," says the man, in genuine contrition. "Too much time hefting cameras." He throws his victim a smile that even she finds disarming. After all, it's not this poor guy's fault that her husband is a dissembling scumbag. So she smiles genuinely back.

"*De nada*," she says, remembering her schoolgirl Spanish.

"Hon, the doctor here is something of a movie buff," says Cassie. "Has to be, if he's seen our stuff!" She looks at Pete in her mirror. "So, when d'you find the time, Doc?"

"Oh," mulls Pete, with a gravity the question deserves. "In between consultations, Cassie, you know. So, David, have you just finished a movie? Just starting one?"

The big man shakes his head. They can see from his furrowing brow that he appears concerned. "Haven't made a movie this year, Pete. Guess nothing has got my juices going. Don't suppose that makes a whole lotta sense to a 'civilian.'"

"It does to Peter," says Julie. "It take a lot to get heem excited."

Pete tries to laugh. "Er… that sounds a bit funny in English, darling."

The acid in her response could corrode the car's expensive bodywork. "Does it, *darlink*?"

As they descend the same twirly mountain road up which a desperate Pasquale led them only the day before, the two impostors watch the pretty town appear through the cloud. The sea beyond seems very choppy, yet the vista is appealing and, at least to Julie, still full of hope. If she could just extract herself from this nightmare her idiot husband has concocted.

"So – how long is it since you left Venezuela?"

Julie is so lost in her thoughts that it is some seconds before she realises that the world-famous director, of whom she has never heard, is addressing her. The nudge from her husband assists, but even once she has processed the question she has no idea how to answer.

"Er…" she hazards.

"Must be over twenty years now, eh, *carino*?" says Pete helpfully, tossing in a term of endearment he googled on a recent rewrite. "Yeah, that's right. 1998. Before all of the troubles. I met Julia when I was in Caracas for a – PTSD conference. A colleague out there – an eminent Venezuelan professor – mentioned her to me."

He pauses and leans forward in the car. He can almost hear his wife's eyes rolling up to the top of her head, but he's on a bit of a roll himself and can't seem to stop. Not that he particularly wants to. "Actually – and I'm pretty sure she won't mind my telling you this, so long after the event – Julia became my patient."

Pete doesn't dare look at Julie now. But he can hear the sudden intake of breath over the sounds of the engine and the wheels churning on the narrow bends.

"Oh, really?" says David Joe Jakes, turning his huge head instinctively to gaze at Julie, as if her entire mental history might be chronicled on her suitably dark and far from unattractive face.

"Yes," continues Pete, before Julie can muddy the waters by saying something true. "She moved to London later that year, so that I could work with her. Away from, let's say, negative influences. And d'you know, it turned out to be one of the most fascinating cases of my career. More than just a case in fact, eh, darling? But I really don't think I should talk any more about that."

From the front comes a brace of sensitive nods. "Totally understood," says Cassie.

Pete hopes they can't see the frustration clouding his face. Or the satisfied smirk on that of his wife.

The conversation tails off as they finally arrive in the centre of town, save for spasmodic mutterings of '*bastardo*' emanating from the seat next to Pete. *At least she's remaining in character,* he tells himself, which has to be some consolation.

"So," announces Cassie, with a certain finality, "this is the main drag. That's the Piazza Tasso right there – great cafés and some darling shops. Where do you want to be dropped off?"

"Here is good," says Julie, hoping to meld into the crowd and never be seen again.

"What are *you* going to do today, Cassie?" asks Pete.

"Well, we know it's not the perfect day for it," she laughs, looking at them in the mirror, "but David and I are going to brave the elements and take the ferry over to Capri. It's only about twenty-five minutes and they do say it's worth a look."

"Lucia warned us not to," adds David. "She said the sea was way too rough today. But hell – we're flying home in the morning."

"*IN THE MORNING?*" screams Pete, which causes his driver and fellow passengers to jolt and Cassie to park sooner and more awkwardly than intended. "Er, well…" he continues, in more restrained desperation, "we're on a flying visit too, aren't we, darling?"

"I wish," mutters his wife as she purposefully opens the door and slides out. But not in time to miss the dreaded, yet not wholly unexpected, invitation.

"So, come join us," says Cassie.

"Oh, that is so kind of you, Cassie," accepts Pete, at exactly the same time as he catches his disgruntled spouse refusing, with a firm "No. *Muchas gracias.* We couldn't!"

"Of *course* we could, darling," says her husband, staring up at her, eyes beseeching. "Don't you want to see the beautiful Isle of Capri?"

"No. No, I cannot, *carino.*" By this time she is standing beside the open door, in drizzle that is rapidly turning to something far stronger. She addresses her seated listeners in character. "You are forgetting this, Peter – the Isla of Capri – what she mean to me."

"Excuse me?" says Pete, in justified bafflement.

The director is ahead of him. "Too many memories, huh?"

At this, Julie gives an enormous Latin sigh, one that appears to shake her entire frame. "Sí. You bang the nail on his head, David. Much too many memories." Another massive exhalation ensues.

Pete has absolutely no idea what is going on. Or what the hell Capri, to which they've never been in their lives, nor ever wished to, has to do with his story. Or indeed with anything. He simply knows that he has to get the show back on the road.

"Ye-es," he begins, trying to eliminate all identifiable sounds of panic from his voice, "but it's all changed since – that *thing* you're talking about, darling. You'll be absolutely fine. Trust me – I'm a psychoanalyst. Count us in, guys. Julia?"

With a sigh of resignation – but by no means defeat – Julie Dawkins slumps back into her seat and slams the door. Cassie starts the car once more, scouring the Piazza to find a suitable parking spot for the day and for the steps down to the Marina Piccola.

"Hasta la vista, baby," says Julie, which causes everyone to laugh and David's reflected eyes to twinkle at her, as the car trawls the square. She throws Pete a swift look, which he can't quite interpret.

He is not sure that he totally wants to.

OTTO!

If anything, Lucia has underplayed the lunacy of taking a hydrofoil to Capri this gusty December 31ˢᵗ.

Or perhaps, thinks Julie Dawkins, *she has simply underestimated the inherent stupidity of her guests.* The only sounds louder than the unrelenting rain and the angry, almost affronted, gales are those of the smattering of passengers bouncing around in their seats like teenagers at a rock venue, but without the drugs.

"*Whoa!*" they yelp as every ferocious wave is surfed, attempting bravado where fear and regret are probably the more accessible emotions.

"Fasten your seat belts, it's gonna be a bumpy night!" says Cassie.

"Bette Davis – as Margo Channing, in *All About Eve*," cries Pete, above the roar of the engines, hoping that this trip will be a bonding experience none of them will ever forget. Perhaps they will laugh about it in years to come, at the Chateau Marmont or wherever such people meet up to reminisce.

"Hey, mister film buff shrink – you are good!"

While Pete is shrugging modestly – hard to notice when an entire body is being contorted by the elements – David's attention turns to Julie.

"You okay, Julia? You're not looking too comfortable."

"I hate the boats," hisses Julie, thankfully still in Latin mode.

Cassie pats her hand reassuringly. "I used to hate 'em too, hon – *whoa!* – but then the kids wanted to go sailing with Pop. So Mom had to come along for the ride!"

"How many kids do you guys have?" asks Pete, finding more common ground by the minute.

"Twins. Boy and a girl. Not identical," says David, with an easy smile. The confidence of this man! "They're sorta grown up now."

"Are they in – the industry?"

"Afraid so, Peter. But Hannah's just landed her first little movie role. So perhaps the Bank of Mom and Dad could finally go into credit!"

"She might just make it as an actress," says Cassie, proudly.

They don't notice Julie looking wistful. "Good for her," she murmurs.

"Got kids, Julia?" asks David.

"Sí. Two boys. Poncho and Pancho."

"*Nicknames!*" explains Pete, swiftly. "For… Jack and Gavin." He leans over Julie, towards his new American friends, although of course the waves have no intention of keeping him at this intimate angle. "It's so ironic, you know – Julia hating boats."

"Why's that, Peter?"

"Sí, Peter," asks his wife, with genuine curiosity, wondering if this might be a time to throw up her breakfast on him and get away with it. "Why is ironic?"

"Well," says Pete, with what he hopes is a professional lowering of the voice. This is how he'd script a psychoanalyst. Which, of course, he has. "I'm sure Julia won't mind my saying this, it's so long ago. See, back in Venezuela, this lady was a famous star. Very famous. In the most popular television soap in that country's entire history… of television."

"You were an *actress*, Julia?" says David. His intense blue eyes, ever in search of knowledge and experience, are locked onto her face.

"No," says Julia. They look baffled. "I was a star. I am still big star." Pete sighs in relief. "It is the soaps that got smaller." The sigh reverts instantly back to fear. *They'll know that bloody reference, Julie!* "Ha ha," she smiles. "Is another famous movie quote, sí?"

David and Cassie laugh. Pete thinks his stomach would be going up and down even if they were floating to Capri on a millpond.

Julie turns to Pete, with great seriousness. "I prefer to forget about all this, *carino*. Is too painful."

"No!" insists Pete. "No, it isn't. *Carino*. It's… therapeutic." He smiles at their listeners, who are clearly hooked on the marital/professional back 'n forth. "Julia played the part of the mistress of a Greek shipping tycoon. And she was very good." Julie sighs, modestly. "Lots of her scenes were supposedly on his luxury yacht on the Gulf of Venezuela. You ever been?"

David and Cassie shake their heads. *Thank Christ for that.*

"Wow! Meaty, Julia!" enthuses Cassie.

"Sí," agrees Julie. "Sometimes I wish I am with him for bloody real."

It's Pete's turn to take her hand. Yet his face has changed. No longer the easygoing holidaymaker, snatching some much-needed respite from his worthy calling, he is now every inch the professional. Ignoring the listeners, he focuses the entirety of his attention on his former patient, almost as if he is staring directly into the woman's confused brain.

"But he *wasn't* real, was he, darling?"

The ensuing silence is so profound, you might almost be able to hear a pin drop; although in truth, with waves crashing and passengers whoa-ing, you would be unlikely to hear an anchor drop or a hydrofoil crashing into a harbour wall.

But Pete does his best, turning to David and Cassie. "Actually, *that* was what the problem was all about. Especially when it came to the fatal stabbing. But hey, enough about boring old us – tell us more about the twins."

"*Shoot!*" says David, shaking his head. "You may not be in our business, but you sure as hell know how to leave an audience hanging on."

Pete simply shrugs, acknowledging their frustration. He dares not look at his genuinely murderous wife, so he stares fixedly towards the prow of the boat.

"That must be Capri!" he says, pointing through the mist and the foam to a dark clump of land. Although he still wonders where in the name of God he is going.

SETTE!

As a pretend psychoanalyst, Pete Dawkins is only too well aware how nimbly the body will somatise the heady maelstrom of emotions that can foment within a troubled mind. So he is fully conscious that he has never felt more utterly at sea than when he sets foot with some trepidation on the solid pier that is the entrance to Capri.

So absorbed is he in these musings, trying to juggle fact and bullshit, that he fails to notice he has left the courtesy of helping his nauseous wife down the gangplank to an almost total stranger.

He is about to retrieve Julie from this unnecessarily seductive American when his own arm is clasped by an unshaven man he has never seen before in his life.

"You like guided tour of Capri, Signor? Very good price."

"Yes, please," calls Julie, from her safe American berth.

"No, thank you," says Pete, who needs to get his show back on the road.

They begin to walk, still a touch unsteadily, through the hovering seagulls and towards the centre of town, fastening their waterproofs tightly around them. The tour guide has already latched himself onto another foam-spattered arm.

Cassie, who seems blessed with an unshakeable optimism, gazes around her, head held high, as if she has just set foot on some unspoilt tropical paradise. "Looks lovely even today, doesn't it?" she enthuses.

Pete, who thinks it looks miserable as hell, nods in agreement. "You can't douse charm," he says poetically, adding "Those are some serious mountains." He looks around the elegant and richly stocked harbour in envy. "And them's some serious yachts."

David still has Julie's elbow lightly in his grasp. "Feeling a bit better, Julia – now you're on *terra firma*?"

Julie, who doesn't appear that much happier, manages a grateful nod. "Sí. A leetle. Thank you, David. You are very kind gentleman." She glares at Pete, the 'unlike this selfish bastard' unspoken.

"I imagine Venezuela is a beautiful country," says the director.

Pete looks at him in admiration. The guy is clearly hooked, but has the skill to allow himself to be reeled in gently.

"Oh sí, very beautiful," says Julie. "Many mountains." Pete nods in agreement. You're pretty safe with mountains, unless you're talking about Holland. "But many problems." She shakes her head as memories of that tortured country move unbidden to the forefront of her mind.

"This much I know," agrees David. "Ever since Hugo Chávez."

Pete, who knows his wife, realises immediately that she has not the faintest idea who Hugo Chávez is. Or was. She has little interest in politics or international affairs. But ask her about theatre…

"Oh sí," she sighs. "Of course, Hugo. I meet him once. We call him Chav." *Okay Julie*, thinks Pete, *quit while you're ahead.* "*Politics*! Hah! My parents," she persists, "my mama and my papa, they are first from Buenos Aires. Is in Argentina. They are knowing Evita." She shakes her head. "They cry for her. Even though she tell them not to."

"*YES!*" agrees Pete, with an enthusiasm that surprises even Julie, adding mysteriously, "*That is it!* My late in-laws were indeed from Buenos Aires. But you're thinking of the musical, *carino*! Madonna? Lloyd Webber?" He turns to David and Cassie, elaborating with some authority. "You *see* the power of popular culture!" To Julie's chagrin, he is practically exultant. "It can often appear more real than reality. So lines get blurred. Sometimes dangerously." He allows himself a wry professional smile. "Y'know, I'm rather glad this has come up. Because – well, it's a big part of our story. Mine and Julia's. I wrote a seminal paper on it for the British Journal of Psychiatry."

He winks swiftly at Julie. Deuce!

They begin their walk into the town. Signs encourage them towards Villa San Michele, in the hilltop town of Anacapri, and the equally popular Blue Grotto closer by, but they appear to be making their way over the wet and now glistening streets for La Piazzetta, the main square.

Pete has the clearest sense that his 'marks' are less entranced now with this famed, romantic isle than they are with the prospect of hearing a story no one, to their knowledge, has heard before – in which the potency of cheap popular culture apparently plays no small part. And who is he to disappoint them?

"So you played a femme fatale, eh, Julia?" says David.

Here we go.

"*David!*" chides his partner, gently. "Leave the poor girl alone."

"You're right, Cass. Sorry, Julia. Me and my damned curiosity. Not the first time it's got me into deep water!"

"That's okay, David," intercedes Pete, magnanimously. "It's so long ago now. Can I tell them, sweetheart?"

"Try and stop you, enchilada."

The rain has subsided to a drizzle, although the sky is still busily threatening. There are cafés nearby as they approach the pretty square, but Pete feels they have to keep walking. Something to do with flow, a phenomenon he couldn't ever quite explain but which he knows is essential to good storytelling.

"When this very special lady and I met," he begins, making occasional eye contact with his patently enthralled audience, but careful not to overdo it, "Julia had been playing the part of the glamorous mistress for quite some time. Actually she was recognised *everywhere* she went. From *bodegas* to *favelas* to society events." (He's not quite certain why he includes the one word he knows for 'slums', especially as it's Portuguese, yet it seems to add colour.) "But you know how the public tends to blur fiction and reality." He senses their nods. "She'd walk in the street and people would happily call her a whore and a murderer."

Now he turns to face them, careful not to catch Julie's disgruntled eye. "You see, she stabbed her wealthy Greek lover to death. In the soap, that is."

"He deserve it," mutters Julie.

"Er, yeah," continues Pete. "Do you know, some people would even spit in her face!"

"God bless Joe Public," laughs Cassie. "What would we do without 'em?"

"Ah, yes," says Pete, his tone taking on a new, far more sombre dimension, in deference to the approaching climax of his tale. "But this time, because of things – secret things – that had happened in Julia's own childhood – disturbing things no one knew about, certainly not the makers of her programme – the blurring had quite a different effect."

He pauses.

Somehow he knows that these intelligent, highly imaginative people will be there ahead of him. And that they'll be thrilled their perception has been rewarded. *Okay, enough pausing.* "*She gradually came to believe she was that person!* Y'know, the person she was playing," he adds, most probably unnecessarily, but you have to dot the 'i's.

"And that's where *you* were called in!" enthuses David. "The respected psychoanalyst. Boy!"

"Indeed." Pete gives a deeply professional yet strangely loving sigh. "And it took years of painstaking work. A voyage of discovery, right back into the past. The buried secrets and the awful traumas. But she's come through it now, haven't you, *carino*?"

He turns to Julie, who is being unusually, yet not unhelpfully, subdued. Pete makes a silent, heartfelt promise to ensure that the remainder of this eventful holiday is the healing break this fine woman deserves. "She knows *exactly* who she is now, thank God," he continues, with a gentle smile. "And she hasn't had what we call an 'episode' or 'fugue' for years."

"Okay! Now that is *enough*, David," says Cassie. "Poor Julia – after what she's been through. She just wants to relax and see Capri. Look at all those darling little houses, nestled up there in the—"

"*AAAAAAAAGGGGGHHHHHHH!!!!!!*"

The scream causes birds in the trees surrounding the small square to scatter and rain-defying tourists to think seriously about doing the same. Glasses and cups freeze halfway to lips. Struck-dumb waiters pause halfway to tables. David and Cassie are themselves stunned to be so close to a human mouth they never thought capable of opening so wide or emitting a sound so chilling.

Pete takes back his recent silent promise.

"Oh my God!" gasps Cassie. "Julia, what is it? You went too far, David. Perhaps I did too. She did mention this place—"

"*Darling!*" interrupts Pete, who feels he should step in. If only to throttle her. "Are you alright? *Carino*?"

Julie says nothing. Her body trembling uncontrollably, she points shakily upwards towards some grand old buildings on a slope above the town. The three of them stare at her. In fact, most of Capri is staring at her.

Finally, she appears able to speak.

"*The hotel*," she gasps, her voice more guttural than ever. "That hotel!"

"What hotel?" asks Pete, fear returning in waves far larger than the ones they have just survived.

Julie continues to point. "That one high up there. For God's sake! The pretty one up on the rock. Do you see? *Do you see?*" Pete recognises the voice now. They had watched *The Exorcist* on an old DVD over Christmas because Julie had never seen it. For a couple of terrifying hours they had seemed unusually together. He finds himself hoping her head doesn't spin round.

"DO YOU SEE?!" They all nod, mesmerised, even Pete, and gaze upwards to where her trembling finger is pointing. They wait, without breathing. "That was the hotel where—" She ceases as swiftly as she began.

David can't stop himself. "Where what, Julia?"

"Where I kill Dmitri."

"WHAT?" yells Pete, who has, of course, read the script.

"Oh. Oh dear. I'm so sorry," says David. Yet still he has to ask, "Dmitri?"

Cassie is shaking her head at her husband in vague warning, but her eyes seem unable to shift from the lovely yet contorted face of the clearly possessed woman in front of her.

"Dmitri Stassinopolopolous – the famous Greek shipping magnate. I was his mistress, you know." The others nod. It's all they can do. "He buy me such lovely things. But he was cruel … cruel… cruel…" The 'cruel's continue at decreasing volume until all they can see is the vivid mouth moving frantically yet silently.

"Perhaps you should go back, Peter," suggests Cassie. "The boat hasn't left yet."

"… cruel… cruel…"

"Oh no," says Pete, shaking his head just a bit more fervently than is generally accepted in conversation. "And it wasn't that hotel at all, sweetheart. Wrong continent. But it's happened before," he explains. "The delusions. They come on… when she's a bit unwell. Who knows, perhaps the rough sea…" He realises that he's clutching at straws here and knows what he'd prefer to be clutching. He glares at his rogue wife with a helpless fury he hopes the others don't pick up.

49

"Julia, darling," he says in the softest, most persuasive tones he can muster, "when I snap my fingers…"

"*Do not you snap at me!*" His darling turns to the Americans, whose kindly, concerned smiles are all over her. "Please excuse. This bring it all up. After the many years. My poor Dmitri. I loved him but I hated him. Is possible, yes?" Cassie and David nod. Of course it is. "And his wife. I hated her more. I kill her too, actually."

"No, you didn't!" corrects Pete helplessly.

"Perhaps it might be better not to talk about it," suggests Cassie, gently touching Julia's arm. "You're shaking, dear."

"I think I should get her back," says Pete, grabbing his wife's wrist with all the strength he can muster. If he breaks it, he breaks it. "I'm so sorry."

"Never apologise, Doc," says David. "The mind is a powerful creature."

Pete just nods. "And so much still to explore. Like the ocean. Maybe we'll see you at the fireworks tonight. If, well… you know. Let's go now, *carino*. It's going to be alright." He yanks her away, looking kind but feeling kind of homicidal.

"*I have killed… I will kill again!*"

"Yes, okay dear."

A seagull drops a recently purloined piece of bread from its beak, as if he can't quite believe it either.

SEI!

Come Back to Sorrento played on the Musical Tesla Coil is a version Pete Dawkins has never heard before, but this time he is far too preoccupied even to remark on it. The Dawkinses actually came back to Sorrento in total silence, due mainly to Julie spending almost the entire rocky journey in the hydrofoil's toilet, to the intense discomfort of the other churned-up passengers.

Her stomach appears to have settled now. In fact, as Pete can't help but notice, it has self-calmed to the extent that she is now sitting in a large but pretty restaurant just off the Piazza Tasso, happily tucking into *paccheri* with ragout of monkfish and a massive side salad. Whilst he can barely stomach a *formaggio* sandwich.

"*What the hell was that about?*" he finally manages to ask, having been barred from speaking until she finds herself completely tranquil and able to respond.

"I don't know what you mean."

"You bloody do! Murder in Capri? Killing his wife too! They weren't in the script. And Dmitri Stassithingy wasn't even his name!"

"Well, they all should have been." She smiles at him.

He notices an uncommon smouldering in those green eyes and a fervid flush on her face that he can't recall having seen for quite some while. Possibly not since she gave her Lady Macbeth, or at least the highlights, on that school evening she arranged for parents to persuade them Shakespeare could be fun. They had thought her quite demented and he's feeling much the same way.

"Oh, come on, Pete," she enthuses. "They're totally smitten! You saw their faces! Now we just have to draw them—"

"Hang on!" cries Pete. "You're getting off on this!"

Julie looks at him as if he is insane. "No. I'm not," she laughs. "Pete, I'm so... not."

"'I have keeled – and I weel keel again'?"

"*Well, how was I to remember the exact script!* I know it was about this foreign lady, who goes a bit doolally and splits into two, yeah? And it all comes galloping back again years later. Forgive me if I can't recall precisely what triggers it off – *mea* flipping *culpa*! But doesn't her hubby have to stop her committing a *real* murder somewhere in London? Probably not Eastcote, although I know at least one woman there who's thought about it."

"Yeah, well, that's the big finish. But not the way you—"

The huge chunk of pasta-parcelled monkfish in her mouth doesn't stop Julie reacting with what she considers perfectly justifiable outrage. "Now you just listen here, Dottore Dawkeens. All I asked for was a few sweet, uneventful days with my husband, before school starts. To... get back on track. Possibly. But oh no, you have to turn it into Mediterranean sodding Murder Mystery Weekend."

"And a nice break's exactly what we'll have," says Pete, not wishing to get into this. "Tomorrow. Soon as they leave. But right now I need to talk you through the whole scenario. Scene by scene. So you don't go blithely wandering off-piste again."

She takes a sip of chianti. "What if I'm not happy with my part?"

For a moment he just stares at her. Making a supreme effort not to yell directly into her chomping face, Pete explains with almost scary softness. "It is *not* your part."

"Is now. Hey, that scream was excellent, wasn't it? Talk about projection!"

"Julie, do you think we're doing the right thing?"

His change of tack is so sudden it takes her by surprise. She realises just how desperate this man has become. "Oh, I don't know, love," she says gently, emptying her glass with a sigh. "We can't keep this up forever, can we?" She smiles as she descends into her Latin register. "*Mi amor.*"

"You are being very odd, you know."

She looks around the busy restaurant, a touch disingenuously. "Dunno what you— *Oh. My. God!!!!*"

Now it's Pete's turn to sigh. The woman is incorrigible. "Oh for pity's sake, Jools. You've no audience now."

She's nodding her head, but this time in total disagreement. The colour appears to have drained from her face, as if a cheap bronzing cream has been washed away in the rain. When she talks, it's almost a child's voice. A very scared child. "Don't look round, Pete. Please. Just stare straight at me."

He does as she pleads but his eyes demand an explanation.

"My headteacher just walked in."

CINQUE!

"*Julie Dawkins!*"

Pete thinks that now might be a good time for turning and staring, as anything is better than watching the person you married losing her reason, her colour and most probably her lunch.

He has, of course, met Mrs Edwina Booth before, but there is something seriously disconcerting about confronting a person in their off-duty mode when you've hitherto encountered them only in a professional capacity. Like seeing the doctor who gave you your first colonoscopy romping with his children at Center Parcs.

Personally, Pete feels it might always be pretty daunting to meet Mrs B, given that she is so formidable a presence. Small in stature, she still looms as large as the volcanic Lucia. He reckons that it has to be a confidence thing, bolstered over years by a more than comfortable upbringing, public school and Oxbridge education, genuine intellect and an accent you could cut with a knife. Choosing to turn around a large yet struggling comprehensive affords her a satisfaction that an already flourishing private institution might not.

Standing beside her, taller by far yet paradoxically occluded by the giant shadow she casts, is a man of similar age, whom Pete assumes is her husband. He can't imagine that this is an easy job and wonders if she has turned him around too.

"*Mrs Booth!*" yelps Julie. "What a lovely surprise." As if he hasn't had sufficient evidence today, Pete marvels yet again at what a consummate actress his wife is, whilst simultaneously feeling guilty for having robbed her of the chance to shine. "Pete, this is Mrs Booth – my headteacher. I think you two have met, briefly."

"Of course we have," enthuses Mrs Booth in a wholly convivial manner that, whilst suggesting that she never forgets a face, still manages to convey that she meets so many people in her important line of work that she could hardly be expected to remember someone of such little import. (Despite himself, Pete is hugely impressed.) "I don't believe you've met my husband. Eric, this is Julie and, of course, Pete."

Satisfyingly, Eric sounds just as Pete would expect a character whom he has named Eric to sound: a tad nasal, a trifle nerdy. The man even looks an Eric, very tall with an unnecessary smattering of mousy hair and an Adam's apple that bobs up and down his throat like a lift in a shaft. Yet Pete suspects that, in his own field, whatever this may be, the man is spectacularly competent, bringing home more in a month than the far more interesting Peter Dawkins earns in an average year. And all his years are unfortunately pretty average. At this moment he reckons that the fast approaching twelve-month is unlikely to buck the trend.

From a nearby table Mrs Booth grabs a chair – fortunately without an occupant, although Pete senses this might not have stopped her – and sits herself down. "Mind if we join you?" she adds, somewhat redundantly, pushing her thick glasses back on her nose to make her gawping, grey eyes even more challenging. "Eric, Julie here is my drama teacher. And Mr Dawkins is, I believe, one of that noble breed – the struggling writer."

"Well, actually…" Pete stops, because this is exactly what he is.

"Novels, is it?" asks Eric in genuine interest as he folds himself beside his wife.

"Television, I'm afraid," elucidates Mrs Booth. Pete waits patiently for her to add that, of course, she and Eric never watch television, affiliating herself to that vast majority of the known universe claiming to lead utterly TV-free lives the moment Pete explains to any of them what he does for a living. "But fortunately for his creative juices, our lovely Julie here has a steady job. Not that drama is a real subject, but it does allow the children to let off some well-earned steam."

"So, what a happy twist of fate," says Pete, with all the natural insincerity he can muster, "you being in Sorrento."

"Not really," says Mrs Booth, who wouldn't give fate the credit for anything. "When our Julie announced in the staff room that she was taking up my kind recommendation, I suddenly heard Vesuvius calling me too. We usually stay in Napoli, there's always a dinky palazzo going, but Eric thought *Novello Anno* in our beloved Sorrento would be more romantic. He's so impetuous, aren't you?"

"Oh yes," agrees Eric.

"I can tell," says Pete.

"Don't want you to think we're stalkers though!" laughs Mrs Booth. "You'll hardly notice us. Where's your hotel?"

"It's not quite a hotel," says Julie. "More of a pretty guest house, up in the hills."

"Way, way, way up," adds Pete.

"How sensible. We're right on the Piazza Tasso and, whilst generally *gemütlich*, it really is terribly noisy. I'm afraid the lager louts have discovered the Amalfi Coast. And tonight there's a fireworks display right in the centre of town. The world and his wife will be there!"

Pete and Julie nod sympathetically. *Tough titties.*

"Do you think your place has any spare rooms?" enquires Eric.

"*What?*" cries Pete. "NO!"

"Pete!" says Julie. "I very much doubt it, Mr Booth."

"Eric."

"She very much doubts it, Eric," endorses the doubter's husband. "They seem incredibly full. Standing room only."

"Oh," says Mrs Booth. "Maybe we'll just give them a ring anyway. Jot down the *número di telefono* for me, dear. It would be so nice for us all to be together on New Year's Eve, wouldn't it?"

If the Booths notice that it takes the younger couple several seconds to respond, they certainly don't let it bother them.

QUATTRO!

The great perennial end-of-year shouting match has to come and the bathroom seems as good a place as any.

Pete has no burning reason for taking a shower – it just crops up as the optimum way to slam a door in fury, without finding himself outside his own room with nowhere particular to go.

He isn't expecting Julie to follow him into the bathroom, but clearly she wants the row to continue. At least he feels that this time it is he who has that rarely attained moral high ground. Although, to be honest, he is not one hundred per cent certain of this.

"Well, what the hell did you *want* me to say?" she screams, above the roar of the plumbing.

"You could have said the Villa Lucia was dirty. Or quarantined for Ebola. Or hey, I know – you could just have said 'no.'"

"*She's my headmistress!* Anyway, keep your hair on. It's not like she's staying here. You were right – there's no room."

Pete steps out of the shower and into the towel she's holding out for him. It's a gesture he notes but finds himself wondering if she simply doesn't want to see him naked for any longer than necessary. Which makes him strangely sad, despite all the other emotions roiling around in the steam.

"But apparently there's room enough to join us for tonight's bash on the *terrazzo*," he moans.

"Yes, wasn't that sweet of Lucia?" Pete looks around for something else he can slam. "Anyway, I dunno why *you're* getting so upset. It's me who's going to be out of a job when she sees her middle-school drama teacher rocking up as a homicidal Venezuelan soap star with a split personality and a voice like Carmen Miranda." He tries to interrupt but she's clearly on a roll. "Oh, and a husband who's blithely doing his Sigmund bloody Freud impression! It's a good school, Pete. They don't like weirdness."

"Just my naffing luck," he sighs, the fight leaving his body like the air out of a party balloon. "And it was going so well."

"*Going so well!*" Now Julie is looking for something to smack. Preferably him. "This was meant to be a quiet little holiday. To get us back on an even keel."

"What do you mean?" he asks, although he knows exactly what she means.

"You know *exactly* what I mean. You can't pretend things are terrific, Pete. Oh, sorry, course you can. You're grandmaster at pretending."

He tries to dry himself but feels a perspiration building that has nothing to do with the shower. "I know it's been a difficult year, Jools," he offers, but is pretty sure even before the words are out that he's shovelling exactly the right fuel to keep her fire burning.

"*Difficult year!*" There she blows. "Difficult sodding decade. Make that two decades. If you've got work, you're worried it's not going to be any good. If you don't have any, you're paranoid you'll never work again. It's like being on that Colossus ride at Thorpe Park. Blindfold. Without a safety bar. And what about *me* – where do I fit in?"

"You LIKE your job!" He's shouting now, which he hates doing but he can't seem to stop himself. "You LOVE teaching kids. And it's STEADY." These don't feel like particularly shouty words but they'll do at a pinch. He wonders for a moment why he so habitually assesses his language as if it's dialogue rather than life.

Julie doesn't appear to be playing. Instead, she contemplates the words he's just yelled at her. "'Steady'. Ah yes, it's steady." She laughs without mirth. "Well, it was until—"

A sharp knock on the door causes them to stare at each other, as if it's an unscripted noise offstage.

"Who's that?" asks Pete.

"Do you know, my x-ray vision doesn't seem to work in Italy. Guess I'll just have to open it and see."

"No need to be sarcastic."

She's already at the door. Pete finds that he can't move, although he realises he isn't looking his best.

"Hi, Julia."

The unmistakeable richness of David Joe Jakes's greeting moves through the doorway like the beam of a smile. Julie is clearly in its orbit as Pete detects, with some dread, the worrisome Englishness of her response. Fortunately corrected in an instant.

"Oh. David," she says, "*Hola*! How are you?"

"More to the point – how are you? Was your boat ride back okay?"

"The boat ride? Oh sí, she was fine." She calls back into the room. "Pedro – is name I call him, means Peter in my country – Pedro, it is David."

"Oh hi, David," says Pete, moving towards the affable visitor. "'Scuse the towel."

"No problem. Sorry to interrupt. We were just, y'know, concerned."

"Very kind of you," says Pete. "I think today brought up a lot of stuff for us, didn't it, Julia?"

"Oh sí. Much stuff. And I nearly bring up my breakfast. Ha!"

David smiles at this. "Well, we'll see you guys later, yeah? At the big party. I'm just off for a walk in the grounds, between showers!"

60

"Oh, I come with you," says Julie. She feels Pete's stare behind her and just hopes he hasn't dropped his towel. "If is alright, David? I need the breath of – how you say? – fresher air."

"Er, Julia?" comes the expected voice from behind, which she chooses to ignore.

"Oh. Well, sure," says David, a touch surprised. "Be good to have company."

"I just grab the jacket." She turns and picks up whatever garment is closest to hand, smiling at Pete. "See you soon, my little tortilla. *Adiós.*"

"*Adiós*," says Pete quietly, as the door closes.

He has never felt so naked in his life.

TRE!

Pete Dawkins can't quite believe that his hostess is actually humming *Come Back to Sorrento* as she happily vacuums the room where they had their momentous breakfast just this morning. She has to be doing something subtly post-modern, he decides. So perhaps, tempted as he is, he won't mention it.

Lucia notices him and switches off the machine. "Ah, Signor Dawkins. I am just making the cleaning. For this night's big party. You had the nice day?"

"We went to Capri."

"Then you must be idiot. Like the Americans."

"And Canadians," comes a voice from the doorway. "We always get sidelined. Hey, check out that fire. Cosy."

Lucia smiles warmly at Cassie. "I tell my husband you go to Capri. He will laugh and laugh." And off she goes to have one of those precious chuckling-at-foreigners moments that boost gross national smugness all over the world.

"I'm so glad she finds us amusing," says Pete, moving towards the crackling fire.

"Yeah. We try. How's Julia?"

"Oh, much improved, Cassie," says Pete, remembering to glide back into doctor mode. At least he doesn't have to switch accents. "She's gone for a therapeutic walk in the grounds with

David." He hopes he hasn't revealed the level of panic underlying this simple fact.

"I sure hope he doesn't drive her back into the ocean with his movie talk."

"No, no," protests Pete. "She'll be fascinated. And excited. It's such an alien landscape to our own." He recalls that this is the land of Pinocchio and has a vision of his nose growing out of the door.

"Seems you've had your share of excitement too, Doc," she says, sitting in a wide hand-carved chair. Quite possibly homemade. "Sorry if we gave you the third degree back there. Old habits."

Pete draws a similarly well-crafted chair up close, hopefully sending a signal to his quarry of discreet but momentous things to come. "Julia and I are very different, Cassie. Most times she keeps things bottled up. I'm someone who... well, who needs to talk. But, of course, there are confidentiality issues—"

"Hey, I wouldn't wish to—"

"—which *can* be overridden, if names are changed!" He fears his voice just went up a few octaves but she seems not to have noticed. What they do notice is a bottle of limoncello and two glasses on a marble side table. He immediately does the honours.

"*Salute!*" she says.

"Cheers!" he replies, taking a sip and steaming on, as if the sweet, local liqueur is already loosening his tongue. "I was just a young psychoanalyst when I first met Julia. She was thirty-five. Eight years older than me."

"So, what – Julia is fifty-six now? You're kidding me."

"Oh," he says, suddenly stumped. "Er. Well, between you and me, Cassie," and here his voice goes even quieter, just in case his former patient is around, "for her fiftieth birthday, I treated her to some cosmetic surgery."

"They did it very well," she whispers.

"Didn't they! Anyway, I knew the moment I was introduced to her – in that 'characterful little apartment in a picturesque part of Caracas' – that I wanted to help her fight her way back to normality. Even if it took me every waking moment of every—"

"Only problem – you fell in love with her!"

"*Not until the second act!*" He really wishes he could retake that bit. "Er – as I think you people say!" he laughs. *Neatly done, Pete.* "Which is what turned our psycho-drama into a romance. And later, of course, into a… well, into a thriller."

"See," she laughs, "you've locked on to *my* wavelength now!"

"Cassie, it's what we psychoanalysts do." He is aware that night is falling all too swiftly. The rain hammers on the windows like a village in panic trying to escape a volcano. From the garden he hears footsteps and chatter moving in their direction and quickens his pace. "Anyway, I knew if I had any hope of finally getting rid of the murderous Isabella, I had to get Julia well away from Caracas. To… to somewhere she wouldn't be recognised and taunted by her fans." *Backstory, backstory!* "Sorry – Isabella was the name of—"

"—her character. Gotcha! And you had to do it before she might actually turn her mind to violence. *Real* violence."

"*Exactly!*" The sounds are growing louder. He builds up his speed even more, trying not to sound too like Alvin the Chipmunk. "And I thought we were getting somewhere with the therapy, Cassie. I really did. But—"

"Always a but. Buts are good. Sorry, Peter."

"—but… well, I hadn't counted on that chance meeting with an old fan – the Venezuelan Ambassador. At Buckingham Palace."

"*Jesus!*"

"Oh, that fire – she look so good!"

They turn to see Julie and David losing their sodden waterproofs but not their smiles, which are still broad and expansive.

"Hey, you guys," says Cassie. "Have a nice walk?"

"Sure did," beams David. "The people you meet on vacation!"

Julie nods in agreement. "I am just telling David. About our story."

Pete tries to maintain his smile. "Oh," he says, casually, "were you?"

"Now before you scold me, Cass, I didn't push. I think Julia wanted to talk." He looks solicitously towards Julie who, to his relief but not Pete's, is nodding. "Okay, come on, honey. We've got to freshen up and have some dinner. Before the fun starts."

Cassie lifts herself from the chair. "My director is ordering a costume change. See you at the party, guys."

Pete waits until they're out of earshot before glaring straight into his wife's eyes, which seem incredibly bright and wide open; and, admittedly, rather lovely, although her looks aren't top of his mind right now. "What the hell did you just tell him?"

"Only what's in the script," she says innocently.

"*You never read the bloody script!*"

"Oh no, you're right. I didn't, did I? Shall we pop into town for some din-dins?"

DUE!

The little hire car is making a meal of the poorly lit, winding road. Pete knows that he has to drive more slowly than normal, in order to limit their chances of bumping into Cassie and David. But his mind is still sending him fairly swiftly round the bend.

"You said *what*?!"

"I said I met you when we were both twenty-four."

"How in God's name could that have happened? You'd have been playing Kostas's – or, in your version, Dmitri's – mistress from the time you were thirteen!"

"In my country," she explains, as Julia, "the theengs, they are different. Anyway, chuck," she continues, dropping the accent, "I don't think the female lead *should* be eight years older than her psychoanalyst. Doesn't work for me."

He swerves to avoid a passing elderly peasant. Or somebody all in black, he's not exactly sure of the classification. "But it's an older woman, younger man romance. That's the whole bloody point!"

"I don't think so, darling," she counters, with some confidence. "And Pete, I know I'm a bit knackered but they can see I'm not eight years older than you."

"No, they can't."

"Oh, thanks a bunch."

"I told Cassie you'd had cosmetic surgery."

The silence lasts three bends and a further abrupt narrowing of the hillside road.

"Pig," she says, finally.

"*Jools…*" He sounds pathetic but sincere. "It's a compliment, really. You look… your age." He turns to inspect her, just to make sure, and is quite pleasantly surprised. "Actually, you're already looking better. Younger! Than when we started. I mean it."

He senses that she is mildly placated, which is a relief of sorts but right now the least of his concerns. "What else did you tell David?"

"Not much," she says. "Just that I have a third personality – one that even you don't know about."

He manages to find a stopping point at the side of the road into which he can demonstrably screech, although part of him feels like finding a rockier one at the very bottom of the crevice.

"*WHAT?*" he screams, thinking as he does so that cries of anguish will soon supplant *Come Back to Sorrento* as the signature theme of their trip. "That doesn't make any sense at all. If I don't know about it, how the hell do you?"

"Because I've been seeing another psychoanalyst. A Scotsman. And we're falling in love."

There is absolutely nothing he can say to this. Because it's clearly a nightmare from which he will soon wake and they'll be happily back home in their small, three-bedroom semi in Eastcote. Impoverished but sane. So all he can do is drive on.

Eventually, however, he finds some words. Although things now seem to have moved on beyond even his gift for language. Tears feel more appropriate. Or the rending of garments. "Julie, this is a complete travesty of my work."

She just looks at him.

There are more cars around now, as they enter a tiny suburb on the flank of town. Coloured street lights are flicking on. People stroll in groups and couples, enjoying a sudden and welcome respite from the rain, before going on to their Novello Anno celebrations. Pete wishes he could share their joy.

"We appear to have artistic differences, don't we?" says Julie, blithely. After a well-timed pause she adds, "David seemed to like it."

Once again Pete finds himself thrown off-balance. "Did he? What did he say?"

"Said it had an almost cinematic quality that made him want to know more."

"Yeah? Except now they've got two totally different bloody versions! Let's pray they don't compare notes."

Julie surprises him by taking his hand. He finds it comforting, which sets him back even more. "Listen, love," she urges, "*forget* the script. You can rewrite the flaming script. You've always said it's the idea that counts. We've got the party tonight and then they're off. Last-chance motel. We get 'em to buy one hundred per cent into our story, y'know, the bigger picture, and once we've reeled 'em in, got 'em to find the narrative totally irresistible, fact *or* fiction, we say *'fine, okay, it's yours – but only if we write it!'*"

"*Our* story? *We?*"

She heaves a sigh worthy of Chulia Carmen Rodriguez thingy thingy. "Okay, you."

"Julie," he has to ask, "are you alright?"

"I'm fine, Pete. Why?"

"No reason." But, of course, he tells himself, there's every reason. He has never seen her quite like this. "Who is this third 'face' of Julia, by the way? Just so's I know."

She turns to him and gives him the sweetest smile. "Still working on that. Your mission – if you choose to accept it – is to hold off Mrs Booth and loverboy Eric. Until we clinch the deal."

"*'Clinch'*. You really think...?"

Julie nods. She really thinks.

UNO!

The breakfast room has been transformed.

Perhaps it's simply that it's night-time and all they can see way down below, from the open terrace, is a sea of sparkling lights, as if Neptune has bought Mrs Neptune a massive diamond tiara for Christmas.

Yet there's also the scent; of flowers perhaps, real logs in the fire, cool Amalfi breeze. But it's the tang of hope too – new beginnings, thick with promise, and a future nobody can yet attempt to describe. Plus, of course, aromas floating through the heady air from Lucia's massive table, now overflowing not with rolls and homemade marmalades, but with fine Italian delicacies and medium-quality Italian wine.

Lucia herself is also overflowing. That firm, burnished Neapolitan skin positively glows in a shimmering, low-cut party gown the colour of flame, affording her entranced guests the indelible image of a walking firework.

"Ah, my good friends from London!" she greets the Dawkinses, who would have to admit they don't look too shabby themselves.

Pete can't fail to notice that there is something curiously enticing and vaguely... well, Latin, in the way his increasingly mercurial wife has decked herself out. Even with the sharp descriptive skills that he knows deep down are his birthright, he couldn't quite capture what she has actually done to achieve this look. It might simply be the enhanced vividness of her make-up or the amount of flesh she is managing to reveal in those same clothes in which she usually appears – at rare Eastcote soirées – attractive yet relatively restrained.

Yet it must also reside in the way she holds herself, standing tall in her best heels with a self-confidence that almost, but not quite, tips over into arrogance. He will not be totally surprised if she dashes out onto the terrace, grabs a random male and rips off a swift but lusty tango.

"You are looking very nice, Signora Dawkins," gushes their hostess. "I think this is good holiday for you, yes?" She winks broadly as she points across the room. "And look, there is stupid Pasquale. It is to him you say *grazie* for this."

They turn to stupid Pasquale, who is laughing with his young cousin and already well into the Lambrusco. He raises his glass and smiles. Pete wonders if *grazie* will turn out to be the most apposite word for this night. Or indeed for this visit. He really has no idea.

A knife smacks hard and repeatedly against a wine bottle.

"In few minutes," announces Lucia loudly to her assembled guests, who number barely more than a dozen but appear to be making the noise of hundreds, "we turn on television. For the counting. And then is fireworks. Ah, and see who has come to say *ciao*!"

This last is apparently directed to Pete and Julie. They look towards the door. Mrs Booth and Eric are striding towards the only faces they know, even if one of those faces isn't quite as they usually know it.

"*Buonasera, buonasera!*" gushes the headteacher, dressed in what Julie assumes is her mother-of-the-bride outfit. Eric is rather smart, if a tad formal, in his chairman-of-the-board suit. "Oh, isn't this more *autentico* than that noisy hotel of ours? Especially tonight, eh, Eric?"

Eric nods. Pete and Julie find themselves wondering exactly what specials are on the Booth menu for this turn of the year. And then try not to think about it.

Lucia puts her strong, expansive arms around her new guests, gripping them as if they might otherwise hurl themselves into the spangled night. "On this evening, the word we say is '*auguri*'. It mean 'I wish you many good thing' for the year that is coming."

"*Auguri,*" repeats Pete.

"*Auguri!*" cries Julie in a very passable Italian accent.

"How you say in Venezuela, Signora?" Julie just stares at her hostess. "I am hearing this is your first country, yes?" Clearly her dubious provenance has been passed on. "Feliz Año Nuevo, I think," suggests Lucia. To which Julie simply nods, wishing Vesuvius would explode just to change the conversation. Lucia has already wandered off to explain '*auguri*' to other merry but ignorant foreigners.

Mrs Booth appears confused, which is a rare and not particularly good look. "What's she talking about… Venezuela?"

Julie turns to Pete as she pictures her hard-won career plummeting to the level of his.

"Poor Lucia, she gets her guests confused, Mrs Booth," explains Pete, swiftly. "Ha. Venezuela."

If he thinks Julie has depleted her stock of New Year surprises, she confounds him once again.

"No – ees no confusion, Signora Boot. You do not know this, but I make maracas in Caracas, ay ay ayyyy!!"

Mrs Booth, as befits her calling as an academic, takes her time to process this. The seconds feel like hours. "Yes… well, you're not at school, and I'm not a schoolmarm. So you enjoy yourself, Julie. In your own way." With this, she drags Eric to the terrace. "Eric, the Asti Spumante is calling us."

"Are you on self-destruct?" Pete asks his wife quietly.

"No… Least I don't think so. For God's sake, I'm setting the bloody scene! For, you know, our friends. I theenk you understand thees, Pedro."

As he watches his peculiar wife become more sultry before his eyes, Pete Dawkins feels stirrings that aren't particularly career-oriented and could indeed create a major distraction from the task at hand. The curious thing is that he is not totally displeased, even though the particular climax he has been setting his sights on will involve another couple altogether.

"Nobody would believe you're fifty-six," he says, rakishly.

"I SHIT ON YOUR DEAD FAMILY!" Which is a lovely South American curse she just discovered on Google, between texting her sons from the bathroom. Julie senses now that it might sound less lovely spoken at volume in a crowded room.

"Whoa – we interrupting something?" says Cassie, whom they haven't noticed until she is standing there beside them. Sensitively, she lowers the temperature by adding, "Hey Julia, you look great!"

"For my age."

"You're younger than us, kid," laughs David, taking in the surroundings and the food.

"Is that what she told you?" scoffs Pete, who can't now recall exactly which story is which. "Quite a spread Lucia's laid out, eh? Bet it beats – what do you guys call it? – location catering."

David just laughs and makes for the deli counter. He looks back to see that Cassie has rested her arm consolingly around Julie's attractively bare shoulders.

"This age business," says Cassie McBride. "Such a load of bull, eh, Julia?" The kindly Canadian smile that accompanies this turns within seconds into a horrified gasp. "Whoa… *Julia?*"

Something in Julie's countenance has caused Cassie to stop mid-sentence and Pete to stare open-mouthed at his wife. The set of her formerly sweet face appears to have subtly changed and hardened. Luminous green eyes seem almost impossibly wide and somehow haunted by a past unspoken. The woman appears to have entered a deeper, darker place.

When she finally talks, her voice takes on a far lower register, as if stones have just dropped into the pit of her stomach.

"BULL!" she intones.

"Er, yeah," agrees a bemused Cassie, just in time to hear this curious woman say "BULL" once again, only louder. "I'm sorry… Julia? Sweetie?"

"You WON'T be…" says the drama teacher from Hull formerly known as Julie. The voice goes even lower, until it's almost a rumble. "When you have spent the night with *El Merido*."

"Er… Julia…?" The panic in Pete's voice sounds like Disneyland compared to the raw fear surging unchallenged through his gut.

"Who the hell is Chulia?" booms the voice. "And who the hell are you?"

Oh God!

"Well," says Pete, in finest psychoanalytic-verging-on-homicidal mode, "I'm—"

"More to the point," interrupts a riveted David, addressing this *new* Julia, his foraging temporarily halted, "who are you, señor?"

"You do not recognise Venezuela's greatest matador?" snaps Julie, with a scornfully throaty snarl.

Pete is in there, damage-limiting. "*Classic!* I'd heard of this, obviously, but never actually— The third personality, David. *YES!* It can be a different sex. With different talents, a different IQ, even different blood pressure." He shakes his head. "Wow – the human mind!"

David looks at Cassie then at Julie, who is doing a deft pass with a festive red table napkin. "This is extraordinary, Pete. Say, even if we stay up all night, we have to talk."

Pete can't breathe. The man is serious. He has never seen anyone so fired up in his life. Except, of course, his own wife.

A loud noise, soaring now above the room's chatter, causes everyone to be still. Even El Merida. The TV has been switched on. A handsome man chats happily in Italian to the room and the wider world beyond as upbeat music pulsates relentlessly behind him.

73

"*Everybody!*" screams Lucia. "*Now is the counting!*"

Cassie knows that she should stay quiet, in deference to whatever ritual is about to unfold. Yet it's apparent to Pete and Julie that the producer inside can't restrain herself. "We hear a lotta stuff in our line of work. But your story – sheesh – it has everything!"

"DIECI!" cry the people on the television, along with Lucia, her family and, finally, her guests as they latch on to the countdown custom of the land. Yet to David it appears to be taking on the function of a checklist.

"It has *drama*," he announces.

"NOVE!"

"*Romance*," adds Cassie.

"OTTO!"

Pete and Julie, who are looking quite sick with excitement – especially Pete – gaze around at the other faces. Ordinary, smiling, comfortable people, totally unaware of the scenario being played out before their shiny, alcohol-fuelled eyes.

"*Suspense*," supplies Pete, who reckons he should keep this particular moneyball rolling.

"SETTE!"

"*Death*," intones Julie, still channelling the disturbing El Merida.

"SEI!"

Julie turns to notice that Mrs Booth and her husband Eric are staring at her quite curiously. She gives them a tiny wave, with just a hint of castanet, and prays they won't come any closer.

"*Charm*," from David, with a smile to Julie.

"CINQUE!"

"*Tragedy*," adds Cassie, resting a comforting arm on Pete, which he finds rather gracious.

"QUATTRO!"

"*Ethical dilemmas*," says Pete, who's struggling a bit now but feels it's important to maintain momentum. He notices that his old mate Pasquale is keeping up his own momentum with his pretty medical cousin in a quieter corner of the room.

"TRE!"

Contributions appear to have dried up, so Pete adds a barrel-scraping, "*Professional rivalry.*"

"DUE!"

"Perfect!" agree the producer/director combo, before adding in unison, "*Jeopardy!*"

"UNO!"

Pete just has time for a swift thumbs-up before David decisively concludes the countdown.

"*And total bullshit from start to finish.*"

"AUGURI!!" cry the TV folk, along with Lucia and all the contented guests at her splendidly hospitable, if rather pricey, villa.

Couples from assorted European countries embrace each other, Edwina and Eric Booth do something weird with the tips of their tongues that Julie wishes she hadn't seen, Pasquale and Maria become kissing cousins and fireworks light up the Golfo di Napoli with a display that might put even a grumbling Vesuvius to shame.

Pete tries to talk above the noise, although somewhere near the surface of his tortured brain lurks a sense that he really needn't bother. "I'm sorry, David? Didn't quite—"

Lucia descends on them, pushing loving heads closer together as she goes. Except for those of her daughter and nephew, the backs of which she smacks quite firmly on her way. "*Auguri,*" she cries. "Now everyone must kiss everyone. Is Italian."

"Oh well, when in Rome…" says Cassie.

"Sorrento," corrects Lucia, as the fireworks reach their first splendid crescendo.

Cassie moves to Lucia and kisses her warm cheek, segueing easily into a buss on the flushed faces of both Dawkinses. Doctor and patient. "*Auguri*, Lucia; *auguri*, Julia and Peter."

"Er, *auguri*," mutters Pete. "David, I didn't totally catch—"

"Would you listen to those fireworks!" says the director.

"Peter, you've gone quite white," observes Cassie. "Past your bedtime?"

"Were we really that bad, Cassie?" he asks, mournfully. He follows this up with a look to David, as if to seal his fate. Yet, to his surprise, the couple shake their heads.

"I told them, Pete," says Julie.

"*You what?*" he yelps. "When?"

"When we went for our walk," says David. "Julie – or Chulia – let me in on what was going on. So we cooked up El Merida. It's a place in Mexico, by the way. Big on bullfighting."

Julie chooses to grunt '*olé*' in her third voice, which right now doesn't augur well for the relationship.

"But *why?*" moans Pete, looking humiliated and – even worse – betrayed.

Before Julie can explain, if indeed any explanation would suffice, Mrs Booth returns, glass in hand. "You are the only couple I haven't kissed," she announces, like an Oxfam team finally arriving at a remote and starving backwater. "Are you still Venezuelan?"

"She come and she go, Signora Boot. Oh, you haven't met David and Cassie. Guys, this is my headteacher. She just… turned up."

"Third act complications! I'm all over it!" says David.

"David and Cassie are filmmakers," explains Julie.

"Oh, how exciting," gushes Mrs Booth, instinctively turning her best side to the light. "Pete here is a writer, you know."

"We know."

"Not that you'll have seen anything of his. Now, I must find Eric – he's like catnip for older, unattached women."

As they watch her return to the babe magnet she married, Pete brings all his despair back to Julie. "*Why on Earth did you tell them?*"

"Because they're nice people, Pete. And because they already knew."

He looks at them. They're actually smiling quite benevolently, not at all like a couple betrayed. Condescending bastards. "Did you really, Cassie? Did you know?"

"We had our suspicions," says Cassie. "After Capri and Dmitri."

"*You see!*" says Pete to Julie, with a curious sense of vindication. And then, not entirely devoid of hope, he addresses Cassie and David in a professional capacity, albeit not quite the profession in which he started out. "So, *The Case of Señora X*? On a scale of 1–10."

Cassie shrugs apologetically. "Not our kind of thing."

"It's *exactly* your kind of bloody thing! Okay, it's not one hundred per cent factual, but it's got drama, excitement, passion…"

"No laughs," says David.

"You don't *do* bloody laughs!" Pete smashes his hand into a nearby *zabaglione*, which makes its own point. "David Joe Jakes movies are wrist-slitters!"

"Then don't you think it's time I opened a new window, instead of a new vein?"

The seconds in which Pete fails to respond are fully taken up by the other guests in expressions of boozy, kissy delight at the display of Neapolitan pyrotechnics beyond the window. A display that leaves Pete Dawkins sadly cold.

"Pardon?" he says, eventually.

"He wants to do a comedy," says Cassie.

"I can do comedy!" yelps Pete, with almost alarming speed. "I've *done* comedy. Sitcoms. Sketch shows. In fact, some say funny is what I do best."

"Pete…" says Julie gently.

"I've got a comedy movie that nearly got bought by… someone. It's on my phone right now. I can email it—" He stops and looks at Julie. "Bit needy?" She just nods.

Suddenly, like the ghosts of New Years Past, Mrs Booth and Eric are back.

"We're back," she announces unnecessarily. "I've kissed you, Julie, but Eric says he hasn't and it would be bad luck to miss someone out."

They're probably all too immersed in the unfolding story to be unduly perturbed by what Eric decides to do with his face, but Julie finally manages to wriggle free with just the slightest display of total repulsion. Unperturbed, or possibly even strangely proud, Mrs Booth asks Julie if she is looking forward to the new term.

"I hope she is, Mrs Booth," says Pete. "Seeing as it's going to be her last."

The women stare at him, even Cassie.

"*Pete?*" mutters Julie, a bit shakily, feeling more scared than she has been all day. Even Eric's continued pawing doesn't distract from what her unpredictable husband just said.

"She's going back to acting, Mrs B," continues Pete. "That's where her heart really lies." When his wife gawps at him as if he has lost what was left of his mind, he tells her, "I haven't seen you so sparky in years... Chulia."

Seeing his formidable partner quite unusually lost for words, it is Eric, the Don Juan of Eastcote, who speaks up. "I would have thought you needed *one* regular income in your household."

"Oh, but we will have an income, Eric," says Julie, finally catching her breath. "Pete's just sold a script."

"No, I haven't."

"Think you might have, Pete," says Cassie.

David laughs his rich laugh, one that even Eric can't match in its swoon quotient. "Guy who tries to sell a movie by pretending it's the story of his life? Ring any bells?"

"Ees called *Going Caracas*," adds Julie/Chulia, clearly off the top of her head.

Pete Dawkins, jobbing writer, father of two, husband of Julie, has no idea what this brand new year will bring. But he can't ever recall finding himself on an early January 1st morning feeling quite this sober yet hopeful. He takes his extraordinary and possibly deranged wife in his arms and gives her an *auguri* that would make the newly twinned cities of Hull and Caracas proud.

"I think you are very happy I double the book for you now," comes a mellow voice beside them.

"Sod off, Pasquale," they respond as one, while *Come Back to Sorrento*, performed on the great organ of St Peter's in Rome, echoes into the sulphur-tinged Neapolitan night.

AUGURI!

THE ART OF LISTENING

Two very dear friends of mine willingly give up a few hours of their free time each week to volunteer on a confidential helpline.

Curious, I happened to ask them an intriguing 'What if?' question. To which they simply shrugged and smiled.

Fortunately the imagination knows no such boundaries.

I have always been a good listener. I suppose I got it from my parents, who barely listened to a thing I said.

That probably doesn't make any sense to you, but I think you can learn a lot from people who do the exact opposite to what you very much hope that you would do.

I imagine it's like people who've been abused wanting to treat their own children with dignity and respect, rather than just repeating the awful pattern. Not that I was abused; dear Lord, far from it. But I actually talk to quite a lot of people in my spare time who have been abused rather badly, so that's why I'm saying it.

I'm getting ahead of myself.

My late parents were both refugees from Nazi Germany. They didn't escape together but they both came over on the *Kindertransport* and met through an organisation set up for just that purpose. They never saw their parents again. Can you imagine that? I try but I can't, not really. Of course Mummy and Daddy didn't help by never actually talking about it.

They were quite old when they had me – well, for those days. Couples today seem to put it off for as long as possible, don't they? I suppose it's a mixture of slow economics and, dare I say it, even slower maturity. But my folks hadn't even believed that they could have children, so a little girl was a complete and, I think – well, I hope, wonderful surprise. But it meant I never had friends I could really talk to. You know, who had parents who'd been through similar experiences. So I never knew if their parents listened to them either.

I do think, however, speaking to other people, that whatever your background or culture, it's a bit of a generational thing. So, of course, my lot have gone the other way, like those clanging steel balls that you see on office desks which are supposed to reduce stress but don't, and we probably listen to our own offspring way too much.

I say to my girlfriends that our kids would tell us their bowel movements, given half the chance. And they're away from home and in their thirties!

But that's another story.

I don't want to bang on about my parents, because this isn't about my parents. I think I now understand why they really didn't take that much notice of my problems when I was growing up. I mean, falling out of a friendship with Jenny Grossman, or even out of a tree with Nancy Rosen, can hardly compare with your windows being smashed and seeing your own father beaten up by work colleagues he'd always thought were his pals.

And crying over getting a C in a subject you thought you were pretty good at doesn't amount to much for people who were yanked out of school and landed up in Liverpool Street Station not knowing a word of English. (Although they were actually rather displeased at my getting that C and that was largely *because* they'd been yanked out of school and, of course, wanted me to attain what they were certain they themselves would have, had times been different. But it still wasn't like listening.)

Now, of course, I've been *trained* to listen.

Yet I do believe you need to have those basic skills already there inside you, like some sort of innate talent, such as music or art or cookery, just waiting to be channeled.

Have you ever heard of *Here*?

I imagine you have. Most people have. You may even have called us. Who knows, I might have spoken to you, although there are thousands of us, up and down the country, all shapes and sizes, so it's pretty unlikely.

Here is one of those charitable organisations this country does so well, staffed totally by volunteers – highly trained volunteers, I have to add – with a local or a national number you can phone if you're feeling sad or upset or distressed. Or just angry and fed-up. Or even, I'm afraid to say, suicidal. We don't know who you are; you certainly don't know who we are. We don't record your calls and we have absolutely no means of tracing them back to you.

So it's about as safe and anonymous as you can get. Which is why people like it and why we have so many unfortunate people calling us at all times of the day and night. It's curious, but in some way, when you hear about all the misery and awfulness some poor souls have in their lives, it makes you realise just how lucky you are.

Sometimes.

***

My husband doesn't know that I come here.

'Here' being a room in a nondescript building in the centre of the town where I live. A large room with three telephones in it, set in small booths, so that we get a bit of privacy when we're talking; but without doors to the booths, so that our fellow volunteers who are on shift with us can offer support if we need it. If, of course, they're not actually manning their own phones. At the very least they can bring us a nice cup of tea. (The amount of tea I drink in the course of my weekly three-hour evening shift, it's amazing I'm not on the loo all night. Perhaps they should put a phone in there too. Joking!)

You probably think that's really weird, my husband not knowing where I am on a Wednesday evening. What sort of a marriage do we have going, with such a big secret? Surely honesty is a basic requirement, you'll say, both in marriage and in *Here*?

It isn't that weird, if you know Michael.

He's a lovely man, don't get me wrong. I wouldn't have stayed married to him for nearly thirty-five years if he was a pig. And I hear about some marriages on the phone, I can tell you. Well, I can't actually, it being confidential – but trust me, there are some tricky people out there. And I don't just mean men, we women can do our share. Less often with our fists or our boots, I grant you, but we have our own weapons of choice. And the damage can be just as lethal.

Sometimes you end up thinking, when you hear these stories, *why on earth did you two people get together in the first place?* But that's rather judgmental, which we're really not supposed to be.

What I always say is: we volunteers are human, we're not saints. Even though when a caller tells us what a difference we made, just by listening and occasionally saying the right thing at the right time, well, we do feel just a wee bit saintly. At least until the next caller rings up and tells us we're all fucking useless. Excuse the language – but that wasn't half as bad as some of the stuff we hear. Actually, I think it has made me a bit more sweary at home, listening to all that every week. Michael has picked up on this and he doesn't approve. So I have to be a bit careful.

I have to be careful of quite a lot of things at home.

And Therapy is one of the things I have to be most careful of. Even mentioning the T Word is tricky. Or the C Word, which isn't what you may think it is (although we do hear what you may think it is quite a lot too). Of course in some homes that we know the unspoken C Word is Cancer, but our particular banned C Word is Counselling.

You see, Michael is not himself these days. Actually, this has been going on for so long that he probably is himself, but I'm pretty sure, what with the bad moods and the overriding sadness that hangs in the air like flowers on the turn or the smell of last night's supper, that it's not a self he's particularly comfortable with. There's no single overriding reason – it's a mixture of a lot of things really.

At least I think so. I can't be totally sure, because the man won't talk. Men don't, do they? Or at least, not the ones our age.

The kids leaving home was probably one of what they call the 'biggies'. And, of course, their doing it at virtually the same time. It's not as if it was some sort of conspiracy – *let's get the hell away from Mum and Dad!* – at least, I hope not. Although that's a natural feeling too, isn't it, for kids, when you get to a certain age and everything your parents do drives you totally round the bend? And vice versa. I remember it only too well myself, which is why I couldn't wait to marry Michael.

They both had their own reasons for moving out and they just sort of coincided.

Adam was offered a good promotion at work, which meant he had the money to rent a nice little flat – they can't own these days and we don't yet have the money to help them onto that ladder they all talk about. Too many snakes around! We live just outside London and you've heard all about the prices here. Shameful, except of course that the value of the little semi we bought over thirty years ago has gone soaring. But unless we move to… I dunno, Huddersfield – so what?

Anyway, at around the same time, Sharon decided she wanted to move in with her longtime girlfriend, Petra. Michael did say a while back that only *our* daughter can go to a disco and come out with another woman. I had to explain that it was a Gay and Lesbian Disco. We laughed at the time but I actually think he was and still is a little upset.

Of course he'd never admit he was bothered or dare I say saddened. Because he's a good man and Sharon is the apple of her daddy's eye. I have to add that we both think Petra is a really special person. She's also a nice Jewish girl and a dentist, so that's two boxes ticked! (And a family isn't out of the question, which just shows you how we've moved on.)

I'm sure there's a lot of other stuff going on too. Michael's a very thoughtful man and his mind is always churning away. And churning him up. But he won't talk to me and, like I say, when I try the T and the C Words, he goes berserk. He thinks they're all cranks and charlatans – even the few we know personally – and that people should be able to sort out their own problems.

I do believe he still thinks you have to lie down on someone's sofa while an old foreign gentleman with an accent you could cut with a knife sits behind you, pad in hand, and asks you what you dreamed about last night, and did you fancy your mother?

I don't even bother anymore.

But last year, when a girl at the local play-school where I work told me that she volunteers at *Here*, I thought this might be something I could usefully get involved with. Something that's just for me and that means… well, that I can give a little something back.

It's only one night a week, so it's not like I've suddenly gone all Médecins Sans Frontières or Mother Teresa or something. But it does seem to help those far-too-many unfortunate people, who often have nowhere else to turn. And, as a lovely by-product, it really takes you out of yourself. Which we all need sometimes, don't we? (Especially as nobody else seems to be doing too much on the taking-me-out front these days.)

The problem is, I had to lie to Michael.

This is something I've never done before and hope I never shall again. But, to be perfectly honest, I didn't think I could go through the inevitable disdain and ridicule. Not week after week.

Michael can be quite sarcastic at times; it's not his most attractive quality. And sometimes you get a bit tired, that's all. Not to say diminished. So it was much easier at the time just to say I was still at the regular keep-fit class at the local sports centre, the one I had been going to for yonks with some of my girlfriends. ('Keep Fat', as we call it.) And that we would probably go on for a cup of decaf and a piece of cake afterwards. Just to put back the calories!

I was intending to tell him the truth eventually. Of course I was.

The girls were in on it and they still are, bless them, although I'm sure they think it's a bit odd. Well, more than a bit. But, as my late Auntie Bea would say, if she were still here, it's only what they call a 'white lie'. Beate wasn't my real auntie, she was a much older Viennese refugee my parents met up with when they came here, and she was celebrated in our family for writing exactly as she spoke. She once put 'three shits' on a laundry list and got the message back: 'not received'.

Sorry about the digression – I'd be flayed alive for telling a story like that in one of my phone calls, even if I was getting on ever so well with the person and an appropriate juncture had somehow come up. Not that I can think of one offhand.

You see, we're not supposed to reveal *anything* about ourselves – not our background, our family, our sexuality, our work. And certainly not our race or religion. It's all about the caller; we're what I suppose you'd call a 'blank canvas' and they can fill us in as they wish. And I imagine they paint their own picture of us just from the way we sound at the other end of the line. The way I guess I do when I listen to somebody talking on the radio.

Our callers do sometimes ask us questions about ourselves; they're only human and I imagine they can feel a bit uncomfortable with the conversation being so one-sided when tonally it's as if we're chatting like friends. But we steer them back pretty swiftly onto what it is they really called about, and that certainly isn't us. We can give out our first name – of course that's allowed and it's a sort of ice-breaker, but some of us don't use our real one, either because it's too unusual or because we feel more comfortable in a sense 'being' someone else. I'm a case in point. My real name is Elisa but on the phone I'm Derek. No, of course I'm not – that was just one of my jokes.

I'm Ann.

As you can probably tell, I'm a bit of a glass half-full person, but with Michael the glass is always a wee bit empty. Well, more than a wee bit. (Except when it's his favourite Scotch, but that's another story.) Please don't think I'm complaining; in a way, it's probably how we've managed so well over the years. They do say that opposites attract, don't they, and I think that together we've made for a pretty full glass, even if right now our cup isn't exactly runnething over.

It's funny, but for all my talk about being a bubbly, open person, there aren't really that many people I can open up to. There are my girlfriends, of course, and they're lovely, but they all seem to have their own problems and worries. As we all do, don't we? It could be our health – we're all getting to a certain age, so we always start off our chats, when we come together, with what we call our 'organ recital'. You know, kidneys, heart, liver, tummy. Spleen, if we're feeling reckless. As indeed do Michael and I, when we're with other couples (although that hasn't occurred too often lately). And after this, we might go on to grandchildren, but as Michael and I don't have any, not yet, our friends are very thoughtful and don't bring out too many photographs.

Curiously, there is one person I *can* open up to and he's the person you'd think I have the least in common with. Antony is a youth worker, mainly in the local Afro-Caribbean and Somali communities, and he's told me that he himself has been involved with some quite bad gangs and some horrible drug-dealing. In the past, of course, when he was younger.

There's a lot of it goes on around here, apparently, but you feel so cushioned, don't you, in your neat little semi in your quiet little suburb. Well, I know I do. Although I do hear a fair bit about it on the phone and I've learned a lot more than I ever thought I'd know.

But he's a wonderful and very brave young man is our Antony, and he has really turned himself around. The fact that he would bother to volunteer for *Here*, when he does all that he does anyway, is extraordinary. Bit like a busman's holiday, I would have thought, but he says he gets a terrific amount out of it and it helps him enormously with his day job. Plus he likes all of us. Which is win-win, as they say these days.

Antony is my regular shift-partner on a Wednesday evening and because we hear so much awful stuff on the phone, it seems to open us up to talking about absolutely anything when we have a break between callers. And, trust me, you do need a break when you've had a heavy call that has lasted the best part of an hour and you've had to listen with your entire mind until your brain and your body ache from the sheer concentration; a few minutes away from the booths just to stretch, offload and get some support from your partner.

Debriefing is what the powers-that-be call it, but I just say it's unwinding. Because you really are like a coil of wire that has been wound and wound. I suppose that's how it works – we get tighter as the callers loosen up, like unravelling and gathering up a ball of wool. Even just being told by your duty-mate that you did the right thing gives you the strength to get back in that booth and prepare yourself for whatever the world is going to chuck at you next.

Sometimes it can be ever so sad.

Antony has told me things about his life as the weeks and months have gone on that I don't think he has even told his parents or his mates. I suppose I have been just as open with him; I hope I have, although it has probably seemed a bit tame, what with no one being stabbed in the belly or ending up in a gutter overdosed on smack.

But when you or I have a problem that's really bothering us, we don't immediately measure it against things that are so much worse, do we, because I don't think this is how our minds or emotions work. It's what I was telling you about my parents. Having another stupid argument with your husband over breakfast doesn't exactly compare with Hitler, or what's going on in Syria, but that doesn't stop you feeling sick to your stomach.

So when I popped into the centre a couple of Wednesdays ago for my regular shift, I was quite looking forward to one of mine and Antony's no-holds-barred, what-plays-in-*Here*-stays-in-*Here* chats.

And then I got the phone call.

***

I knew it was Michael the moment he said 'hello'.

Of course, I had spoken first. You don't answer a phone call with silence. But all I had said was, "Hello. We're *Here*. My name's Ann." I suppose I must have a 'phone voice'. Everyone does, don't they? We all want to sound our best and come across as the person we'd like others to think we are, even if it's not actually how we do come over day-to-day. And I try to make the first words they hear seem caring, especially as this might be the first time they've ever heard them from anyone. (I know this makes me seem like I'm as false as anything, but I don't think I am. I hope I'm not. It's just that striking the right note is so important.)

Fortunately, I could tell by his tentative and softly spoken "Hello, Ann" that he didn't immediately recognise me. And why should he? My name is Elisa and I was at Keep Fit. But that didn't exactly prevent me from feeling like the light supper we'd eaten together just before I left him was about to shoot right back up my throat.

I assumed of course that my not being around was exactly why he had chosen a Wednesday evening to get in touch. And because he'd used our local number, not the national one, he had come straight through to us. He probably didn't even know that there *is* a national number and had maybe just noted down ours as he passed the building one day on the slow drive to his office. Actually he doesn't work too far away, so if he pops out for a lunchtime stroll, which I hope he does, he'll probably walk right by our door.

There are rules in our organisation. Very strict rules. With penalties to match.

And one of them is that if we think we actually *know* the person who is calling, we should excuse ourselves – sensitively of course, because this is tricky territory – and gently pass the caller on to a colleague, as you would with something precious that you wouldn't wish to break. Or you might simply ask him or her to call the national number rather than their local branch, in

92

the reasonable hope that the next time they'd connect to someone hundreds of miles away.

I don't know what took hold of me at that moment. Shock, I suppose. Yet I knew in an instant that there was no way I was handing my poor husband over to Antony or to any other Hearer in this country or on this planet. But I didn't dare let on to my sweet fellow volunteer, who was not yet on a call and was smiling over to me, just to check if I needed any support (which of course I did – a stiff brandy would have been good!), that there was the least little thing amiss.

So I just continued the call. In an accent that was no longer my own.

I could feel Antony staring at me from the other booth, where he was sitting and waiting. As indeed I too would be staring, were I to hear someone whom I had always believed hailed from East London, with just a hint (so I'm told) of something vaguely continental, sounding like they had just taken the first train down from Newcastle. (I would later tell my shift-mate that I had been to college there – which is true – and that I was picking up the familiar accent from the caller himself, which can happen if you have too good an ear.)

"Is there something I can call you, pet?" I asked, in order to begin this brand new relationship with a man next to whose warm body I had woken up only a matter of hours before. Which sounds a lot more steamy than it was.

"Er, yeah, okay," he said, a bit hesitantly. "My name's… Howard." Which is his brother's name, but Howard is estranged from Michael and living in Vancouver, we think, so he's hardly likely to find out. But it was interesting to note that I wasn't the only one playing games, although my mystery caller's name-change hardly matched my own duplicity. And we had only just begun.

"I'm listening, Mi— Howard." *Jesus!* "How can I help you?"

If there's one thing I do well, it's recall conversations. Perhaps it's a natural ability, but it's certainly a part of the training. There's nothing more crushing for a caller than if you totally forget what he just told you or make a daft mistake when you're referring back to things he has said. So I'm pretty sure that what I'm remembering now is what actually went down, as they say. Although, of course, it didn't go down anywhere, except in my reeling head.

"I'm a bit low," said Howard. (I'm sticking to his *nom de phone*. I was going to say to avoid confusion, but that would be quite a stretch in the circumstances.)

"A bit low," I repeated, which is quite a good thing to do as it shows you're listening. And by God, was I listening – even while my voice and, I believe, my whole body, trembled like an office block in an earthquake zone. Make that a jelly at a children's party. "Why's that, Howard? Are you able to tell me?"

And did I really want to know? Of course I bloody did.

"It's my life, really," he said. Then he stopped.

"Uh huh," I said. "Could you be a bit more specific, love?" I know that down here calling a stranger 'love' can sound like you're being a bit too familiar, but up North, in my experience, 'love' and 'pet' are fine. And it wasn't like I was going to launch into a chorus of *Blaydon Races*.

"Well, it's everything," continued Howard unhelpfully. "Sorry Ann, I don't know how this works. It is, you know, totally confidential?"

"Nothing will go any further than you and me," I assured him, which was truer than he would hopefully ever know. "And this is a safe place to tell me anything you want. No one's going to judge you here, Howard."

No one but your wife, that is.

If I had a guilty conscience at this point – and I'm pretty sure I did – it was getting soaked up in the far more heady mix of fascination, disbelief and pure, undiluted terror. But I'll tell you one thing: my mind definitely wasn't wandering.

"Thank you, Ann," he said sadly, and my heart melted. "If my wife knew I was doing this, she would laugh her head off."

"Oh, I'm sure she wouldn't," I said, perhaps a tad too vociferously. I wanted to add, 'She might nod a bit too smugly and grin to herself like a Cheshire Cat, but laugh her head off…?' I held back.

"I'm just a bit… you know… sad."

He paused again and this time it went on for a good few seconds. I found myself wishing that he would just get to the point; the tension was tying my gut in knots and all over my body I could feel the sweat that I should have been letting out at Keep Fit. But you have to allow your callers to go at their own pace. It really is a big deal making that decision to phone us.

For a start it means admitting to yourself that you have a problem, which can be quite a step, and also realising that it might just take the kindness of strangers to help you through it. (I know that's a quote from some film but it's always stuck with me as summing up what we are really all about.)

"Sad?" I found myself almost crawling into the phone. "Has something happened, Howard," I said softly, "to make you feel this way?"

"No," he said, which kind of reassured me, as I truly wasn't aware of any such occurrence. "Quite the reverse, actually."

"The reverse?" What was he on about?

"Yeah. Nothing's bloody happening."

I'm sorry?

"What do you mean?" I could hear myself totally losing the Geordie in my anxiety to discover what he had to tell me. So I added a 'petal', just to get us back on track.

"Well, take work for example. I'm bored bloody stiff."

"Oh. Oh dear. What do you do, Howard? For your work. You sound… professional." An assumption I really shouldn't have made – and how on earth does someone sound professional when not actually practising their profession? – but I thought it might somehow boost him just a little.

"Do I?" He seemed surprised, but not unpleasantly so. "I'm an accountant."

I tried to sound impressed. 'Ooh' was as much as I could, and indeed should, manage. It's not like he was Secretary-General of the United Nations.

"Been doing it for years and years in the same small ruddy firm, and at 59 I'm not even a partner! Pathetic, isn't it?"

Well, I don't think so. Not pathetic. But I've told him for years his bosses are taking advantage and he could do so much better elsewhere. Will he listen?

"No, I don't think it's pathetic, Howard. Not at all. But it's not about what I think, is it?"

That was when he surprised me. Well, surprised me even more. "No. It's about what my wife thinks."

I was silent for a moment and not by intent, but of course you can't be doing this for too long or callers think you've hung up or simply died of boredom.

"I'm sorry?" I managed.

"She's thought for years I should branch out. You know, set up my own firm. But it's a risky business, Ann. Especially at my age. Who's to say my clients would come with me?"

"Oh, of course they would," I blurted out unthinkingly.

"How would *you* know?" Which was, as they say on quiz shows, a correct challenge. And he had me stumped.

"Well," I blurted, "you just… you sound so competent, Howard. Like somebody you could trust."

"I wish I could give you my wife's mobile. She thinks everything I touch turns to shit. Excuse my French."

Do I? I'm sure I don't. *Do I?* I really wanted to change the subject.

"Do you have any children, Howard?"

"No."

No? Whose were those bloody bedrooms we recently had to fumigate? Was I going mad? Perhaps this wasn't Michael. Oh my God!

"So… you don't have any children," I continued, feeling like a fairy-tale character lost in the woods. But not a princess.

"*What?*" he replied, quite loudly for him. "Of course I have! … Oh, sorry Ann, I thought you meant at home. I'm not thinking straight. I – we – don't have any at home. Not anymore."

Well, that was a relief, I can tell you. I thought for a moment we were going to have one of those conversations with someone totally pretending to be someone else. (Okay, with two people pretending.)

"And this makes you sad, does it, Howard? Your children being – what? – at university? In their own flats… homes?"

He didn't say anything, not for a while. I wondered if he was still there, but sometimes you don't want to jump in too swiftly. Then I heard it. The man – the caller – was crying.

My husband was crying.

"It's alright, Howard," I reassured him, because it was. No, it wasn't. The man never cries. Well, not to me. This was breaking my heart. "Talk to me when you're ready. I'm not going to go away. Love."

I could sense Antony approaching.

His call had obviously been a short one. Sometimes they are, but it doesn't mean they aren't important or beneficial to the caller. I really didn't need someone hovering, however solicitous they might be, not right now. So I cradled the phone under my chin, like a violinist, and made the letter T using one finger from each hand. Off he toddled with a kindly nod. He knows how I like it.

By now, Howard's terrible crying – well, terrible to me, probably quite cathartic for him – had subsided to the occasional wrenching sob, so I felt it was probably a good time to interrupt. But before I could say a word, he spoke.

"I miss them, Ann."

"I know you do."

I don't know why I said that or where it came from. Because, truthfully, I didn't know that I did know, if this makes sense. Howard

97

– Michael – had never said that he misses them. In fact, when we spoke about their absence, it was usually with a sense of relief, and even unrestrained joy that we had the house to ourselves. Having post-university kids back home can be a total nightmare – all my friends say so – because the place they most want to be is anywhere but with their farty old parents. Excuse the language.

"Do you?" he said. "How do you know?"

Er… "Because you're crying, pet."

"Well, you're more perceptive than my wife, that's for sure, Ann. She thinks I'm glad to be shot of them."

"Does she?" He's right. I thought I was the one who had a little cry to myself about it. Well, more than a little, to be truthful. But – when I think about it – only on my own. "Maybe it's because she hasn't caught you crying, Howard."

"Yeah, maybe," he muttered, somewhat begrudgingly, I thought. "But women don't want to see their menfolk cry, do they?"

"Why not?"

"Well, I dunno." He hesitated for a moment, wondering perhaps how far he should go or perhaps just thinking. He's quite a thoughtful man. It's probably one of the things that attracted me to him, all the way back when he was a thoughtful schoolboy, at the boys' grammar school down the road from my own. "It's not very masculine, is it?" he decided.

Before I could disagree, although I wasn't totally sure whether this would be as Elisa or just as Ann (which sort of bothered me), he continued very quietly, "And things aren't particularly good in that direction anyway."

Oh dear.

Antony could see the look on my face as he came in with the tea. In fact, it was the look on his own face that warned me I had quite a look on mine. I just shook my head to reassure him that things were okay, although of course they were far from it, and returned to Howard.

"I'm sorry, Ann, I— I have to go now. You probably have much more important calls to attend to."

"No one right now is more important than you, Howard." Which suddenly didn't seem simply a reassurance that we give to those dear people who feel – quite wrongly – that they are stopping someone with a 'worse' problem from getting through. I really didn't want to let this one go, even though I was utterly terrified as to what I might hear.

But then he threw me once again, speaking very urgently this time, as if something had instantly changed.

"I have to say cheerio. Sorry. I— I can hear my wife coming home."

That would be a good trick. But it was either someone else opening our front door – pretty unlikely these days – or he couldn't bring himself to continue. Not after what he'd just said. Curiously, I felt quite abandoned.

"Yes. Okay, Howard. You take care now."

"I will. Thank you." I thought he had gone, and was halfway through a massive sigh, when he said, "Ann…?"

"Yes, Howard?"

"Can I— may I call you again? Next Wednesday, if you're there?"

"We're not supposed to make arrangements like that, Howard." *Yes, of course you can!* "But everyone here is a good listener."

"Please, Ann. You sound very… caring."

He seemed so plaintive. What could I do? I could gently but firmly say 'no', that's what I could do. Nip this insanity in the bud. "Howard, that would be fine," was, of course, what I said. I lowered my voice before adding, "I shall look forward to it. Petal."

The phone went down and I could feel myself flopping back into the chair, totally spent, drained and sighing for Britain.

Of course, Antony was there in an instant, looking caring but also quite curious. It's human nature, we always want to know what sort of call our partner has taken, to support and reassure them but also to wonder whether we ourselves might just have handled it better – or at least differently. I'm not sure how Antony would have got on with my last caller, but I'm almost certain he wouldn't have been sharing a bed with him the same evening. To be honest, I was a bit daunted about the prospect myself.

What the hell had I got myself into?

I have no idea how I handled the remainder of that evening's calls. I hope I didn't do our callers a disservice – that would have been unforgivable. I don't think I did. Do you know, sometimes, other than an 'uh huh' or an 'oh dear', I don't actually say anything at all? The people might be lonely or sad or simply want to vent and get something off their chest. They're just thankful there's someone at the other end prepared to listen. Which I always am. And gladly so. From 7pm to 10pm every Wednesday.

Yet not, apparently, to my own husband.

***

I felt more of a liar arriving home that evening than I had done for the entire year and two months I had been lying. Suddenly I felt I had been sprung into the 'major league', as the Americans say, like the occasional shoplifter deciding overnight to do a smash-and-grab at Cartier. I didn't know if I could look Michael in the face. What if I called him Howard?

"How was Keep Fat?" he yelled from the living room, as he always does when he hears me clump exhaustedly into the hall.

I usually big up some of the exhaustion, because I always talk a bit breathlessly about how our merciless instructor Geraldine the Sadist really puts us through our paces. (She's a real person, by the way, as I painfully discovered for the months I was her victim, before *Here* saved my aching muscles).

"Oof, she worked us hard tonight," I called back, as he knew I would. And, for the first time, it made me think. Why hadn't my husband noticed that for well over a year I hadn't felt any firmer or looked any slimmer? This upset me more than I can say.

"Hi, love," I greeted him as I entered the living room, before remembering that I don't ever call him 'love'. Thankfully, he wasn't really listening. He had his feet up, a bowl of Morrison's mixed roasted nuts and rather a large Scotch by his side, with the BBC News channel on full-blast to make him even more miserable. I tell him not to watch it and he always says, 'well, how will I know what's going on?', to which I usually reply, 'I think they'll manage without you'. In fact, I was about to say the same thing that night, before thinking that people managing without him is probably what he fears most in the world.

"How was your evening?" I asked. "Any calls?"

"No, very quiet. The kids didn't ring."

"Well, you know, they've got their own lives," I said gently, which probably wasn't necessary. But the memory of hearing him sob down the phone just a couple of hours earlier was still breaking me up. When did we start pretending to each other? Or had we always done so?

"Suppose so," he said, and we didn't pursue it. "Girls okay, were they?"

"The usual moans and groans," I chuckled. I suddenly thought that if I could video this Wednesday exchange and play it back, we'd both think 'seen this one, it's a repeat'. Yet while everything was exactly the same as always, it was also more different than it had ever been.

We didn't talk much that night. I think I was pretty talked out. My brain was still reeling from what had happened just hours earlier. But when we lay there, in the same bedroom where we'd slept for well over thirty years and occasionally – in fact, quite regularly, in the less recent past – more than slept, I couldn't stop looking at him. I don't think he noticed. He was either deep into one of those heavy history books about World War 2 that he loves or he had his eye mask on and was trying to get off to sleep. (He hates the early morning light – we just can't seem to stop it seeping in through the curtains).

I knew he'd be up a few times during the night. As he'd tell you himself, he's a martyr to his prostate. I've also read that regular early-hours waking, which he always does around 3.30am, could be a sign of depression. Whenever I've asked him, he's just pooh-poohed it and muttered 'what've I got to be depressed about?' So you see, I have tried. Although possibly not hard enough.

I lay there thinking, *I have no idea what to do.*

Curiously, knowing what was troubling Michael made me feel more impotent than not knowing. I couldn't reel the kids back home, could I? And the joy of that would probably only last through the first mealtime, what with both of them making their own weird food, or checking their phones all the time in case – God forbid – they miss a text or an Instagram, or telling us about their days and not asking a thing about ours.

Nor could I suddenly tell him he was a star in the accountancy firmament, not after years of nagging him to man up and move on. (That's not an expression I ever actually used, but it's what they say these days, isn't it?) I suppose I could stop doing that last bit. To be honest, I thought I already had.

And then I realised, about 4.30 in the morning, when the snoring had resumed beside me, that it probably wasn't about *doing* anything at all.

It was simply about listening.

***

"Hello, is that Ann?"

"Yes," I said, and then lowered my voice, so that eagle-eared Antony wouldn't cotton on. "Hello Howard, pet."

"I've been trying for ages. You've been really busy, haven't you?"

It had been a busy evening and I had had to fight the sense of disappointment in my gut each time I realised that the caller wasn't my husband. *How funny*, I thought as I heard his familiar voice. Like a lovestruck young girl, I had been wondering if my man-of-the-moment would phone.

I remembered that feeling so well. The thumping in the hollow pit of your stomach, where the food you couldn't eat all that endless waiting day should have been. Of course, we didn't have mobiles back then. You just had to linger in the hallway or on the stairs, feigning nonchalance and pretending you really weren't that bothered, with your parents – well, mine – muttering that it was hardly like waiting for the Gestapo to pound on the door.

"Yes, it has been quite busy," I agreed, "but I'm here now, love, and I'm all yours."

He laughed at that. He actually laughed, not loud but still quite a chortle, and I realised with a start that it was a sound I hadn't heard for ever so long. So, of course, I laughed too. Both with him and at myself.

"That sounded worse than it was meant to," I said, with a Northumbrian smile to my voice.

"Are you married, Ann?" he asked me. *Oh, Howard, of course I am.*

"We can't really talk about ourselves, Howard," I said, kindly but firmly.

"No, of course. Sorry. I bet you are." I said nothing. "Well, if you are, your husband is a lucky man."

I laughed at this. Out of what, I don't know – embarrassment, at the pure irony of it all, or maybe just because it was so sweet that the man was flirting with me, in his own clumsy, innocent way. But I had to ask my next question, although of course, I didn't have to do so at all.

"And what about you, Howard? Are you a lucky man?"

"I think I am, Ann. Yes, I'm sure I am. To have found a woman like— like— Lena." *Lena? She's our cleaning lady!* "But I'm not sure…"

I gave him a few seconds. You can't just rush in.

"Not sure of what, petal?"

"That she's a lucky woman to have me."

Why did that old song *Don't Go Breaking My Heart* (Elton John/ Kiki Dee) come instantly whooshing into my head? Concentration is a funny thing. You think you're focusing every molecule of your entire being on an important call (in this case, probably – no, definitely – the most important phone call of my life) and still your mind is whizzing all over the place, making associations which, whilst still vaguely connected, aren't actually very helpful. Especially when the artistes involved in this particular tangent are singing at the tops of their voices in your brain!

Yet perhaps this is what I needed at that point to stop me totally falling apart. Or, even worse, telling Howard that he's really Michael and that his wife – not Lena but his real wife, Elisa – to whom he happens to be talking, despite the bland made-up name and northern accent, does in fact think she's lucky.

Or at least, she thinks she thinks she is.

Before I could respond, I could see Antony mouthing at me through the glass panel that separates our booths, yet still allows us to be of some support to one another. I think he was saying 'are you okay?' Of course, he couldn't say it out loud because he was on another call, but I got the message. I nodded with a grateful smile and gave him the most insincere thumbs-up I've ever offered a fellow listener.

"Hello… Ann?" came the shaky voice. "Are you still there?"

"Er, yes, sorry love. Howard. I was just… processing what you've been saying. Why shouldn't – Lena, you say? – why shouldn't Lena think she's as lucky with you, y'know, as— as you are with her?"

"Well, it's like I told you last week. I haven't gone as far as she'd like me to."

"In the bedroom?" *Why did I say that? It just came out! Bloody hell!*

"What? Eh, no! Well, maybe that too. But I meant in my work. In, you know, providing."

I took a sip of the tea Antony had kindly brewed for me. I would have killed for a bikkie but it meant walking across the room with my phone. And biscuits make such a crackling, crunchy sound that the callers could worry there's someone else on the line.

"Do you not think," I said, my drying throat now mercifully lubricated, "that maybe you're doing yourself a disservice, Howard? You've given her a lovely home, supported your family, taken her on a nice holiday every year…"

Bugger!

"How do you know about the holidays?"

"Howard, petal," I chuckled amiably, trying not to throw up, "you told me when we spoke last week. *You* may not remember, but we're trained to."

"Oh. Funny, I don't— Are you keeping notes on me?"

"*No*, Howard! You're only in my head." *That's for bloody sure.* "Why would your Lena find you… wanting?"

"Oh, I don't know, Ann. But, I mean, look at tonight. She flounces out to her Keep Fit without a backward glance." I didn't flounce, not this time, I'm sure I didn't. "She can't wait to be with all her pals. You know, having a laugh. She never asks me what *I'm* up to."

Oh. He was right, wasn't he? *I don't.* "And what *are* you up to, love?"

"I'm pouring my heart out to a total bloody stranger, aren't I? On a suicidal chat line!"

I'm not usually stumped, and I have to tell you that we hear things on our shifts that, as my oldest pal Judy likes to put it, are 'very different from the home life of our own dear Queen'. Yet the sheer bloody poignancy of this exchange was leaving me lost for words. And I had no idea where we were going.

"We're not only here for the suicidal, Howard." I took a breath. "But now that you mention it…?" You have to ask, don't you, if the subject arises. Not that I really believed I was on one of those devastating calls.

"I have considered it, Ann."

Oh my God. No, Michael!

"Have you, love?" I could barely speak. "When— when was this?"

"Oh, I dunno. I don't mean I've been planning to throw myself in front of the next train to Euston. They're never on time anyway. Or, you know, take something. Too much of something. I just sometimes think it could be better for everyone, if one morning…"

"One morning?"

"You know, I just didn't wake up."

He mumbled that last bit, like he knew somewhere that it was too awful to say out loud.

"Oh, Howard," I said, with what I'm sure he could pick up as genuine despair. "You honestly think this would be better for everyone? To lose a— a husband, a father, a soulmate, a provider? I'm just asking," I added swiftly, "not judging or persuading…" There are rules as to what we say. We're not – what do they call it? - moral guardians. We believe in a right to choose.

"They'd get over it. And there's insurance."

"I'm not sure there is pet, if you kill yourself. You'd have to check."

Why am I talking about insurance when my lovely, gentle husband is pouring his heart out? Does this say something about me that I really wouldn't like?

I could feel Antony staring. This isn't the usual way such conversations go. So I sort of shrug and roll my eyes in a way that hopefully suggests the caller and I are totally on the same wavelength and are getting on just fine.

"Howard," I continued. I could hear the shakiness in my voice. "Have you ever talked to—" *What the hell was her/my name?* "LENA!" I almost yelled it in triumph, so I had to make a concerted effort to calm down. "Have you ever talked to Lena? You know, about just how bad you're feeling." I paused, but there was nothing coming back to me down the line. "Sometimes we *think* the other person knows what we're going through, but often they simply don't. Pet."

"She'd only reckon I was some sort of wimp, Ann."

"*She wouldn't!*" I wouldn't.

I could almost hear him mulling. After a while, he spoke, but he sounded just a bit more spirited, as if something had clicked inside his head. Not necessarily one of the largest cogs, but an important one nonetheless.

"Perhaps—"

"Yes, Howard?"

"Perhaps I'll talk to her tonight. I dunno. We don't really talk that much these days. Except about, you know, the mundane stuff. I think that could be my fault as much as hers. Who knows? And it might be that she doesn't – well, like you said. Anyway, Ann, I'll tell you next week."

"Yes, okay, Howard." I could feel a sense of relief but also the most incredible fear. Dread, almost. I wasn't sure that this time I would even be able to get up from my chair. And then I said the stupidest thing. *Here*-wise, I mean. "Same time next week."

Antony was on it in a flash the moment I set down the phone. I think it's often the younger volunteers who are real sticklers for the rules. And, to be fair, rightly so.

"'*Same time next week*'?" He said it quite quietly, because he's a respectful man and I'm considerably older. Although he has been a volunteer significantly longer than myself.

"Oh, don't," I replied. I so didn't need this. Not with what was clearly waiting for me at home. "Sometimes, *you* know, Antony, the callers work out when you're on duty and call back deliberately on that shift. I know I shouldn't have said it, and I'm very sorry, but if it keeps him alive for seven more days…"

Antony, bless him, just nodded – a sort of 'well okay, Elisa, I'll overlook it this time' nod – and sweetly cleared the air by offering his smiley, two-fingered 'T' enquiry.

I nodded back, wishing I could work out a multi-fingered 'extremely large G 'n T' response.

***

You remember how I said, when I was lying in bed on that first Howard Wednesday, that I just had to listen harder to Michael? Well, I had done, all that week. *Really* listened. With both ears and an open heart and mind.

Yet it's hard to listen to someone who isn't really saying very much, or at least not much that isn't about the price of cherries these days or the parking permits the council have now decided we have to buy just to park outside our own front door.

But get him on the phone to a stranger…!

I realised as I walked into the house on the evening of our second chat, with a clarity that felt almost blinding, that I had to be Ann (although it might be prudent to lose the Geordie). It remained to be seen if he was going to present himself as Howard.

"How was Keep Fat?" he yelled, as he heard the front door close and my footsteps in the hall.

"Oof, Geraldine the Sadist worked us hard tonight," I responded. So no change there then.

Yet when I walked into the living room, I was quite surprised to find that Michael wasn't slumped in his usual chair, with End-of-the-World-News 24, his favourite whisky and assorted unsalted nuts.

He was standing in the centre of our small but, I believe, tastefully cosy lounge, looking like he had been wearing a hole in the carpet and had simply paused when someone invaded his space.

His face looked sadder than I had ever seen it, yet it wasn't simply an upgrade on the usual grumpy sadness. It was as if whatever structure had been holding his usually tense muscles so precariously in place had suddenly collapsed, like a demolished building, leaving him looking totally vulnerable and without support.

"Michael, are you okay?" I asked, and realised immediately that being Ann wasn't going to work. Not this time. Not in this house. I was Elisa, his wife, and there was no one else I ever wanted to be.

"Elisa," he said. "Can we talk?"

***

We talked for nearly three hours that evening.

Well, that night really, as we didn't flop into bed until after two. And the extraordinary thing is, it was so easy. You probably think, 'why wouldn't it be, you've been married to each other forever'. But when you've spent years not doing so, not *really* talking, you can lose the skill. You just get out of the habit. Like sportsmen, I suppose, or musicians, who've injured a crucial limb.

Of course, he didn't come right out and say that he'd been pouring his heart out to some anonymous Northern woman on an emotional helpline – heaven forfend – or even admit that his thoughts had veered disturbingly towards the morbid.

But we did discuss his work. How he felt that I was crushed by his lack of ambition and drive – and I admitted that there were times when I had been, but I now genuinely understood that his fear of the new far outweighed his dissatisfaction with the old and that not everyone was born to lead.

I also acknowledged – and discovered, as I said it, that I actually meant it – that he had done the lion's share of providing for and supporting us. And that, whilst we didn't necessarily have the lifestyle of some of our wealthier friends, what with the cars and the cruises, and even a bit of nip and tuck, we really hadn't wanted for much over the years. Certainly nothing worth making himself stressed and unwell over. Dear Lord there are people out there, I almost shouted, poor lonely people who would *kill* to be like us. (Not something I would ever suggest to Howard!)

For once, we talked about what we had, not about what we hadn't.

Yet, perhaps most importantly, I was able to reassure Michael that he was a good man, a decent man, a man who had been there unfailingly for me, especially in those early years, when my despair with my parents and my frustration that I could never please them grew to combustible proportions, as my own self-esteem dwindled to virtually zero.

At one point, in this most pivotal and, I have to admit, thoroughly unexpected conversation, I felt I had to ask him what event or change had suddenly brought on this 'opening-up'. For some reason, I hoped with all my heart that he might mention *Here* and, with its mention, consider at least to himself that Ann's job was done and that Howard could now move on with his new strategies, deeper realisations and, hopefully, a more understanding and responsive wife.

"It's been coming on for a while, darling. I think I just had to find the nerve to bring it up."

Well, okay. I suppose I had to settle for this and, to be honest, it was quite sufficient. I didn't need that pat on the back – I had something much more important. I had Michael back. Actually, I had Elisa back too.

We made love that night. For the first time in… well, for the first time in a very long time. And if, occasionally, it might have been Howard and Ann finding joy in the crisp Costco bedding, then I was fine with that too.

As we lay there, sleepily sated, in the early morning darkness, I mused on what the hell had just happened, whilst thanking God that it had. Wondering also whether the phone would ring the following Wednesday. And hoping, with all my heart, that it might not.

But it did. Only not quite in a way I could have imagined.

***

"Hello, Howard. How are you?"

I looked around to see if Antony was hovering, but fortunately he was heavily into a call, from someone whom, it's safe to assume, wasn't his partner of thirty-four years.

"Not great, Ann," came the low-key reply, which I have to say deeply surprised me, as I had thought we had been having the best week since I don't know when.

For a start we had made love three more times that week, which could be a record not just for us but for our entire social circle these days, unless the girls I mix with, who vie with each other as to the unresponsiveness of their couch-potato spouses, were just playing a bit coy and were in reality at it like rabbits.

"Oh dear," I sympathised, although sympathy was not my emotion of choice. "Have things not been going too well with you and Lena?"

Was I going mad?

Had I totally misread the past few days since his last call? *Come on Howard, petal, stop playing the 'poor me' card.* We'd talked ourselves hoarse, screwed each other rotten, laughed and cried together over photo albums unvisited for years, had our kids for Friday night dinner, which hadn't happened since Lord knows when. (It was as if they had sensed a new energy in the regular, and just as regularly discarded, invitations and, before they could think of a good reason not to, had responded in an unusually positive – even enthusiastic – way).

We had even discussed our jobs, our finances, our pensions and our security, which actually looked quite a lot better when you set aside the fears, the disappointments, the jealousies and the regrets.

So what the hell do you want, Howard – blood?

"Actually, Lena…" He paused. Yet he didn't sound simply hesitant, he sounded confused. And more than a little sad. I didn't dare tell him that he'd addressed me – Ann – by his made-up wife's name. "Actually, things are going far better than I might ever have expected. Or even dared hope."

I sighed with relief, yet was still confused. Had I, in my state of stress, misheard the man just now? "Well, that's wonderful, Howard. But forgive me, you came on the phone and said things weren't too good between you?"

"Sorry. I know it must be a bit confusing." *A bit?* I could almost hear him shaking his head. "I'm more than a bit confused myself. And if I'd called you yesterday, then this might have been a totally different conversation."

Well, it certainly would have been, Howard. You'd have probably got Margo, who is forty-six and lovely, but isn't the lady you sleep with. Nor is Samesh, who's divorced and works at Argos. But I had to join the dots – and swiftly.

"So… did something happen today then? To – y'know – change things?"

"I think it did, Ann. Yes. It did. A new client came into my office." *So? Where is this going?* "With a view, you know, to handling her financial affairs." *Get on with it, man!* "The name hadn't meant anything to me when our secretary mentioned it. Until the woman told me her first name was Geraldine. And that she was a fitness instructor."

Oh shit!

"Oh, yes?" I said, although I really have no idea how I was able to make any sounds come out past my trembling lips, other than yelps of pure terror.

"Anyway, my wife's Keep Fit instructor on a Wednesday, well… right now actually, is called Geraldine. Geraldine the Sadist. That's not her real name." *Might as well be!* "So, we talked. And I put two and two together…"

"Well, you're an accountant." *Why the hell did I say that?*

"And I said to her, 'Ah, then you'll be seeing my wife tonight. You know, Elisa?'" He gave this big sigh. "Okay, Ann, my wife's name is not actually Lena. It's Elisa."

"Pretty name," I said. *I've always liked it. One of the nicer things my parents did for me.*

"She's a pretty woman."

Oh!

"But do you know what this Geraldine said?" he continued.

'She hasn't been to my class in over a year'? "No, Howard, what did this Geraldine say?"

"'Elisa hasn't been to my class in over a year.'"

I said nothing. I couldn't think of a single thing to say.

"What do you think of that? Ann?" he persisted. He sounded desperate for a palatable explanation from someone who would know about these things.

"Well, these people do so many classes," I hazarded. "They probably can't be expected to remember *everybody*." *Clutching at straws, Elisa.*

"I said the very same thing," said Howard. "But this Geraldine was adamant. She'd noticed that Elisa had stopped coming and she'd asked some of my wife's friends about it. They'd seemed a bit sheepish, apparently, but just sort of gave out that she'd had enough and the class wasn't for her." He paused for a moment, but I didn't interrupt. "Then it was Geraldine's turn to look sheepish, poor woman, like she'd revealed some sort of secret."

"Oh, well, I'm sure there's a perfectly reasonable explanation. And you and – Elisa, is it? – you've been getting on so well, haven't you, petal? From what you've said. Even, you know, romantically." I felt it was important to stress this, although my well satisfied, albeit not terribly firm, body was feeling like a lump of quivering blancmange right then.

"Well, that's one of the first signs, isn't it, Ann?"

Now he really had lost me. "First signs of what, Howard?"

"Out every Wednesday. Physically responsive and loving at home. Trying to make me happy and free from any sort of doubts and cares…"

"Ye–es…" I said, gazing at the chatting Antony for the support he would never in a million years be able to give.

"Ann," said my husband. "I believe my wife is having an affair."

What could I say to that? Only one thing.

"I'm listening, Howard. I'm here."

THE WATCH

When I was, quite briefly and not very competently, a young divorce lawyer, I was fascinated by how often a client would tell me that he/she and their respective spouse couldn't live with each other – yet curiously couldn't seem to live without each other.

Some even confided that sex with each other was so much better now that they were apart.

As a young and still single man, so much that I heard I found rather confusing – including that quarrels in a marriage can arise not from monumental differences but from the tiniest misunderstandings.

From not quite hearing one another…

The day Doug Brownridge left his United Supporter's watch by the kitchen sink, in the house where he had lived with his wife and children for fourteen years, was the same day he left home, resolving never to return.

Until he realised he had left his watch.

***

The dusty white van is parked with its loading doors wide open outside a sixties terraced house, in a small town on the south coast. You can just about read the writing printed on the side of the van beneath the grime: 'Douglas Brownridge, photographer. Weddings a speciality.'

If the neighbours in the chilly morning street find this ironic, they keep it to themselves. They are far too busy watching, from the pavement, their gardens or behind veiled curtains, the drama being enacted before their unashamedly riveted eyes. After all, it's not every day you observe the physical evidence of a marriage in fragments being loaded into the rear of a truck usually employed for quite the reverse.

The man, who is obviously the one doing the leaving, doesn't appear to be a great reader. Or much of a fashion plate. He does, however, have quite a collection of CDs and DVDs and what looks, to the discerning eye, like a comprehensive collection of programmes from several decades of home games played by the town football team. Not the finest team in the world, or the country, or even the area, but one that has apparently earned his unfailing loyalty over a good number of years; possibly even from childhood, as his own children, a gawky teenage boy and a younger girl, appear to be struggling under the weight of even more overflowing boxes.

"Doing a bunk, eh?" asks the local postman, whom by this time Doug knows quite well, but not well enough to keep him fully informed of the progress of his marriage. "Kidding! Garage sale or charity shop run?"

"You got it," replies Doug, who really doesn't want this conversation. But the postman is already into one of the boxes Doug is holding.

"You can't get rid of these! United v. Derby, FA Cup 1998 – first round. *I was there!*" He waves the programme at an encumbered Doug. "Can I?"

"No, you bloody can't!" says Doug, grabbing it back with his teeth.

He feels an anger suddenly surge up inside him in a way it hasn't really done before, even in the last few difficult months. Not that he is exactly prone to anger; indeed, this was one of the qualities – or deficiencies – about which his spikier, more inflammable wife would become most incensed. As if an easygoing disposition was just the layman's term for mental cruelty.

He begins to tremble and sweat and his arms start to feel shaky, so he hurls the box inside the rapidly filling van, spilling precious memorabilia onto the dusty floor.

"Oh. Okay," says the postman, trying to regain his dignity. "Got some mail for you. Just a load of bills and a postcard from your auntie. Want 'em?"

"Not my problem, mate," smiles Doug, attempting – not altogether successfully – to restore equilibrium as he returns to sorting out his van. But the postman appears even more confused, as if he has strayed into territory beyond his pay grade, more disturbing than a vicious dog or a potentially lethal letterbox.

It takes a small, twelve-year-old girl to help him out. "It's not a charity shop run," she tells the bemused but far from disinterested postman. "We're breaking up. Mum's staying here with my nerdy brother and dad and I are going round the corner to my gran's."

"Yes, okay, Kaz," says the girl's father. "Not everyone has to know."

"Everyone does know," she points out. "Most of them are watching right now."

The postman manages to look both compassionate and as if all his birthdays have come at once. "Oh, I'm sorry, mate. I had no idea." He says this as if employees of the Royal Mail are normally the first to know these things. "Well, I hope… you know…"

He walks up the path, to find the other party to what is becoming an evermore public dispute standing at the open doorway with a lanky lad of around fourteen hovering just behind her.

The boy manages to look both lost and deeply protective at the same time. The postman has no idea what to say in these circumstances, yet feels curiously obliged to say something, although his better instincts are telling him just to deliver the letters and sidle across past the front bay windows to the house next door, without doubling back down the path and encountering the departing husband once again.

"Your husband – well, your ex or whatever – he's told me what's going on. I'm really sorry. You seemed so…"

He knows this sounds ridiculous as he has only ever seen them for seconds at a time, except perhaps at Christmas, when they would slip him a little envelope and a standard message. But he can't help thinking that they did look so right together, the wife compact and warmly attractive, in an efficient, no-nonsense sort of way, the burly husband friendly and amiably placid. But, of course, as he's always saying, you never can tell what goes on behind closed doors.

The woman shrugs and takes the bundle from the deeply uncomfortable man's hands. The postman notices that the young

119

lad seems like he is trapped in the doorway, not knowing whether to slip in to collect more boxes or to stay loyally by his mum's side and deal with the new domestic situation.

Observing the man's discomfort the wife offers a grateful smile as she nimbly manoeuvres past him towards her husband, her daughter and the van. For one brief, fanciful moment the postman wonders if he has single-handedly succeeded in reconciling the couple. He decides he will wait until tomorrow and see if the vehicle is still there.

As she reaches the van Molly Brownridge sees that the packing is almost complete. "You've not been putting all those heavy boxes on top of your clean clothes!" she says.

Doug turns to stare at her and she knows that she has already crossed some sort of line, but she has no idea exactly where these lines are drawn as she has never done this sort of thing before.

"No, Molly, I have not been putting – that!" he responds crossly yet automatically, as he has no more idea than his wife where such emotional boundaries are drawn. And, of course, he has been committing exactly the offence of which she just accused him. "But I could have, if I'd wanted to," he adds, defiantly.

"Fine. Well, it's up to you now. I'm not bloody ironing them."

"No one's asking you to."

She starts to tidy up the spilled boxes. She knows that she shouldn't do anything of the sort but she can't help herself. She hates disorder. Doug knows that he should stop her. But surely a bit of tidying doesn't hurt; in fact, it reeks of maturity and cooperation, and he really doesn't want to do anything petty in front of his daughter, who has probably seen enough.

To be fair to both himself and Molly, he does feel that they have tried their very best to keep whatever altercations they may have had away from the children as the marriage slowly eroded and its occupants grew irrevocably apart.

"Good," says Molly, from inside the van. "Well, I'm not going to."

"Fine. Well, don't," says Doug, who can't quite recall, with all the thoughts spinning around inside his head, exactly what she has said that she won't do anymore.

"I won't," says Molly, as she re-emerges, brushing the dust from her denims. And then she adds, more softly, "Well, that's it, then."

"Yeah," says Doug, almost to himself. "That's it."

For a moment they just look at each other, as if they can't quite believe that this is actually happening, after all the months of talk and planning. Curiously, it reminds Doug of a family holiday, such as the ones they saved up for but only occasionally managed: that day on which you suddenly find yourself on the beach, something you knew was the inevitable consequence of all the effort and time expended, yet something in which you never quite trusted until your bare feet brushed warm sand.

"If the cat comes back, I want half," says Kaz, instantly shattering a moment neither of the grown-ups appear to want to let fly. The young girl is wearing a woolly United cap on her head, half-buried under a faded hoody. She carries a tall, black metal clothes rack in the shape of a curvy woman. Molly looks at her and immediately tries to tidy her up.

"Mum, get off!" yelps the young girl.

"You can't go looking like that," protests Molly, although what she wants to say is 'you can't go'. She understands the daughter's loyalty to her father, misplaced though it might be, but feels aggrieved that she can't keep the remnants of her family together. At least, she comforts herself, the girl isn't going far.

"I don't look like that. Anyway, how's a tug-of-love child supposed to look?" Molly just sighs. "I'll see you."

"Tomorrow?" says Molly. "I'll make a nice tea."

Kaz simply nods. "When Lisa Norris's parents split up, she got to live in Amsterdam."

"Better luck next time," says Doug, hefting the final and largest box into the van.

"Mind your bad back."

"My bad back is fine, Molly," he replies. "And even if it isn't, it's my bad back now, isn't it?" He says it like this is a plus, then realises this might not be the case.

"I was only…"

"Yeah, okay." He notices his son, standing halfway down the path towards them. Or halfway up the path away from them. He is never quite certain with Ryan.

"Call you tonight, Ry," he says, adding jokily, "if you're not at a rave."

His laugh is unechoed, which is par for the course. He knows that the fourteen-year-old, their firstborn, is on his mum's side and he wishes that the kids hadn't chosen to take sides at all. He supposes it was inevitable and has to admit that he is quite relieved his daughter came down so firmly on his.

Before he slides into the van, Doug Brownridge takes one final look at Molly. When this becomes too much for him and the poignant reality of it sears his soul – even though he knows that it is right and he will very soon feel relief and the lifting of a huge weight from his stomach – he turns away, to see that a huddle of neighbours are now openly watching from across the road.

"*Is this the end for Doug and Molly? Join us after the break!*" he announces loudly.

An embarrassed Molly storms off, passing Ryan on her way to the house, in which she will sleep alone for the first time since her wedding night.

***

When Ryan Brownridge comes into the kitchen some time later, wanting to check on how his newly-separated mother is managing on her own, he finds the floors wet, the chairs upturned and Molly on a set of steps, scrubbing away at the woodwork above the window. She sings *I'm Going To Wash That Man Right Out Of*

122

My Hair from South Pacific, a particular favourite of her own late mother. Which is how she manages.

Without saying anything, because he knows that a sudden sound could cause her to fall and possibly break her neck, Ryan decides to make some tea. Next to the kettle, which fortunately is already full, there is a wooden mug tree with four mugs, each one bearing the hand-painted name of a member of their small and now fractured family. He decides to turn around those mugs belonging to the recently departed, so that their names won't compound his mother's sadness.

"DO YOU WANT SUGAR, MUM?" he calls above the singing and the boiling. Although he is aware that she is normally sugar-free, he has heard that it can aid people in trauma. It might well need to, as he gives her such a shock she almost topples off the ladder.

"Thanks, love," she says, stepping down gingerly as her heart races." Two, please." She accepts the personalised mug and smiles kindly at him. "You know, Ryan, some lads would have run a bit wild, with all this happening." He nods. "I'd understand if you ran just a little wild."

"It's okay," he says, going to fetch her a spoon from the tray by the sink. "Oh, look what I found."

Molly turns to see that her son is holding a man's watch, with a vividly striped band sporting the same colours as the fraying bobble hat in which her daughter left. She moves closer, although she knows exactly what it is.

"That's your dad's United Supporter's watch! I bloody gave him that for his birthday. Went especially to the little stall at the ground, on a rainy match day, and— and he's gone and bloody *dumped* it!"

"Maybe he just forgot it," says Ryan, who rarely stands up for his father.

"His favourite watch? I think not, Ryan. I think not. You know I would never speak ill of your father, but this was malice."

She holds out her hand to her son, who realises that she wants the item he's holding. Very shortly after this he finds himself wondering if perhaps he should have held onto it, pending his next meeting with his dad. Yet he can only stand and stare as his mother takes a wooden meat pounder from a rack, drops the special birthday gift into her sink and systematically pulverises it into dozens, possibly even hundreds, of tiny mechanical pieces.

Ryan is the one who hears a sharp knocking on the front door. Molly is far too preoccupied.

***

It is only when Doug arrives with Kaz at his mother's house, which is a good mile away from the former marital home, that he realises he is not wearing his watch.

He can't quite recall where he left it as the morning has not been a normal one, and even he would admit that he is not quite thinking straight. He assumes that he must have packed it somewhat automatically, along with the few other items of male jewellery he happens to possess.

Doug wouldn't even have cause to check his watch at this point, as he is not a man who runs his life by the clock (something his wife has never understood), save for the fact that his mother appears not to be at home. He does have a key but feels that, as a matter of principle, on the day your only son leaves his wife of fourteen years, a woman of whom you've never really approved, with your young granddaughter at his side, you could at least remember to be there to let them in.

And a cup of tea wouldn't hurt.

Curiously, Kaz seems less bothered about this than whether, in these new but not totally unexpected circumstances, she and her dad can still go to the United match tomorrow.

"Poppet, I've got to work tomorrow," Doug apologises.

For the first time today, and indeed since this whole uprooting was mooted, his daughter slumps to the ground and bursts into almost uncontrollable tears.

124

As he kneels to comfort her, Doug tells himself that she is a child in the midst of a marital breakdown and that what is now happening is simply a trigger for all the roiling emotions she has resolutely been holding in check. She's too young to understand but something was bound to open the inevitable floodgates.

"I'm not crying about you and Mum," she says, looking up at him, "in case you're wondering. I just want to see the fucking match!"

Doug doesn't know quite what to make of this slightly precocious self-awareness, so he tells her off for swearing.

***

His mum is still pounding the ex-watch to smithereens in the sink when Ryan walks back into the kitchen. Molly has been so preoccupied that she hasn't noticed him leave and she is still too involved to observe, on his return, that he is not on his own.

"Trust something to go wrong just when you don't have a man around," says Molly's best and oldest friend, bearing a large plant in both hands, as she watches the frenzied sink activity from the doorway. There are so many ways in which this statement is misguided that Molly hardly knows where to begin.

"Nothing's 'gone wrong,'" she says, turning round, with the pounder still in her white-knuckled hand. "It was a— a cockroach. Yuchh. How are you, Dawn?"

"No, Molly," says the woman, peering between fronds, "how are *you*?"

Molly can't help but notice the look of pure sadness, verging on grief, that is not so much clouding her friend's kindly face as transforming it.

"I'm fine," she says, smiling wearily at the other, considerably larger, woman of a similar age, who is shaking her head of tight auburn curls like she's trying to rid herself of a troublesome wasp swarm. "Dawn, I am. Really. I'm terrific."

Dawn isn't having any. She seems to be unable to stay still or even look at Molly, so she walks around, plonking her plant on a shelf and tidying as she goes. Glancing into the sink, she is puzzled to see shattered remnants of what clearly wasn't anything remotely cockroachian. She recognises the still intact watch strap with its celebrated colours, but decides she won't pursue this as she wouldn't know where to start.

"You were playground sweethearts, Molly. Like me and my Raymond." She turns the mugs round on the mug tree, so that all the names are on display. "It was like a fairy-tale."

"Except most fairies aren't four months gone." Dawn gawps at Molly, then looks around. "It's alright, Ryan can count."

Ryan decides that he can leave his mother now, so he retreats to his room. The women watch him go.

"Back to his computer?"

Molly nods. "I wish he'd have a few less friends on the Pacific Rim and a couple more on the south coast."

"He needs a man around," says Dawn, before bursting into tears.

Molly moves the huge plant to a windowsill, blocking most of the light, and goes to comfort her friend, who is drawing her home-knit blue cardigan around her like a shroud and appears inconsolable. "Oh Dawn, please don't cry. It's alright. It'll be fine."

Dawn's disagreement is quite violent. "It'll never be the same, Molly. *We'll* never be the same. I blame myself, I really do."

"It takes two, Dawn," says a slightly mystified Molly. "And you weren't either of them."

Gradually the tears subside and Dawn accepts the offer of a cup of tea and a biscuit. Her closest friend randomly grabs the mug with Doug's name on it and sets Dawn off all over again.

But Molly is still thinking about the timepiece that is lying quite dead in her sink.

***

By the time Doug's mother rolls up it is evening and Doug has forgotten once more about the watch.

He and Kaz have taken their first supper as a newly-truncated family and what it lacked in taste, being little more than eggs and some toast, it made up for in intimacy. Kaz spent the early part of it explaining to her father, for the umpteenth time, that Molly was never right for him and that her friend Olivia totally agrees (but as a consequence of what was an inevitable severance, her own chances of a lasting relationship have probably gone down the toilet).

Doug puts this insight down to an excessive amount of television and possibly also to the *Cosmopolitans* littering his mother's cosy kitchen-diner, a room to which the young girl has often been drawn, partly because of the atmosphere at home but mostly because her widowed grandma talks frequently and inappropriately about sex.

He is dozing on his mother's TV chair, his feet on her faux leather pouffe, when the singing wakes him up.

"*I dreamed a dream in times gone by, when hopes were something something…*"

"Grannie!" yells Kaz, rushing to hug the old lady.

Annie Brownridge is a slim, smartly dressed and colourfully coiffured woman in her sixties, whose absence of natural warmth belies a love for her granddaughter which is almost feral, whilst appearing quite in keeping with her disdain for the rest of the world.

"Oh bugger, it was today!" she says. She still has her Cumbrian accent, although she has lived down in the wimpy South for well over half her life.

"*Where've you been?*" asks Doug, his outrage carefully tempered by the knowledge that he is imposing on his mother and her valued solitude at a time in her life when she fully expected to enjoy her own company and the opportunity to bring home elderly men whenever the occasion should arise. It is when she turns back to the open hallway that her son realises one such opportunity had presented itself only this evening.

"Sorry, love," she apologises, to whoever is lingering eagerly by the front door or leaning heavily on a stick. "I forgot I had company. Well, me son." Doug assumes her shrug of regret is echoed by the gentleman caller, who can be heard returning disconsolately into the dark. "Ahh, his little face," she smiles. "We went on a coach trip to see a matinee of *Les Misérables*. You'd love it, Douglas. Especially now."

Kaz resumes cuddling the tall woman, which Doug imagines is like hugging a tree. But Annie does at least stroke her granddaughter's hair as she upbraids her son for the look of filial outrage he is making little effort to disguise. "*You* decided to leave your missus and come live here."

"It was a *joint* decision! And you know I can't afford two homes."

"Much as it sticks in my gullet, your bossy wife wasn't wrong about you earning some decent money."

Doug doesn't need this conversation, not today and certainly not with his daughter listening to every word. *We might as well be back home,* he thinks, *if this is how it is going to be.* He sends the young girl upstairs with a kiss, before making another futile attempt to justify his existence.

"She was always on at me with her crazy ideas," he protests. "'Put in a one-hour processing lab, Doug'… 'Extend the studio, Doug'… 'Wash the van'…" Even he is sufficiently perceptive to realise that he may have blown it with this last one, so he gives his mother a peck on her still cold cheek and makes for the hall. "Anyway, thanks Mum, for… you know. Must get off to bed. Doing a wedding tomorrow."

"*On a home game day!*"

Annie notices the look of desolation on her son's face.

"Whole new ball game," he says, with a sad shrug. Yet suddenly his look changes to one with which both people are far less familiar. It might almost be determination. "And a new beginning. *Yes!* From today, Molly Brownridge is… yesterday!" He seems unusually excited. "What's the date?"

"How should I know?" says his mother. "I'm retired."

Instinctively, he rolls up his sleeve to check his watch, and shakes his head as he finally remembers exactly where he left it.

"Just got to pop out for a few minutes, Mum."

***

It may be totally subconscious but Molly has not been able to stop twisting her wedding ring around her finger since the day began. What she is far more conscious of is that her oldest school friend has returned and is stocking her freezer with enough ready meals to feed a women's refuge for a month.

"You know what will happen, Molly," says Dawn, the look of concern on her face by now almost as frozen as the items she is transferring from her freezer bags. "You'll sink into a depression, you won't bother to cook and you'll just start to wither away."

"Well, at least I'll be able to get this fucking ring off," says Molly, suddenly aware of what she has been doing. Dawn appears settled in for another good solid cry when the door opens and Doug enters the kitchen.

"*AAGGHH!*" screams Dawn, the colour immediately retreating from her usually rosy cheeks as next Friday's main course drops with an icy crunch onto the spotless kitchen floor.

"I didn't die, Dawn," says Doug. "I just moved out."

"And now you're bloody back," says Molly in outrage. She slams the door of the freezer, only just missing Dawn's shaking hand.

Molly knows why she is so inordinately angry and it isn't just because of her husband's sudden reappearance, inappropriate as this may be. Yet she isn't going to offer him the satisfaction of an explanation. This would simply be playing into his spiteful, bare-wristed hands.

"Next time, you ring the bell. Like any other visitor. And then you push off."

Doug has known his wife long enough to be able to categorise the rages and this one does appear to be at the higher end. "So Dawn, how have you been?" he asks, hoping for at least one friendly response on what has not been the easiest of days.

Now that the shock of his arrival has receded, Dawn is feeling incredibly uncomfortable. She realises that it was inevitable she would see Doug Brownridge again. It is a small town and the husbands are the closest and oldest of friends. She simply hadn't expected it to be so soon and for her own best friend to seem not so much desolate or bereft as almost preternaturally angry, which isn't how she would picture herself feeling were a similar, albeit unimaginable, scenario ever to present itself. She still hasn't been able to eradicate from her mind the sight of that merciless pounding.

"I'm okay, Doug," she manages to say, trying for a casualness she doesn't in the least feel. "Thank you."

"Are you still—"

"Married? Yes. To Raymond."

"—going to the Lakes this summer. Without us, I mean."

"Oh. Oh yes. But it won't be the same. Well, the Lakes will be, but—"

"Look, I'd so love to talk holidays," says Molly, mercifully stepping in, "but it's very late, I've still got work to do and – what else? – oh yes, Doug… we're separated!"

"I'm not stopping, Molly," says Doug, trying to ignore the unanticipated blasts of cold fury wafting in his direction. "I've just come for my watch."

If Doug Brownridge hears the tiny yelp emanate from his wife's best friend, it clearly doesn't register. But he does wonder momentarily why his wife should be looking quite so shocked.

Shooting a warning glance at Dawn, Molly responds with a calmness she most certainly doesn't feel.

"What watch?"

Molly wishes that the other woman wasn't staring so fixedly at the sink.

"*You* know, Molly – my United Supporter's watch. The one you got me for my birthday from that little stall at the ground." She doesn't say anything but gives an 'oh, that watch' kind of nod. "I took it off this morning because the sink was blocked."

Molly's outrage is all the more vehement for now being totally without justification. "When did *you* ever unblock a sink? Only time you even saw a plunger was that fancy dress party at the kids' school, when you went as a Dalek." She shakes her head at his blatant effrontery. "Well, I'm sorry, Doug, I really can't be picking up after you anymore."

"I'll just be off then, Molly," says Dawn, grabbing her depleted freezer bags and sidling uncomfortably towards the door and sanity.

"No need, Dawn," says Doug, kindly. "I'll just fetch my watch then I'll be on my way."

Molly makes the face of someone who has come up with a passingly plausible alternate theory, although she does wish Dawn would just get on with her going. "Did you *deliberately* leave it here, just so's you could come back and bother me?"

For a moment, Doug Brownridge wonders if this could indeed be the case without his even realising. Because, to his chagrin, he has to admit that Molly is quite often right about these things. "Why in God's name would I do that?" he still protests. He suddenly turns to Dawn, who appears, for some reason, to be flattening herself against an available wall. "What do *you* think?"

"Ohhh," says Dawn decisively. "It's possible, I suppose. But…" She's looking at Molly, wondering where her loyalties should lie. "It's been so great seeing you, Doug. Send my love to your mum. And Kaz."

She scurries off and along with her goes any memory in her dear friends' troubled minds of her ever having been there, save of course for a freezer that will soon be too stuffed even to open.

Molly crosses her arms and stares at Doug, with the look of someone on whose side right has firmly been all along. He realises with a jolt that he still finds her attractive, even when she is glaring at him, and wishes that he didn't. He decides that it is beyond foolish to believe that this purely animal thing suddenly dissipates at the moment of separation. Lack of appeal is clearly something you have to work at.

"You could have just phoned. Kaz is coming tomorrow – she would have picked it up."

"No, Molly," says Doug, in his most grown-up voice. "I just wanted to make a clean break. Now. Today. No hangovers."

"That'll be new for you." She gives a smile that says she's not really making a joke and he returns one that says he's not in the least amused. "Well, I'm sorry, Doug, I know how much you liked that watch but I haven't seen it and, as you've probably failed to notice, I've cleaned up after you everywhere. So it can't be here."

Doug seems genuinely puzzled. "I was so sure. Hey, maybe I left it in the bathroom. Would you mind, Mol? Please?"

With an enormous sigh, she stomps off towards the stairs, muttering loudly. "Like I've nothing else to do." From the hallway she calls back to him. "And don't *touch* anything. Not yours now – remember!"

He winces at this. "'Not yours now, remember,'" he repeats in poor but deeply offended imitation.

Doug glances around the familiar kitchen in which he has spent so much of his married life and feels a pain that seems to scorch him from stomach to throat as he realises that this really isn't his kitchen anymore. Perhaps, in pure monetary terms, at least fifty per cent of it is; yet in his heart it has wholly gone.

He finds himself welling up as he looks around at the school photos on the fridge, the fading kids' drawings, the wipe-off 'to do' list of things he rarely bothered to do (although, to give him his due, he did unblock the sink), the personalised mugs on the rack. He recalls how he would infuriate Ryan by making his coffee in the mug with his son's name on.

He notices that the mug inscribed with Molly's name has been used and set back in the sink, most probably because the tiny dishwasher is already full. It wouldn't kill him to rinse it for her. He looks around the sink as he does so, as if Molly might have overlooked the watch or it has mischievously slunk under a dishcloth, unwilling to leave, but it's clearly not here. Even though there's no logical reason why it should have dropped into the nearby waste bin, he decides to check this anyway, just to be sure.

When he opens it, he's sure.

He picks out the gaudy strap from under a large sliver of browning lettuce (which should, of course, have been in the black bin by the sink, so she's not so perfect either). As he lifts it, what little remains of the savaged casing drops off to join its fellow lifeless cogs and homeless screws in the bin.

The deliberate thuds of Molly's return afford him time to toss the dregs of his treasured watch back into the bin and move well away. He's checking out the photos on the fridge when she steams back in.

"No. There's no watch," she announces. "You definitely must have packed it somewhere." She stares at him, noticing the unfamiliar stiffness in his still familiar body. "Doug? … *Doug!*"

He looks for a moment as if he is about to confront her, and with some force, but instead he just nods and turns away. "Yeah. Well, it's likely in one of the boxes. Haven't even begun to unpack yet." He knows that this will resonate with Molly. He recalls weekends away and family holidays they have taken together over the years. Her suitcase would be emptied and everything stored and drawered before he even had time to check out the available TV channels.

Doug walks to the hall. She follows him in some relief. "Anyway, how's Ryan?" he asks concernedly.

"Mutengke Ronuka from Papua New Guinea says 'chin up.'"

He nods.

Molly opens the door for her husband, trying to act as normal as she can without, of course, knowing exactly how 'normal' looks in these circumstances. "So – tell Kaz I'll see her tomorrow. After you've been to the match."

"She's going with Olivia and her dad. I'm working."

"*On a home game day?*"

Jesus! "YES, on a home game day!" He opens the front door then turns back to her. "Well, if you do find the watch, Mol…" He doesn't finish the sentence but just walks to his van, without looking back. He is unsurprised that she insists on the final word. She usually does.

"You bloody took it *with* you!"

He may be at the other end of their path but it's no distance and she knows that her insistent voice is far too loud, so she is not surprised to see curtains lift across the otherwise sleepy road.

What she doesn't see, because his back is towards her, is a smile remarkably like triumph appearing on her soon-to-be ex-husband's formerly disgruntled face.

***

In a local churchyard the following brisk afternoon, Doug Brownridge looks around impatiently for the bridal car and checks the time once again. Not on his own watch as this would be miraculous, considering the state in which he recently discovered it, but on the unnecessarily sophisticated mobile phone of his young assistant, Ansel.

Ansel, who has renamed himself after his hero, the great American landscape photographer Ansel Adams, is a cheerful nineteen-year-old of Afro-Caribbean origin, who is almost as good-looking and talented as he thinks he is. Ansel finds it hard to keep still, even for a time-check, as he is forever walking around 'framing' shots that aren't yet his to take. Today, however, it is his boss, usually so laid-back, who seems like he is the one dancing on hot coals.

"Chill out, Duggie," says Ansel, peering down the road along with most of the evermore concerned wedding guests. "They'll be here. The match has started anyway."

"It's *Doug!*" insists Doug, as he always does, although he wonders why he bothers. "And I'm not thinking about the match. I've just got to get to that United Supporter's stall before it packs up."

"Your rattle break again, did it?"

"No, that's fine. What I'm looking for is—"

"Not really interested," says Ansel. "Hey, howsabout when the bride comes, I catch her reflection in the wheel of the car?"

Now Doug isn't really interested. Especially as he can spot the ancient white Bentley finally approaching. Even before the bridal car has come purring to a halt outside the churchyard, he rushes to the rear door and practically yanks the bride out.

"*Where've you been?*" he cries, realising that somewhere he is losing it.

The father of the bride appears more than usually apprehensive and it soon becomes apparent to everyone that the young woman in the plush back seat isn't budging. Doug, who can already envisage the tiny stall at the ground shutting shop, is in no mood for anyone's cold feet other than his own.

"Look, love, everyone's waiting," he urges, as he watches her dig her ivory satin heels in. "Three of the choirboys' voices have just broken." He knows that humour can sometimes work where cajoling fails miserably. Not today, apparently.

They remain there, locked in place, bride and photographer, as if in some deathly showdown. Finally, in a small, trembling voice, she asks him, "Are you married?" Which is the last question he was expecting and hardly seems relevant. He just nods, hoping this will cover it, but she has more. "Do you love your wife… you know… till death do you…?" He nods again, wishing he wasn't having this conversation today and that he could just hoick her out of the car and propel her down the aisle. "Kids?" He proudly shows her two fingers, but she is still shaking her head. What's she going to quiz him on now – mortgage repayments?

He looks at her, so young and so nervous. And despite his irritation, Doug softens as he remembers. This time when he speaks, he realises, to his own surprise, that it isn't totally fuelled by self-interest.

"Hey, it's okay, is marriage." He smiles. "Most fun you can have with your clothes neatly folded." He can detect the tiniest smile in return. "It's just two people who love each other enjoying each other's company. Y'know, sharing things."

He doesn't mention waste bins and meat pounders because she is staring at him, sweet and slightly moist blue eyes seeking – and, curiously, finding – assurance in his gentle, clearly moved and only slightly saddened face. The minuscule lines of worry on her own are just beginning to recede.

"Listen, sweetheart, do you love him?" asks Doug. She nods without hesitation. "He love you?" More nods. "Then come inside before your mascara runs, marry the poor sod, live happily ever after."

Ansel is watching from some distance away, through a lens of his own, and notices the young woman gently sobbing. Misinterpreting the situation, he struts over and smiles warmly. "Don't you let old Duggie upset you, darling," he says. "He only split up with his missus yesterday."

"*Drive!*" cries the bride, smacking the chauffeur on the back of his neck.

They watch the Bentley speed off.

"Looks like you'll get to that stall," says Ansel, who sees light at the end of most tunnels.

***

As Doug Brownridge moves with unusual purpose towards his spiritual home, showing an unprecedented lack of interest in the final score, Molly is visiting the last person on Earth with whom she was expecting to make contact on this first full day of freedom.

"Look, Annie," she says to the older woman, who is already rolling her eyes at her from the doorway, "I know we've never liked each other…" The older woman simply nods, which Molly, who can usually give as good – if not better – than she gets, finds curiously disconcerting. "… and I've grown to accommodate this."

"Aye, it's comfortable," agrees Annie, not stepping aside to let her daughter-in-law into her home, as she assumes the younger woman isn't staying. "He's doing a wedding, so you've wasted your valuable time."

To Annie's surprise, Molly shakes her head. "It's you I came to see."

"Oh yeah? You're worried I'll be a bad influence on your daughter," nods Annie. "Well, it wasn't me who had my wedding list at Mothercare."

Before Molly can respond, Annie turns away so that the younger woman can follow her in, which has to be considered progress.

"I didn't 'trap' him, you know, Annie," protests Molly. "Maybe he wanted to leave home."

"He's settled back in quick enough." Annie turns back to her at the threshold of her kitchen-diner, blocking further intrusion. "So, what is it you want?"

"Ah, that celebrated northern hospitality. Never leaves you." Molly watches in begrudging admiration as Annie heaves a sigh that doubles up as a scowl. "I just want to leave things… y'know… tidy."

Molly doesn't notice the older woman's puzzlement as she is already rummaging in her handbag. She finally fishes out a gleaming United Supporter's watch, complete with gaudy strap.

Complete also with a tiny price label on the back, which she immediately scrapes off before her mother-in-law can spot it.

Molly appears to the older woman strangely uncomfortable as she explains. "I once gave him this. In a fit of kindness. You must have seen it. Can you tell him that it had fallen behind the tidy-unit on the sink. I've polished it up a bit. See. Good as new."

She appears exhausted from her explanation. Annie takes the watch from her slightly trembling hand.

"I'd best get back," says Molly, turning with some relief. "Kaz is coming round for supper. Probably misses the cat."

Annie suddenly softens, stroking the newly 'retrieved' watch. "I've known *you* since you were her age." Molly smiles. "You always were a right little madam."

***

Doug Brownridge has only one notion in his head as he stands in his local pub this early evening enjoying a pint with his closest friend Raymond and a loyal but fairly bored Ansel. It's something he is quite desperate to share. So the photographer is really in no mind to hear the older of the two men's kick-by-kick recap of the match he was obliged to miss earlier in the day. Especially as Raymond has a manner of delivery that would suck the life out of a battery. He is barely listening as Raymond suddenly leaps topics in order to discuss Doug's newly attained 'single man' status.

"I'm surprised you're here, Doug," he says, with a curious smile, "when you could be, you know, on the razz. Although, of course, it is only seven o'clock!"

Ansel has clearly never come across this expression but Doug understands it sufficiently to protest that twenty-four hours is hardly enough time to learn a new postcode, let alone segue into full footloose and fancy-free bachelor mode. He does, however, know his old friend well enough to realise that this is Raymond's clumsy but well-meaning way of trying to make Doug feel slightly less wretched about his lot, one which genuinely saddens the contentedly married man – even as a smidgeon of envy adds some noticeable tang to the mix.

"Better not let your Dawn hear you talking like that," says Doug, if only to stem the flow.

"Dawn can't hardly hear anything over the sound of her own crying," says Raymond. "Talk about clingy. She insisted on standing next to me at today's match. Which, I have to tell you, didn't impress my sergeant one bit. Not that there were any reportable incidents…"

"Yeah, yeah," says Doug, whose desperation to move on from his friend's constabulary ramblings and share his own recent masterstroke is causing him to shuffle in place so violently that he almost spills his beer. "You know that United watch Mol gave me?" The men nod, not knowing what this has to do with anything. "Well, I left it in the house yesterday, y'know by mistake, and she only went and smashed it to bits! I found it in pieces in the bin."

The men do Doug the courtesy of looking totally appalled. Clearly such wanton destruction is beyond the imagination of either drinker. Which is saying something, considering one of them is an officer of the law.

"I hope you cautioned her," says Raymond.

Doug shakes his head with a glee that his listeners find curious. "I never let on I knew, Raymond. But you know what? Instead of coming clean, like you or me or any normal person, *she tells me I must have taken it with me!*"

The men simply shake their own heads, too stunned to speak.

"You're not going to leave it like that, are you, Duggie?" says Ansel, who knows that he for one wouldn't let such an outrage go unpunished.

"*Doug,*" corrects Doug as, from deep in a pocket of his jacket, he produces a brand new watch, identical in every way to the one so cruelly and recently dispatched. Peeling the tiny price label from its back, he straps it showily around his naked wrist.

The men stare at it then at their elated friend, awaiting with some eagerness the explanation that currently eludes them. He stares back as if they must be beyond dim to not fully comprehend.

"*I'm going to pretend I found it in my pocket!*"

Raymond simply nods at this but Doug notes the younger man's total confusion. "Hang on, Doug," says Ansel. "Molly knows you couldn't have found it."

"*Exactly*, Ansel!" beams his boss, which clearly doesn't enlighten the young assistant one bit. "For pity's sake, man! She'll only reckon I must've gone over to the little stall and bought myself a brand new watch especially." Ansel looks at Raymond and can see that the nodding constable is firmly on the case. "Cos I was so awfully choked up at losing the one she gave me."

"Because of how much it meant to him," explains Raymond.

"It'll make her feel wretched for weeks," concludes Doug. "*Result!*"

Ansel still looks baffled. "But Duggie – why bother?"

"You'd have to be married to understand," says Raymond, to which Doug just nods and contentedly drains his pint.

***

"You've lost weight," says Molly to her daughter.

"You only saw me yesterday."

It is Kaz's first visit to the place that used to be her home since she left it the previous morning. She doesn't find this situation particularly uncomfortable as she often stays nights with her grandmother down the road, so in truth she considers both houses her home. And if her mum does anything to make her bedroom upstairs something less than a shrine, words will be spoken.

What she does find more uncomfortable, or perhaps simply more annoying, is having once again to share the same air as her nerd of an older brother, who – for reasons best known to himself – has taken his mother's side.

It is Molly who is feeling her way in all this, as she has always supposed that in a marital break-up, unless there is self-evident neglect or abuse, the children remain with their mother. Indeed, this has been her observation as a legal secretary, and she feels slightly embarrassed at the uncommonly precise division that has occurred within her own domestic arena.

"I bet the Merry Widow's too busy to feed you. Or if she does, it's fast food rubbish."

"Then I'd be fatter, wouldn't I? Dad doesn't make all this fuss," says Kaz, although relatively little fuss has as yet been made.

"Your father thinks salad is a punishment," responds Molly, before vaguely recalling that she and Doug had pledged not to disrespect each other in front of the children.

"I dunno why I came back," mutters Kaz, who is actually quite happy to have done so and is enjoying the more than usually expansive and relatively unhealthy supper her mum has laid out.

"Neither do I," says Ryan, who isn't too bothered whether his sister is here or not and just wants to get back to his chat rooms.

Their mother looks suddenly very sad. "It's hit you both really hard, hasn't it?" They stare at her. "But sometimes— well, sometimes parents just don't get on. It doesn't mean we don't love you."

Ryan turns to Kaz. "We've had this talk, haven't we?"

Kaz nods. "It's 'cos she feels so guilty."

"Excuse me?" says Molly, but no one is really listening.

"It's Doug who should feel guilty," says Ryan, taking his second slice of cake. "He's the one who hasn't been supportive. The poor woman's had to do everything."

"Ryan," explains Kaz, patiently. "It's Molly who humiliated *him*."

"No, I didn't," protests Molly.

"Mum, we're talking," snaps Kaz. "She made him feel like he was a waste of space, Ryan. She might as well have cut off his—"

"*Karen!*" shouts Molly, who only uses her daughter's given name in emergencies. She has every intention of developing this

141

into a full-blown rant – she knows she is on a pretty short fuse – when the door opens and Doug walks in. "*Oh, bloody hell!*" she explodes, as the fuse is blown.

"Hi guys," he says.

"We won 3-1," cries Kaz. "*United*!" Doug shares her joy with a nod.

"Doug," says Molly. "Can I explain 'separation'?"

Doug shakes his head, yet he is smiling benevolently and appears unusually affable. Molly isn't certain whether to be displeased or relieved, but settles for mature, as the kids are there.

"Don't worry, Mol," he says, "I'm not stopping. I just came to show you something." He rolls up his left sleeve. "Da daaaa!"

He waits for a moment to allow Molly to gawp. The children, of course, have no idea what is going on and care even less.

"You'll never guess, Mol – it was in my pocket all the time! *What am I like!* I knew you'd be scouring the house for it – y'know, cos of how very much it meant to me."

"Oh, yes," says Molly, nodding vigorously. "I had a good… scour."

"So that's it then. Clean slate. As they say, pastures new." He throws Molly his best smile. Rolling down his sleeve, he turns to go.

"I'll come with you," says Kaz. She grabs a final slice of cake for the journey. "Can we have an extra large KFC bucket tonight, *please*?" She smiles at Molly.

"With or without chocolate sauce?" says Doug.

Molly, who in usual circumstances would react to this with all the disdain she could muster, simply looks uncomfortable, because these circumstances are light years from usual. "Listen… Doug…" He turns, with an amiable smile. "Before you go back to your mum's, there's something I should tell you."

He grabs a chair, sensing that this could be the best moment of what hasn't so far been his favourite weekend. Even the ring on the doorbell doesn't distract him. Ryan gets up to answer it, grateful for the chance to slip away from a situation that is seriously confusing him.

Kaz follows her brother out. "I'll wait in the car. Bye, Mum." They exchange waves as she goes.

"They seem okay… don't they?" says Doug, gently closing the door.

"The expert speaks. Oh, I don't know. I hope so. Listen, Doug…"

"It's okay, Molly. We're all square. New lives."

Molly looks anxiously towards the hallway. "No. Wait, Doug. Please—"

Before she can finish, or even start, the door swings open and Dawn swoops in, bearing a massive bunch of flowers that almost obscures her face. Through the blooms she spots Doug.

"Oh! *Doug!* You're back. Again."

"It's okay, Dawn. I'm just going."

"No!" insists Dawn, slapping the flowers between two ravaged cake plates on the table. "Don't. I can go. STAY!"

"It's alright, Dawn," says Doug, kindly. "You're not interrupting anything. I just came to tell Molly…"

Dawn instantly begins to talk extra-loud in an odd sing-song voice, like someone who really doesn't want to hear a final football result before they have a chance to watch the match. "*None of my busi-ness!* But, actually, I'm really glad you're here, Doug. Because guess what I found when I was clearing out my coat?"

They can't guess. Neither can they imagine that they could be the least bit interested. For once, they are totally wrong.

Dawn fishes in her pocket as she explains. "I must have picked it up by accident when I was here yesterday, *eh, Molly*? Silly old me. And I know what it meant to you both." She finally discovers and brandishes a remarkably pristine United Supporter's watch. "So, all solved."

She lunges for Doug's left arm. Before he can move away, she deftly rolls up his sleeve, then pauses, transfixed.

"*Oh my God!*" she cries. "What's that?"

"It's my watch, Dawn," says Doug calmly.

"But… it can't be!" protests the confused visitor.

"Can't it, Dawn? Why not?" asks Doug, with a smile.

Before she can stop herself, Dawn makes a pounding motion with her arm. "Because Molly—"

"Because I *found* your old watch, Doug," says Molly swiftly, "and I gave it to your mother this afternoon."

"My mother?" says Doug, suddenly wrong-footed.

"His *mother!*" exclaims Dawn, then realises she shouldn't have. "So, how is she?"

"Er, fine, thanks Dawn," says Doug. "So, where did you find it, Molly? My watch."

Molly feels that she might just be returning to safe ground. "You'll never guess, Doug. Behind the sink-tidy! Yeah. Must've fallen down." She wishes Dawn would stop staring at the sink in question like it was a crime scene. "But hey, I appreciate you – both of you, actually – trying to make it right. It was… well, it was very sweet of you."

Doug can't quite understand how momentum, so solid only seconds earlier, can dissipate so fast.

"Best to be straight, eh, Molly?" he manages.

"I think so."

They notice that Dawn's arm appears to be waving quite forcefully in the direction of the door. "As we're getting on so well," she beams, "are you okay if I bring Raymond in? He's a bit embarrassed, Molly, cos of – you know – being on Doug's side."

"There's no 'sides', Dawn," says Molly, in her best grown-up voice. "We're all adults here."

Dawn trots off, leaving Doug and Molly to continue being adult.

"Your mum seems well," says Molly.

"Yeah. Still tricky but fine. Hey, funny the watch being round at her place now. The original."

Molly is still chuckling at the oddity of this when Dawn walks back in with a slightly sheepish Raymond.

"I haven't bothered Raymond with all the silly details," she says. "We're just happy everything is all cleared up."

"Yeah," agrees Raymond, in some relief. "Hey, Molly, I bet you felt better smashing Doug's watch to smithereens."

For a moment no one speaks, but there are a lot of eyes darting around and focusing on other eyes.

"Not that bit, Raymond," yelps Dawn in alarm.

"Oh *Dawn!*" says Molly, quite mortified at her friend's indiscretion. She turns to a stunned Doug and the look she gives him is genuinely contrite. Yet she can't help but notice that for some reason her best friend is shaking her own head quite vigorously.

"No, Molly," cries Dawn, almost in tears. "I *never* told Raymond that bit. I never said a word to you about Molly smashing up Doug's watch in the sink, did I, Raymond?"

It is Raymond's turn to shake his head, which leaves Molly even more bewildered.

"But who else could have told him?" she asks, then looks at Doug as it slowly becomes clear. "You *bastard!*"

"Me?" protests Doug. "You smashed the watch!"

"And you *knew* all the time! My God – of course! You must have seen it in the bin. And you *still* couldn't get totally unreasonable about it. Like any normal husband! Ex-husband." She looks around the kitchen. "I'm sorry, guys. I've got to slam something."

"Cupboard doors are always good," suggests Dawn helpfully.

"Dawn!" admonishes Raymond, but her friend has already taken up this invaluable household hint and is rabidly pulling open doors all over the kitchen, simply for the infinitely satisfying release of sending them noisily, one after another, back into place.

"Oh no, Douglas Brownridge can't just get cross like any decent human." *Slam!* "Heaven forbid. He has to go all round the fucking houses, buying new sodding watches with— with his kids' inheritance." *Slam!* "Trying to make me feel even worse than I already was. I cannot believe you would do that." *Slam, slam!* "I cannot—"

"Molly—" the offender attempts, but his lone voice can't compete with the kitchen percussion.

"*Shut up!* Anything to avoid a healthy, honest-to-goodness marital ding-dong!"

"If we're going to talk honesty—"

"I told you to *can* it!"

"So, you two," intervenes Dawn, with a lightness of tone she hopes will prove infectious. "What time were you at the Supporters' stall this afternoon?"

"Dawn, why are you interfering in their marriage?" asks Raymond.

"I was simply thinking we could have met up. And I'm not interfering."

"You are, Dawn," says Raymond.

"I most certainly am not, Raymond!"

"Hoy, you two – this is our row," says Molly. "Or at least what passes for one in this house."

"No, tell you what – you three carry on," says Doug. "I don't have to be here. I'm separated, remember?"

"*Then why the hell do you keep coming back?*" says Molly.

To his credit, Doug pauses for a moment to ponder this. But he's not sure it's a question he can fully answer. "Okay, Molly," he says instead, "my new life starts now." He rolls back his sleeve once more. "Synchronise your watches."

Dawn checks the watch she is still holding. "It's exactly thirteen minutes past—"

Raymond grabs the brand new watch from her hand. He sets it down on the table, well away from her. Doug takes one final look at Molly and walks out of the door.

Before he has even left the hallway, Molly grabs the most recent watch from the table and walks over to the sink. Like an action replay, she calmly picks up the meat pounder and totally obliterates the offending item. This time even the strap doesn't survive unscathed.

As they back away, Raymond mutters, with some regret, "I could have given that to one of the kids."

"Don't worry," says Dawn, removing further items from her pocket. "I bought enough for all of you."

***

"I thought we were separated," says Kaz, who feels she has been waiting rather a long time in the van.

"Yeah, well, we are now," says Doug.

He remembers something he has been wanting to do. He shoots out his wrist and removes the watch. As he starts the engine, he hands the timepiece to his daughter, whose eyes light up.

"*Wicked!*" she says, then points to his bare wrist. "But what about you?"

"It's okay, poppet. Your mum's just bought me another one." He drives off. "It's waiting for me at Grannie's."

Kaz looks at him. She seems puzzled as she attempts to work things out in her sharp, but still only twelve-year-old, brain. "I thought Mum didn't like you."

"Yeah, well," explains Doug Brownridge, "you've got to be grown-up about these things."

***

The woman smiles at her partner as she gazes around the restaurant.

"This is pretty classy," she enthuses. "Rob a bank, did you?"

"No," laughs the man. "But I didn't half sell a lot of watches this afternoon."

BETTER LATE

I worked in an advertising agency many years ago, with someone whose father had sadly died a few months before this colleague was born. She told me that she always wished she might have met him.

Some time later I stayed in a house which I heard had a certain curious history.

And two strands slowly drifted together.

The crash came in the middle of the night. Although, of course, it's always 'the middle of the night' when something happens that is so shattering it awakens everyone around it in dark, switch-scrabbling panic.

Because they all knew that this was something beyond awful; something bound to happen, yet the one thing they hoped and prayed never would.

It began with a scream. For some the scream never ended.

DO I HEAR ONE?

David Ramsden is learning to speak Finnish.

There is no particular reason for him to do so; he has no intention of ever going there. The country, like the language, sounds particularly dark and cold and he prefers his holidays, if he ever bothers to take them, in places that don't disturb his equilibrium. Like Devon, or at least the northern part. Anyway, when you've lived in the Cotswolds for every one of your forty-four years, why would you wish to venture further afield?

He is learning Finnish to keep his brain active during the many car journeys he is compelled to take for work, and as something to occupy his mind on his bracing morning strolls in the hills around Cheltenham. David isn't particularly fond of music but neither is he comfortable with leaving his mind disengaged, because he knows that such vacancies furnish opportunity for unsettling thoughts, premonitions of danger and hazard, to sneak in like mice through a rotten skirting board. You can't think of anything else when you're learning Finnish.

'Could you please speak more slowly?' says the amiable Fin on the cassette in his car. She is an old car, a Volvo, but she is safe and solid and she knows the Gloucestershire roads by heart. '*Voisitko puhua hitaammin?*'

"*Voisitko puhua hitaammin?*" repeats David Ramsden quite accurately, realising that this is clearly a most useful phrase for a first-timer in, say, Helsinki, which he knows he will never be.

He is on a narrow country road near Winchcombe, a road he hasn't had cause to visit for a while but one which he rather likes, with its coil of sharp curves you have to take really slowly and fields in whose uncomplicated lushness you could really lose yourself, if you didn't have to keep your eyes fixed firmly on the road at all times.

Yet the bang still comes as a surprise.

Something has smacked hard against his passenger door, just as he is carefully rounding a particularly treacherous bend. David Ramsden halts immediately with an unpleasant screech and looks out of his side window. He can see nothing save for a rather grim Victorian house on the corner, shrouded in laurel, with peeling windows and a 'For Sale' sign on its front lawn. It is, he realises, his final destination, and he wonders sadly if this might also be the case for whatever he has hit.

"Oh my God!" he yelps, then adds, "*Hyvanen aika!*", priding himself on his foresight in having looked this up just the day before.

He repeats both phrases with mounting alarm as a small wizened face suddenly appears in his side window. The body attached to it is clearly hoisting itself painfully up, using his door handle for leverage. He has never seen this face before and indeed he has never seen a face like it, suffused as it is with what he can only suppose is terror in its most raw and primal form. A terror redolent, he senses immediately, of far more than banging into a slow-moving and very old Volvo.

"Are you *him*?" enquires the face.

David notices that the voice, even through the closed window, is still remarkably strong. As he winds the window down the elderly woman clings to its edge, until she realises that this is sending her in entirely the opposite direction and she has to keep clambering back up to prevent herself from sinking into a heap beside his front wheel.

"*Mr Ramsden? Are you Ramsden?*" She infuses the words with such frantic desperation that he would have said 'yes' had he been someone totally different. He wonders for a brief moment how being different might feel but dismisses it in light of more pressing concerns, especially when she adds, "Thank God you've come!"

David Ramsden knows that auctioneers and house clearers are not the most despised members of humanity, but only rarely are the heavens invoked to celebrate their arrival, so he can only wonder what else might be going on. He tries to open the door, hoping that the woman will take this as a signal to rise and move away. When she glides round with it, light as a feather, he finds himself slipping swiftly out to support her before she is crushed like a tiny bird.

It is only when the old lady is safely – and, for him, embarrassingly – in his arms that she points back to the crumbling house behind her. "You going in, then?" she asks, her feverish eyes searing into his own, as if this is more a challenge than an invitation. David courteously gestures 'after you', but a disturbingly violent shake of her wispy, grey-capped head dictates that he had better lead the way.

David can't help thinking, as he walks to her open door, that this lady, clearly his new client, really is a very odd person. So he will probably not ask Mrs Eileen Ballard why her house, on this pleasant spring day, is so bitterly cold.

DO I HEAR TWO?

"One Victorian burr walnut Sutherland table on turned underframe..."

The old lady can't keep still.

David is too polite to say anything but the woman's antics are really putting him off. She's like a senile squirrel that has found its way into the house but hasn't the brains, or is just too petrified, to find a way out. He wonders if, when he plays it back, the tape from his pocket dictaphone will have picked up all the sighs, moans and tiny yelps emanating from the clearly troubled owner of the property in question.

"Set of six Regency rose dining chairs, two with arms... very nice. Set of Charles and Diana ceremonial corgi cruets... not so nice." He turns to find Mrs Ballard almost up his backside. "Can't think why you'd want to leave this place, madam. Getting too big for you?" He finds it's this personal touch that has made the establishment for which he works so successful, even if it hasn't been overkeen to share that success with its head auctioneer.

"'*A most desirable period residence in traditional Cotswold stone*,'" she responds. "'*Beautifully maintained and appointed. Delightful English country garden...*'"

"Exactly!" agrees David. "So why..?"

"I sodding hate it!" says the old lady, her frightened face crumbling even more.

"… Georgian mahogany chest of drawers…"

From somewhere outside they hear the roar of what sounds like a motorbike. The old lady suddenly utters a short but piercing scream and clings to an Edwardian standard lamp as if the house is buckling beneath her.

"It's only a— Is everything alright, Mrs Ballard?"

David Ramsden has a strong feeling that everything isn't. For a moment it makes him think of his own mother, who is probably about ten years younger than the lady quivering beside him but who also lives on her own and has her little ways. Although, of course, she has her only son close by and most probably always will. Even a brief marriage, he thinks to himself, took him only one suburb away.

He wonders if Mrs Ballard has anyone but she doesn't seem in the mood for conversation. And, to be honest, he would really like to put some distance between them. She is making him quite nervous and he hates to feel unsettled. It – well, it unsettles him.

"Is there anything up in the loft?" he asks, praying for a negative response. Curiously, some of his colleagues love lofts, but as he tells them – rather wittily, he thinks – there's no love loft with him.

He turns to catch the old lady in a wide-eyed stare, as if he has asked her whether she is still sexually active and happy to frolic. Finally, she nods far more manically than required.

"Would you care to show me?" he asks. The nods, which haven't yet stopped, convert immediately to head-shakes of equal vehemence. He wouldn't be surprised if the bloody thing fell off and rolled across the fading Axminster. But she just points up the stairs, waving a bony arm to the skies, and retreats into the kitchen, still shaking.

"Old woman, late nineteen-thirties. Demented."

DO I HEAR THREE?

At least, thinks David Ramsden as he climbs up the potentially lethal wooden steps into the darkened loft, *I can be on my own up here.*

He wonders sometimes whether it's totally healthy to be on his own so much, but he tells himself that he does have those rollicking times back in the auction house with his colleagues and their banter, some of which he actually understands. Then there are the auctions themselves, of course, and most of all, his long-widowed mum. His life is really so full.

A shower of dislodged wood shavings falls into his eye as he scrabbles for a light-switch. He discovers it but there's either no bulb or the resident has served its time. He's accustomed to this, which is why he never goes anywhere without his rechargeable torch. Switching it on as he heaves himself up into a chamber that is even icier than the rooms below, he realises fairly swiftly that, like most lofts in his experience, it is not exactly an auctioneer's Shangri-La.

Trying not to rest his arms or legs on anything that might be concealing a rotting floorboard, he manages to make purchase on timber that feels reasonably sound. But, of course, you never really know. The hospitals are full of auctioneers who haven't paid due care and attention. At least this is what his mother has been telling him since he first began as a trainee in this most hazardous of professions.

David does occasionally wonder what occupations or activities she doesn't actually regard as fraught. He recalls her being the only mum amongst his classmates who wrote him a 'please excuse...' note for choir practice because of the potential damage to his larynx.

He begins his tentative foray into the semi-darkness. He assumes that the near-Arctic chill, making him shiver beneath his old but still smart Dunn & Co jacket, must be the wind seeping through what have to be pretty large gaps in the tiles. The dust swirling in the beam of his torch seems like a swarm of flying ants.

As he moves the trusty tool of his trade around him in narrow then more expansive circles, he spies several items of varying size, wrapped in old, yellowing sheets of newspaper. David knows that he will have to rummage through all of these parcels in due course but he's not expecting much. This is not to say that treasures aren't occasionally found – these are the stuff of auctioneers' dreams, and indeed anecdotes when they get together after another gruelling day. Yet, spotting an early but highly distressed gramophone and a rusty three-wheeled pram, his hopes aren't terribly high. He realises after a few minutes that he should be inventorying into his machine and wonders why the old lady downstairs has unsettled him so much.

"One child's buggy – broken. One vacuum cleaner – obsolete. Not exactly Tutankhamun's tomb... don't type that bit, Avril. One battered— *aagghh*!!"

David recoils with a start, sending the torch beam whirling madly around the loft like a manic mirrorball in a deserted ballroom, as he glimpses a shadowy figure in the gloom. He soon offers the machine and the universe a self-deprecating laugh. "One tailor's dummy!" He shakes his head – that's one for the lads. The old lady really has managed to put the wind up him. It strikes him, in a rare moment of self-perception, that this might not be the most onerous of tasks.

"Hello, Davey."

This time he freezes.

No frenetic torch beam. Not even a gasp. The instantly petrified auctioneer dares not turn round. He cannot bring himself to face the direction from which he senses this greeting – if greeting it was – has emanated.

Finally, after several seconds glued to the unstable floorboards, he manages to send a few ragged words into the chill yet musty air. "Who's— who's there? How do you know my name? Which is *David*, actually."

With a chuckle, the voice continues. David recognises a Gloucestershire accent, such as he himself has, only more pronounced and clearly younger. "You wouldn't believe me if I told you."

David forces himself to turn slowly around. He sees a once-elegant, early Victorian chaise longue that has clearly fallen on hard and lumpy times. On it reclines a shadowy yet clearly languid figure. David can make out unfashionably long dark hair and what could be the glint of leather. And teeth which seem unusually white.

"I warn you," says David, "I'm a green belt in karate."

"You're an auctioneer at that lardy Harbottle and Webb."

"I could be both," challenges the auctioneer, before wondering how the younger man knows this – and what on earth 'lardy' means.

"Well, are you both?"

"No. Who are you?"

For the first time, David allows his torch to shine fully onto the figure. The beam trembles along with his hand, but still manages to illuminate a striking young man, rather pale, who he reckons can't be more than twenty-one. David wonders why this particular number occurs to him – why not twenty or twenty-two? – but he doesn't linger on it as he is too taken with how singularly mesmerising this figure is. With his roguishly blue eyes that seem to play with whatever light is available, two-day growth and tall, Brylcreemed quiff, he looks like a Cotswold James Dean; especially clad in his tight denims and a leather, bike-boy jacket, with the insignia of the '59 Club on his shoulder, whatever the hell that means.

There's a cocky bravado here, in the way the younger man is smiling directly up through the quivering torch beam at a bemused David. Yet, despite this, he is looking almost as stunned and fearful as the older man gawping down at him.

"That's better," says the reclining man, sitting up for a clearer view. "I've been waiting for this, Davey." To David's surprise, the man's smile instantly fades, to be replaced with a desperate sadness that seems quite at odds with the youthfulness of his face. "I've been waiting for forty-four years."

David shakes his head. He knows now why this man is kept in the loft. It's for his own protection – the poor fellow has what they would call these days 'learning difficulties', or is what David's mother would term, somewhat mysteriously, 'mad as cheese'. No wonder old Mrs Ballard appeared so disturbed.

"Forty-four?" repeats David. "Sorry, but you can't be more than – what? – twenty-one." That number again. "I can get you help. I know a first-class consultant in Tewkesbury." David turns to go – he has to proceed with his task. "He collects Georgian trephines – they used them for drilling holes in the skull. Not that I'm suggesting—"

The young man's laugh stops him. "You look so like your mummy."

David turns back. This is getting creepy and he doesn't do creepy. "How on Earth do you know what my mum – my mother – looks like?"

"'Cos I married her," explains the young man. "I'm your dad."

DO I HEAR FOUR?

"In for four, out for seven…"

David and the young man, who has just caused him to hyperventilate and pass out, sit side by side on the old chaise longue alongside the old broken gramophone. David's head is practically inside the gaping mouth of the machine's brass horn, which is the closest thing to a paper bag his helper could think of on the spur of the moment.

"What if you just breathed in and out without counting?" suggests the young man, whose name, if he really is who he says he is, which of course David knows is impossible, would be Rick. Rick Ramsden. The very late Rick Ramsden.

"I've been breathing in and out for longer than you have," echoes David from inside the gramophone. "In for four…" He shakes his head vigorously in disbelief then decides this might be less painful were he to remove himself completely from the vintage metal container. "No. This isn't real. I'm just exhausted, that's all," he tells himself. "You can't work at the cutting edge of Gloucestershire auctioneering without having the occasional meltdown."

He senses the young man beside him stand up, although strangely he feels no change in the distribution of the lump-ridden furniture on which they're both sitting. But the curious fellow is now laughing fit to bust.

"What's so funny?" asks the auctioneer.

"I was pulling your leg, sunshine. Bit cruel, I know. Using your poor old dad like that. I'm just the old lady's son, Terry Ballard. Gave you a scare, eh? Woooohhhh! But you gotta learn to cool it, man. Life is too short."

David is beyond relieved. So much so that he even laughs with his new and clearly deranged acquaintance, something he is not given to doing on a regular basis. "Oh, right," he says. "I don't know why you would do that, but never let it be said David Ramsden can't take a joke, eh?"

Rick holds out his hand and David reaches out gratefully to clasp it. As his fingers discover that they're gripping nothing other than air, his body falls straight through that of the younger man and lands on the dusty floor, just missing a broken dolls' house. He immediately smacks his head on a stretch of rotting wood. Noticing a small knothole in the crumbly floorboard, David realises that he can see right down into the small bedroom below.

Through the pain he can hear elated laughter that verges on the demonic. "That was *brilliant!*" exults Rick. "Did you see that? *Splatt!* Right on my whispering hole! First laugh your old man's had since 1975."

David, who is also hysterical but not in a good way, picks himself up and immediately bangs his head on an unexpectedly low cross-beam. This time his deceased father doesn't laugh but seems genuinely concerned.

"Ow!" empathises the young and spectral figure. "Davey! You okay? You know what works on bumps? – dab of butter. Your poor mum taught me that. What a worrier that woman was."

"Still is," mutters David through the pain, which causes his young dad to smile. Even the older man – his son – can't help but recognise that beneath the sadness there is some relief here. The woman made a widow so prematurely is clearly still around.

161

For a moment Rick Ramsden is lost in memory of an age gone by, when his world was ripe with time and possibilities. So it is a few moments before he realises that David has backed away towards the staircase that leads down to relative sanity.

"No! Don't go," pleads the father. "Davey – please. We've only just met."

Whilst lunacy is not an atmosphere in which he especially thrives, David finds himself halted by the tearful break in the young man's voice. Perhaps he will stay just a few moments more, then, of course, try to forget that this ever happened. Because, as he tells himself, he has more than enough going on his life, without the surreal and paranormal.

A thought occurs to him, one of many he supposes might reasonably flood in, when confronted with your long-dead father, whom you've never met.

"How did— how did you—" He finds he can't quite get the words to form.

"How did I know it was you?"

David just nods.

Rick wanders over to another part of the loft, gesturing for David to follow with his torch. The young man directs the beam to a large bundle on the floor wrapped in fading newspaper. David recognises the wrapping as an inside spread from the regional weekly of a few years ago.

"Read it in the local rag, didn't I?" says Rick, with an enthusiasm that could only be described as boyish. "It's all I seem to get up here. Talk about purgatory." He smiles with what could almost be pride, as he recites from memory: "'*David Ramsden of Harbottle and Webb...*'" – she named you after her old dad, I wanted to call you Harley – "'*... gave a very interesting talk at the Local History Society entitled 'My Crazy Life as a Cotswold Auctioneer'. Tea and biscuits were served.*' Doubt that."

"They do a very good biscuit," protests David. "Oh. You mean... It *was* very interesting, actually." Something occurs to

162

him that sends his head spinning even more. "You *made* me come here, didn't you? You scared poor old Mrs Ballard so much that she just wanted to sell up and get the hell away!"

"Calling Harbottle and Webb… Wasn't sure it would work, but…" Rick suddenly begins to cry. "My own little lad. After all these years." He wipes his eyes. "Sorry, son. Yeah – even grown-ups cry sometimes."

For a brief moment David is genuinely moved. Until reality kicks in. "Oh, stop it!" He begins to smack his own head. "You're just a figment of my imagination." He stops the smacking because he's not great with pain and he knows his mum can spot a bruise anywhere, even when it's only on his heart.

"Ooh, somebody got his eleven plus," mocks Rick.

"I did, actually," counters David, sniffily. "*And* I went on to the grammar school. Then on to the local university. Almost got a 2:1."

"Oh, Davey," sighs Rick. "I had such hopes for you."

"*What, didn't you hear…?*" David finds himself strangely hurt by his newly encountered father's disappointment. "Anyway, you never met me. Never even knew what sex I would be. If you hadn't gone and electrocuted yourself at work, when poor Mum was four months—"

He doesn't get to finish. The stunned look on Rick's face in that stone-cold loft freezes the words on his tongue. "Is that what she told you – *electrocuted*?"

Suddenly David's phone, in the front pocket of his plain white and now not-so-crisp shirt, begins to vibrate.

"Bloody hell!" yelps Rick. "You're a fucking robot!"

David answers his mobile. "Ramsden. Hi, Quentin. No, still at the Ballard house."

Rick is just staring. "That is spooky!"

"Coming from you." David sighs down the phone. "Yes, okay, I'll list it all tonight… I do know we have a big sale on tomorrow. I'll be in first thing, Quentin."

"That is never a phone! Jesus."

David puts it away but Rick simply slips inside his son's body to take a better look. This is quite enough for the older and unwillingly invaded man. "Okay, I'm going now. Got a—"

"—big sale tomorrow. I heard. I was sort of hoping for a footballer. Or a fighter pilot."

"I'm in line for a partnership! My boss is having a serious mull, even as we speak." David can see that Rick is seriously unimpressed and finds himself weirdly eager to correct this. "My life is— is just how I want it, thank you. I'm very settled. I'm in the Rotary Club!"

With this *coup de grâce*, David Ramsden edges away with as much dignity as he can muster. He turns his back on the younger man, even if this means going down the loft steps in the most hazardous manner for any auctioneer. *If I had as many hot dinners,* he muses, *as there have been injuries doing this.*

The cries behind him pummel his ears and his heart.

"Davey, son – you can't leave your old man. Not now... YOU CAN'T LEAVE YOUR DAD!"

David, standing the wrong way on the ladder, twists his head uncomfortably for one final retort, before he returns to normal, un-ghostly life. "I never knew my dad. My dad's dead!"

"Then you should show him a bit more respect!" Rick looks thoughtful for a moment, clearly not a look with which he is overly familiar. "I oughta be in heaven, not stuck in a musty old house. There must be some reason why they're not letting me in."

"I can think of several."

"Don't leave me here on me ownsome, son. Not after I went and done all this scary stuff to get you called in." He can sense that this is having no effect on David, who is both resolute and shell-shocked. So Rick Ramsden decides, in his desperation, to change tack. "You NEED me!"

David stares at him one final time before descending back to normality. He slams the loft ladder shut with an angry crash.

He is halfway to his Volvo before he wonders what his dad was doing in Mrs Ballard's house in the first place.

A little boy plays with wooden blocks in a sunlit English garden. Roses bloom all around him but he knows to stay away from the sharp prickles and to keep on the grass.

Suddenly he feels himself swept off his feet by a gigantic, leather arm. The man swirls him around effortlessly with one hand, laughing as he does. In the other firm hand is a toy of some sort, zooming around along with him, just out of reach. The boy can't quite make it out – there are wheels and perhaps a handlebar...

Now there comes a sound so loud that it frightens him. Is it coming from inside the big man's massive mouth, that deep, toothy cavern? Or is it the song of something far more scary?

DO I HEAR FIVE?

The roar behind him is so fierce and real that David Ramsden's road-time reverie vanishes in an instant.

Instinctively, he looks in his mirror but the country road is deserted save for a distant tractor turning off down a dusty farm track between two fields of wheat. Yet the sound is growing stronger. He thinks he must be going insane and simultaneously wonders what sane man wouldn't, when confronted (possibly) with his barely-out-of-adolescence yet long-dead dad, someone he had never even encountered in life, let alone in a creepy old house in Winchcombe.

And, to cap it all, someone is speaking in tongues from the inside of his Volvo. He realises with some relief that it is simply the current language tape continuing unperturbed.

Must have a holiday, he thinks to himself. *Nowhere foreign.*

The roar is now almost on top of him. It is as if this hellish sound is actually inside his car. Or inside his head. But it could, of course, be something right beside him, in his blind spot. That has to be it. Instinctively he swerves to avoid it, whatever it is, and ends up careering blindly into a ditch.

The next noise he hears, which could be five minutes later or considerably more, is that of a police siren. In his concussed state he has no idea whether to be relieved, embarrassed or just mightily pissed off.

***

"Not like you to be out of control, Mr Ramsden," says the driver of the police car, addressing a bruised and disgruntled David in his rear-view mirror.

David just shakes his head, realising that his whole body is doing a similar amount of shaking without any instruction from him. "I was sure I had a vehicle of some sort up my backside," he tells the older of the two Gloucestershire policemen, both of whom are local and known to him. He realises that he doesn't sound hugely convincing.

"*That was me!*" announces an elated voice from the seat beside him. "*Been practising that for years.*"

David instantly jolts, as if a spike has suddenly shot up through his own seat, and spins with a speed that causes the men in front, whose instincts are so much swifter than our own, to gaze at each other and wonder vaguely what's up with the poor chap.

"Oh God!" moans the shocked auctioneer. "Oh no!"

"These things happen, Mister R," says the younger policeman kindly, bemused by the man's overly dramatic reaction. "Not the end of the world."

David reckons that this could be a serious understatement as he watches his long-departed father bouncing around with a glee he has previously associated only with overstimulated children or the mentally ill. At one point the rebounding Ramsden's head surges right up towards the sky, which is all the more impressive as the patrol car isn't a convertible.

"I'm FREE!" yelps an ecstatic Rick Ramsden, late of that old house on the bend. "After forty-four crappy years. Dunno how, but what a blast!"

"This is a nightmare," mutters David.

"Oh, that old car'll be as good as new," reassures the driver. "Those Volvos are like tanks. My mother-in-law drives one, more's the pity."

Rick leaps out of the open window of the patrol car and for a few seconds begins to race it at a ghostly clip, waving at David as he maintains an easy, sweat-free pace. "Look at your dad, son. He's still got it." He can see David's unsurprisingly confused face, as he zooms back into the car through an open window. "Speed, pal. What life's all about. And death, come to think of it."

They reach a built-up area, rows of social housing on either side of the road, attempting to match the sandy Cotswold stone in colour if not in texture. "This used to be all fields," says Rick, with some sadness. "Hello world, Ricky's back. Rick the Ram!" He beams at his son, his long flowing hair moving not a millimetre in the breeze. "Must be *you* done this, Davey!"

"No!" yells David, in serious denial. "I'm hallucinating! I DON'T BELIEVE IN GHOSTS!"

"You sure you don't want us to drop you at the hospital, Mr Ramsden?" says the driver, who isn't big on weird stuff.

Rick is now sitting on the driver's knee, running long, spectral fingers over the controls and puzzling over the built-in sat nav. "What the fuck?" he muses.

"Look," shouts David, who isn't a fan of bad language, "why are you here?"

"Why are any of us here?" responds the younger policeman, surprising even his colleague with a hitherto unrevealed existential bent.

Rick is back beside his son, stroking the older man's face with wondrous, loving hands that David can't feel but still isn't thrilled about, as he tries to make sense of the miracle that has clearly just occurred. "It's gotta be *you*, son," he decides. "Stands to reason. I'm here for YOU!"

"I never had a dad," insists David. "I don't need a dad."

"We all need a dad, Mr Ramsden," says the older policeman, who can't quite get a grip on the conversation but is game to try. "Y'know, someone to look up to."

Rick takes this as a playful instruction to lie flat on the roof of the police car and dangle his head upside down outside the windscreen, waving between the coppers to his long-lost, joyfully found son.

David Ramsden has never given credence to either heaven or hell up until this point. Now at least one of these locations has gained a new believer.

DO I HEAR SIX?

The rattled auctioneer can almost hear the sigh of constabulary relief as the patrol car drives speedily away from the small, modern semi-detached house in which David Ramsden chooses to live, a house deliberately lacking in any of those older, finer and more collectable elements that make up such a large part of the rest of his life.

"It's very *you*," says the ghostly figure beside him.

"Thank you," says David.

"Wasn't a compliment, son," adds his younger dad. "Let's hope the little woman has made it a bit more homey inside." He suddenly smacks David on the shoulder. The older man watches in morbid fascination as a ghostly hand disappears into his more corporeal body. "Hey, how many grandkids have I got? Four, five, six? Do I hear 'Dave the Ram'?"

"There's no little woman," says David, moving to his front door but holding out little hope that he will be able to block his uninvited new relative from home, hearth or head. "We're divorced."

"Oh," says Rick, in evident disappointment. "She take the kiddies with her, did she?" David is silent for a moment. It tells Rick everything he needs to know but not what he wishes to hear. "Ah. Okay. Right."

He stares at the charm-free house disappointedly. Through the picture window he can see a particularly uncluttered and boring living room and thinks almost wistfully of his loft, which may have been layered in dust and debris, but at least had character. Then the door to the room opens and a small, white-haired figure enters, pushing a vacuum cleaner.

"At least you got yourself a lady-who-does," says Rick proudly.

"I've got bad news for you," says David, who can't quite believe he's having this conversation. "That old lady with the Hoover is your wife."

This time it is the ghost who passes out, which isn't something David would have thought psychic phenomena actually do.

**

The old vacuum cleaner, which needs a good service or a mercy killing, reminds David of the noise in his head that nearly did for him less than two hours earlier.

He realises now – although he knows that any idiot would have worked it out sooner – that it had been the sound of a motorcycle, travelling at terrifying and highly illegal speed. How his late father had managed to replicate this awful noise he has no idea, nor indeed why the long electrocuted man would have wished to.

The woman who has always told David how hazardous these machines are, along with every other activity known to man (other than perhaps reading and origami) hasn't heard him come in. A morbidly obese black cat, however, snoozing fartily on the sofa, suddenly leaps awake with its back arched, hair like furry porcupine quills, and launches itself in pure terror onto the old lady's shoulder, sending her off course and into the – thankfully unkindled – fireplace.

"*Keith*!" shouts a horrified David from the doorway. "Get off Mummy! Down, boy."

The large cat obeys somewhat sullenly and slinks into the corner, becoming a cowering black furball and eyeing its master with new suspicion.

"Hello, David," says his startled mother, switching off the machine. She is about to question him on his early arrival when she notices his face. "Are you alright, my darling? You're white as a sheet." She looks out of the window. "I didn't hear your car – where is it?"

For a moment David thinks he might be alone, then realises his fellow traveller has revived, in his own way, and is now standing right beside him, mouth and eyes wide open, former garrulousness lost in a haze of nostalgia or pure horror. "Had a bit of an accident with the Volvo, Mum," says David, then immediately wishes he hadn't.

Mrs Ramsden is trying really hard not to panic but failing utterly, as indeed her son knew that she would. "Oh my God, David! You're not hurt, are you? Did you go to the hospital? Mrs Jackson's older sister in Cirencester thought she was perfectly okay after her accident until three weeks later when the whiplash killed her, just like that, by the cosmetics counter in Boots. Something about a clot in the—"

"Mum," he reassures the worried lady, who is by now hugging him and gently examining his body for fractures, "I'm fine, really."

He can't help but wonder at this point whether he actually is fine and resolves to have himself checked out once this nightmare is over. He also wonders, looking at the leather-clad spectre beside him, whether in truth it ever will be.

"Were you listening to an over-stimulating language?"

"Just Finnish." He realises this sounds more like a progress report than an answer.

He watches Rick helplessly, as the young man moves in closer to his own widow's lined but still pretty face, checking out her every feature with trembling hands, from her attractively crooked little nose to her flashing and currently alarmed hazel eyes. He

172

carefully avoids her wrinkles and the double chin. "Is this *really* you, Wendy?" he asks her, tears forming in his own disbelieving eyes, but of course receives no reply.

"Have you taken your blood pressure, sweetheart? Remember a sphygmomanometer is for life—" David nods, as he joins in. "— not just for Christmas."

Keith, in the meantime, bares his sharp little teeth and makes a noise like an angry growl, a sound his humans have never previously heard, before retreating even further into his corner.

"Keith!" chides Wendy. "It's only Daddy come home perturbingly early."

Rick looks at David in confusion, but the latter just shakes his head. There's a line of enquiry he has decided to pursue and he is not going to allow anything to interfere. He stares as meaningfully into his mother's eyes as his soft and somewhat pudgy face will allow.

"There was this motorbike…" he begins.

His mother's entire body freezes, whilst she tries with her smile and her voice to remain casual. The effect is both implausible and seriously disconcerting.

"Motorbike?" she throws off, picking up a feather duster to keep her hands from shaking.

Rick walks around Wendy, his leathers glistening in a light whose source David can't quite discern. "Yes, Wendy," he says, although he knows she can't hear him. "A Triumph T120 Bonneville, actually. With five-speed gear—"

"They shouldn't be on the road!" says the pensioner. She lifts a small vase and gives it an unnecessary wipe.

"You didn't say that when you were keeping my bum nice and toasty en route to the Ace Caff," chuckles Rick, remembering. "With your little hands wandering and The Beast just feet ahead of us."

"*What?*" yelps David, receiving a look of total confusion from his mum.

"So where did you see this motorbike, did you say?" she asks him, as if she isn't terribly bothered.

David remains thoughtfully silent for a moment, then says quietly, "Old Mrs Ballard's house. That little Victorian, right on the corner of Finster Road."

The vase his mother is dusting slips quietly from her hands and disintegrates on the fireplace's tiled surround. Keith shakes his head and leaves the room.

"Oh, yes?" she says, bending down to pick up the shards with her trembling fingers. David stops her before blood is spilled.

"That did it, old son," chirps Rick. "You never forget where your old man kicked off." He moves over to the poor woman, who is trying desperately to hold it together and not shatter into as many pieces as the vase. "Remember, Wendy, that awful Monday? After we'd had that…"

Wendy walks right through him and out into the kitchen. "Now you just put your feet up, David. I'll fetch the dustpan and brush."

Rick watches her go, shaking his head. "Why'd she lie to her little boy all these years?"

"So he wouldn't turn out like you?"

"Well, that bit worked," agrees Rick, sadly.

David checks himself out in the mirror above the fireplace and nods approvingly. He sees nothing there to be ashamed of. Rick joins him and sees nothing there at all.

"Shame. I was bloody good-looking." He looks at his son. "You've got my— well, you've got my ears. I see your mum in you." David turns to look at him. "She used to be such a goer, that little woman. *Jesus!* Couldn't get enough of the old Ram-rod!"

"That's my mother you're talking about!"

Rick calls fruitlessly into the kitchen. "*I never stopped loving you, Wendy!*" He looks suddenly stricken. "We broke the bloody bed on our wedding night. That was just two days before I died."

David stares at him. "*What?*"

174

"Oh. Didn't she tell you about her old dad and our 'shotgun'—"

"*Kanisteri me juoruta jokseenkin jokin jokin?*"

Rick moves over to his son, hands outstretched in strangling mode. "My God, if I could just shake some ruddy life into you!"

In an instant, Keith, protective interests revved to the max, is back in the room and leaping straight at Rick. With nothing to break his journey, the overweight cat flies straight through the unwelcome spirit and stuns himself on the living room window.

"Should've worn a helmet," says Rick. David isn't quite sure whether he's talking about the cat or himself.

DO I HEAR SEVEN?

"I'll never forget the sound that night… the screamin' tyres, the bustin' glass, the painful scream that I heard last, oh where…?"

"Will you SHUT UP!" screams David, from his spot next to his dead father on the bed.

He wonders, for a moment, why he is scrunching up at one end – it's not like ghosts take up that much space. Indeed, he muses, all they are is space. Yet David still feels, as he tries to plough through the sheaf of work papers on his lap, that he is now sharing his room with a seriously uninvited guest, who appears to have no intention of moving on. And who, indeed, finds sleep surplus to requirements. "I need my rest for tomorrow's—"

"Big sale," completes Rick. "So what is it, Chippendale chamber pots?"

"Assorted memorabilia, 50s through 70s. Not my type of thing, but needs must."

David ponders on why he is justifying his working day to a ghost but reasons that this isn't just any ghost. And, to be honest, it's not entirely unpleasant to be discussing his career with his father, after all these silent years, the way he assumes most sons are wont to do.

He recalls his long-ago schooldays, the sadness he felt as boys went on about their dads, or indeed, went off with them. Fishing trips, football matches, cycle rides. He remembers how fathers would stand in the cold, breath like cigarette smoke, punching the air as their lad scored a goal. Or how they'd sit in the summertime sun, surreptitiously sipping beers, while their offspring smacked a six. Of course, his mum always gave him a note for games, but perhaps, had his dad been around, those 'please excuse David...'s would have remained unwritten.

It's not as if his mother asks him for details – it's rarely more than a vague 'had a nice day, love?' Just occasionally she will tell him a fact she's read, such as in the United States last year more people lost their lives to furniture than to terrorism, so he had better be careful of those Victorian *armoires*.

"I'd like to go to sleep now," he tells Rick, "if it's all the same to you. I've got to be up at seven."

"Want me to tell you a bedtime story?"

"I'm forty-four!"

Rick looks over at the older man and smiles tenderly. "Never too late, son. You know, I may not have lived long, but at least I've lived."

David can see where this is going, where this might forever go, and he suddenly feels that he has had enough. "*Can't you see?* – I'm doing just fine. Good job, nice house, stable life. So, nothing to worry about any more – rest in peace." He switches off the light, only to find that his late father glows in the dark. "Bugger," he says.

"David," continues Rick, "I reckon I've been sent to give you the benefit of my experience."

"Well, if I ever need to know how to smash headfirst into a brick wall, you'll be the first person I'll call. Meantime, I'm going to sleep. Play dead!"

"And the Beast said to the Ram, 'you can sleep when you're six feet under'..."

Despite himself, David switches on the light once more. "The Beast? The Ram? Is this some sort of hippy fairy-tale?"

"The Beast weren't no fairy, boy," smiles Rick. "And Rick the Ram ain't no hippy. Bravest biker I ever knew was old Beastie. No one could touch him on that Norton of his. I remember one moonlit night – the road down to Oxford. Picture the scene, son…"

"No!" protests David. "Can't you take a hint? What are you waiting for?"

Rick looks thoughtful. "Dunno. Some sort of sign?"

"I'll give you a bloody sign!"

"Now, now, no tantrums! We've got forty-four years to catch up on. How did the breastfeeding go?"

David looks at his father for what he hopes is the final time and switches off the light.

Yet even in the dark, as his own eyes are closing on this most extraordinary of days, he notices a tiny smile on the younger man's face, a smile so disconcertingly abundant in mischief and cunning. And the trace, too, of a perturbing glint in his eye – almost as if Rick Ramsden knows something that David Ramsden doesn't.

But of course, this is impossible. The man has been stuck in a musty loft since 1975.

David falls asleep, and dreams again of a little boy.

The bicycle is tiny, but to him it looks as high as a horse and just as daunting. He can hear the big man's laughter in his ears, ringing as loud and clear as the bell that is all he dares touch on this fearsome new object.

He wants to ask the laughing man about the little wheels, the ones he has seen on other 'starter bikes', the ones that keep the new rider from falling off and hurting himself on the pavement.

There are no wheels.

Perhaps, he thinks, they are too expensive. Yet he knows, as the big man lifts him up in the air and sets him firmly down on the tiny plastic saddle, that he is supposed to ride his new two-wheeler as just that.

A big boy's bike.

He trusts the smiling man. Nothing bad will happen.

DO I HEAR EIGHT?

In the morning, as he slowly wakes, David Ramsden feels a lump at the bottom of his bed. It takes him a while to compute that, as his father is currently both absent and weightless, it must be Keith, who is very far from either.

With a sense of relief that is not quite as potent as he might have anticipated but nonetheless quite real, he starts his day. As always, he talks things through with the cat, who listens without interruption or criticism, unlike his ex-wife; or indeed his mother, who will fuss over him until she dies and quite possibly, given his recent experience, thereafter.

Yet perhaps yesterday was simply a dream, like the curious ones he is currently having, as there is no shred of evidence that his late father was ever here. Not that ghosts are known to leave an abundance of reminders. He has heard of something called ectoplasm but has no idea what it is, although it sounds disgusting and something his mother would probably hoover up before anyone could trip over it.

"And my talk *was* interesting," he tells Keith defensively. "Mrs Harkness cheered, dementia or no dementia."

He showers swiftly, dons his most rakish cavalry twill, gulps down the healthy (if binding) muesli his mother makes by the barrel-load and heads for the door. It is only when he begins to talk Finnish that he recalls he has no car.

He returns inside and calls a taxi.

***

The Montpelier district of Cheltenham is one of the most fashionable and attractive in this beguilingly Georgian-white spa town. David Ramsden feels a great sense of pride that he works here and that people know him by name. See how he nods to shopkeepers and local businessmen and watch how they nod cursorily back. Respect like this doesn't arrive fully-wrapped overnight. It has to be diligently earned and prudently maintained.

There is an uncharacteristic lightness to his step this morning and not just because of the unfamiliar pleasure of having been driven to work. Yet he can't quite puzzle out whether it is due to the extraordinary encounter he possibly had yesterday or the fact that it has left no visible trace today.

He even dares to gaze in the window of that new lingerie shop which just opened, to the disapproval of some of Montpelier's older residents. An unbelievably well-proportioned mannequin is wearing a policewoman's uniform that he is quite certain has yet to be officially sanctioned, unbuttoned as it is to reveal not-entirely-regulation lacy underwear.

David Ramsden regards himself as a man of the world, so whilst he might be intrigued, he is hardly shocked. He is more shocked, however, to see his late father standing in the same window, very close to the female PC, with a disgustingly leery look on his face.

This is how Elspeth Martin finds David when she passes the shop on her way to her job at the auction house. "Morning, Mr Ramsden."

David catches her reflection in the window. It is a second or two before he can turn round, somewhat sheepishly, to greet her.

"Oh. Elspeth. Good morning."

"She's a black girl!" yells the figure in the window, pointing at the colleague.

"*We've got black people in Montpelier now!*" calls David, disapprovingly.

"I know!" says Elspeth. "Isn't it exciting? See you at work."

"You're in there, son," says Rick, walking in and out of the policewoman. "Boss and secretary. I won't stand in your way."

"Elspeth is a Fine Arts graduate and a trainee auctioneer. And what's more…" He notices passers-by staring at the man berating thin air, so he takes out his mobile. "And what's more," he repeats, "the bidding will only start at eight thousand."

"Didn't no one tell you it's rude to ignore your elders?"

"You're not elder, actually. And I'd just rather my customers didn't think their local auctioneer is drunk or losing it."

"Got it," nods Rick. He leaps out of the window and takes in the passing throng. He notices an unshaven man approaching, dishevelled and looking like he's talking to himself. "Phone in his ear, right?"

"No, he's drunk and losing it. Morning, Neville."

Rick isn't listening. He stands in the middle of the road allowing cars, of which he has never seen the like but adores on sight, to pass right through him. He's allowing young men and women to do the same as they cross the road, and is clearly fascinated by the tattoos and the face furniture. He beams at David, as if all his birthdays have come at once and this brave new world was created just for him.

"So, that Elspeth," he calls to the pavement, where David is edging away from that shop, "she seeing anyone?"

"She's married, actually. To Sandy. Short for Alexandra."

"Fucking hell!" says Rick, but not before a few delicious moments have passed.

"You're not going to cope here. Things have moved on."

Rick is right next to him, watching the world – mostly female – go by. "You ain't moved anywhere, lad. You're stuck on the hard shoulder. But Daddy's here. Just waiting for that sign."

"Here's a sign for you," says David and thrusts two spread fingers right up his late father's nose. Or into thin air, depending on how you and the population of Montpelier choose to look at it.

The morning had started out so well.

DO I HEAR NINE?

The 'Why the hell did I throw mine away?' sale is being prepared. At least, this is what the employees of Harbottle and Webb call it as they dust and polish the fifties-to-seventies memorabilia scattered all over the cavernous, brick-lined chamber.

As David walks in, a stooped, white-haired old man slumps slowly past him, laboriously hefting a gleaming jukebox to the rear of the vast room. David finds it painful to watch as this frail but dignified gentleman, who should be enjoying his retirement by now, struggles to find a safe berth for the precious object. A fag dangles from his mouth, the ash almost as long as its host.

"Here," says David, moving towards him, "I'll take that for you."

"*Leave it!*" comes a voice like a chainsaw from a nearby office.

"Morning, Quentin," says David, stopping mid-assist. The old man shrugs and shuffles off.

"Quentin bloody Harbottle!" yelps Rick, staring at the portly owner with his drinker's face and belly. "Of course! He was a poncey mod with a scooter back in the seventies. You're working for a poncey mod!"

This is not entirely news to David, at least the poncey bit, but he finds himself taking offence at his father, who has never shown the least interest in his son's world owing to a totally avoidable early interment, passing judgment on the people by whom his only living heir chooses to be employed.

"You look like a distressed commode," says the employer, scrutinising David through unattractively bleary eyes.

"Pillock!" mutters Rick.

"Sorry, Quentin," says David, ignoring his father. "I was doing the Ballard list until the early hours. I'd better just go help poor old—"

"Future partners, chummy, do not heft. Get on with what I pay you for."

As soon as the irascible man strides off, Rick is in there. "You gonna let him talk to you like that, Davey?"

"He gave me the job." David knows he is looking, and probably sounding, like a ventriloquist and finds himself wondering whether he could still do it whilst drinking a glass of water. "I owe him a lot."

"Not your bollocks, son. A man's gotta stand up for himself, or he's no son of mine."

"Some threat," retorts the son of his, but Rick is already prancing around the auction room in unashamed wonder, gazing at objects of nostalgia as if the wondrous childhood world he so unwillingly left long ago has been carefully preserved just for him.

He glides in and out of familiar Oxo tins and Ercol recliners and Dansette record players, passes through Mickey Mouse dial phones and Agas and Subbuteo sets. He even has fun trying to leap out of 'modern' Swedish wardrobes and scare people, but when he realises they can't see him and couldn't care less, some – but not all – of the fun wears off.

Meanwhile, the elderly ash-stained gentleman is still shifting objects excruciatingly slowly into the yard, each one appearing to send his bending back another centimetre closer towards the ground, where he doubtless will lay in entirety before long.

"How's your delightful mother?" calls Quentin Harbottle from his office, without regard for those other employees who might be listening.

"Oh. Er… she's fine, thank you, Quentin."

"She tell you about our intimate little dinner the other night? She fought all the way." He smiles. "For her son, that is."

Rick is out of his wardrobe in a flash. "*He's after my little Wendy? The randy old—* Over my dead body!"

This time he whizzes all over the shop, bouncing angrily off walls and windows, shooting out via the ceiling and back through the door again. David thinks he is simply showing off, but has to admit it's quite impressive.

Suddenly there's a huge crash from outside, followed by a mournful, drawn-out groan.

"Go and help him," sighs Quentin. "Shoot him if necessary."

David rushes outside into the yard, followed by Rick, who is still glaring at Quentin.

They find the aged man struggling under the weight of a vintage but lovingly well-restored motorcycle, minus its name badge and number. Despite its years, it looks like a gleaming baby compared to the decrepit body pinned and wriggling beneath.

David rushes to hoist the classic but potentially lethal machine off his writhing colleague.

"I've died and gone to heaven," exclaims Rick, as he watches the rescue take place.

"I wish," says David.

He manages to shift the motorcycle sufficiently for its victim to raise himself up, although the shocked man doesn't seem hugely keen.

"You know what this is, don't you?" asks Rick rhetorically.

"It's an old Triumph T120 Bonneville," says David.

Rick stares at him, as if his little boy just began talking in Serbo-Croat. (Which is, interestingly, the next one on his list – language number nine, but Rick is unlikely to know this.)

"She's a 'Bonnie' alright," sighs Rick. "In fact, just like…" David notices that Rick is finding it hard to finish the sentence and believes he may know why. "She is so beautiful."

His father is clearly choked as the emotion wells up, giving if not colour to his cheeks, then at least an interesting change of pallor. But David is more surprised to see that the incident is having much the same effect on the poor shifter.

"Had her in the shed for donkey's years," explains the old man. David realises that this is actually the first time he has seen this admittedly splendid object, although he has catalogued others, equally lethal, in the past. "Then a few months back I had the notion to restore her." He looks at the auctioneer pleadingly. "I was thinking we might put her into the sale today, David. If it's okay with you, of course. And the boss… See, I need the cash."

David looks almost embarrassed. "Ah. Well, I'm not sure – it's just that I don't know that Quentin would exactly approve of his staff just—" He hears a loud cough beside him and looks at Rick, who is staring at him quite sternly – in fact, as sternly as a twenty-one-year-old hell-raiser of possibly arrested development might stare. "I'm sure we can fit her in."

"Thanks, lad," says the bruised but clearly much-relieved dogsbody. He strokes the Triumph with what can only be perceived as a true and profound love. "Real beauty she was. In her day. Until…" He shakes his head and David can discern a genuine sadness. "Never mind. I hope whoever ends up with her lets me visit her now and again."

The emotion is too much for him. His rheumy eyes seem on the cusp of streaming. Brusquely, he picks up the bike and wheels it proudly, if shakily, away.

This time David doesn't hang back. "Here, I'll help you, Walter." And they both carry it together.

He hears the intake of breath behind him.

"Walter?" repeats the ghost. "Walt— Oh my God – *it's the Beast!*"

"THE BEAST?!" screams David, causing Walter, aka the Beast, to drop his end of the proudly restored Triumph T120 Bonneville onto David's left foot.

"Nobody's called me that since…" The old man sniffs the dusty air. "Can anyone smell Brylcreem?"

Instinctively, Rick runs a delicate hand over his quiff. "Beastie, what did I do to you?" He tries to caress the bike. His hands pass gently through it. "*You kept my bike!* You kept Bonnie all these years? But you never told Davey here, did you, about what happened?" The answer occurs to Rick and he shakes his head. "Wendy must've sworn you and every last soul in town to secrecy." He turns to his awestruck son. "Davey, my boy. I think we just had our sign."

David stares into his father's weepy yet curiously suspect smile and has a horrible feeling that this will all end in tears.

DO I HEAR TEN?

"I am *not* buying a bloody motorbike!"

The seats are out and the buyers are in. Alert men and women of all ages, Gloucestershire gentry in Burberry and Barbour, local dealers with pockets full of catalogues and blarney and cash. Hip flasks glint under lights designed to show off the lots to their best advantage and bids at their most discreet.

David Ramsden would rather not be seen talking to himself as he walks to the podium, but he finds he just can't let this go. Fortunately, there is so much hubbub in the crowded room, the chatter of anticipation melding with fake indifference, that he isn't noticed. He wonders vaguely whether this is what tinnitus is like – a constant, annoying buzzing in his ear. Although tinnitus probably isn't life-threatening, whereas Rick Ramsden most definitely is.

"I can't buy it anyway. I'm the bloody auctioneer."

Rick points upwards to the cheap chandeliers and the high timbered roof. Or perhaps beyond. "But *He* wants you to, son. That's why He sent me the Beast."

"Walter has been here for years. And mum never said you were religious!"

"Being dead can change a man, David. You have to listen to what He says."

"God wants me to buy a sodding Triumph?"

David thinks he may have said this just a bit too loud as the background noise instantly fades down. Many of the familiar faces have known him for years but never realised he was one of those who based their decisions on diktats from above. It immediately changes their long-held perceptions of him and has them churning over past encounters, to see how they conform to this faintly disconcerting world view.

Then she walks into the room.

David has never seen anyone like her in his life.

Possibly because people like her don't usually frequent auction rooms and people like him – well, exactly like him – rarely venture outside them, except perhaps to visit houses for valuations.

Yet, at the same time, something about her is hugely familiar, especially since yesterday, because she is dressed entirely in leathers, as if she just stepped off a motorcycle of her own. And she holds a bright red helmet confidently in her hand, as other women might carry an accessory that perfectly defines who they are and without which they would never countenance being seen at all.

She is not beautiful, or at least not in a way that David, who admittedly knows little about these things, has defined beauty up until now. Yet there is a freshness and an honesty about the young woman, a compelling directness in the way she strides down the aisle towards him, past rows of bemused customers, staring unblinkingly into his astonished face with eyes he would categorise professionally as lapis lazuli blue, under short hair as black as her jacket, No-nonsense practicality, an economy of movement, seem to inform every muscle of her body as it flexes under the hugging tightness of apparel that she may wear for safety yet read distinctly like a statement.

"Hello dollface, and who are you?" says Rick, adding a whistle of approval that makes David think with some relief how far his sex have come. Yet he finds himself staring at her in a way that causes him to wonder if there's still some way to go. It's not attraction, surely, not for a young biker in perhaps her late twenties. Rather a fascination, as if in the hours since ten o' clock yesterday morning, he has entered a distinctly alternate realm.

But he still knows that the gaze he is offering, reflected in her own slightly combative eyes, is one of cool disdain. Despite her bravado, she seems as if she has walked into totally the wrong place – almost into a different social stratum, and everyone else in that suddenly stilled room feels the same.

"Hear you got a Bonnie," says the young woman, in an accent more upmarket than he was expecting, from his admittedly limited knowledge of the biking fraternity. "Triumph T120 Bonneville?"

David stares at her in amazement. "How on Earth…? It's not even in the catalogue!"

She shrugs. "Small town. You hear things. And Walter comes into where I work."

"And where is that?" asks David, thinking a supermarket perhaps, or a charity shop, but then he hears a loud coughing start up behind him: Quentin, who mutters that it might be fun to have an auction some time soon.

"*Don't let her get it, Davey!*" says Rick. "Take it off the shelf for later. Don't let that beauty get away."

David turns to his father, with a smile that is almost cruel. "Could you tell me your name, Miss?"

"Gosforth. Daisy Gosforth."

David believes he hears a gasp from beside him, which is obviously something basic and involved with sex. So he simply removes his beloved gavel from its felt-lined box and offers the expectant crowd a firm but welcoming nod.

He doesn't notice the surprisingly gentle smile Rick is affording the auction room's newest and most unexpected arrival.

DO I HEAR ELEVEN?

It is eleven o'clock at night and Rick Ramsden is still crying.

"For pity's sake, man…"

"'Dad'. At least call me 'dad.'"

"Will no one rid me of this troublesome ghost!" says David, which he can't help thinking is rather clever, although he knows instinctively that this will fall on dead ears. He also feels more tired than he believes he has ever been, save for that time when his ex-wife spent the entire night listing the reasons why she was leaving him and that his imploring her not to in five different Eastern European languages was just compounding the problem.

What bothers David Ramsden the most, as he sits in his favourite and only armchair, nursing a larger supermarket Scotch than he has drunk in years, is that there seems to be a sense of normality setting in. It no longer feels quite so surreal to be sharing his home, every waking moment and most of the sleepy ones, with the spirit of his juvenile, twenty-one-year-old father, an emanation who can talk only about women and bikes and women on bikes and, bewilderingly, women who are bikes. Or, of course, how his only son is squandering his birthright.

Yet he really does wish he could find a way to send Rick Ramsden back to purgatory or heaven or at least the Ballard loft. It's not like you can Google it – and he caught *Poltergeist* once by accident on the TV, so he's not going anywhere near that. He'd also like a still vaguely concussed Keith to come back in from under the shed.

But right now he'd settle for a way to stop Rick the Ram bawling his head off.

"*It's a flaming bike!*" says David. "The weird young woman wanted it, she bought it, she's got it. She's happy, Quentin is satisfied and Walter the Beast is ecstatic. Job done."

"But it was meant for you, Davey. Your inheritance. It was the one thing I could give to you. That has to be why Beastie was fixing it up."

David shakes his head in disbelief and finds it still hurts from the accident, so he stops. "What was I going to bloody do with it – frame it on the wall? Oh, I know, I could have had it turned into a modern sculpture and planted it on your grave."

Rick stops crying. "You'd do that, for me? Nice thought, son. But, actually, I wanted you to ride it."

"You have got to be joking."

"You wouldn't have been on your own – I'd have been there to teach you."

"Bit like Captain Smith of the Titanic giving sailing lessons."

The ghost gives an enormous sigh. "I'd have been better off staying in my little loft. You are such a disappointment."

David is surprised to discover how much this hurts. It has to be some sort of nadir when even the dead don't have a good word for you. But it makes him more determined than ever to return to the status quo. He's way behind on his Finnish.

"Okay," he says, finally. "What would it take to get you out of my hair and back into that loft?"

"Would you still come visit me?"

"Not sure how the new owners would feel – if it ever gets sold – but we'll see. Now, what am I bid for your disappearance?"

"You've got that bird's address – the leather girl?"

"She's not a 'bird' – and Elspeth must have it written down. For our books."

"Then take me to see my bike."

DO I HEAR TWELVE?

"Well, I never expected this," says Rick Ramsden, gazing in awe at the shop window. "I think I've died—"

"—and gone to heaven," completes David, staring along with him. "I really wish you'd stop saying that."

David thinks this is the most dispiriting retail establishment he has ever been cajoled into visiting, save perhaps for those dress shops with his mum when he was a little kid and had no dad to be left with. It is only a small shop yet motorcycles and their enthusiasts take up almost every inch.

Displayed in those rare corners where machines are not erect, propped or dangling are gleaming helmets, crisp new leathers and all the accoutrements of the roaring road. There's even a black T-shirt that proclaims in white lettering on its back, 'If you can read this, the bitch has fallen off', which David doesn't understand, but is pretty certain wouldn't be a favourite of the young manager, one Ms Daisy Gosforth.

"Didn't think I'd see you here," says the young woman, still in black but not this time in leather, from behind her mysteriously cluttered counter.

"Nor you," says an intrigued Rick, after which the silence grows even more uncomfortable. He tries to nudge his son, without success. "Say something, boy. Be sociable."

"Why?" demands David, then sees the quizzical look on the young woman's face. "Why, it's all part of our service. At Harbottle and Webb. To see if our purchasers are completely happy."

"Well, I am," she says, "completely happy. Thanks. Though I wasn't so happy with the look you gave me when I came into your place yesterday."

"Ah. What look?" Although he believes he recalls the look.

"You know. The old 'what's someone like you doing in a lardy place like this?' look."

"'Lardy'?" repeats David. He's come across that curious word recently, but can't quite recall where. *Something to do with baking?*

"Short for la-de-da," explains Rick. "Ain't heard that for years! Well, go on, man!"

In the ensuing lull, David finds himself moving closer to the counter and the young woman. As if unable to shift his gaze, he stares unblinkingly into her eyes, and the tiny piercings in her nose and ears that he hadn't noticed before. *Why do people do this?* he wonders. *A face would be fine without them. Well, at least this one would,* he decides. He has known some that might just be improved with wire mesh.

"Anything else?" she enquires, as the silence persists.

"*You've got bloody pins in your face!*" cries Rick, who clearly hadn't noticed them either.

"You've got bloody pins in your face!" repeats David instinctively, as if this had been a prompt and not simply an observation, swiftly adding, "Which is totally fine by me," an addendum that doesn't really ease the situation.

He glares at the ghost. That, he decides, was a final line crossed. Or, as his mother would say, for reasons best known to herself, 'a fridge too far'. *Enough! I should be at work,* he tells himself, *not insulting innocent young women with metalled faces in bike shops.* He really has had his fill of Rick Ramsden.

"Phew!" says Daisy Gosforth. "I'll certainly sleep easier tonight, knowing you approve. Anything else you wanted. Latest *Bikers' Monthly*?"

Rick says something that changes David's life and world forever.

"If she lets you ride her Bonnie, just the one glorious time, I'll be out of your hair forever," he promises. And this time he sounds totally sincere. "I'll have passed something fine on, from father to son, and my job will be done." He smiles, almost embarrassed by his earnestness. "Sounded like a poem, didn't it?"

David looks directly into Rick's pale eyes. He's not going to make the mistake again of talking rubbish out loud, but the stare he's drilling into the far younger and only slightly deader man's face is one that demands total reassurance. The ghost simply nods. A deceased man's word is his bond.

David Ramsden turns back to the young woman and moves even closer, until he is leaning on the counter. Quietly, as if he doesn't want anyone else to hear, he gently murmurs words into her intriguing face that he never thought he would hear himself say in a million years.

"I want to ride your bike," he whispers.

He expects a response with an element of surprise in it, but not quite as much element as he receives.

"Get out of my shop, you fucking perve!" says Daisy Gosforth, quietly but firmly.

***

It takes David Ramsden a good twelve minutes to convince Daisy Gosforth of the innocent literality of his request.

Twelve minutes which aren't aided by the sound of almost hysterical ghostly laughter shooting directly into his left earhole. Hearing the spirit of one's long-deceased parent talk about wetting himself, a phenomenon even David suspects goes way beyond the most outer of limits, is an experience he will not easily forget.

David is finally rewarded when the young woman agrees to meet him on Sunday at an ageing and abandoned airfield on the outskirts of town. It turns out that the never-less-than-surprising Ms Gosforth is a qualified motorcycle instructor, a calling she combines most efficiently with running the shop.

"Well, we'd better get you geared up, hadn't we?" she says, with an enthusiasm even her future pupil can detect as containing more than a note of amusement. She is pointing to an array of clothing that David Ramsden wouldn't normally be seen dead in, although he feels that this could be exactly the state in which he might soon be found. "And I have to tell you, an old Triumph T120 Bonneville, however lovingly restored, is so *not* a starter bike for a guy like you."

"It's gotta be my old bike, Davey," urges the voice beside him, "or I'll haunt you until the end of your days, morning to night, Cotswolds and beyond the A40…"

"Yes, okay," hisses David to the air around him, ignoring his previous vow. "That has to be the bike, Ms Gosforth."

"I'll need you to fill in a form," says Daisy, handing him some printed sheets from a drawer under the counter. She taps them firmly. "There's a big section on health." Staring straight at him, she adds, "I'd pay particular attention to the mental health bit."

David's cheeks grow red, as the insinuation slaps him. "Are you suggesting I've got… problems?"

"You're a middle-aged auctioneer who suddenly decides he has to ride a powerful bike he only just saw the day before. No, you're firing on all cylinders."

"You're in there, Davey!" says Rick Ramsden, which even in all the surrounding madness has to be the barmiest thing David has heard all day. Yet he feels he has no choice, if he wants his old life back.

One session should hopefully do it. He will have to go along for the ride.

DO I HEAR THIRTEEN?

At least the weather is fine, thinks David Ramsden, clutching at straws, as he drives his newly repaired Volvo to the old airfield. His Fin-Begin tape is playing at full blast, if only to drown out the over-excited rambling from the seat beside him.

'*Kuinka paljon kalaa on*?' says the tape.

"*Kuinka paljon kalaa on*?" repeats David.

"What the hell is that?" exclaims the Fin-Beginner's father finally. "And can't you go any faster?"

David switches off the tape. "No. And it means 'how much is the fish?' in Finnish. It's very useful."

"Going to Finland, are you?"

"Why would I do that?"

"Jeez. Aren't you just a bit fired up, son, about this morning?"

"You're the one who's a bit 'fired up'. You didn't stop talking all night. I'm a bit terrified-up, if you must know."

"There's nothing to it, bike-riding," laughs Rick. "Easy as falling off a log."

"Or smashing into a brick wall."

"If there's one thing I'm gonna teach you before I die – before I leave – it's to stop being so negative."

"Perhaps it's being so negative that's kept me alive twice as long as you. Why were you riding at such speed round the corner that night?" David can't even look at Rick. "You were about to become a dad. My dad."

"Practising, son. Obviously."

"Practising? For what – euthanasia?!"

"Don't, Davey. The ladies don't go for cynicism. I was practising for the Isle of Man TT."

"*What on Earth is that?*"

"Only one of the most dangerous sporting events in the world."

"Well, that's responsible. Didn't even make it to the bloody ferry, did you?"

"No." Rick pauses for a moment. "But there's still time."

David Ramsden turns to stare at the ghost of his late father who is sitting there in the seat beside him, looking paler and more agitated than his son has ever seen him, yet also, curiously, more determined.

"Keep your eyes on the road, son. We're here."

***

There are around twelve or thirteen motorcycles and dutifully helmeted riders at the airfield and as many instructors, male and female, yet David spots Daisy straightaway. And it isn't just because she is standing beside the gleaming Triumph, a sight over which he can hear his rapt companion immediately begin to slaver. At least, he assumes the 'hello, baby' and 'hi, you little beauty' are addressed to the bike.

David can't help noticing that whilst she is possibly the most practical and down-to-earth person he has ever come across, there is something curiously other-worldly about Daisy Gosforth, as if she is firmly rooted on this planet, yet inextricably linked to somewhere and something beyond. He can't quite explain it and thinks perhaps it is because he has never met anyone, young or old, who appears so comfortable and almost unnaturally serene in their own skin, seemingly untouched by the earthly forces surrounding her.

He also can't help but notice once again, berating himself even as his eyes remain stubbornly fixed, how well that skin is contained within worn, but undeniably fetching, motorcycle leathers. He puts this uncharacteristically crude observation, directed at someone who is so far removed from his limited social (and even more limited imaginative) circle, down to the strain of the occasion and the fact that he is being driven round the bend at almost exactly the same speed as his clearly possessed father took that fatal curve so many years ago.

"Good enough to eat, that is," mutters the ex-biker beside him, reminding David gratefully how much attitudes have moved on. He just wishes he wasn't thinking exactly the same and supposes the difference is that these days, you just don't say it out aloud.

David never had robot toys as a child and doesn't go to those movies in which robots play a major role. Yet, as he struggles out of the Volvo clad in his spanking new – and to him, ridiculously expensive – leathers, he feels that he is moving and creaking exactly like a machine designed to function as human but leaving plenty room for more work to be done.

"Morning, Mr Ramsden," says Daisy Gosforth, striding towards him. The professionally welcoming smile can't quite cloak the apprehension on her make-up-free and hitherto unlined face. "Are you sure?" she asks gently.

"Too tight?" he asks, assuming she questions his dress sense.

"Probably, but I meant about all this. You know. The Triumph."

David doesn't say anything until a voice beside him says, "Unless you don't want a sound night's sleep ever again, tell her you're more than sure."

"I'm more than sure, Ms Gosforth," says David, without much conviction. "I've never been more certain of anything in my life."

"And it has to be that Triumph," comes the prompt.

"And it has to be that Triumph," repeats David, adding "although I've done my research and know that I must go to full licence to be legally permitted to ride this one on the roads." He can't believe he is actually spouting this rubbish and that he should be demanding instruction on the one machine that is specifically programmed to kill Ramsdens.

"Fine," she says, shaking her head. They walk across the recently restored tarmac towards the threatening machine. "Well, I normally start my pupils off by comparing and contrasting riding a motorcycle with riding a bicycle." She is about to elaborate on this when she notices his face. "What's wrong, Mr Ramsden? … Mister…?" The first lines begin to appear on her brow as the horrible truth dawns. "Can't ride a bike, can you?"

David shakes his head. "My mother wouldn't let me near the things. I could never work out why – well, not until last week."

"Oh shit," says the spectral voice beside him, adding ominously, "I might be here longer than we thought."

DO I HEAR FOURTEEN?

The difference between learning to ride a motorcycle and learning to drive a car is, of course, that the practising biker will eventually need to confront the highways entirely on his own.

David Ramsden, however, is never on his own.

At each point on his journey from that first tentative mounting, an almost invisible passenger rides pillion, whispering fervid instructions into his apprehensive but strangely determined son's ear.

Yet something almost as momentous, and possibly even more surprising, is happening to David.

It occurs on the very first lesson, when he manages to uncreak his encased legs sufficiently to clamber onto the huge and terrifying machine. He was once lifted onto a mangy donkey on a seaside day trip in a rare moment of abandon by his over-cautious mummy, and began immediately to cry because he suddenly found himself helpless and unimaginably far off the ground. He feels much the same right now.

For about five seconds.

It could be the encouraging, if certifiably overexcited, voice in his ear that only he can hear. But he doesn't think so.

Something is happening to him, something deep inside, not just corporeally but within his very soul and essence. His inner Dave.

And it happens the very moment the terrifying machine on which he sits with such ingrained reluctance bursts into roaring life.

To the utter astonishment of his instructor, himself and most probably everyone around him, David discovers that he has a natural sense of balance; more than that, an instantaneous, almost inexplicable affinity with the machine that throbs so powerfully and unforgivingly beneath him, like a tiger straining at the leash. As if his own ignition has simultaneously been switched on.

This comes as absolutely no surprise to his father, who always knew his progeny would have bikers' genes. What comes as more of a surprise is that David, rather than feeling stolidly hostile to this turn of events, finds himself totally elated – even as this same elation scares the middle-aged shit out of him.

He gradually senses that the undisguised admiration of those other new learners around him, most of whom are at least twenty years his junior, isn't purely for the exquisitely restored 1974 Triumph T120 Bonneville.

"Well, I never thought I'd find myself gobsmacked," says Daisy Gosforth, shaking her head, as the first lesson draws to an end. "If I didn't know better, Mr Ramsden, I'd say you were a born biker. Are you sure you haven't done this before?"

David is sitting on the Triumph and shaking his head, wondering for a moment if he might be possessed or schizophrenic or a victim perhaps of multiple personality disorder, like someone he saw on a documentary once. But he can sense the shake of another equally triumphant yet completely weightless head directly behind his own.

When Daisy moves off incredulously to write something on her chart, David turns to Rick. "It's you, isn't it? Keeping me upright."

"I'm a ruddy ghost, sunshine. This was all your own work. Born to ride, you are."

"Don't be ridiculous," scoffs son of ghost. "This is just to get you off my back, you understand. Literally."

"If you say so. And a Ramsden always keeps his promise." David doubts this with every fibre of his being. "Oh God, Davey, did you not feel the thrum?"

"The *what*?" Somewhere, David Ramsden knows full well what his transported dad is on about, though he dares not admit it. Not yet. Because it frightens him too much.

"The thrum!" enthuses Rick. "You know – the throb of her. The sensation of man and machine as one. The not knowing where she starts and you ruddy finish. It's better than sex, Davey, even with your mum. Although, mind you, sometimes riding her wasn't unlike—"

"*That's my mother you're talking about!*" yells the outraged son.

Daisy, who happens now to be making a very swift phone call, looks back at him in puzzlement. "No, it's *my* mum I'm talking to. She's not been well." She ends the call and returns to the bike. "Why would I talk about yours?"

"No reason," says David. "Shall we book another lesson, Ms Gosforth? Saturday the fourteenth? And I hope she gets better soon."

"Thanks. And sure, if you want. Can I ask you something, Mr Ramsden?"

"David," whispers Rick.

"David," mutters David, a bit shyly.

"David… why are you doing this?"

"When I have enough adventure in my life…?"

"*What?*" yelps Rick. Daisy seems a bit lost for words. The man doesn't appear to be attempting sarcasm.

"If I told you, Ms Gosforth," says David, "you wouldn't believe me."

"Oh, I'm sure I would."

He takes off his helmet and she looks into his pale blue eyes. There's a disarming, crinkly warmth to them she hadn't quite spotted before. And they are currently wide open. "No, you wouldn't," he insists.

Despite her usual cynicism, she finds that she is drawn to the almost painful innocence of the man, as if life has managed to leave no trace, save for the natural effect of years passing. Somehow she knows instinctively that if he did tell her something, she would believe him.

"Okay, well let me get my calendar," she says, tapping into her phone. David unzips every zip in his new leathers, save for his fly, with increasing frustration, until he finds his own small pocket diary.

He can't feel the nudge his father wants to give him but knows that there is an active virtual-nudger beside him.

What perturbs him most about the morning is that he is actually looking forward to the next encounter. Whether it's with Triumph Bonneville or Daisy Gosforth he is not entirely certain. He finds either scenario equally disconcerting and, for a man who has just discovered an unexpectedly acute sense of balance, he feels in grave peril of disturbing a long-established and reputedly comfortable equilibrium.

So he won't think about it, and just let the days crawl by until the next lesson.

***

The days do indeed crawl, as if in defiance of the build-up in speed occurring on the converted airfield.

David tells himself that if he takes on more lessons with Daisy, perhaps early mornings or even the occasional lunch hour, it will accelerate the departure of what is most haunting him. In his rare but precious quiet moments, he wonders if what is most haunting him may not be his late father after all. And this is what disturbs him most.

There is a part of David that is genuinely beginning, against every sane instinct, to share the excitement Rick Ramsden feels each time the ghost sits on that old Triumph, behind (or sometimes even in front of) his son. The younger man's transparency, David thinks with something almost bordering on affection, isn't simply a feature of his spectral state.

"For the first time in my life, I'm proud of you, son," says Rick as they stroll down the busy street towards the auction house, some weeks after their first 'spin'. David is less self-conscious about talking to his father in public now, mainly because he is wearing those earphones he recently observed on more worldly souls, with a microphone attached to the wire.

"Weren't you proud when you read about my success in the auctioneering field?"

"I was excited to read about *you*. That you were alive and still living nearby. But be honest, Davey, what father could say he's proud of a son who's an auctioneer?"

"Most fathers, actually."

"Not when their boys were born to be bikers," insists Rick. "Just ask your new lady friend." Before David can protest, although either notion is too ridiculous to merit comment, Rick has a revelation that sends him leaping into the air, where he lingers until he can calm down. "*Of course!*"

"Of course what?"

"Bloody hellfire! Your mum was riding pillion with me until she was four months gone. It's all making sense now. You were *there*, Davey! And, blow me – you were conceived in my bloody bike shed! Right next to the Bonnie! Little Wendy popped in wearing her tight T-shirt and spanking new hotpants that steamy Sunday morning. Just when I was polishing my—"

"AAHHH… ummmm… ooooohhhhh…"

If the worthies of Cheltenham wonder why their local auctioneer has burst into a song which sounds vaguely foreign, with choreography to match, they wisely keep it to themselves – at least until they can pass the news on to everyone who might be interested.

Unfortunately, Quentin is one of those interested.

And a fortnight after this, when David is up to three lessons a week with a bemused yet never bored Daisy Gosforth, the older man ambles corpulently over to David's desk and asks his senior auctioneer to join him for a lunchtime drink.

David grabs his new leather jacket from the rack beside him. Which is probably his first mistake.

"What the hell is that?" asks Quentin, pointing to the garment as if it has just been sliced off an available cow.

"Do you like it? I bought it for— for a change."

"It has tassels, David," the older man mutters. "We need to talk."

"Wanker," says Rick, and David knows for once that his dad isn't talking about him.

***

The old Victorian pub, with its high ceilings and minstrel gallery, would readily be described in local guidebooks as characterful, but as David and Rick look around, they see that it's mostly full of characters with whom they wouldn't wish to spend that much time. The tourists are okay, the Ramsdens kindly concede, as are those who come for the overpriced gourmet food, but it's the regulars with whom David is finding less and less affinity.

In the past he has been able to do small talk with relative ease by simply making a show of listening avidly to the beer-guzzlers and borderline alcoholics whilst they rabbited loudly on about themselves or foreigners. But these days, to his astonishment, he finds that he yearns to tell them about his other life, one in which they would be at best disinterested and at worst appalled. He has recently read in newspapers about people who 'identify' as something of which first impressions might signal quite the reverse. He wonders, as he gazes at his father, whether he is beginning to identify as – God forbid – a 'biker'.

Thankfully, he is not totally lacking in perception and finds himself almost hoping that his boss will simply tell him to grow up, pull himself together and stop pissing around.

Quentin has almost downed his first lunchtime pint, but probably not his last, before he even contemplates speaking to his head auctioneer, who nervously sips a large lime and soda.

Of course, someone else won't shut up.

"I can't bear the thought, Davey." David dare not ask Rick which unbearable thought, although he's pretty sure he knows. "That porky old fart's grubby hands all over my little Wend. Bad enough she looks like my granny – or at least her mum – but she deserves better in her old age."

"How's your lovely mother?" asks the porky old fart finally.

"You probably know as much as I do, Quentin," says David. "I haven't seen a lot of Mum lately." Which is true, what with living 24/7 with his exhausting dad, and also trying to hide from her exactly how he currently spends his free time, which he knows would distress his poor mother hugely.

"She's been through a lot in her life, David. You don't want to be upsetting her even more, do you?"

"No, of course not," he says, suspicion growing as to where this conversation will lead.

"Well then, grow up, pull yourself together and stop pissing around."

There you go.

It is becoming increasingly apparent to David that everyone, aside from him, has been aware for years of how his father died and that there has been a ruthlessly observed conspiracy of silence. He feels quite angry, which is not a common emotion for him, or hasn't been until his dad arrived back on the scene.

As Quentin stares at him, David suddenly realises exactly what is going on. At age forty-four and a half, he is finally rebelling. It may be around thirty years too late, decades beyond a time when most males go through it, but it has to be better than nothing. He has heard of mid-life crises, so he suspects he could also be having one of those, save for the fact that he is slowly beginning to realise that he may not actually have had a life to be in the midst of. Or perhaps, appropriately, it has been one only half-lived.

"Get on that stupid ruddy bike again and you can whistle for your partnership," threatens Quentin.

So, of course, Rick Ramsden begins to whistle. Something David could have predicted a mile off.

What David couldn't have predicted is that he would whistle too. Right into Quentin's glowering face.

The portly man, glass frozen halfway to his rubbery lips, is too shocked to respond. So David – who is, of course, equally shocked – turns to his father. He assumes, quite naturally, that the younger man will be beside himself that his son has finally grown some balls. He is surprised to find Rick Ramsden shaking even more than he himself is.

"Can we get out of here, please, son?" says Rick, rather quietly for him. "I never expected this."

David, deciding that he is hardly likely to astonish his stunned and reddening employer more than he just did, sidles away to continue his apparent conversation with thin air.

"What?" he addresses the ether. "That your milksop son finally stood up to his bully of a boss?"

"No. Well, yeah. Respect for that, son." Rick reduces his quavering voice to a whisper. "But this is something much worse."

"What could be worse than a man losing everything he's ever achieved or striven for, in a moment he may well later – well, in about five seconds – regard as total madness?"

"Davey, I think this pub is haunted. I've just seen a bloody ghost."

DO I HEAR FIFTEEN?

If there's one place David Ramsden would never have expected to find himself, especially on a working Thursday afternoon prior to a full day's auctioneering, it is in the poky back room of a small motorcycle shop on the outskirts of the town in which he has lived, or at least existed, all of his life. And, quite as unpredictably, he is drinking coffee, a caffeinated beverage off which he has been warned since childhood, as it leads to excess excitability and is the sworn enemy of nourishing sleep.

This shows the full extent of the hedonistic mire into which the man has sunk. But, as he tells the young woman sitting beside him, who temporarily quit her post fifteen minutes earlier to minister to her never-less-than-bewildering pupil, if an angel like him can't raise a little hell now and then, he is unfit to wear the jacket.

"David," she says to him, gently but firmly, "babe, do you not think you're sort of running a little bit before you can walk?"

No one has ever called him 'babe' before, or at least not that he can remember, and it confuses him, as it confuses the unseen but omnipresent figure beside him. Indeed, when David glances at his father's young yet ageless face, he wonders at the look of deep puzzlement upon it, as if the man is slowly working something out. To David, suddenly, all seems crystal clear.

"No, Daisy, I really don't think I am. I've had what I believe they call an epiphany. It's time for me to cast off the shackles of responsibility," he announces poetically, although it does sound like something he might once have read, "and start the life I was born to lead."

"So you're going to leave your job?"

"Don't be ridiculous. Why would I do that?!"

"Oh sorry, I just thought—"

"No, I'm going to apologise profusely to Quentin then explain to him that if he wants the best auctioneer in Gloucestershire – in fact, dare I say, in the whole of the Cotswolds, including the Oxfordshire borders – he has to accept that he's also getting the first auctioneer in history to win the Isle of Man TT."

"*That's my boy!*" exults Rick, then pauses. If a ghost can be seen to go pale, this one does. "WHAT?"

Daisy says nothing, at least not immediately. To David's astonishment, yet by no means displeasure, she reaches out and takes both his trembling hands in her own small but noticeably firm ones.

"David?" she says. He just nods. It's all he can do. He's sitting down yet everything is going too fast for him. "Are you listening?" He nods, again. Finally, she says the words he would never expect Ms Daisy Gosforth, nor indeed any confident woman of any description – or, to be totally honest, any woman at all – to say to him.

"Can I take you out to dinner tonight?"

He is understandably speechless. And, for once, his father is too.

DO I HEAR SIXTEEN?

The establishment to which Daisy Gosforth has invited David Ramsden on this sultry late spring night, perched on a major road just outside Tewkesbury, is not one that he already knows. This could be because he never ventures inside restaurants, unless he has to make an assessment, preferring a homemade sandwich for lunch and quite often also for dinner.

This particular evening, however, he puts it down to the fact that the rendezvous of choice is, not entirely unpredictably, a bikers' café and, of course, he is not yet fully a biker. So he could only ever have arrived here in his Volvo, which would stand out in the car park in a way that might make him at best, self-conscious, and at worst, terrified.

Which is exactly what his Volvo does as, to his slight disappointment, Daisy has arranged to meet him here, rather than accepting his invitation to escort her. Perhaps she had known he might be intimidated by the array of bikes, with leathery-faced and jacketed smokers milling beside them, and would want simply to drive them both on as swiftly as possible.

To the passenger who takes up no room and needs no invitation, Syd's Place is the Savoy. And the fact that Syd is a voluptuous lady biker only adds to Rick Ramsden's joy. He wishes this had been here in his time – he'd never have gone home. David reckons if his dad tells him he thinks he has died and gone to heaven one more time, he will undoubtedly arrange it.

Ramsden Junior is sufficiently nervous as it is.

The last time he went out on a date was with his ex-wife, and look how well that went. The fact that Daisy Gosforth actually invited him has sent him into a state he hasn't known since he discovered an early Thomas Girtin watercolour in a rundown Tudor cottage near Painswick. And that was sixteen years ago.

He reckons he must have washed and showered at least three times, although observing his fellow guests as he enters the steamy room (confusingly famed, according to its blackboards, for its all-day and all-night breakfasts), he muses that this gives him a lead of at least three on the majority. He immediately berates himself for being judgmental, especially as he will be one of their number before long.

David would like to engage them in some biker talk and just wishes that he hadn't chosen to wear his best suit, the one he wears when accompanying his mother to church or a funeral. He supposes he should have realised that a place called Syd's would probably not be the classiest of eateries, although who really knows nowadays? But he doubts anyway that Daisy Gosforth is exactly flush with cash, especially not when she has just forked out on his dad's old Bonnie. (Not that he will allow her to pay the bill, he isn't that modern.)

Curiously, he realises as he looks around the room and at the bemused diners staring up at him (most assuming he is either lost, slumming or a sanitary inspector) that he doesn't feel overly daunted, choice of wardrobe aside, in talking motorcycles. He reckons that this is because bikes have formed a particularly large part of his discussions at home with his dad – discussions which, to his own surprise, he has grown to enjoy.

To be honest, David had thought that Rick Ramsden might have been a tad more gracious about a son wanting to finish the job his dad had started and to compete one day in the celebrated race that eluded him. The son puts this down to sadness and regret, and perhaps just a tinge of totally understandable yet petty jealousy.

In the meantime, he knows that his father is more than impressed with the incredible progress his lad has been making. And the son realises that it is the constant voice in his ear, albeit infuriating at times, that has been helping him to blossom so swiftly. This and the fact, childish though it might be, that he wants to make Daisy Gosforth proud of him.

Surely, he thinks, to train a pupil up to those standards David fully intends to attain must be like, say, a piano teacher coaching a youngster to first place in the International Tchaikovsky Competition. Only better.

Who would have thought that he, David Ramsden, could find something in common with such a lovely young woman? He wonders if this evening they might become something more than teacher and pupil. He also wonders where the hell she is.

"Reckon she stood you up?" asks Rick, as they sit down at a wooden table. "Birds like that come round once in a lifetime. You can't let this one go, son. Y'know I really think I can smell that bacon."

Suddenly all the doubts that David has been trying frantically to park alongside his old Volvo come karooming back in with the speed he intends one day to attain on the Bonnie.

Ten minutes later, just when he has had to apologise yet again to a very pleasant waiter with a heavily tattooed face and an increasingly sympathetic expression, and explain that he is waiting for a friend who has probably become delayed in traffic, Daisy Gosforth walks in.

"Told you she'd be here," says Rick, although he has never said anything of the sort.

David's relief and delight that his 'date', if this is indeed what she is, has finally turned up (a delight reflected in the faces of other customers) is somewhat thrown by the fact that she is holding two motorcycle helmets in her gloved hands. *Has she brought someone with her?* he wonders, his heart plummeting down to his sturdy brogues.

Daisy doesn't say anything. She just tosses one of the helmets to David then turns back to the door. He looks to his father, totally perplexed as to what is going on and exactly what he is expected to do. It could be a modern mating ritual that hasn't as yet appeared on his admittedly imperfect radar.

"She wants us to go with her," decides Rick, a man of the (nether)world.

"Us?" says David, who has already stood up, because this is what you do for ladies.

"I'm as intrigued as you are, sunshine. Thought we was gonna have a nice quiet dinner, just the three of us, with some good bike talk."

"So did I," says David, making for the door. The remaining clientele heave a communal sigh of relief. The suited guy talking to himself was starting to become a touch worrisome.

They aren't the only ones who are troubled. By the time David joins Daisy outside, she is on her Triumph Bonneville. The bike that he has, after so many lessons, curiously begun to regard as his own. Or at least as part of the family.

"Get on!" she tells David, which sounds very much like an order, one which clearly he will not be permitted to refuse. And indeed, why would he wish to, as it would mean riding on a machine he has grown to love whilst holding on tight to the woman he— well, he's not sure what his feelings are, but he knows they are nothing like he has ever felt before.

How strange, he thinks, for someone who has just begun to relish speed, to feel that things are going far too fast.

DO I HEAR SEVENTEEN?

"Put your arms round me," commands Daisy Gosforth. "Don't want you falling off."

David has donned the helmet, which is clearly fresh from the shop, and climbed onto the back of the familiar bike with ease. But the usual confidence he exudes on Bonnie completely deserts him when he finds himself so very close to the head and body of his teacher, whose shape he admires and whose particular scent he can inhale even through all her layers of protective clothing.

This understandable hesitancy isn't shared by his late father, whose hands and body are rolling around the oblivious young woman with a zeal that only the still-lustful dead can muster. He winks at David as he urges his son to do, if not exactly the same, some acceptable twenty-first-century equivalent.

"I remember when your mummy was just seventeen—"

"*Oh, grow up!*" cries David, as his rider starts the engine. He realises, of course, that this was one of many opportunities sadly denied to his father by the very bike on which they're now sitting. Fortunately Daisy doesn't hear.

"Come on then, David," cries Daisy. "And hang on for dear sodding life!"

Whilst this doesn't sound quite the language David Ramsden would expect from a conscientious bike-trainer, it certainly makes its point. Tentatively, he stretches his worsted arms out until his fingers are clasped firmly around her taut waist. He finds himself thinking of his father and mother that hot morning in the bike shed, then decides that he won't go there.

"Ready?" she cries above the roar.

"I'll say," cries Rick.

"Where are we going?" enquires David, thinking that perhaps she knows a more intimate, less middle-of-the-A-road sort of place, where his smartest suit might find fellow travellers and he can discover whether this really is a date after all.

"You wouldn't believe me if I told you."

He wonders where he has heard this before.

***

The exhilaration David Ramsden feels when powering the Bonnie down an airfield at full pelt is as nothing compared to the vomit-inducing sensation of riding pillion with a biker who appears to know no fear. Especially on roads where caution is not only advised but almost mandatory.

He can't as yet understand why Daisy Gosforth feels impelled to move quite so fast. His only assumption is that she has made reservations at somewhere rather exclusive and that these are not the sort of people to hold a table for even a second beyond the diarised time. But then why arrange to meet him at Syd's? Unless this is a very 'in' biker joke to which he is not yet, but happily soon will be, party.

David knows he won't be overheard if he whispers into a nearby phantom ear. "Dad, why are we going so fast?"

Silence. From one rarely silent source. For an unexpected reason.

"I'm moved, son," says Rick gently, after a few moments.

"Yes, I'm moved too," says David, not understanding. "My bloody bowels most of all. Answer my question."

Rick can't talk. He's too choked to make a sound. Finally he manages, "I'm moved, son, because you called me 'Dad.'"

"Did I?" said David, genuinely surprised, but then he too finds himself unable to speak as he recognises exactly where they are. It's the same road he drove along just a few short weeks and a lifetime ago. He was in the old Volvo and was well into his Finnish when, about a mile or two further on, beyond a few tight and winding corners, a horrified old lady ran smack into his side.

He can tell by the intake of ghostly breath that his father recognises it too. They look at each other, but neither says a thing. No need.

The speed at which Daisy is taking the curves makes David more terrified than he has ever been in his life. Not that he has ever done anything the least bit terrifying, but his mother has made quite certain that he remains terrified of anything he might do. He can't for a moment believe that his 'date' is staying within those speed limits on which she has insisted in every lesson she has given him.

David suddenly wonders if she is going slowly – or indeed, quite rapidly – insane and whether he is a contributory factor. He doubts it. Why would anyone like her go mad over someone like him? Yet why also should she wish to send an innocent pupil careering at 100mph round the bends, their fragile heads and bodies now at such an angle as to be flying almost parallel to the most treacherous road in the area?

He tries to yell into her ear but her helmet, the rabid scream of the engine and perhaps her downright contrariness make any warnings futile.

It is with particular horror – amidst all the terrors of this impending night – that he sees the fatal bend coming up. He can only pray that Daisy Gosforth sees it too, because so far she's offering him precious little evidence. Indeed, it feels to him (and all that he has right now are extreme bodily sensations) that she is going to smash headlong into the very same bend at which—

"*NO!!!*" screams David Ramsden.

"*FUCKKK!!!*" screams young Rick, the older.

The brickwork, which must have been replaced at the time of that fatal crash, is looking like it might soon need replacing again because Daisy and David – and, of course, Rick – are charging straight for it.

History is going to repeat itself. Incredibly loudly. And bloodily. And—

And yet it doesn't.

A nanosecond before the inevitable and undoubtedly fatal crash, Daisy executes the most exquisite glide, front wheel rearing like an obedient stallion, back wheel eating up the grass verge bordering the deadly wall, until she can safely land and screech to a screaming halt some good distance ahead.

"We're here!" she cries, as the roar dies down and two generations of Ramsdens begin to cry.

DO I HEAR EIGHTEEN?

Sitting on the front wall of a deserted old house, eating homemade sandwiches his host has been storing in her leather pocket, is not how David Ramsden had expected the evening to unfold. Although, to be fair, he has been far too on-edge to hold out any expectations whatsoever. So he has to admit, as his heart rate and blood pressure return almost to normal – although they may never fully do so – that this isn't the worst of outcomes. (The expression he has heard about some eating establishments – that people would kill for a table – has a hitherto unappreciated resonance.)

Finally, he has to ask. "Ms Gosforth… Daisy…?"

She stops him with a nod. "I know. What the fuck was all that about…?"

"Well, I wasn't going to—"

"Yeah, what the fuck was all that about?" echoes Rick, who was going to. He still feels curiously hungry. Must be from the spectre of those all-day breakfasts at Syd's.

"You were going too fast, David."

He stares at her. He wasn't the rider who nearly killed them both… so she must mean their relationship. But he's not sure there even is one – and anyway, wasn't it she who asked him? "I'm confused, Daisy."

"Can I tell you a story?" He just nods. "You won't believe a word of it, so take it as a fairy-tale. Although—" She pauses and looks back up at the darkened house. "Although it's probably more of a ghost story."

This time it's David and Rick who exchange glances.

"About eighteen years ago, when I was a little girl, I lived in this house." She points to a small front bedroom but neither man can take their eyes off her face, a face that appears to be growing younger by the second. "That bedroom, right up there."

David hears a gasp, which is more like a shocked sniff. As if Rick suddenly knows exactly what's coming. "Oh my God," whispers Ramsden senior..

"There was a little hole in the ceiling," continues Daisy. David recalls the small knothole, seen when he collapsed onto the rotten timbers in Mrs Eileen Ballard's dusty loft. "And I was sure someone was whispering to me through it as I slept."

"It was totally dark, son. I only whispered – I never peeked," insists Rick, although the thought hadn't even occurred. "I never thought she'd hear me."

"It was a young voice," she continues, "the voice of a young man. A local man. And he told me how, about twenty-five years earlier, he'd been practising on his bike for the big race – it was a Bonnie T120, like the one I just bought – and he'd crashed. Into this very wall."

"Or the wall that this one replaced," corrects David pedantically, but Daisy doesn't hear him. She's a little girl again, back in her tiny, doll-strewn bedroom. Listening to a ghost.

"He was going way too fast, poor guy. And not wearing a helmet. And doing a lot of other daft things young men do when they think they're immortal." She looks at David. "Older men too."

David can hardly speak. "So, what did you do?"

She seems puzzled. "Do? I didn't do anything, David. I was a child. I forgot all about it."

"No, you didn't," says Rick. But now he's smiling and his eyes are wide open.

"Well, I thought I'd forgotten. But look where I ended up. Look at what I'm doing. I hated school, although I'm far from stupid." She pauses, as if waiting. Rick gives his son as near to a nudge as he can manage.

"Far from it," agrees David. "You're one of the brightest people I know."

"Exactly. And thank you. It was only when I saw the Bonnie – y'know, the one Walter was restoring – that it all came shooting back. And I had to have it. Hey, maybe it was even the same one!" She shakes her head at the lunacy of the notion.

"But why—" He finds himself too confused to complete the thought.

"Why did I nearly kill us both?" He just nods. "I wanted to warn you. The way he— it— whatever it was warned me."

"Warn me? About what?"

"Well, about taking risks. Okay, I know we all have to take risks in our lives…"

"I don't," says David. "Well, I haven't until now."

"There are risks and risks, David. I mean, accepting my invite this evening was a risk."

"I'll bloody say," says Rick, still panting.

"But wanting to ride a bike round the most dangerous circuit in the world? At your age? Just because you've discovered some – I dunno – hidden aptitude." She stares at him with those scarily honest yet curiously knowing blue eyes, and he feels the stare exposing his soul. "How stupid is that!"

"Very stupid?"

"Wasn't actually a question. But yes, very stupid. You knew somewhere that you needed… well, something else in your life."

"Did you ever try to find out who the man was?"

"I told you, I'd forgotten. Or at least my conscious mind had. I suppose I could try now. But he must have killed himself over forty years ago. Why bother?"

David can sense a movement beside him. Rick is bouncing up and down, shouting as loud as he can. "I knew it. I knew in my water it was you!"

"*Rubbish!*" responds David. He watches the hurt rise on her face, like one of those sudden and unexpected allergic reactions his mother has always warned him about. And the pain in his own heart is unbearable. "No – Daisy! I wasn't talking to— You're right, Daisy. I'm sure you are. What did you mean, I needed something else in my life?" He looks around, as if for guidance. He can't understand why his reckless young dad is suddenly looking so – hard to admit, but undeniable – very wise. "What did I need, Daisy?"

"You needed me, David Ramsden."

The silence around them and between them is quite beautiful. Until a voice right next to him cries, "*Result!*"

"Daisy Gosforth," says David Ramsden, wondering if he might be going slightly insane, yet curiously not feeling too worked up about it. "There's somebody I'd like you to meet."

DO I HEAR NINETEEN?

The loft feels far less chilly this morning as David Ramsden slides opens the hatch and clambers back up for his second visit. He also notices that he is taking the dodgy ladder with a lighter spring to his step, hoisting himself onto the fraying timbers with the sprightliness of an auctioneer half his age.

"Are you sure you want to stay up here… again?" he asks the figure just ahead of him.

"It's my home, Davey," replies his father, looking around as he hops into the dark, familiar chamber. "Until my maker sees fit to—"

"Yes, well, all in good time."

They sit down beside each other on the old chaise longue. Neither speaks for a while, which is a huge strain on at least one of the parties. Finally, David has to say what has been on his mind.

"You never wanted me to try for that race, did you?"

"And bloody kill yourself? Course not, son."

"Then why—"

"I wanted you to meet people. Not stuffy ones like… well, like you. Real, decent people."

"Like bikers."

"Yeah. And like Daisy. She was my sign. Well, her and the Bonnie. I wanted to see you happy, Davey. I wanted you to have what I missed." He looks at his son, who is still wearing his leather jacket. "And I don't mean a trophy."

"You mean a life."

"And a kid."

"Well," nods David, with a shy smile, "maybe you'll get your wish."

"When are you two moving in?"

"The nineteenth. When the sale goes through." He shakes his head. "I'll say one thing – when a house is haunted, you don't exactly have to fight off other buyers."

"See how parents can help their kids onto the property ladder! So, what does your mum reckon, about you and our Ms Gosforth?"

"What do *you* think?" David's sigh of frustration seems to reverberate around the dusty loft. "Daisy isn't exactly what she envisioned."

"She'll come round. Hey, would you like me to talk to her?"

David stares at the man and begins to laugh, in a way he doesn't think he has properly laughed in his entire life. "One day. Perhaps. Maybe."

"Are you two going to be up there all day?" calls Daisy, from the landing. "I'm not cleaning this dustbowl on my own."

"Coming, my love," calls her fiancé, the auctioneer. "So, Dad," he says, smiling at the younger and deceased man. "You okay?"

"Couldn't be happier. You know where I am, Davey. Until He—"

"Yeah. I do. And you know where we are. Or will be very soon. Just don't scare us away. Or peek!"

"*On yer bike!*" laughs the ghost of Rick Ramsden (1954–1975). "On yer bike, son."

MISSING

Recycling is the mother of inspiration.

I created a comedy series for the BBC in the late eighties that was BAFTA-nominated and ran for six years. My favourite episode of this series involved a scenario not unlike the story coming up. I always felt it merited a separate life.

Which it now has.

Only it has turned out, in the writing, to be something totally different.

A few weeks after the third miscarriage, he brought home a dog.

It was a curious-looking animal, an unplanned meld of German Schnauzer and something the Schnauzer happened to meet in the park. Or so he assumed. He found it odd that, unlike other species that come to mind, dogs seem happy to mate with anything. But then he looked at his wife and himself and realised that humans were probably not so different.

He had always thought, until now, that the attraction of opposites was what made them such a team. But now he was at a total loss. He wanted so deeply to say or do something that would diminish her pain, yet the stoicism, the silences, the just-getting-on-with-things were so agonising that he could hardly bear to be in her presence. He thought it would be so much easier if she just broke down and went to pieces or punched him or screamed at the God she never believed in for a moment and was hardly likely to turn to now.

Whenever they went for a walk these days – and they had always enjoyed walking, because open spaces and greenery appeared to make the trickiest conversations far easier and a niggling problem that much more solvable – they would encounter children. Swarms of them, legions, multitudes. In buggies or wellingtons, running, climbing, sloshing, screaming. It was as if some government agency had alerted the local public that their town was about to be bombed to oblivion, so anyone under the age of ten must be evacuated forthwith to the nearest nature reserve.

He knew that a dog, even one as cute and cuddly as this, with its shuffling gait and hairy face like a dour old Scottish schoolmaster, couldn't replace a baby. He wasn't that stupid. He also knew that, so far as he was aware, she wasn't really a dog person.

Yet he needed so desperately to do something for her, if only as a gesture, an acknowledgement, and this was all he could come up with. Perhaps it might serve, he reasoned, as a preamble to the adoption conversation that they would need in their own time, but not too far from now, to pursue. For some reason, he thought of those 'smart babies' they give teenagers to take home to make them appreciate what having a child entails. *Maybe one day,* he mused, *these are what everyone will have.*

Naturally, he couldn't parcel up the creature and watch her face as she undid the string and removed the festive wrapping. But he did observe her as she slowly opened their front door to his unexpected knock. He was taken especially by her large grey eyes (Schnauzer-grey, now he thought about it), as they followed his own eyes downwards. These had always been his favourite of her features, along with her soft, full lips, now gently parting to say, "Get that fucking thing out of my house this minute."

He had expected a ticklish conversation but the enduring silence that evening threw him.

In his head he had pictured her initial and quite natural reluctance to entertain the new arrival transforming in time to at least some appreciation for the misguided kindness that had prompted the purchase. And a sort of tentative yet inevitable bonding thereafter. The finality of 'one week – either it's out of here or I am' had rather taken him by surprise. Although, in retrospect, had he been thinking straight, it probably shouldn't have.

Perhaps he might also have computed that, whilst he went out to his office every day, she worked from home. But he promised faithfully that until a new and more appropriate family could be secured for Gerald (the dog's given name, the refuge insisting that a re-christening would be one change too many), he would walk, feed and do all the socialising with their temporary guest.

He was as good as his word. For five days, morning and evening, he tramped the streets of the quiet suburb in which they had lived since they first got together, talking to Gerald about life, love and everything in between. He could honestly say that these were the most convivial conversations he was having at this point – Gerald was an excellent listener. Talk at home, when it occurred, was mostly about bills, elderly parents and household chores. It certainly didn't touch on anything emotional. Or canine.

On the sixth day, Gerald went missing.

This apparently had occurred just minutes before the man came home that evening. A door, improperly closed, had blown open and Gerald, quite ungratefully and with a speed rarely associated with his lineage, unless greyhound was somewhere in the mix, had scooted off.

The man was thankful that his wife agreed to accompany him on the search, although he suspected that this could be attributed more readily to a small but appreciated measure of guilt than a genuine concern for Gerald's welfare. He had a feeling, however, that the quest – whatever its outcome – might not be totally unproductive.

As it was dark by this time, he carried a large torch. They tried to ignore the looks they were receiving from passers-by as they called out the errant animal's name into the crisp night air. It made him think for a moment that these people, commuters and strollers, would possibly assume that the couple had lost a child, which of course came close to the truth, but they would have been more careful and wouldn't have named him Gerald.

It was well over an hour later that they hoarsely abandoned their search of possible haunts and hiding places and returned in some frustration to their small, empty, terraced house.

Sitting on the doorstep, looking genuinely hangdog, was the escapee.

The tears and sobbing could probably have been heard from there to the local nature reserve and beyond. Anguish and pain, so long contained, seemed to bounce off the walls of the sleepy little houses like gunfire.

"Finally," came the gentle voice.

He turned to look at her in surprise as the tears continued to stream down his face. It was some days before he asked her, half-jokingly, as they all walked together, if it was she who had let the dog out.

SOUNDING OFF

BBC News. July 2006: A Geordie woman has apparently woken in hospital after a stroke to find her distinctive Newcastle accent had been transformed into a mixture of Jamaican, Canadian and Slovakian.

This story caught my eye some years ago.

And – as a Geordie lad shipped to Glasgow aged eleven – my ear.

WAN/ONE

The week in which Dr Sandy Robertson of Glasgow turns English begins much the same as any other: with a rousing speech.

"Pupils of Thornliepark High, I'm supposed to respect you as individuals. Understand your '*problems*.'" The inflexion the big man dumps on this final phrase, rolling his 'r' at his audience like a bowling ball aiming for a strike, suggests to the thousand pupils – most of whom make only the vaguest attempts to look like they are listening – that this might not be their headteacher's – or 'Heed's' – most prominent concern. Which comes as no big surprise to many of them.

Sitting behind him on the stage, which still bears evidence of the recently concluded school play, *The Slab Boys* by John Byrne (the inspired and only slightly inappropriate choice of the bright young English teacher, whom Sandy has himself recently poached), are his Thornliepark staff.

Staring fixedly at the broad, gowned back of a person many of whom would like to stab or push off the stage is not their favourite part of the day, although it does give them the not wholly unwelcome opportunity to fantasise.

Unfortunately, widening their focus hardly serves to improve their morning, encompassing as it does an almost syncopated display of adolescent yawning, nose-picking and arse-shuffling that is amongst the most unedifying yet sadly familiar spectacles known to members of this once noble profession.

Yet these teachers know, even whilst gazing distractedly at the restless youngsters, many of whom come from the most deprived homes in Glasgow, or indeed the whole of Scotland, that there is evidence that this once-failing school is slowly turning around. A bit Titanic-like, but the results speak for themselves. Hard to believe, admittedly, with parents whose expectations often range no further than that their kids will actually turn up and stay the day, hopefully without being knifed or arrested; and boys and girls aged from eleven to eighteen, most of whose school prayers consist of little more than 'please God, make the auld fucker shut up'.

But the auld fucker has actually begun to make a difference, which paradoxically causes many of those staring at him from both angles to resent him even more.

"Fine, but out there," the man continues, in proudly sonorous tones, marinated in humble beginnings and reeking of almost Olympian bootstrap-pulling, "the respect you get is the respect you *earn*."

It is a voice well-known to television viewers north of the Border – at least, those who care about education. Even the assorted group sitting behind him, whose eyes are becoming more glazed by the second and who silently disapprove of his rampant and indiscriminate brusqueness, can't fail to admire the consummate skill with which he projects clear intellectual superiority, whilst remaining quite patently a man of the people. Just a smart local guy from this same fatally ignored, underfunded and, sadly, still dangerous neighbourhood. Or, as his staff like to say when assured that they have a sympathetic and, most importantly, discreet audience – nae breeding.

"I'm not expecting you to do '*the best you can*' – that's for your ma and pa," he concludes, with a smile that has precious little warmth in it. "I'm expecting *the best*. You hearing me?"

Of course they hear him. The pigeons on the roof can hear

him. The children, who know his cadences by now, sense with some relief that it could be almost time for the routine/ignorable announcements and then the real business of the day will begin.

They won't see Doctor Robertson again until the following morning unless they have the misfortune to be summoned to his office, which is rarely good news; or they catch his celebrated bark resonating down a corridor, ordering them to walk slower, move faster, chatter less or smarten themselves up, accompanied sometimes by a firm wee smack on the head – which of course is hardly acceptable, but as the parents generally admire Doctor Sandy and what he is doing for Thornliepark, he knows that, short of branding the school crest on an errant child's torso, he can pretty much get away with anything.

"And, as this night is Burns Night," he continues, "although these days I fear many of you have absolutely no idea who or what I'm talking about and think I'm giving you *carte blanche* for another acid attack…" He awaits the obligatory appreciation for this cutting-edge wordplay to arrive from those behind him. Suitably rewarded, he continues. "… I'm going to recite to you – not read, mind, but *recite* – one of the greatest poems this man, or indeed any man, e'er wrote: Robert Burns's *Address tae a Haggis*." You can almost hear the groans echoing down the rows. "And to make it even more palatable, I've ordered haggis for anyone who wants it in the dinner hall this lunchtime."

It doesn't particularly, as the majority of diners prefer their chip butties or turkey twizzlers, but the wiser ones behind him know that this will be yet another self-serving item to make the day's *Evening Times* and a splendidly topical picture for the school's already groaning website.

"*'Fair fa your honest, sonsie face…'*"

TWA/TWO

The Robertson tartan is predominantly red with navy blue and forest green. The Robertson knees beneath it are predominantly craggy, yet still a joy to behold this chilly, late January evening. At least, this is how their owner feels as he stands admiring himself from all angles in the full-length, cloak cupboard mirror that dominates the hallway of his fine red sandstone house.

The Robertsons live comfortably, but not inappropriately, in a recently gentrified part of the city, on a quiet street that can still claim to be within the same postal district as his barely gentrified school.

"You look fine," says Laura Robertson, daring to intrude into his reflected space. He nods, which his wife knows could have been gratitude but is pretty sure was accord. Carefully, he adjusts his well-hung dress sporran.

"I will come, Sandy. If you want me to," she tells him, in that refined West End accent he still finds attractive. Like the purr of an expensive engine, but one that you keep only for best or show. The silence continues. "Okay, enough said."

He feels suddenly irritated, as if his wife has set out to spoil a very special evening, one about which she really has not the slightest idea. "Och, you've been before, Laura. Anyway, you told me you had something…"

"Just a wee drinks party with the Law Faculty." She tries to smile. "I've never heard you do The Toast."

"'To the Lassies'? It's very rude."

"I can take rudeness from you, Sandy Robertson."

He wrenches himself reluctantly away from the mirror, wondering fancifully, as he sometimes does, but thankfully only to himself, whether he might one day leave his reflection there awaiting his return, so formidable is his presence.

"Anyway," he says, barely glancing at her, although she seems more than presentable. But then she has always appeared effortlessly smart and attractive, a handsome, well-bred, impeccably turned out woman. Whereas he knows, to his constant frustration, that whilst his persona may be faultless, looks aren't his greatest asset and the dress sense needs work. She waits for his opening to have a conclusion but unusually he appears to have lost his thread.

"Anyway...?" she prompts. Not that she is desperately interested, now that he has hinted so clearly that she isn't wanted on the voyage.

He pauses for a moment, as if struggling for an answer that won't quite come. "Angus Miller will be there," he remembers. "Aye... Chairman of the School Board?"

"I *know* who Angus is... You still think he's gunning for you?" There is just his trademark grunt in reply. "And it'll be provocative to have a lawyer by your side."

He turns to her. Curiously, whilst the last thing he wants right now is a conversation, it still seems to be what they do best. Provided it isn't about family, home improvement or, of course, their relationship.

"We're in an economic war-zone, for pity's sake! Kids can't get jobs – unless you call drug-running a career, knife crime hasn't been this bad since Macbeth, and the man *still* wants me to be all touchy-feely."

"As opposed to the school of hard knocks."

He takes the notes for tonight's address out of his jacket pocket, just to reassure himself that he has them. She recognises the familiar handwritten scribbles that seem to wind in and out of the badly-typed lines like bindweed. "Oh, it's okay for you," he scoffs, "sitting there in— in the Kelvingroves of academe." He pauses, as if expecting her to clap. "Lecturing the future masters of the universe."

Laura could respond to this in any number of cogent, well-reasoned ways, combining a legal mastery of the relevant facts with an argument that would floor any opponent, but as she was telling a trusted colleague only this morning, sometimes she really cannae be arsed.

The sound of footsteps down the stairs is immediately followed by an apology from their maker, as he picks up the tension. They look up to see an uncomfortably tall young man of seventeen, wishing he were anywhere else.

"Oh, for God's sake, Struan, do you have to apologise your entire life away?"

"Sorry," he says again. Struan Robertson, only child despite their best efforts, pushes his straw blond hair out of his eyes, although it immediately falls back as if for protection. "Why are you in a kilt?"

"Because I'm going to an *eisteddfod*. Why do you think I'm in a bloody kilt?"

"Oh, is it today?"

"Aye," says the young man's father, managing to infuse even this uncontentious syllable with disdain as he grabs his heavy winter coat from the cupboard. "Any danger of some *burns* to the midnight oil tonight? Oh no – let me guess – it's your 'photography' class." He says the word as if it is a euphemism for child abuse or training for the ministry.

Pausing only to roll his eyes at Laura, which is something she can never abide, the big man opens the door. He is almost out onto the chillier side when Struan talks again.

"Did Mum tell you?"

240

Sandy swivels round, the red rising instantly on his jowly face in a way that Laura has always found disconcerting, although she is never quite certain whether this concern is for the health of her husband or for the domestic fallout.

"Tell me what?" asks Sandy quietly, aware that his audience knows, as his audiences always do, that this is simply the deceptive intro to the more thunderous theme to follow. His eyes are totally on Laura. "Tell me *WHAT*?"

"Och, it's just something Stru and I were talking about."

"And the boy couldn't tell me himself?" He nudges the door shut again. The blast of freezing winter air recedes.

"I want..." The young man is painfully hesitant. "I want to study photography."

"Well, you are, aren't you? Unless you're spending the money on sweeties."

"He means for real, Sandy. At college." The 'don't be obtuse' remains unspoken.

As expected, the father takes this news, if indeed it even is news, with customary scorn. "Just what the world needs – another snapper! Christ on a bike, laddie, kids come out the womb these days wi' a phone that takes photos. I cannae talk about this right now – but the answer's no."

Struan doesn't say anything. He just stares at his father. Not exactly like he might wish to kill him, although he undoubtedly entertains the notion; more as if he wants the man to notice the tears in his own son's eyes, even as this same son is so deeply ashamed of them. But of course the man isn't looking, so the boy turns and stomps back up the stairs. Even the stomp itself lacks the requisite thud a really good stomp demands.

"What *is* it with that boy?" says Sandy, before that boy is even out of earshot. "I tell you, Laura, if—"

"If you had him at your school... I know."

Sandy Robertson looks suddenly uneasy, as if he has something tricky to say and is searching for the best way to say

241

it. She waits. "Listen Laura, I— I need to stay on for a bit tonight. And – you know – cosy up to Angus." He tries to smile. "Show him my feminine side."

"Good luck with that. So I shouldn't wait up then?"

"Best not. And I'll need to check in with Pa on my way home. Poor guy's usually up pretty late these days, with the coughing."

"Well, send him my love." As her husband opens the door once more, she murmurs, "Sandy – kiss?"

"Oh aye, sorry." He gently brushes her cheek with lips already cold. "Enjoy your soirée."

"And you your Lassies."

THREE/THREE

The call comes from the hospital at around four o'clock in the morning.

It is only when she is jolted by the ringing that Laura Robertson realises her husband isn't lying there beside her. Usually he manages to disturb her sleep on his return, either by the effect of his bulk on the creaky floorboards of the old house or the massive displacement when he slumps between the sheets. For a moment she simply assumes that she has slept more soundly this night, perhaps because she enjoyed a drink or two at the faculty. But now she is awake and unsettled.

"Mrs Robertson?" the efficient yet kindly voice enquires. When it receives the requisite groan, it continues. "This is the Glasgow Royal Infirmary. We have your husband here."

"Oh my God! What…?"

"He wants to speak to you."

The sound of his voice, a touch shaky but still recognisably and powerfully him, immediately reassures her.

"Hello – Laura?"

"Sandy, what—"

"I'm okay. It's alright. Well, it's not, but it's not critical. I've had what they call a TIA."

"Oh. I know what that is. It's a wee stroke, isn't it?"

"Aye. But just a wee one. The T stands for Transient. I'll need to be monitored *ad infinitum*, but thankfully it looks like there's no real harm done for now."

"How can you—"

"They seem to know these things. My recovery was pretty quick, which is reassuring, apparently. I'll just need to be – maybe – a bit careful. Lose some weight, cut down on the fags, that sort of—"

"Did you drink a lot?"

"Not too much. Aye, a wee bit. I left my car at school – it was in the cab that I had my... turn."

"The cab from the school?" She has no idea why she asked this.

Sandy seems suddenly snappy, as if he is being challenged. "Aye, of course from the school. Where else would it be coming from, woman?"

Laura wonders why such an innocent enquiry should be exercising him so and realises in the same moment that sparking this reaction, albeit unwittingly, will hardly aid recovery.

"Oh, sorry. I thought maybe you'd already visited your pa. Or, you know, dropped someone off. Or…"

She has no idea what the final 'or' could be and then realises what has been puzzling her. Why the Royal Infirmary? Wasn't the Queen Elizabeth closer? Perhaps it was a question of facilities. Or beds. Or something. The cabbie might have known the situation and made a judgment call.

"Will I come and collect you?" she asks. "What am I saying? I'm on my way. I'm so sorry this has happened to you."

"Aye," says her husband. "Be quick, will you, Laura? I hate hospitals. But mind how you go. The roads are a bit icy."

Laura Robertson is out of her bed before they have even said goodbye. She wonders when it was that her husband last needed her. And already knows that this time will be as transient as what just happened to him in the cab.

FOWER/FOUR

It is when she is in the shower the following morning that she hears it.

At first, she puts it down to the water streaming into her ears and fatigue flooding her system after a broken and difficult night.

She had persuaded Sandy, quite forcefully, that he should allow her to phone the school and tell them what had happened, not in detail, but simply that he wasn't too well and would be taking at least this one day off. The secretary was most sympathetic and wished the headteacher well. She was certain that his depute would cope. There was practically no sarcasm in the remark, perhaps simply a touch of relief.

"You were bloody lucky, Sandy," calls Laura over the water's comforting rush. "Thank God it happened in that cab to your pa's and not in the street." She hears a non-committal groan from the adjoining bedroom. "But it was telling you something, pal. I just hope you're listening."

"A warning shot across the bows," comes the reply.

"Aye," says Laura, a wee smile in her voice. He can still make her smile and she is heartened he makes the effort. "Who talks like that?"

"Talks like what?" responds Sandy, a bit confused.

"Like that fella you're doing. Oh, don't tell me now, it's off a film, isn't it?"

"I wish I knew what you're blethering about," he calls back. Yet suddenly he does. And it scares him more than anything has in his entire life. More even than the events of last night.

When she emerges from the bathroom, her towel covering a figure that she, at least, regards as nothing to be ashamed of – Jesus, she puts the hours in – Laura Robertson is surprised to see her husband still in pyjamas, talking quite seriously to his own reflection in their ornate mirror. At first she simply thinks he is practising some lecture he is about to give, albeit in curious tones, but soon she worries that the trauma of last night could have affected his mind. Especially as he is spouting, in this peculiar way that as yet she can't quite attribute, "*Sandy Robertson... this is Doctor Sandy Robertson... testing one, two, three...*"

"Sandy," she interrupts, a bit hesitantly, "what are you—"

"'*Wee, sleekit, coorin, timorous beastie...*'"

She has to wonder why the man is so assiduously reciting Burns to himself in an accent that sits uncomfortably somewhere between that of Sir Michael Caine and Sir Winston Churchill. And suddenly she isn't quite so amused.

"*Sandy...?*" She stares at him in the mirror as the look of pure, open-mouthed, bulging-eyed terror that has frozen onto his face slowly finds its fellow on her own.

It takes the horrified man some seconds before he can force his mouth to make the noises he least wants his wife, or indeed anyone, to hear – including himself. "I sound different, don't I? ... Laura, how do I sound?"

"Well... different," she hazards, not daring to venture a jot beyond wherever he has gone himself. "So you're not... having a wee joke?" she adds, which doesn't appear to add much to the world's most peculiar conversation.

"No, Laura," he says, his whole frame now shaking almost uncontrollably, "I am not having a wee joke. It feels more like someone is having a wee joke on me. How do I sound? And don't just say fucking different!"

"Well…" she tries again, her gifts for advocacy and eloquence serving no purpose whatsoever. She can actually watch her face in the mirror as it speeds through its repertoire of kindness, gravity, tact, empathy and total incomprehension. "Sandy," she decides. "You sound English."

***

The doctor at the Glasgow Royal Infirmary, when the staff finally find someone sufficiently qualified, is having similar problems with his face. It cannot seem to decide between professional empathy and a feeling that all its birthdays have come at once.

"It's a rare side effect of a stroke, Doctor Robertson," explains the man. "And can also happen apparently after a wee bang to the head. But it's very rare. So rare in fact that I doubt anyone at this hospital, perhaps at any of the city's hospitals, has ever come across it before."

"Could you possibly keep at least a smidgen of the excitement out of your voice?" says the patient, who proceeds to look incredibly embarrassed at how that just sounded. Not the sentiment – he meant every word, but the pathetic and unfathomably alien manner in which it has been delivered. He finds himself wishing that the doctor, a kindly man in his late thirties of Pakistani descent, didn't have a Glasgow accent so much more authentic than his own.

"I do apologise, Doctor Robertson. I realise, of course, how terribly disturbing it must be for you. Especially this close to its onset. And all the more so for a man in your position. I've seen you on the TV." The responding glare suggests that this might not be the most productive of tangents. "If it's of any comfort, I honestly don't believe it reflects an actual worsening of your physical condition."

247

"It isn't. And it feels a lot fucking worse to me."

"So, you have heard of it before, Doctor?" says Laura, anxious to move the conversation on.

"Oh, indeed," says the man gratefully. "It's called Foreign Accent Syndrome. I mind there was a case a wee while back of a Manchester woman, I think she was, or was it Liverpool? Anyway, overnight she started to sound West African."

"*West African?*" echoes Laura, as if this is so much worse.

"Aye," continues the doctor, warming to his subject, whilst his patient sits on the bed in the stark hospital room listening in total despair. "She had no connection with the place. None whatsoever. Never been there, no family ties. Couldn't even find it on a map. You see, it's not about the patient's own history or experience, not at all. It's purely – well, how would you describe it? – mechanical. Aye. Something clicks, I suppose you could say, in the vocal region. You know, the way the sound comes out. And really it's all about… well, the listener's perception."

"In the ear of the beholder," says Laura, musing on how a turn of phrase can present itself so elegantly in even the most taxing of moments.

"*Exactly.*" The doctor appears quite delighted with this.

Sandy finds himself wishing he were standing up like the other two instead of sitting abjectly on the hospital table. He has heard how folk in wheelchairs feel ignored by the 'grown-ups', but it would appear weird and a touch overcrowded to raise himself now.

"And we do tend to judge folk by how they sound, don't we?" says the doctor. "You only have to listen to the radio." He pauses for a moment. "Now that we're on the subject, I recall reading – must've been back when I was in medical school – about a poor woman in Norway, I believe, aye, during the last war – she began to sound like a German."

"What happened to her?" asks Sandy, feeling that the conversation is somehow running away from him.

248

"She had to flee the country. Folk thought she was a spy."

"Well, that's reassuring," says the patient.

"I don't think we feel quite that way about the English," says the doctor kindly. "Well, not yet."

FIVE/FIVE

Kirstie Newton is packing up for the evening when the receptionist knocks on the door and walks into her tiny room.

"Kirstie," she says, "there's a guy here to see you."

Kirstie is not expecting a guy at this time, either professionally or personally. The second circumstance might cause her some regret but the first, very little, as she is tired and it has been a long day. She has promised to collect some supper on the way home for herself and her best pal, who is helping her to spruce up the new tenement flat in Shawlands she has just rented. She really doesn't want to be late.

"I've no more patients, Mrs Gemmell," she tells the older woman. They're all older in this place – she's very junior and she knows that she still has a lot to learn. Which is fortunate, as her fellows in the department know that they have a lot they can teach her. "I'm done now. And done in!"

"I'm not exactly sure what he is, dear. But he knew your name. It's all he said but he did sound awful insistent."

Kirstie seems surprised. She's not yet at the being-asked-for-by-name stage. And, as it's the NHS, she's not certain that such a request cuts much ice anyway.

"Oh. And what's *his* name?" she asks.

"He said you'd know him when you saw him," says the receptionist, who loves a bit of intrigue and can see that this has all the makings. "See, I think I recognise him, but don't ask me how or why."

Kirstie just sighs and asks the lady to send the guy in. Mrs Gemmell does so with a smile as she bids Kirstie her own goodbyes.

The first thought Kirstie Newton has on seeing her old headteacher after so many years is that an undiscovered malfeasance, long assumed to have escaped detection, has finally caught up with her and expulsion is not far behind. She can almost smell the school on the big man as he looms in the doorway.

Yet there's something about him that isn't quite right. He's still as large and as scary as he has ever been, no change there, even if it is a good number of years since she fled Thornliepark. But for a man who has always appeared so centred, grounded in whatever piece of earth is given the privilege of supporting him, there's something disquieting here. Perhaps it's simply his being outside his comfort zone, although she would have assumed his presence was actually more prone to cause discomfort to anyone else zoning around him.

When a more rational reason for his visit occurs to her, which is probably only a few seconds after he has shut the door, the blood seems to leave her body as if drawn out by a giant syringe. "Oh my God, Doctor Robertson. *My wee brother!* Something's happened to Calum."

Sandy shakes his head then waves his arm to maximise the reassurance. Yet he doesn't say a word. For a man who loves the sound of his own voice, Kirstie finds this deeply disconcerting. She wonders for some reason if he's going to strangle her, but has absolutely no idea where this came from other than seeing too many rubbish films on her own late at night.

"Would you like to sit down?" she offers, pointing to a hard wooden chair that suddenly looks so ill-equipped for his sizeable

251

yet curiously sagging frame. "… Sir," she adds instinctively, then silently berates herself.

The man nods and slumps into the seat, once again surprising Kirstie Newton, who has never imagined this particular man slumping. Ramrod straight on the podium, giving his glowering, sermonising pep talk of the day; or equally erect in the big leather chair behind his intimidating desk, with all his framed certificates on the wall behind him; never slumped as he is now, in her small, hospital-grey room, looking so – what would she call it? – despairing.

As he settles himself, an old speech rushes into her head, one she has always recalled because of the uncomfortably public namecheck he gave her.

'*When a writer called Alan (something something – she can't recall that bit) had three hit shows on Broadway at the same time, somebody said to his pa, 'Your Alan's a lucky wee guy.' To which Pa replied, 'Aye, and you know what? The harder wee Alan works, the luckier he gets!' The only luck you'll have, ladies and gentlemen, the only way out, is hard work. Results. That's what I'm talking about, KIRSTIE NEWTON! Grades. Exams. Right, young lady?*"

The man still isn't talking. He just stares at her, as if taking her in – who she is and what she has become. This is getting creepy. Yet a natural compassion prevents her from berating him for his odd behaviour or showing him the door.

"Is there something I can mebbe do for you, Doctor Robertson?" she asks finally.

"Aye, Miss Newton," he says, after an uncomfortable pause, "I think that mebbe there is."

Kirstie Newton is speechless. Which is never an ideal state for a speech therapist. But she has absolutely no idea why this man, whom she so feared and who regularly made her young life such a misery, should have silently plonked himself down in her poky wee office, only to put on a funny English voice.

"I'm sorry, Doctor Robertson. Maybe I'm being a bit dumb – like you always said I was – but I'm not getting who you're meant to be."

"I'm not doing a bloody impression, Miss Newton. And I never said you were dumb."

"Mebbe not in so many…" She stops, although the puzzlement doesn't. "Why *are* you talking in that voice?"

"You tell me, Miss Newton."

"I have absolutely no—" He's staring at her now, and there's still defiance there in the cool grey eyes and face like a Trossach. But there's also something new to the mixture, as if the familiar formula has been radically revisited. And suddenly she knows. "Is this why you came to see me?" The shock is too great for her. It makes her laugh. Not loud but not silent. *Oh Jesus. Kirstie!* "Oh! Oh my Lord!"

The hurt in the big man's eyes seems so much worse for being such an infrequent visitor. "Do you laugh at all your customers?"

She finds herself pausing, not knowing which of the errors in that statement to correct first. The pause clearly doesn't go unnoticed, which makes her almost garble the words that follow it. "No! *Sorry.* Not at all. They're called— we call them patients. Doctor Robertson, what happened to your voice? That voice?"

Kirstie has to admit, albeit begrudgingly, that it is – was – a marvellous voice. Whether on the podium, in his office, echoing through the corridors, booming over the school loudspeaker system or pontificating on Scottish television, it was quite unmistakeable.

Sandy seems almost relieved to return to his home ground of facts. He speaks unemotionally, yet the young woman already knows that every word is being wrenched screaming from some desperate, hurtful place. "It's called Foreign Accent Syndrome. I doubt you've heard of it. Apparently it can happen after a stroke or some sort of assault to the head. Something changes in the way the sound comes out."

"Aye, I have heard of it, actually," corrects Kirstie, although she's not altogether certain that she has. "You've had a stroke?"

"A mild one. TIA they call it. No permanent damage, so far as they can tell." He smiles wryly. "Well, no other permanent damage. I need to be careful, obviously, and they're doing more tests. They're quite fascinated, apparently."

"Aye, well, they would be. Foreign Accent Syndrome? Must be awful rare."

"I'm sure you feel *awfully* excited."

"Please don't, Doctor Robertson."

"Don't what?"

"Use that tone of voice."

"Well, that's what I'm here for, isn't it?" says Sandy, in his curious manner, with a smile he doesn't mean.

"I'm not talking about your accent," says Kirstie quietly, although quiet isn't quite how she feels.

"I have no idea what you're on about."

"No, well, you wouldn't." She sighs a bit too loudly. "Anyway, why have you come, *Doctor* Robertson?"

"Why the hell do you think I've come, *Ms* Newton?"

"There are loads of wonderful speech therapists in Glasgow, most of them far more qualified and experienced than me." She adds, for his benefit, "And surely far brighter."

He mutters something, but so quietly that even her young and professionally alert ears fail to pick it up.

"I'm sorry, Doctor Robertson?"

"You know how I used to sound... Kirstie."

SAX/SIX

There are not many things that make Gourlay Robertson laugh.

In fact, his own brother has been heard to say that the man draws all the fun out of dourness. So to find him practically rolling around on the floor of his nearest and dearest's kilim-strewn, book-lined living room, laughing so loud he almost singes himself on the sit-in fireplace, is a sight that Laura Robertson finds quite discomforting.

To Sandy, it was, sadly, only to be expected.

"I'll wait till you're done, will I?" says the unamused sibling.

"Ye'll be waitin a while," replies the chortler, the laughter reignited each time his elder brother opens his mouth. "Och, I'm not laughing about the stroke, Sandy."

"That's heartening."

"But can ye no see the irony of it?"

"Sorry," says Sandy, glaring at the smaller man, "and I'm usually so hot on irony."

"Dear God, I never thought it possible. You've become even more condescending since you turned English! Mind you, they are a condesc—"

"I HAVE NOT TURNED ENGLISH!"

Sandy knows that he has even more reason these days not to raise his voice or lose his temper, yet something lunatic inside his head keeps telling him he might simply scream his new voice away into the ether. Surely his younger brother's heartless goading and its accompanying relish are more than any sane man can bear.

"My brother, a walking – I dunno, you're the 'linguistics' expert – a walking metaphor? Analogy? Symbol? Aye, that'll serve. A walking symbol."

Laura finds a rare opening. The men appear to have forgotten she is even present. "*Symbol*, Gourlay? Of what, for heaven's sake?"

"Of what, Laura?" laughs her brother-in-law, but with less amusement. "Of what's been happening in this country over the past few centuries. We've all gone bloody English!"

"Utter nonsense," responds Sandy, before Laura can say a word.

She finds herself relieved that her husband is arguing. He has hardly opened his mouth since he saw that speech therapist a couple of days ago. As if he is ashamed of what he has become, even in front of his wife.

Laura has no idea what went on in that office but she knows that it wasn't by any stretch a full session, because he had just barged in – typical Sandy – and the poor girl was on her way home. Apparently they're having their first proper appointment tomorrow, which is hardly NHS speed, but the therapist, fortuitously an ex-pupil, is clearly going the extra mile. Laura can't help wondering what this young woman really thinks of her husband. Perhaps she got off particularly lightly at Thornliepark, one of the school's few natural high achievers?

"The country's got its own parliament, for pity's sake," says Sandy, enumerating on still shaky fingers. "They make their own wee laws. They get more than their share of the national pot."

He wishes he could smash the stupid smile off his brother's face with his huge fist, a fist he has used many times in the distant past and quite often on his brother.

"Scraps from the rich man's table! The world and his faither ken the majority of folk here'd still vote to stay glued to your pals.

Like they did last time round. It's filtered into our DNA. It's got stuck in our bloody voice."

"Bollocks. You nearly won last time. With Mr Salmond's fake oil bonanza. Snake oil more like."

Gourlay edges towards him, favouring his profile. "Sorry pal, didn't quite catch that. Can you say it again please, in Scottish?"

"*Gourlay!*" chides Laura. "Give the poor guy a break. He's still in shock."

If there's one thing Sandy Robertson is discovering that he hates, it is to be discussed as if he isn't there. Especially as it elides with the awful feeling that he is slowly disappearing.

He has told school – or rather, Laura has – that he is taking indefinite leave, until the doctors pronounce him fit and well. But, of course, he hasn't mentioned the 'syndrome'. He has no idea how the school will cope without him yet this is not foremost on his mind. A fact which concerns him almost as much as the curse itself.

"Och Laura, it'll just be temporary," says Gourlay, with a reassurance clearly tempered with regret. "You told me yourself the CT scan was clear. Let a man enjoy this miracle while he can."

"They do say it can take a while, Gourlay," warns Laura, without looking at her suddenly silent husband. "And no one really knows whether—" She stops abruptly, before she wades in too deep.

"Well, he cannae go back on the telly like this, can he? 'Here's Sir Ian McKellen to tell us about the state of Scottish education.'"

Sandy moves towards Gourlay until there is nothing between them but spit. "Gourlay, you are NOT to talk to anyone about this, you hear me? You *understand*?"

"Not even the guys down the—"

"I'm not jesting, Gourlay. The media love a freak show. Channel 4 would do a documentary before you can say—"

"Auchenshuggle," suggests Gourlay, which doesn't help. "'*The Scot who turned into a Sassenach.*'"

257

"I'm from Govan, for pity's sake," says the man, who sounds less like he's from Govan than anyone they've ever met.

He sinks down into his chair, staring up at Laura. The need in his eyes is pitiful, yet she knows the man doesn't want to be pitied. He simply wants to be helped.

She really doesn't know if she has the energy.

SEEVEN/SEVEN

"I want to be *me* again, Miss Newton."

Whilst Kirstie Newton can totally appreciate why this should be a fervent desire of the patient sitting directly opposite her, she can't help thinking that there has to be a lot of people out there who wouldn't exactly share it. His staff, his pupils, perhaps even his poor wife and kids. Who knows?

She realises that the last thing she should be, in these sorry circumstances, is judgmental, but she tells herself that knowing and, more to the point, understanding a patient in all his or her contexts (and indeed, the actual *causes* of the condition) can quite often be key to making any progress.

Not that Kirstie is absolutely certain progress *can* be made. She has consulted textbooks, Google and her colleagues and is frankly none the wiser. She is almost ashamed that she feels such chagrin over the fact the bastard is most probably right again. The decision to choose her was well-placed.

She knows his voice by heart.

"You owe me this, Miss Newton."

Now this she didn't expect. "I *owe*…?"

She wants to plunge in, to answer the man back for once and have the argument that has been brewing for years. Festering, more like. She has forever anticipated such a golden moment, but never dreamt... No, she's a grown-up now, not a child. She'll wait until session three.

"Well, I'll do the best I can, Doctor Robertson." She knows these words will rile him, but it's only the truth. "Could you tell me exactly what happened? Please. In as much detail as you like."

"It happened. Isn't that enough for you? And I need you to make it unhappen."

"The full story please, Doctor Robertson." She wonders why she is enjoying this so much, although she doesn't wonder for long. Yet she finds the hesitancy peculiar, especially from a man who she recalls so used to love talking about himself. Perhaps, in his eyes, only wimps get TIAs.

"I'm a public figure," he protests. "I turn schools around. If this 'condition' gets out... I'm relying on you, Miss Newton – and on our mutual respect." If he picks up the look on her face, he wisely lets it pass. "I appear on TV, for pity's sake! Well, I did."

"Doctor Robertson, whatever you tell me in this therapy room stays in this therapy room. It's like... Las Vegas."

"I think you mean the confessional."

"Aye. That too. So where were you, when it happened? ... Doctor Robertson?"

He shakes his large head. "The irony of it is I'd been to a Burns Supper. At the school. I was giving The Toast to the Lassies."

"And was Mrs Robertson giving The Toast to the Laddies?"

Kirstie Newton has no idea why she asked this; it sounded intrusive and can hardly be relevant, yet the moment she sees his face – and she is so used to watching faces – she realises she might have inadvertently stumbled into something beyond her legitimate sphere of exploration.

"Er, no," he mutters. "She had somewhere else she had to be that evening."

"Okay," says Kirstie, moving on, "so you had your stroke at the Burns Supper. See, sometimes, if you get a wee bit nervous..."

"I don't get nervous," he insists.

260

"You seem nervous now."

"Are you certain this is confidential? Not that there's anything…"

"'*Dare to be honest and fear no labour*,'" she responds, because she has just remembered.

"Are you quoting Burns back at me?! You always were a wee chancer, Kirstie Newton." The young woman just shrugs. Aye, she was. Still is, clearly. He shakes his head. "The stroke happened… afterwards."

"So you were at home then. I thought the other day – when you came in – you said something about a cab."

He seems suddenly impatient. "I was in the flat of my new English master. He and I were discussing college applications. Stuff that couldn't wait. Okay? Perhaps I got overtired. Pressure of work. I started feeling weird there – we called a cab to take me home but then it got worse, so the cab took me to the nearest hospital. The voice thing came on a day later. Is this sufficient for your purposes, Ms Newton?"

"Aye. Thank you, Doctor. It could have been a lot worse, you do know that?"

"*Than turning bloody English?* It's like something out of Kafka." Kirstie looks blank. "*Metamorphosis*? Except in my case I've been turning a wee bit *less* fly every day."

She is shaking her head. "I still don't understand the half of what you say. And that's not the accent. Now, do you have any recordings of yourself? I'm sure you do."

"Of course I have. Why?"

"Well, it might be an idea to listen to them. Watch them, if they're on video. See, I work with stroke victims all the time. And the mission is to just help them talk again. You know, to be intelligible. This is different. You have no trouble talking, Doctor Robertson. But you want to talk like you used to. It's almost as if you have to do an imitation of yourself. Your old self."

"Aye. Well, that makes sense." He sounds almost begrudging, like he should have been there way before her.

"Good. And maybe you can bring some in next time, so we can listen together."

"If I can stand it," he sighs.

Aye, and if I can, she thinks, but tactfully doesn't say.

ECHT/EIGHT

Sandy isn't certain whether his son ushers the school's depute head into their living room out of stupidity or malice.

He suspects the former, which doesn't raise his spirits in the slightest. Fortunately he has heard the chatter from the hallway and manages to switch off the video an instant before the door opens. But he has no idea whether Aileen McKay has just caught the echo of her headteacher in full Anglo-Saxon flow..

"Dad, it's—"

"I can see who it is," snaps his father crossly, before realising that he has immediately revealed his condition to the kindly but astonished visitor.

Aileen McKay, a sparrow-like, prematurely greying woman in her late forties, is wearing a thick, woollen coat and the well-meaning face of someone who can make a sick person feel instantly worse. Her head is already cocked to one side and her voice sensitively lowered, as if the best one can hope for is a relatively painless release.

"I just popped in to see how you are. How are you, Sandy?"

Sandy, who is thinking that just maybe his concerned visitor has not yet absorbed the one thing that will concern her even more, mutters, "I'm fine Aileen, I'm fine" in his best but still pretty ropey Sandy Robertson imitation. He finds himself looking to his son for support, but Struan is already backing clumsily away, unsure exactly which mode and timing of departure will incur the least wrath.

"Well, that's grand, isn't it?" says Aileen as the door closes. "Everyone at school sends their love."

Sandy has his doubts about this. He has few illusions about the regard in which he is held by many of his staff, but respect for what he has achieved and a begrudging admiration have usually sufficed.

"Thank you, Aileen," he says, keeping his volume down low in an attempt to postpone for as long as possible the inevitable consternation. He can already see it begin to furrow the bemused woman's hitherto satin-smooth brow.

"Er, Sandy, do you mind my asking – is there something with your voice?"

"Nothing a wee dose of speech therapy won't sort out."

"Oh right. You sound…"

"I *know*, Aileen. But I'd prefer that the rest of the world didn't."

The confused woman just nods. She fancies sitting down – it has been a long day and she's been feeling quite apprehensive about this visit – but a seat hasn't been offered and she suspects that to sink into one of those fancy but cosy armchairs on her own initiative might be considered presumptuous.

"Aye, okay," she says. "We don't want to give Angus Miller yet another stick to—" Aileen feels his glare beaming up at her and is even more uneasy. "You know, Sandy, perhaps this might be a good time to – well, to heal a few wounds. While you've the sympathy."

Sandy finds suspicion gaining the upper hand over reticence. "What's this about, Aileen?"

"Well… I hear Angus has been speaking with some of the governors." She pauses, waiting unnecessarily for his next question. If she is being totally candid, she wants to hear that extraordinarily transformed voice again, in order that she can describe it more vividly to her husband. But the boss simply sets his eyebrows to quizzical. "About your… style?" She adds the question mark in the hope it makes it sound less damning, which it doesn't.

"My *style*? There is nothing wrong with my 'style', as you call it, Aileen," he responds, with as much contempt as his pathetic new voice can muster. "Ask the kids out there with GCSEs. With Highers. HNCs. No, ask the kids out there with jobs."

The depute head, catapulted into a role she neither sought nor imagined, seems suddenly even more uncomfortable, yet somehow resolute. An idea has occurred to her and she is going to broach it, regardless of the consequences. She even dares to pull up a small, finely carved wooden stool nesting beside her, which may well be exotic but is quite the most uncomfortable piece of furniture her small body has ever encountered.

"Talking of jobs," she ventures, "do you mind Kirstie Newton?"

Sandy is immediately uneasy, which Aileen takes as an unexpected lack of recall. "Davy Boyd's younger sister? Well, half-sister. The guy you expelled. There's still another wee one—"

"Davy Boyd was *dealing*, Aileen!" He had completely forgotten the connection. Dear Lord, has the stroke affected his memory? He is normally so hot on all this. "He let the school down. He let *me* down!"

"So he had to go. Uh huh. I was just thinking, his sister—"

"Aye," says Sandy, pretending to recall. "Bright girl. Bit lippy. Wouldn't do her work – well, not until I— I know what you're going to say, Aileen, but nae worry, the hospital are on the case. I don't need favours from old pupils."

"No. Of course not." She shrugs uneasily. "*Anyway*—" Sandy has always found the elongated way she says that particular word, up on the first syllable, descending on the second, as if she's about to launch into a song, intensely irritating. He realises that he notices it even more now, as if he is becoming hyper-attuned to the way people sound. He just wishes some of it might rub off on himself. "What will I tell the school?"

265

"*Nothing*. You'll say nothing, Aileen!"

"I just meant about your coming back."

"You simply tell them the Doctor will be back very soon. He'll be back one hundred and ten per cent!"

It is at this moment, like a well-made play, that Laura Robertson returns from work. She has heard Sandy's determined, if weirdly uttered, vow from the hallway and can't help checking it out subtly with his depute, whom she knows and likes. Sandy watches the look pass between them as Laura comes in.

Aileen rises immediately and gratefully from her stool of pain. "*Anyway…*" she sings again.

"Don't go on my account, Aileen," says Laura. "It's good of you to come."

The unexpected guest is already edging towards the door. This visit has clearly been an uncomfortable one for her, in every sense, and more troubling than she could have ever imagined. If she considers victims of a mild stroke, which she rarely does, they might perhaps have some impediment of movement, hopefully temporary, or a lopsided face with maybe some unfortunate slurring in their speech. Turning English has been beyond her wildest imagination. 'I could've been up nights and not come up wi' that one' is how she will present it to her spouse. She is ashamed of herself for feeling such an urge to share this incredible secret with someone she can trust.

"I must be going, Laura. They're saying there'll be snow the night. Your man's doing very well."

"He's getting there," responds Laura, although everyone in the room knows that she doesn't mean it.

When Aileen has finally scurried out, Laura finds her husband staring at her with absolutely nothing to say.

She realises that this man, who Lord knows has always loved the sound of his own voice, now simply can't bear to hear it. Naturally she feels compassion – who wouldn't? – but she can't help wondering why she should also be feeling so angry.

Is she just picking it up from the atmosphere, as if it is swirling around the ether waiting for somewhere to land, or has it been simmering inside her for quite some while and has come to the boil at possibly the least appropriate juncture?

Something is niggling at her but she is either concerned that she doesn't know what it is or concerned that she does. Laura is well aware that Struan is angry too, angrier than she has ever known the poor boy, even though he says so little.

Sandy leans over and switches on the video once more. The familiar yet somehow historic voice pervades the room like a ghost.

NINE/NINE

"So how does Mrs Robertson feel – about your new accent?"

Kirstie Newton knows that this is most probably a daft question and really none of her business, yet she is also aware that a supportive family can be crucially important in the treatment and progress of a patient. So she tells herself that she is simply and quite conscientiously doing her job. (But she knows it's really none of her business.)

Sandy appears strangely uneasy. "Hasn't said," he mutters.

"I'm sort of wondering if things are a wee bit strained between you anyway." The immediate glare she feels almost singeing her NHS uniform brings back memories she could quite happily live without. "See, Doctor Robertson, stress and tension are the enemies of good recovery." Who talks like that? She knows she is walking a fraying rope bridge over a bottomless gorge, but she just can't help herself.

"*Excuse me?*" says her patient, his outrage diminished somewhat by the weird voice, but still scary.

"Er… well, you had a stroke when you were with a young member of staff."

"Aye. So? What *exactly* are you insinuating, lassie?"

"Not a thing, Doctor Robertson. And please don't call me

lassie – I'm not a dog. But I mind that English department – you've only the one new teacher in it and she isn't a master. Even my wee brother fancies her."

Sandy begins to rise and Kirstie Newton feels she has lost him. Along with, quite possibly, her barely inaugurated career. She is still cursing herself when he sits back down again. She can almost hear the chair sigh.

"Enjoying this, aren't you?" She makes no comment, yet she feels sick inside. "After all I've done for you."

"*Done* for me?"

"Are you married, Miss Newton?"

"No, but I've got— well, I had a—"

"Then don't presume to know about things you don't understand."

"Aye. Okay." She wishes desperately she could think of some way to move the conversation on. "I expect Mrs Robertson would still like the old you back." That sounded more ambiguous than she had intended.

He grunts at this. "A relationship is more than how you sound," he opines, without a great deal of conviction.

"Of course it is. Certainly. Aye." She hopes to God she comes across as sincere. "So, have you been listening to yourself? On your old tapes."

"Uh huh. Every day. I know all about doing my homework."

"Well, if you don't, who does?" she laughs. Alone. "And have you been listening to them *with* Mrs Robertson?"

"Is that a personal question?"

"No, it's a professional suggestion. And an important one. She knows you better than anyone. Now shall we carry on with the treatment, Doctor Robertson?"

He stares at her for a moment. She has no idea what he is going to say and finds herself suddenly terrified.

"Sandy." She looks at him. "You can call me Sandy."

"*Some folk would say you're actually pretty old-fashioned in your teaching methods,*" *says the interviewer.*

"*And some would say I'm aheed o' the curve,*" *comes the immediate and combative response.* "*The psycho-boffins are all telling us now that we shouldn't be lavishing praise on our children willy-nilly. 'Bravo, wee Jimmy, for coming second-to-last in the egg 'n spoon race.' All it does is make them set their sights too low. Then they wonder why the heartless world out there isn't quite so impressed.*"

"All it does— all it does— is make them set their sights— make them set their sights too low," repeats the large man, sitting on his own, staring at the screen, in the cold, high-ceilinged room. "All it does is—"

"Bloody hell, Sandy, it's like an ice-house," moans Laura, from the darkened hallway, shaking the snow off her coat. Ignoring this, he once again switches on the video he has been attempting all day to mimic.

She stands by the open doorway, remaining respectfully, if sceptically, silent. Laura finds it all so weird, as if she is living with two Sandy Robertsons, but has no idea which is the impostor. "How's it going?" she asks finally, although she is not overkeen to hear the response.

"How do you think it's going?" he snaps, which is the response she wasn't overkeen to hear.

"It's early days. You've only seen that young woman of yours a couple of times."

"More than a couple." He switches the machine off. "Not sure she's got what it takes. Listen to me, Laura. To how I sound. Can *you* hear any improvement?"

"You know something? I reckon I can. Not huge, but aye." She gazes around the room, suddenly engrossed in admiring her own handiwork and effort. "Well, at least you're not getting any worse."

"What – like turning into Prince Charles you mean?"

"Heaven forfend! Oh, by the way, Gourlay phoned me."

"Why's he phoning *you*?"

"The man's scared you'll bite his head off. And it's about your Pa."

Sandy looks suddenly concerned. But she senses that this is not simply for his ailing father. "What about him? Is he okay?"

"You'll have to speak to the poor guy some time, Sandy. You can't put it off forever. Gourlay thinks the two of you should take him to the match on Saturday."

"In this weather? With his chest?"

"It's between you boys. I'm not getting involved." She makes for the door. "Now you know I'm giving that talk tonight – to the worthies in George Square."

"Are you? Oh, yes. You did say. I forgot." He seems suddenly and quite surprisingly forlorn. "Laura, do you have to— Aye, of course you do."

She decides the chubby, kilim-covered cushions need some vigorous plumping. "You're alright, Sandy. You can manage fine on your own now. And Struan's home soon, if you need anything."

"Cartier-Bresson? *He's hardly talking to me!*" He sighs, defeated. "You're right. I'll be fine." He turns back to his tapes, then stops and talks over his shoulder.

"Sweetheart?"

When was the last time he called her 'sweetheart'? When was the last time it mattered? She gives an 'Mm?' from the cushions, which by now have gone more rounds than a heavyweight contender.

"It doesn't make *that* much difference to you, does it? The voice, I mean."

She hesitates just a fraction too long. "No. No, of course it doesn't, Sandy. You're still… well, you're still you, aren't you?"

He has to think about this, as if she has posed some profoundly metaphysical query, rather than a casual, throwaway remark. He feels less like Sandy Robertson than he has ever felt in his life. Not that he has ever paused for an introspective nanosecond to wonder who he is. Why the hell should he? He always knew.

"*Of course I'm still me!*" he announces emphatically. "Of course."

"Well, there you are then."

"It's like when I have a bad cold, isn't it? I just don't sound like myself."

"Aye. It's just like having a cold. See you later, okay?" She finds that she can't wait to get out of the house.

"Kiss goodbye?"

"Must run, Sandy."

TEN/TEN

"And some folk would say I'm aheed o' the curve…"

Kirstie Newton is unsure how to respond. The man who has just spoken into her microphone, the big guy who sounds like a posh old Englishman doing a criminally bad, verging on the offensive, impersonation of a Scot, is looking at her like a puppy awaiting a pat and a treat. As a therapist she has found that just occasionally jargon can move the day on, if not necessarily save it. Hopefully, this is such an occasion.

"Okay," she says, taking a breath as she switches off the machine. "Well, there's clearly no problem with your understanding and processing of language, Doctor Robertson. Which is good. Very good. The problem is in what we call your output and expression. Your speech. The reason I'm recording you just now is so's I can make what we call a baseline documentation. You know, to chart your progress."

"If there is any," he grumbles. She thinks the man may have lost weight, either by design or the familiar worry-yourself-slim diet. She could hardly call him gaunt, but his face appears to have taken on a hollow, haunted look.

"I'm afraid you'll just have to be patient." She smiles. "That's probably why we call you guys 'patients' in the first place."

"It's actually from the Latin word '*patior*' – meaning to suffer."

Well, fuck you very much, she replies, in her head. "Aye, okay," she says, adding with a gracious smile, "You'll be pleased to know you don't have dysarthria or dysphasia. I'm sure those terms don't need any explanation."

"Touché."

She hardly hears him; she's on a roll. How often do you get the chance to impress your old headteacher, the one who most probably thought you'd amount to little more than shelf-stacking at the local ASDA or being voted cockiest kid at the job centre. She recalls reading that the millionaire owner of a well-known range of pubs named them after the teacher whose hopes for him were zero-rated. Way to go!

"Your articulation and co-ordination are good, so the disorder is with the rhythm at word and particularly sentence level." Who talks like this! Yet she sees him nod wisely. He seems determined to show her that he understands every word she says – that he is in fact boulevards ahead of a mere 'speechie' in his total comprehension of the problem and its potential solution.

Kirstie Newton finds this stance quite pathetic but also, against all her best instincts, sadly moving. "We'll begin with recording stuff that's very repeatable – this way it'll be easier to hear the changes over time. Okay?" He just shrugs. "Can we try the days of the week, starting with Sunday?"

"I know when the bloody week starts!"

She presses her record button as, begrudgingly, he gives her his seven correct answers.

"Very good," she says.

"I'm pretty damn sharp with the months and the seasons too."

"It might help you if you don't get so angry, Doctor Robertson. You could give yourself a stroke."

"Ha bloody ha."

"I wasn't being facetious. TIAs are like wee nudges in your brain. Undue stress right now could be really harmful, Doctor— Sandy."

"I'm intending to get back to *exactly* who I was, Ms Newton."
Sometimes first names just don't cut it for him. "Strain or no. That
is your brief, okay?"

"You still *are* who you were, Doctor Robertson. It's just your
speech… your voice…"

"I AM my fucking voice." He clearly wants to boom this out
but can't quite find the boom. Yet even in this bizarre accent of
his, far less stentorian in tone and one which she still finds great
difficulty in pinpointing with total accuracy, careering as it does
across counties and class, the message is clear.

He shrugs an apology. No excuse for bad language.

Today is not, of course, the first time Kirstie Newton has
experienced how entwined a person's voice and their identity can
be. She recalls having worked with an elderly Scottish actor during
her training who had been desperate to retrieve his 'instrument'.
Yet she is aware that this is of a quite different and far more
dramatic order. Doctor Robertson's problem is no simple slurring
or hesitancy, a hide and seek of lost words, some unfortunate but
obvious deviation from his norm. It is what her patient perceives
– not without some justification – as the imposition of an alien
and patently inferior personality onto the one he calls his own. He
sounds like someone else, some person he doesn't know yet whom
he totally despises. Someone, at least in his eyes, quite pathetic.

"I *am* my voice," he repeats, in more measured but equally
insistent tones.

What he says next sends her right back to a time she would
prefer to forget.

"Would you have listened to me then if I'd sounded like I do
now?" She doesn't respond. "Kirstie Newton…?"

"Kirstie Newton!"

"Yes, Doctor Robertson?"

*"Jabbering again in assembly. I'll be needing a wee word with
you afterwards. Aye, that's it, Miss, you groan away. Do you know
about Scotland and the tall poppies?"*

"Me, sir? No, sir. I gave them 50p last November, sir."

"Don't laugh, ladies and gentlemen. It's a syndrome with which us Scots are particularly afflicted. We don't want to be the tall poppies, the poppies that stand out from our brother or sister poppies. You know why, Kirstie Newton?"

"Me again? … No, sir."

"Course you don't. If we stand out from the crowd, we can be cut down to size. And that's what Scots are most afraid of. Folk thinking we've got 'above oorsels'. So we cut ourselves down first, just to save them all that trouble."

He catches up with her again in the corridor. "You had no idea what I was talking about, did you?"

"Not a clue, sir."

"You could be a tall bloody poppy, Miss Newton. So could one or two of your pals. So could've your wayward big brother. But you're not taking in enough good stuff – enough 'nutrients' – to make you grow."

"Into a poppy?"

"I'm being metaphorical."

"Is that something to do with the weather, sir?"

"Are you being deliberately thick?"

"No, sir. Yes, sir. I'm doing my best. I've a lot going on right now. Sir."

"But not a lot going in. Buck yourself up, lassie. What are you going to be?"

"A tall poppy. Sir. I've got Mr Fairman's Geography…"

"Well, don't get lost. I want to see you up at least ten per cent on every subject this summer, Kirstie Newton. Or you'll wish you'd never been born."

She is standing up and staring down at his chair. He catches her eye. "Are you sitting comfortably?" she says.

"Then we'll begin." Seeing her bemusement, he explains. "It's how they used to start kids' stories on the radio. Back in the day."

"Ah. Right. You should keep listening to the radio, you know. And the TV. The Scottish programmes. Not the English."

"I'll set *Braveheart* to play on a continuous loop."

"Well, if old Mel can learn our accent, there's hope for anyone." She smiles, willing just one, even a wee one, in return.

"But then I'd be acting, wouldn't I?"

"You'd be *observing*, Doctor Robertson. Look at children – they learn by imitation. What are you doing this weekend?"

"Why – like to take me to the pictures?" She doesn't respond. "They want me to go to Ibrox with my pa on Saturday. Rangers are playing at home. But he's got emphysema, amongst a dozen other things. Old men shouldn't be venturing anywhere in this weather." He looks at Kirstie, as if there's more to say but he hasn't the nerve to say it. She banks on silence as the best form of encouragement. "I don't think I should see him just yet."

"I think you should."

"Oh, *do* you? And who are you to pronounce, young lady?"

She determines not to be intimidated. She won't backtrack or apologise. Not to this guy. "Part of recovery, Doctor, is to follow your old routine as much as possible." She's not absolutely certain whether this is true or she just made it up, but it sounds plausible. So why is he glaring at her? She knows why. "You really don't like being told what to do, do you?" She switches on the recorder. "Well, that's Saturday done. So what's next?"

"Eh? Oh." She can see the effort straining every sinew of his large, sad and currently very pallid face. "Sunday…"

"Sunday," she corrects. In Scottish.

ELEEVEN/ELEVEN

Even in all the pre-match hubbub, one hacking cough stands out. Yet the old man persists in talking through it, as though what he has to say is so important that it can only be improved by an injection of phlegm.

"Well, it could be worse," expectorates the man.

His son, who is talking as quietly as he can, without being totally drowned out by the shivering yet already feverish Ibrox crowd, asks, "*How*? How the hell could it be worse?"

"You could have turned Catholic."

Despite the coughing and the cruel Glasgow chill, Hughie Robertson manages to laugh himself silly at this, the drawn yet still impish face wrinkled in mirth, his slowly shrinking frame shaking with what seems like pure, unsullied joy. In this he is happily encouraged by his other son, the younger, less celebrated but still vociferously Scottish one, wrapped up like every other Protestant around them in this massive stadium in a thick blue and white woolly scarf.

Struan, sitting next to his grandfather, trademark Nikon strung round his neck and rarely far from his eye, appears genuinely concerned by this. Even his own father, however, isn't quite certain whether the concern is for him, silent victim of such hilarity, or for the older man, who is clearly far from well. Although Sandy has a pretty good idea where the young man's affections lie.

"Very amusing," grunts the hapless victim, before turning solicitous. "Are you okay, Pa?" he asks, over the coughing.

"I'll outlive you, Whispering Jack Smith. Especially if any of the folk round here catch you talking."

"That's why he's got his scarf roond his mooth," says Gourlay, whose own accent is becoming more Glaswegian by the minute. "Hey Sandy, lucky this isn't the England-Scotland match. You wouldna know where to sit."

Struan, to his father's surprise, suddenly decides mid-snapping to stand up for his old man. "Can you not see my dad's really troubled by this, Uncle Gourlay?"

Gourlay looks chastened, the smile converting to a ruffled frown at almost cartoon-like speed.

"I *can* defend myself, Struan!" says his father ungraciously at a volume he hasn't hitherto employed. "And are you incapable of looking at anything except through a bloody viewfinder?"

"The guy's a photographer," says Gourlay, adding unnecessarily, "a chronicler of the Scottish scene."

"We don't need you encouraging him," mutters the chronicler's father.

The match is about to start but the Robertsons clearly feel they haven't yet exhausted the current topic, despite what is going on down below.

"Hey, Prince William," shouts Hughie, above the roar, "when does your daftie voice get back to normal then?" The old man begins to cough again, but this time the sound is different. Where once there was a deceptive strength in the hacking, Sandy notices a weakness. A diminution in even the ability to get the bad stuff out.

"Won't be long," the older son assures him, "you'll see. Few weeks, mebbe. Pa, it's far too cold out here. You shouldn't have insisted. You should be home in your bed."

"*I'm here and I'm bloody staying,*" says the man. "I'm eighty-fower, for pity's sake. If I die, let me die laughing."

Struan takes off his own scarf and wraps it round his grandfather. The smaller man's face almost disappears into the wool.

"Hey, Pa," says Gourlay, "your man's agreed to do a Party Political Broadcast for the SNP. 'This could happen to YOU!'" As he says this, he offers Sandy a placatory shrug, as if he's imploring his older brother to bear with his mischief for the greater good. Sandy, whose every instinct is to be belligerent, decides to hold fire.

Sandy Robertson has never seen his father look so unwell yet so at peace. He can't say he is thrilled to be the source of such contentment, but he won't begrudge what he fears could be the old man's last laugh.

As he watches the Robertson menfolk minister to the older, dying man, he can't quite define the particular species of turmoil inside him. Perhaps, he surmises, this is because he has never had cause to venture into the heart of himself in the past and has precious little sympathy for those who do. He is aware that he is about to be visited by grief once more, as he was when his poor mother passed away so many years ago, yet somewhere he can't help but sense that the mourning has already begun.

Curiously, far from felling him, it only makes him more determined.

Turning to the players down there on the field, defying the cold, he is reassured once again that it really is all about winning.

*TWAL/*TWELVE

"You didn't have to come today, Doctor Robertson," says Kirstie, looking into his weary face with such compassion that he simply wants to close his eyes and blot her out. She reminds him of Aileen McKay, his depute, with her cocked head and her sympathetic smile.

"I just want to get this nonsensical business done and sorted, Ms Newton. And it's on my way to his hospital. Truthfully, I'm amazed he's lasted the week."

"He's got your resilience."

"Aye, and then some. They think mebbe tomorrow…" He shakes his head. He can't seem to speak, but he's damned if she's going to slither in through his silences with another bloody platitude. "I suppose I should derive some comfort that one of his last vital signs was laughter – even if it was at me."

"You can't bear folk laughing at you, can you, Sandy?"

"Please don't start being my shrink. Not at your age."

"Nae fear! But you know, laughter isn't always such a bad thing, if we go along with it and claim it for ourselves." She smiles thoughtfully. "Sometimes… well, it's a way of getting through the pain."

He looks at her and wonders, just for a moment, if this time she's talking from experience and not simply from training, then reminds himself that this is his session, not hers.

"Aye. And sometimes it isn't," he grumbles. "Now my time's a wee bit limited, Kirstie. Can we just get on with the next exercise? I feel I'm getting somewhere, don't you?"

She nods with what she hopes registers as enthusiasm, because in truth she feels no such thing. But what's that rubbish he used to spout about something being ninety per cent perspiration?

Well, the man is certainly sweating like a pig.

***

He had hoped that by turning both bathroom taps and their wind-up radio fully on, he would have turned off Laura Robertson, but she is clearly determined to goad her husband from here to bedtime.

"*He was your own father!*" she yells.

"It's late, Laura. I need my bed." He is not sure that she hears and not certain that she listens. But he has a curious feeling she is making herself sound more Scottish these days just to spite him.

"I know you. You'll have had that eulogy done and dusted since the poor soul gave his first wee cough."

He walks back into the bedroom but doesn't look at her. "It's not the words," he mutters.

"I do understand that, Sandy. I'm not as dim as you sometimes like to think." He shakes his head. Dim is the last thing he thinks. "Even your Miss Newton, she says you should just continue to do the things you would normally do."

"And I'm forever making speeches over dead faithers."

She finds herself wishing he might cut down on his Scottish vernacular until he gears up on the delivery. But now isn't the time. "You'll be surrounded by friends tomorrow. People who cared about your pa – and who care about you."

"And snigger behind my back."

"Friends don't do that," she insists, as she prepares for bed.

282

He notices that the sheets are fresh and the duvet a pretty floral one he doesn't recognise, which he also has to concede means nothing, as they could have had it for years.

"Sweetheart, you didn't grow up where I did," he tells her, although she may just know this. "They imbibe jealousy with their mother's milk. It only takes one of them to snitch to the press, then the whole bloody world will know."

Laura can't help it. She starts to laugh. "What makes you think you're so awfully fascinating?"

He looks at her. She has her back turned to him as she slips into bed. Sandy finds himself admiring her slender figure as the nightdress catches in a fold of the unfamiliar linen. When did he last do this?

"What is *up* with you, Laura?"

She takes her book from the small table beside her and finds her glasses. "Up with me?" She says this a touch disingenuously – or at least she hopes this is how it comes across.

"Aye. You've been acting offhand for days."

"Maybe I'm just sad," she says, turning over a page she hasn't yet read.

"About my pa?"

"*Inter alia.*"

He slips into bed beside her. "Talk more Latin. You know what it does to me." She ignores this and carries on not reading. As if she knows what is coming next. "Laura…?"

Sure enough.

"Sandy, I don't think we should." She doesn't take her eyes off the book, but recalls a time when fresh linen was more potent than rhino horn.

"For God's sake," he protests, "you're not going to give me a stroke – just by giving me a stroke."

"Always the wordsmith."

He moves closer to her, feeling the warmth of her body, if not her disposition, on his skin. "I need you, Laura." This sounds to her more plaintive than lustful. And it isn't just the voice.

"Oh?" she says, still not looking at him. "Since when?"

"What do you mean?" He knows fine what she means. "Say it, go on. It's the voice, isn't it? Bloody turning you off."

"No," she says uneasily, "of course it isn't. Doesn't."

"I thought you, of all people…" He remains staring at her, as if the sheer force of his gaze will draw her away from the paperback in her hands.

"Because I'm a saint. Because I'm a woman of substance."

"Because you're my wife."

"Duty-fucks, they're the best, aren't they? Do they come before or after pity-fucks? I forget." He finds himself unable to respond. "Oh for God's sake, Sandy, let's not stray totally into the land of fantasy. Our love is not a red, red rose. Unless you include the pricks." She finally sets her book on the bedside table, her back to him as she talks. "Haven't we just been going through the motions?"

"The motions?" He tries to sound casual, but the fear is so strong inside him it's almost nailing him to the bed.

"Come on, man, it's your burr you've lost, not your memory."

He sighs. He knows what this is about. "Och, Laura, I know things have been difficult. I've been so absorbed, you know, with school politics. Aye, and all my TV stuff."

"And your new English teacher."

Sandy Robertson could not be more static in his bed at that moment if rigor mortis had set in.

"She phoned. To see how you were. Wasn't that kind?"

Curiously, he feels almost relieved. His body sighs. "Did she? She's a very caring young woman. It's what makes her such a good teacher."

Laura is staring at him now, resting her weight on one elbow, as if this is the most casual of conversations. "Well, of course, you're the expert now on voices. You and your wee ex-pupil. But from my admittedly amateur perspective, most of the folk who phone us these days sound solicitous. You know, concerned. Anxious.

Which is just that wee bit different from sounding shit-scared and contrite. *Guilty*, your honour! You forget, Sandy Robertson, I used to be a practising barrister. And so I checked her out. She lives not far from your hospital of choice."

She waits but he isn't saying anything. "Lost for words? Well, this is a first, isn't it? In any of your accents." She rises from the bed, grabbing her book and her pillow.

"Are you going to leave me, Laura?" he asks, softly. "Or have you already left?"

"Get some sleep," she urges from the doorway. "You've a full day tomorrow."

THERTEEN/THIRTEEN

The days hang heavy in a drab, diagram-splattered consulting room on a cold, grey morning, in one of the least attractive suburbs of Glasgow.

"… Tuesday…Wednesday… Thursday… Friday." The equally grey-looking man stares at his young therapist and sighs hopelessly. "No change, is there? No fucking change at all."

The young woman ignores the language – she has heard worse and from far closer to home. "I wouldn't say that. Early days, Doctor Robertson."

"So folk *keep* telling me. 'Rome wisna built in a day.'"

"Now that I never said. How was the funeral?"

He mutters something so softly that she fails to pick it up. Or at least she hopes she does. So he repeats it, but each tiny, strained syllable seems to cause him even more anguish than usual.

"I didn't go, Kirstie." She says nothing, because she can think of nothing to say. So she waits. "The CT scan may have come up gangbusters," he continues, "but I'm afraid paralysis is slowly setting in."

She shakes her head. "How do you mean?"

He gives a sigh that sounds more like surrender. "I canna talk, Kirstie! Okay, to you mebbe, in this sad wee room, but I had to give the cab driver a scribbled note just now, with the address on it. I couldn't speak to him."

"Oh. I'm so sorry. What about your family?"

"As they're hardly talking to me these days, that's posing less of a problem than it otherwise might." She stares at him. "I'm going under, Kirstie. You've got to help me. I *need* Sandy Robertson back."

"And this'll make everything okay, will it?"

She has no idea why she's being so confrontational – would she really talk to any of the others this way? Yet she can feel the frustration inexorably building inside her. And she knows that this time it isn't merely something she is picking up from a patient.

"Are you *judging* me, Kirstie Newton?"

"I don't believe in judging, Doctor Robertson. I think that's your speciality." She switches the tape on again. *Let's get this show back on the road.* "Okay. Seasons, please."

"Winter... Spring... Summer... Autumn... Winter... Winter... Winter..."

***

When Sandy Robertson doesn't turn up for his next session, nor for the one after that, Kirstie Newton decides to do something that she has done several times in the past, but usually pre-announced and with patients too immobilised to come to her. Yet, in a way, she suspects that this is not altogether different.

"Good evening, you must be Struan," she says to the puzzled young man opening the door. She feels her eyes straying off his face, amiable and un-Robertson-like as it is, in order to inspect the smart, brightly lit hallway, which is as large as a room in her flat.

"How did you know that?" asks Struan, not unreasonably.

It has just begun to snow again outside. He finds himself wondering whether he should allow this stranger into the warmth before or only after she reveals her identity. He decides to do it on the move, allowing her to shuffle past him into the glow as she swiftly introduces herself.

287

"Your dad talked about you. I'm Kirstie – Kirstie Newton. Your father's speech therapist." She laughs nervously. "Well, I think I still am."

"Oh. Aye," he nods, "will you come in?" As she already has, he calls for his mum.

When Laura appears wearily from the kitchen, the first glance she gives Kirstie transforms instantly into a glare. Kirstie knows at once that the older woman, whom she immediately finds both attractive and daunting, thinks that Kirstie is the enemy. Which is why Kirstie says, "Oh – no, I'm Kirstie Newton," a statement that even she thinks sounds strangely defensive.

The woman, however, immediately softens and smiles. "Goodness, you're so young. Mind, isn't everyone these days? Our MP is about twelve! Struan, love, will you make us some tea, please? And one for your dad."

Kirstie catches the look that passes between mother and son before the young man slopes off into the kitchen.

"My husband's upstairs, Kirstie, in his study," says Laura, pointing. "Has been for quite some time, as you know. Will you come up?"

Laura walks up the richly carpeted staircase. Kirstie follows, unashamedly looking all around her. There are bookshelves everywhere, especially on the large mid-floor landing, overflowing with weighty works.

"Would you look at all these books!" she says. "And so many lovely paintings!" Then she realises that she should appear more like a medical professional and less like she's about to buy the house. "I've been talking to some colleagues, Mrs Robertson," she says quietly, "and apparently folks with this… syndrome… well, they can get awfully agoraphobic. It goes with the depression. See, I suppose, when you don't know who you are anymore…"

"I know the feeling," says Laura, which is a touch oblique for Kirstie, but she's not going there. "Excuse me. Aye, it must be scary. But if he's not even going to go to speech therapy…"

"Then the therapy can come to him."

Laura stops outside a closed and hugely impressive oaken door. Kirstie feels slightly disappointed that all the other fancy doors are closed too. She'd love a wee peek. "I don't know that he's going to see you, Ms Newton."

What Kirstie says next causes Laura to stop, her fingers resting on the gleaming brass handle. "I wasn't talking about me, Mrs Robertson."

Laura looks at the young woman blankly until the words finally register. "You mean *me*?"

"Aye. And your son." Laura meets her gaze. *Good luck with that.* "There's so little evidence on this, Mrs Robertson, but – well, it's my feeling that if you talk to Doctor Robertson, you know, *really* talk – set time aside for it, not just 'pass the sugar' and 'what's on telly?' etcetera… He needs to hear your voices. Familiar voices. So he can mebbe connect and click back with his own."

Laura laughs, but there's little joy there. "Has he told you? That we don't—"

Kirstie doesn't let her finish. She doesn't want to know. "I can't say what he told me, Mrs Robertson. All I can say is, if he wants to get better and back to the school, it has to be worth a try."

"You do know, dear – yes, I'm sure you do – that the good doctor is not a man who'll settle for second best."

"Maybe that's why he chose you."

Laura shakes her head. "I'll say one thing for you, Kirstie Newton," says the older woman, as she opens the door, "you've a way with words yourself."

FOWERTEEN/FOURTEEN

To hear *Tam O' Shanter*, one of the greatest works of poetry ever penned in the Scottish vernacular, recited in an accent that careers from stage-Cockney to Received Pronunciation, often within a single syllable, is to be offered an unenviable glimpse of hell. At least this is what Laura Robertson thinks as she ventures into her husband's study the day after his speech therapist's brief visit.

"*The storm without might rair and rustle, Tam didna mind the storm a whistle…*"

"May I come in..?" asks the visitor, braving the storm.

Sandy finds that he can't actually look at his wife. He feels that he has become entombed in what used to be his favourite chair, where once he penned speeches that would inspire the world.

"To what do I owe this honour?" he mutters.

"I just wanted to see how you were."

"How did I sound?"

Laura isn't sure, for a moment, whether he's asking for a general diagnosis or a progress report. She opts for the latter. "Do you know, better. Mm hmm. I'm sure. A wee bit closer."

"Maybe Berwick-on-Tweed?"

"… Maybe."

"So still fucking English then."

How can the man make her so angry so swiftly? *It's almost a gift,* she thinks. "Don't play games with me, Sandy Robertson! Just don't." She sits down close to him but not too close. "We need to talk."

He nods and gives a wry smile, still without fully engaging face-to-face. He plays with a silver ptarmigan grouse-foot brooch that used to belong to his mother and now sits on his desk and repulses Laura on a regular basis. "Here it comes. Well, we haven't sold Pa's flat yet. So will I move myself in there this week?"

Laura doesn't speak for a moment. Frankly, the idea is not without its appeal. "No," she decides. "Not yet, anyway." She is finding this so difficult. "I'd like to *converse.*" She smiles, almost embarrassed at her choice of words. Especially when his eyes shoot up. "We haven't really had time, have we, these past few… well, years? I've been wrapped up in my university stuff. You've been wrapped up in— in whatever or whoever you've been—"

"Laura…"

"Let me finish, Sandy. Please. Or I'll lose my thread. How many couples are just like us? Not really talking, just giving bulletins. Soundbites from life's front line. Or, okay, even if we are talking, maybe we just aren't listening."

"Loving the sound of our own voices."

He says it before he has time to think and the words suddenly make him cry. "*Oh God!*"

This is the first time in all their married years that she has ever witnessed her husband lose control, other than in anger, and even then she can usually sense the calculation. Not this time. He is suddenly bawling like a baby and she has no idea what to do. So she does nothing, says nothing and just lets the sobbing, as mortifyingly wrenching and helpless as it is, take its course.

Finally, he is able to speak. It begins as a wry laugh. "It's like that song, isn't it? You know – '*Suddenly, I'm not half the man I used to be.*'" He shakes his head, seemingly furious with himself. "Sorry! So sorry, Laura. I don't have time for self-pity, do I? No. I'm going to be the old Sandy – you heard it here first."

291

"Are you?" she says, more than a bit warily.

"Aye. And I'm not going back to school until I am. Laura?" She looks at him, nodding gently as she draws her skirt down over her knees. "Will you be staying with me?"

Laura is quiet for a moment. "I think we've more talking to do, Sandy."

"I'm listening."

She takes the old book from his lap and begins to read out loud. "*'When chapman billies leave the street, And drouthy neibors neibors meet...'*"

He finds that he can't take his eyes off her face.

***

"*'While we sit bousing at the nappy, And getting fou and unco happy, We think na on the lang Scots miles, The mosses, waters, slaps and stiles...'*"

When the older man looks at her, Kirstie immediately thinks of her wee brother, standing on his primary school stage at Christmas, staring into the crowd, one errant and very pointy angel's wing threatening to poke his jittery neighbour in the eye. It is this same yearning for approval, the same misplaced pride in a job they reckon is consummately well done.

"I do think I'm getting there a wee bit... Eh, Kirstie?"

"Aye, I think so too," says Kirstie, because actually she does. A wee bit. "You've been practising, have you? With Mrs Robertson?"

"I have, yes," he says and then, to her surprise, he smiles.

She realises that he has quite a kindly smile, or he can have, when it's not infused with sarcasm or superiority or derision or—anyway, it's not so bad a smile.

"It's funny," he continues, "we've been talking more than we have done in... well, in a fair while." For an instant she catches a new sadness. "Fighting more too." He stares at her, an almost

292

comically determined set to his mouth and chin, like Desperate Dan from the old comics. "Okay, so from now on I want to see you every day. I know that's not the NHS style. So I'll pay you, Kirstie. A fair price. For your services." The smile returns, with just a touch of the old cleverness in it. "We're going to go for the Burns."

"It's not about the money—"

He stands up and towers over her. "Kirstie, I'm *dying* here."

"Doctor Robertson…"

"Sandy."

"Sandy," she says, more calmly than she feels, "will you sit back down, please?"

He remains standing for a moment, then does what she asks. But not without a meaningful sigh.

"You've had a stroke," she says gently. "It takes time. If you get worked up like this…"

"You mean you're just not up to it."

Despite herself, the anger – which she realises has always been simmering – boils up once more. "No, I do *not* mean that."

"You mind what I told you, all those years ago, about the tall poppies?" Kirstie is so amazed that he should remember this, one conversation amongst so many, that she can only nod and await what's coming. "You're so scared of failing that you don't want to take the risk. Better just to let me tick on infinitesimally. Same time next week, Doctor Robertson… same time next year, *Sir*… next decade, Sandy. Baby steps. Spring, Summer, Autumn, Never… Well, I'm sorry, Ms Newton, I am *not* buying that. No bloody way."

Kirstie is not hiding her anger now. The gloves, surgical or boxing, are off. She knows she may say something she can never take back but she knows also she may not get an opportunity like this again. "If you're so 'fearless', Doctor, such a fine tall poppy, why aren't you going back to school now? Today. This minute!"

"I'm sorry?"

"You heard me. Hiding yourself away in your grand old house with all your fine books and your pictures. Or— or coming here, expecting bloody miracles."

She looks in the mirror beside her and can see the fury spreading like a rash across her face. Unfortunately, she can see her patient's huge face reddening to the same angry rhythm.

"*Miracles!* Oh, well, that is just typical. You kids! When the going gets tough, the snowflakes sink back into their gluten-free, skinny, decaf lattes."

"Now you just listen to me," snaps the outraged young therapist.

"Not exactly why we're here, is it?"

"*Well, it fucking is today!*" she roars back. She wonders if her fellow therapists can hear her splenetically berating a recent and uniquely afflicted stroke victim. She tries to ratchet it down but feels that perversely this makes her sound even more angry. "The reason I don't want to push you too hard is not because I'm scared of failing, *sir*. It's because I'm scared of *killing* you! Or, more to the point, of you killing yourself."

He shakes his head in a way that makes her want to punch him. She starts to wonder if she should be in this line of work at all. She has always regarded herself as quite controlled. Isn't this how she got through her childhood and her schooling? Isn't this how she managed, against all the odds, to end up here?

"Oh, please," he scoffs. "That is not your responsibility. But if you're not up to the job, I'm sure there are plenty around who are."

Dear Lord, won't the man ever stop?

"WILL YOU JUST LISTEN, FOR CHRIST'S SAKE!" *Good going, Kirstie. Security are probably on their way.* She tries to lower the temperature. "Sandy, please. We're not all geniuses. We can't all rise from the slums of Govan and get our PhDs and be on the telly and turn our rotten schools around. Some of us are… well, limited." He's staring at her but is he actually listening? "We work *within* those limitations. We're fine with those limitations. Because we don't regard the world as—" she struggles, as if she's

294

lost in the thicket of her own thoughts, "—as an Olympic event. It's just the place where we wake up in the morning."

"Have you finished?"

She had but she hasn't now. He's just made her mad again. "No. No, I haven't finished, *Doctor* Robertson. You just can't push everyone beyond their natural ability, or all you'll end up doing is destroying them. And, funny thing – making them do even less than they otherwise could."

Kirstie is expecting more anger from this patient, but he surprises her by speaking quite calmly, in that bizarre voice that by now has become almost as familiar as the old one.

"Then just answer me one question, Miss Newton." She stares at him then offers the briefest of nods. "If I hadn't, to use your own words, pushed you *beyond* what you term your 'limitations', would you be sitting just now in your own wee office, a highly qualified health professional, savouring this rather heated conversation with your old headteacher?"

She pauses for a moment as she processes this. "Oh, very clever!" she says finally, and, as she has to realise, a bit feebly. "I know you can run rings round me with words, Doctor Robertson, whatever your accent. But all I'm saying is that if you can't accept – no, make that *won't* accept – that you may never be 'perfect', may never be one hundred per cent top of the form, dux, cock of the walk, best of the best, then you're going to be a very unhappy – and quite possibly very sick – gentleman."

Kirstie knows how she would like the man steaming in front of her to take this message and also knows instinctively how he will receive it.

"Finished? Had your say? Got your own back?" The young woman just shrugs, as you might do at a lost cause. "Well, now perhaps we can resume—"

An excited knocking on the door interrupts them. Without waiting for a response, the receptionist peers round. "Sorry to interrupt you, Kirstie."

"Mrs Gemmell, I've a patient." She is almost grateful for the interruption but knows she has to go through the motions.

"Aye, I know," says the older woman. "Sorry again. It's just – well, there's some reporters outside. You know, from the newspapers. I thought you should know."

"*Reporters*? What on earth do they want?"

"To talk to you and Doctor Robertson."

Kirstie observes her patient's face, as every dash of colour that his recent anger has aroused is replaced instantly by a pallor she finds even more alarming.

"I think you'd better see this evening's *Times*," continues the older woman, in some excitement. "They even have a photo of you, Doctor Robertson. Coming into this place. Is Struan Robertson any relation?"

FIFTEEN/FIFTEEN

When the doorbell rings in the tenement flat that used to be his pa's, Sandy Robertson is in two minds whether to answer it or simply hurl abuse through the peeling woodwork. But he soon realises that the hurling of abuse in the freakish manner in which it will undoubtedly be projected, irrespective of its wit and pithiness, might be exactly the reason why those outside are ringing.

He wishes he had been able to persuade the stubborn old man to have a peephole fitted. Yet this, like so many things, smacked of being posh. The After Eight of door accessories.

Fortunately the person doing the ringing is one step ahead.

"It's not the press, Sandy," shouts Laura. "The press don't even know about Pa's flat."

"They soon will," mutters Sandy, as he unbolts the door. When he sees Struan standing there beside his mum, he turns away with a disgusted groan and stomps back into the kitchen. "I bet they already bloody do!"

"Hi, Dad," calls Struan.

Laura squeezes her son's bony arm, offering a reassurance she seriously doubts is well-founded.

Mother and son find Sandy in the dingy living room, slumped in an armchair that looks as wrecked and hopeless as he does.

The TV is locked onto the BBC News channel, which the current resident feels is the only thing likely to make him feel better about his own miserable situation. Only it doesn't. Somewhere inside he knows that he is simply waiting to be one more of those quirky items they append to the more resonant bulletins of the day. *'A headteacher in Glasgow woke up one morning to discover that he had turned English overnight…!'*

Sandy continues to watch as his family look silently on.

"Surprised you can show your face here." They all know that this is addressed to his son.

"The guy wants to explain, Sandy," says Laura.

"It's okay, Mum. I can talk for myself."

Struan knows that he doesn't actually feel like talking. He has been so on-edge about seeing his father, and still is, that he hasn't once taken into account how it would feel to return to his grandpa's flat so soon after the old man's death.

He can't help looking around the familiar room at the faded, tobacco-stained walls and faux velvet seventies furniture with its stuffing coming out, which always reminded him of the old guy's hit-and-miss shaving; photos of people long gone, but also several of himself at various ages and stages, looking for all the world like he'd prefer to be behind the camera. The knick-knacks are all still there, the ones about which Struan's folks would quietly snigger; souvenirs from Hughie's holidays with Grandma or of classic Rangers games. Remaining there also, unbinned and scattered around, are those half-emptied bottles of Scotch and singed sea shell ashtrays. Or perhaps, he muses now, some of these are his dad's.

The young man is almost taken aback when his father asks him a question. "Were you expecting me to congratulate you on the photo?"

"No." Although he does know it was rather good.

A thought strikes Sandy. That it didn't occur to him straightaway simply feels like another sign of how his mind is slowly deteriorating. "It was your uncle, wasn't it? Gourlay put you up to this. Him and his Scottish Nasty Party."

"*No!*" Struan feels strangely offended by the insinuation that he couldn't come up with such a betrayal on his own.

"It wasn't Gourlay, Sandy. Gourlay has been very sweet about it," says Laura, only to be met with an almost theatrical snort. "I had to stop him coming here."

"I'll bet." Finally, he turns to his son, but on his face there is far more sadness than anger. And the voice sounds no more Scottish. "Then why on earth did you do it, son? Why did you tell the world?"

Struan says nothing. He is either searching for the right response or he reckons that none can possibly make this any better. When he does finally speak, the words come without any sense that he has even summoned them. "Because I'm tired of secrets." His parents stare at him yet his voice barely falters. "The house is groaning with them."

Sandy's glare, dimmed as it is, focuses accusingly on Laura.

She shakes her head. "You can't keep things hidden, Sandy. He's got a reporter's eye."

Silence fills the room, like the smell of grandpa's roll-ups as it would forever linger in the fuggy air. Struan thinks he can still catch it and wishes with all his heart that the old man were here to make things right. "There was another reason too," he tells his dad.

"Come on then, Robert Capa."

The boy is shaking now, but his voice remains strong. "I didn't want you to die."

Laura finds that she can hardly breathe. She looks to Sandy, certain that the effect of these simple words will be almost too profound.

"So you set the hounds on me. Sorry, old son, the dots just aren't quite joining."

As Laura gasps, she sees her son faltering once again. Does the poor kid really have to spell it out?

299

"I thought— I thought that if it was there, you know, in the open, you couldn't pretend any longer. Everybody'd know. And then you could start – well, learning to live with it. Instead of—" He doesn't finish, perhaps because he senses that he has crossed a final line. Or it could be he's just hoping that his belligerent, superior yet infuriatingly childlike father might for once in his life be on the same bloody page.

After an endless few seconds, Sandy finally nods. He looks at Laura as he speaks. "Instead of waiting for something that ain't going to happen. Not in a million years."

She doesn't move a facial muscle – this isn't her call. He shakes his head and smiles sadly.

To Sandy Robertson's surprise, his wife moves to the armchair and kneels awkwardly beside it. "Folk will still listen to you, Sandy." She smiles herself now, but can't conceal some last hints of regret. "You haven't changed as a person."

Sandy looks at her then up at his son, who seems glued to his spot on the worn and faded carpet. A Breaking News strip on the TV announces that there has been another school shooting. To his bewilderment, Sandy begins to sob. Probably not for the victims… yet who knows?

Who knows anything?

He finds himself wanting to respond to his wife, although it wasn't a question.

"Oh, I think I have, Laura," he says.

SAXTEEN/SIXTEEN

The pupils of Thornliepark High have had no advance warning that this morning's assembly will differ from any other Monday's, yet somehow they know. Messages in the form of vibrations, unseen and unlocatable, seem to be passing through the air, causing buttocks to remain unsquirmed, nostrils unexcavated, mouths unexercised. Something is in the wind but only the Lord, and possibly the depute head, knows what.

"Good morning, school," says Aileen McKay. "I hope you had a good weekend." The depute waits a moment, almost as if she is expecting the entire student body to list the vacuous ways in which it has squandered its leisure hours. She continues with the word which, to the knowledge of everyone assembled in that hangar-like hall save for her, has become her much imitated signature. "*Anyway*, before I read out the day's announcements, we have somebody here who wants to talk to you. Somebody you know very well indeed."

They knew something was up!

And they've a pretty good idea what. You can almost taste the excitement – they've all seen, or at least heard, what was in the papers a few weeks back. And that the big guy had gone to ground. Some thought he might even have topped himself – it's what they would have done. This could be the best assembly ever, although in truth the bar was never set particularly high.

And, sure enough, here he comes. The man himself, striding in from the wings as if it's the most normal of mornings.

The guy certainly looks okay. *Braw*, as their grandparents might say. Many of them have heard of strokes, even if they haven't had personal experience within their families, and what they've picked up is that victims can walk a bit funny or their faces can slope down on one side. Nothing like that here.

The headteacher, if indeed he still is headteacher (and it looks very much like he is, more's the pity), looks the same as he ever did. Perhaps a bit paler and a wee bit less weight on him, but nothing critical. Both of his 'clipping-roond-the-heed' arms appear to be functioning perfectly and his glower seems to be in good working order.

But of course, he hasn't opened his mouth yet.

And from the way he's standing there, just staring out at the eager crowd, eyes moving across the rows like a sat nav locking on to a signal, it looks like they could be in for a long and quite agonising wait.

When he does finally begin to talk, the communal gasp can probably be heard from here to Falkirk.

Oh Jeez!

"Aye, it's me. And I— I don't mind you laughing." None of them have succumbed as yet, at least not out loud, but the pressure to do so is palpable and in several cases is causing noses to run and eyes to water. He smiles, but not unkindly. "I'd laugh too, if I was sitting where you are. I'd probably be wetting myself, which one or two of you may well be doing even as I speak."

He waits until the permitted laughter begins and then subsides. Yet it is far from raucous – pure disbelief appears to temper the volume and diminish the blast. Sandy thinks he can also hear the odd snigger coming from the benches behind him, but this could be his imagination.

"You can stop now, please," he tells his audience. "And just listen."

The buzz dies down. The sniggering goes underground as they realise the guy's not putting it on. Not at all. This is his voice. This is him. And it's not funny. Well, okay, it's hysterical, but it's not *just* funny. And man, when the fella starts up with his Burns again...

"'*O wad some pow'r the giftie gie us, To see oursels as ithers see us!*' I never fully understood those words until now."

They still don't understand them, especially not delivered in that astonishing voice, of which they're manically, excitedly, head-hurtingly struggling to make sense. Who does it sound like? Some actor off the telly? A politician never off the telly? Despite themselves, they are totally fascinated, as you would be by some unfortunate whose deviation from the norm is not so much repellent as unfathomable. And the bugger has clearly only just begun.

"There's— there's an old Scots proverb (and yes, ladies and gentlemen, I am still a Scot, despite anything you may suspect to the contrary): '*When I did well, I heard it never. When I did ill, I heard it ever.*' How Scots can you get!" He smiles, but almost to himself. "An ex-pupil from this very school taught me over the past weeks that a wee bit of praise and understanding can work as well as a big stick." At this he turns swiftly to his staff behind him, who immediately switch faces from astonishment to acknowledgment. "Okay, *nearly* as well."

They smile politely. He tries not to catch the eye of his young English teacher, who certainly isn't overkeen to catch his.

Sandy turns back to his by now slightly more appreciative audience. "But she also taught me something else, ladies and gents. Something so profound it rattled me to ma very core. And you've never seen me wi' ma very core rattled." He shakes his huge head. "She showed me the importance of simply doing the best you can."

He looks across the vast field of – what? – uniformly sized poppies. Standing at the very back by the door, eager not to intrude but not wanting to miss the occasion, are his wife and his son. He has begged them to come, to hear and to support him. Sandy Robertson knows that their being here is one more gesture, a massive one, on the list of things for which he needs to thank them and to make some amends.

He has no idea how long this will take, or indeed, if it will ever fully resolve itself. He suspects not – he only knows it is time to try.

As they nod to him, almost imperceptibly, he loses his way. "Er, doing the best you can… aye." No, it's fine. He's on it again. "And you know what I had to learn along the way? Maybe *you* knew all this already."

What did they know? How could they know anything the big guy doesn't? Now they're all ears.

"Who you are isn't— well, it isn't just what other folk think you are. Or what you've achieved. *Or* how you sound. Your identity – now there's a braw wee word—" He can see, as he knew he would see, kids turning to each other, as if surprised for a moment that an 'English' guy is speaking their language. "Your identity is who you are right *inside* yourself. Aye. Every one of you, you're a mass of different stuff, a huge barrelful of ideas and feelings. Aye, that's what I said. Feelings. Bet you never thought you'd hear me use that word. I was never allowed 'feelings' when I was a kid. Bruises, aye. But feelings? No way! By Jesus, I'm bloody making up for it now."

The kids looks at each other. Did the head curse? Did they hear the Doctor say Jesus?

"What I mean is… well, there's got to be something *under* your kilt. Don't snigger, Finlay Gordon. And a school – aye, a school – is more than what its precious results and its league tables say it is." He shakes his head and begins the final descent. "Okay, so you're probably thinking, 'the big guy still likes the sound of his own voice'. Aye, well to be frank with you, I don't. Yet I do too. Make of that what you will."

He pauses for a moment, savouring the silence. Especially his own. He looks behind him, to a staff who now don't look quite so amused. Turning back, he smiles gently at the boys and girls, *his* boys and girls, all of whose names he prides himself on knowing – and if he ever makes a mistake, are they seriously going to tell him?

Finally, he takes in an old girl of the school, almost hidden at the very back of the hall. Still looking just a wee bit *feart* of a detention for being a few minutes late. They nod to each other as he concludes.

"Pupils and staff of Thornliepark High, I have only four wrongly pronounced words for you. 'The *heed* is back!'"

There is silence. Has he finished? Has that weird voice run its course, at least for today? When those assembled decide that it has, they begin to applaud; a few brave kids at first, then a few more and finally most of their number. It doesn't reach ecstatic heights, but it's more than respectful and hopefully not without some spattering of admiration.

Before it can totally dissipate, Doctor Sandy Robertson takes a deep breath and walks down the central aisle, right through the mass of pupils, who have already begun to dissect amongst themselves the most curious assembly they've ever witnessed. This is one to tell their grandchildren, their future colleagues, their probation officers.

He is making for his guests of honour.

Sandy nods to his wife and son. They nod back, with what he thinks – or at least hopes – is a tad more warmth than in recent weeks. But it is to a visiting professional that he turns his immediate attention.

"Thank you for coming, Ms Newton. So, how did the patient do?"

"Not bad," the young woman replies seriously. "Seven out of ten, Doctor Robertson."

The big man nods. "I can live with that. Aye, that'll do me fine."

He strolls out of the hall to begin his first day back at work.

Th'end

'THE PERFECT
MURDER'

*I never heard this story from anyone.
So far.*

TSC

The Script Clinic — *where scripts can only get better*
46 Chiswick High Road, London W4 2LU
www.thescriptclinic.co.uk

Mr D. Crispin   August 14th 2018
PO Box 1463
Oxford OX1 2LG

Dear Mr Crispin,

Re: 'The Perfect Murder'

Thank you for sending us the above script, which we really enjoyed reading.

We have taken into account that this is the first movie you have written, so we've tried to be as helpful and constructive as we can. (We appreciate that you have chosen to use traditional mail, but should you prefer, you can also email us at any time.)

You will find our detailed report attached, but writers often find it useful to receive a brief summary of our thoughts.

1. The story is quite simple, possibly too simple, and whilst the characters are interesting, they are perhaps a bit too one-dimensional.

2. We can quite understand why your main character might wish to murder his wife, given her appallingly cruel and callous behaviour towards him. (Endorsed, as you say, and even compounded, by her devoted, equally awful mother.) But to make him a man utterly without flaws, and her a woman with absolutely no redeeming features, doesn't quite allow, in our eyes, for sufficient light and shade, and perhaps strains credibility too much to make for a satisfyingly well-rounded story.

3. Your choice of a murder weapon – the exotic and apparently undetectable poison – might well work in terms of making the murder perfect, but we do not believe that he could simply buy the item over the internet, in the manner you suggest (otherwise everybody would be doing it!). And do remember that the husband is nearly always the first person to be investigated – as he usually has the dominant motive!

4. We suggest that you work on developing the characters and find a method for the killing that is totally plausible, yet one that we, the audience (and hopefully the police), have never seen before.

We hope that this isn't too discouraging and look forward to reading the next draft.

Yours sincerely,
The Consultants at The Script Clinic

***

TSC

The Script Clinic — *where scripts can only get better*
46 Chiswick High Road, London W4 2LU
www.thescriptclinic.co.uk

Mr D. Crispin   September 2ⁿᵈ 2018
PO Box 1463
Oxford OX1 2LG

Dear Mr Crispin,

Re: 'The Perfect Murder'

Thank you for submitting the above script once again, and for marking your revisions so clearly in blue. Please find our detailed report attached.

Writers often find it useful to receive a brief summary of our thoughts.

1. We are afraid that we still have the same note vis-à-vis your lead characters. The benighted husband does again appear to be a paragon of virtue, whilst his soon-to-be-despatched spouse and her mum are like the creatures that hell forgot. Today's audiences, in our experience, demand a tad more nuance.

2. Whilst it is readily accepted that people can on occasion be 'scared' to death, we think in reality that you might find this a somewhat more difficult task than your script supposes, especially given that the wife, inconveniently, has no prior heart condition. You could, of course, provide her with one – she is your own creation, to do with as you will. But pretending to hang oneself in the bathroom (page 35) is not only quite a difficult and possibly dangerous effect to pull off without

serious injury – it might also, if the marital relationship is as disastrous as you describe, be in truth a source of some relief to the lady on her return from a major shopping trip. (Rather than the guaranteed road to oblivion that you envisage.)

3. Once again our recommendations are a) concentrate on character and b) find that elusive, foolproof murder method, if this is indeed what you wish to be the core of your story. (This is far more difficult than it might appear, and there is nothing to say that audiences really *want* someone to get away with it. They actually love the elements of detection and deduction – the winnowing away of suspects. Think of Hercule Poirot.)

We hope that you have found these thoughts helpful and look forward to reading the next draft.

Yours sincerely,
The Consultants at The Script Clinic

***

TSC

The Script Clinic — *where scripts can only get better*
46 Chiswick High Road, London W4 2LU
www.thescriptclinic.co.uk

Mr D. Crispin   September 23rd 2018
PO Box 1463
Oxford OX1 2LG

Dear Mr Crispin,

Re: 'The Perfect Murder'

Thank you for submitting the above script once more, and for marking your latest revisions in puce. It makes for an easy contrast to your earlier blue.

We have attached our detailed report, but writers often find it useful to receive a brief summary of our thoughts.

1. We appreciate that you have so readily taken on board our notes about character but do feel you may still need to advance this a little further. Making the wife both a marriage and a bereavement counsellor could, in some way, diminish her almost total vileness, whilst adding a welcome touch of irony that the audience might enjoy. And giving the monstrously-put-upon yet almost saint-like husband a secret life as a sniffer of ladies' bicycle seats does indeed take his character in a new and uniquely gross direction. ('Snurd' is a word none of us had actually come across, so thank you for this.) But we do think that these pursuits, whilst colourful, feel slightly 'bolted on', as opposed to what might be more usefully organic.

2. Perhaps some sort of back-story, provided it is not too laboured, would provide further insight into how your

husband and wife arrived at this parlous state. And furnish the reader of your script – hopefully also your audience – with sufficient clues as to what could possibly have brought them together in the first place. Audiences are people – as are, occasionally, script-readers at film studios – so they are intensely interested in human nature and why people behave as they do.

3. Yet again, the exact mechanics of murder appear to be the pivotal problem. We cannot emphasise too strongly that if your desire, as your scripts suggest, is that this crime be totally undetectable, and your newly widowed hero is to sail (or in his case cycle) blissfully unshackled into the sunset, it shouldn't be a crime that any of we armchair/cinema-seat detectives could ourselves solve quite happily before the lights go up.

4. It is for the above reason that we think a hit-and-run when the wife walks home from her Pilates class might be quite tricky to pull off. This is not to say that we are totally dismissing the car as murder weapon, but streets do have houses with windows and nosy neighbours, and bodies struck at a speed necessary to ensure fatality usually tend to leave their impression on the metal that connects with them. (And the only cameras we should be thinking about are those at your director's command!)

5. At Script Clinic we pride ourselves on seeking out solutions as well as problems. So we have been scouring your script for, as it were, clues to assist you in your quest. You mention in passing (on page 21) that the wife is an insomniac. She uses a CD recorded by her hypnotherapist to assist her in gliding swiftly off to sleep. A certain haunting piece of music on this CD would appear always to do the trick. Currently this has no plot significance and is simply a neat piece of observation, allowing Norman to lie in bed and fantasise undisturbed on life without Doreen. (Indeed, you have a long dream sequence

to this effect, which is possibly the most imaginative, albeit superfluous, feature of your script.) We wonder if something currently no more than a fleeting tangent to your plot might in fact be of more practical use? This is purely a suggestion and could be totally unworkable, but we offer it in the spirit of constructive cooperation. (And think about the soundtrack possibilities!)

We hope that this is of some encouragement and look forward to reading the next draft.

Yours sincerely,
The Consultants at The Script Clinic.

***

The Script Clinic — *where scripts can only get better*
46 Chiswick High Road, London W4 2LU
www.thescriptclinic.co.uk

Mr D. Crispin   November 22nd 2018
PO Box 1463
Oxford OX1 2LG

Dear Mr Crispin,

Re: 'The Perfect Murder'

Thank you for submitting the above script once again. We must commend you on your indomitable spirit. It is this type of determination that turns scripts into movies!

And we are grateful, as always, for your marking your revisions in another colour. The script is taking on the aspect of a rainbow, which is no bad thing.

We have attached our detailed report, but writers often find it useful to receive a brief summary of our thoughts.

1. You appear to have taken our note on back-story quite literally. However, we are not entirely certain that revealing the beleaguered husband, in flashbacks, to have come from a home bathed almost to the point of drowning in kindness and civility, whilst the wife appears to have been brought up with the Borgias, actively advances your story. We are not saying that backgrounds don't serve to establish character, it is rather that you have still to find a way to make these characters totally credible.

2. If we can give one note that might help – you seem to be totally in love with Norman whilst despising Doreen with a

vengeance. Sometimes observing your protagonists through a less jaundiced and more dispassionate lens can subtly allow the audience to make their own judgments. They will learn to hate Doreen for themselves, as we all do here at TSC, which will be far more gratifying.

3. Concerning the murder itself, we are intrigued at how enthusiastically you have taken on board our suggestion as regards the Sleep CD. If indeed the playing of that particular piece of music induces an almost instant slumber in Doreen, then contriving to slip it into a CD that the husband himself has made for her is very interesting. (Assuming, in the present state of their relationship, that a 'mix-tape' would still be something he would make and that she would readily accept.)

4. However, most people don't carry portable CD players around with them anymore, as they tend to have their music on their phones. And the likelihood of Doreen listening to that particular 'sleep track' at the exact moment she is strolling in front of a speeding juggernaut is unfortunately relatively small. In a perfect murder you can't really afford to be hit 'n miss. (Excuse the pun!) If you are intending to submit a further draft – and we suspect that, unless you have run out of colours, you most probably are – then it is this area on which it might pay to concentrate.

5. Might we suggest that you devise a situation in which Doreen would gratefully accept such a CD from Norman, and a foolproof manner in which the playing of that particular somniferous track could lead to her sudden death? In an earlier draft you suggested tampering with her car. Might Doreen be driving this same car, but instead of monkeying with the mechanics, Norman has simply popped a CD into the player, and the 'killer track' plays at the moment it will do the most damage?

As ever, we trust that you have found this feedback constructive. We look forward to reading the next draft, should you decide to consult us once more.

Yours sincerely,
The Consultants at The Script Clinic

***

TSC

The Script Clinic — *where scripts can only get better*
46 Chiswick High Road, London W4 2LU
www.thescriptclinic.co.uk

Mr D. Crispin   December 21st 2018
PO Box 1463
Oxford OX1 2LG

Dear Mr Crispin,

Re: 'The Perfect Murder'

I have to say that, here at The Script Clinic, we have all been thoroughly looking forward to reading another draft of 'The Perfect Murder'.

It is not often we find a script by a brand new writer that, whilst perhaps lacking as yet in several basic elements of craft, is written with such white-hot fervour. It is unusual indeed to read a 'passion project' in this particular genre.

We are, of course, grateful yet again for your marking your revisions in another colour. Perhaps if this doesn't happen as a movie, you might consider submitting the script itself to the Turner Prize judges. (Just our little joke!)

We have attached our detailed report, but writers often find it useful to receive a brief summary of our thoughts.

1. We are interested to note the new and helpful additions since the last draft. Whilst the husband's taking out a massive life insurance policy on his wife will inevitably focus even more suspicion on him, it does, of course, provide him (and ourselves) with a useful extra motive for murder, alongside the fact that Doreen is irredeemably horrible.

2. The above will, as indeed you have anticipated, add yet more fuel to the flame of homicidal perfection. There must be no conceivable way that the crime could be attributed to the husband. We shall return to this, as we have had some thoughts.

3. Your suggestion that Norman and Doreen are on holiday somewhere with narrow mountain roads and treacherous bends is an excellent one. Playing an instant-sleep CD whilst driving on such a road would increase enormously the chances of a nasty – and dare we hope, fatal – accident. Especially on a wet or icy winter's night.

4. However, your idea that Norman can simply leap out of the passenger seat at the appropriate moment is fraught with dangers. Especially for Norman.

5. So here is our suggestion – he isn't in the car at all. Not only is he not in the car, he isn't even in the vicinity. He could indeed be miles away. A remote murder – and a murder somewhere remote – would add a new wrinkle to a well-worn genre. Does this notion appeal to you?

6. Should you honour us with another draft, perhaps we shall find this conceit developed. What is, of course, especially appealing, is that were the murder to be successful and the vehicle, along with poor Doreen, to end up a total write-off (or, indeed, even if Doreen is the only thing 'totalled' or 'written-off') no one – not even the keenest of investigators – will be the least bothered about a CD that was playing at the time. Why would they?

We look forward once again to your next draft, should you feel we might still be of assistance.

We wish you and your family a very merry – and hopefully not too murderous (!) – Christmas.

Yours sincerely,
The Consultants at The Script Clinic

***

TSC

The Script Clinic — *where scripts can only get better*
46 Chiswick High Road, London W4 2LU
www.thescriptclinic.co.uk

Mr D. Crispin   January 10th 2019
PO Box 1463
Oxford OX1 2LG

Dear Mr Crispin,

Re: 'The Perfect Murder'

Happy New Year. You've done it again!

Once more you have set our combined creative juices here at The Script Clinic sizzling – or whatever juices do!

Firstly, can we say once again that your use of different tints for each set of corrections adds both colour and convenience to our world.

You firmly requested in your covering letter that we 'forget the character stuff' for the time being. Clearly and, in our opinion, quite wisely, you would prefer to prioritise plot. So here goes:

1. Your latest draft tells us that Norman, who is a highly successful, self-made businessman, has given his wife, as a surprise Valentine treat, a week in a remote Snowdonian cottage, an area she has loved since childhood. This is apparently a gesture of rapprochement on his part (although we, of course, suspect quite the reverse).

2. As the cottage is high up on a mountain road and there is no internet access, we agree it is quite plausible that Norman should decide to venture down into the local town on the fateful day to pick up and send important messages.

3. Furthermore, he thoughtfully wouldn't wish to leave Doreen in such lofty isolation without a car. Rather than using the push-bike you say he has brought with him, which would make his journey on the steep hill both long and treacherous, especially his return in the dark, might we suggest that he uses a local cab company?

4. He can book his cab from the working landline in the cottage the same afternoon on which he expresses a need to make such a journey. This way there would be independent evidence that he was nowhere near the scene of the crime. (And the one cab company in town, should they even be questioned after the event, would confirm that no further cabs to return back up the hill were booked at any point by Norman).

5. Your reason for getting Doreen to make that hopefully fatal downhill drive is fraught with dangers – but not, as yet, of the right sort! In your script (page 72), Norman calls her to say that he has had a nasty accident on his bike and is seriously ill in the local hospital. If Doreen's feelings for Norman are as you describe, we would suggest that this – or indeed any other misfortune to befall him – might not immediately cause her to drop everything and dash recklessly towards him in blind panic. (Although she may indeed play a lively CD when she eventually gets going!)

6. You have described Doreen's devotion to her unspeakable mother in some detail – perhaps too much detail – in every draft. What if Norman calls Doreen from the town, quite late on that winter evening, and tells her that he has just received a distressing call from her mother's neighbour? (Someone who has only their mobile numbers to hand, but 'apparently' couldn't seem to get through on Doreen's.)

   • Norman could explain that this concerned person has just told him some awful news: Doreen's poor mum has suffered a really terrible fall, slipping on her path and smashing her head on the steps of her house. She was rushed away by an ambulance just minutes ago.

- Norman tells Doreen not to make any calls – the ambulance won't even have arrived at the hospital yet. She must simply drive to town just as quickly as she can and pick him up by the town hall.

- As you know, we are very drawn to the sleep-track being on a mix-CD that Norman has made. But whilst 'favourite songs of Doreen' might work in less distressing circumstances, perhaps 'favourite and meaningful tracks of Doreen's poor mum' will better serve Norman's purpose on this occasion. (Songs from the shows etc, with some easy listening thrown in.)

- Norman could tell Doreen on this final phone call that, by the purest chance, he had made such a CD as a gift for his mother-in-law, and that it was already in the car's CD player, awaiting Doreen's final approval. Norman feels certain that it might truly bring some comfort and calm to Doreen while she drives to meet him.

We humbly suggest that this combination of panic, excess speed, daughterly affection, winter darkness, an emotional musical selection – and, of course, the interpolated instant-sleep track – could be sufficient to send the driver and the car into a fatal tailspin on a notoriously treacherous road. End of Doreen, end of car (and CD), end of story. And, of course, who would suspect that it was anything other than a dreadful accident? His poor wife was just driving down to the little town to meet her devoted husband for a romantic Valentine's Day supper. (Perhaps Norman should book a restaurant table for two that evening in the town, just to dot the final 'i' and provide a reason for his earlier phone call to the cottage, should anyone bother to check.)

Of course, these are only suggestions. We look forward to reading how you choose to develop them.

We hope 2019 will be your year, Mr Crispin.

Yours sincerely,
The Consultants at The Script Clinic

***

Abingdon woman dies in fatal Snowdonia plunge

Mrs Davina Cracknell of Eastbury Villas, Abingdon, died on Valentine's night when her BMW plunged off a mountain road in a remote region of Snowdonia.

Mrs Cracknell, who was driving to meet her husband, Abingdon businessman Neville Cracknell, for an intimate Valentine's dinner in the nearby town, is assumed to have died instantly.

A local farmer, Mr Robert McKee, who witnessed the incident from the window of his cottage, noticed a car driving at enormous speed then suddenly going out of control. "It started just weaving all over the road," he said, "like the poor driver had lost the plot and suffered a stroke or something. Next thing I saw was a massive ball of flame."

The deceased, who was a JP and Relate counsellor, leaves a husband and a mother.

***

TSC

The Script Clinic — *where scripts can only get better*
46 Chiswick High Road, London W4 2LU
www.thescriptclinic.co.uk

Mr D. Crispin   August 14th 2019
PO Box 1463
Oxford OX1 2LG

Dear Mr Crispin,

Re: 'The Perfect Murder'

As it has been some months since we last heard from you, we are just writing to say that we trust you have been satisfied with our service to date.

We are currently offering a reduced rate on script consultation for our valued clients. If you would like to send us your latest draft of 'The Perfect Murder', or any other script, we would be more than happy to read it.

If, on the other hand, you have found a *productive* home for 'The Perfect Murder', do please tell us. We are always delighted when something on which we have hopefully assisted comes to happy fruition.

Yours sincerely,
The Consultants at The Script Clinic

Acknowledgements

I'd like to thank my brilliant agent, Christina Pickworth, for all your help and encouragement and my dear friend Karol Griffiths for your unfailing support.

And hats off to a new and most welcome addition to my writing day. The wonderful BrOOKS of Pinner. How many authors can experience the pure joy of writing in an independent book shop, that is also a coffee shop and a café (and a bar!)?

Thank you Sarah and Peter and all your lovely colleagues.

Finally, my gratitude to all of you who have taught me the Art of Listening.

PAUL A. MENDELSON graduated from Cambridge with a first in Law, which did him little good as he very swiftly left legal practice to create award-winning advertising campaigns. He then moved from 30-seconds to 30-minutes to create several hit BBC comedy series, including BAFTA-nominated *May to December, So Haunt Me* and *My Hero,* then back to ITV for the highly acclaimed Martin Clunes cancer drama *Losing It.* He co-created *Neighbors From Hell* for DreamWorks Animation and writes regularly for BBC Radio 4 Drama, most recently adapting *The African Queen* with Toby Jones.

Paul's first novel *In the Matter of Isabel* ('a wonderfully funny debut novel' The Independent), for which he has also written the screenplay, has been bought by a major Hollywood producer. His first novel for children, *Losing Arthur* was published by The Book Guild in 2017 and is being developed as an animated movie.

Paul is married with two daughters and lives in North London.